STORIES AND SCENES FROM MOUNT LEBANON

Mahmoud Khalil Saab

STORIES AND SCENES
FROM MOUNT LEBANON

Translated from the Arabic by
Tammam Abushakra

SAQI

British Library Cataloguing-in-Publication Data
A catalogue record for this book is available from the
British Library

ISBN 0 86356 570 0
EAN 9-780863-565700

© Saqi Books, 2004
This edition first published 2004

SAQI
26 Westbourne Grove
London W2 5RH
www.saqibooks.com

To the one
who crowned my existence with her perfection
and adorned my life with the pleasantness of her character.
To my wife, Najla Mahmoud

Contents

Contents

Contents

Translator's Foreword

by Tammam Abushakra

I am not a professional translator, but I felt qualified to undertake this English language translation of *Qusas wa mashaahid min jabal lubnaan* (*Stories and Scenes from Mount Lebanon*). Apart from believing I had sufficient language proficiency for the task, I had a personal connection to the work that I felt would enable me to understand, and hopefully convey in English, both the letter and spirit of the text.[1]

The author, Mahmoud Khalil Saab, was my grandfather. Though I was only three years old at the time of his passing, he has always been a part of my life, through my direct memories of him and through all the members of our family in whose hearts he remains alive. Jiddo Mahmoud, as I have always known him, was one of those uncommonly selfless individuals who spared nothing of himself in giving to those he loved, and sometimes even to strangers. With his wife Najla, to whom he dedicates the book with beautiful adoring words, he raised a family that has carried his legacy with them to their new lives as part of the vast Lebanese emigration he frequently writes of in this collection of stories and scenes. Jiddo Mahmoud lived almost all of his life in his hometown of Choueifat. He witnessed Lebanon's birth and its development through the first three quarters of the twentieth century. A bright and diligent young man, he excelled in school and went on to earn a degree in political science from the American University of Beirut. After a teaching stint in Iraq, he returned to Lebanon and to the AUB for a master's degree in political science. He taught political science and public administration at

---

1. My special thanks to Imad Harb for his valuable help with editing the translated text and the translator's footnotes.

the university, and later became Director of an elementary and secondary school, *al-kulliyya al-wataniyya* of Choueifat.

A few years later he became Director of Public Relations for the Trans-Arabian Pipeline Company (Tapline) which built and operated an oil pipeline from eastern Saudi Arabia to Lebanon. He held the position for over two decades, doubling as Choueifat's *ra'is baladiyya* for five of them. He served his hometown admirably, even using historic maps and documents to persuade the national authorities to recognize Choueifat's jurisdiction over Lebanon's international airport. The airport had been considered part of Beirut and other municipalities that were reaping its benefits at Choueifat's expense. Jiddo Mahmoud refers to this event in passing in this book, modestly mentioning in a footnote that he happened to be the *ra'is baladiyya* of Choueifat at the time.

It was in the late stages of his life that Jiddo Mahmoud began writing this book. He had experienced disappointment in an unsuccessful bid for Parliament, but still took great joy in his family life and pride and passion in his literary project. He collected and assessed the facts scrupulously, driving hours to different towns to interview witnesses and record their recollections.

Jiddo Mahmoud passed away before he could see his stories and scenes in print. He had submitted the manuscript to his publisher before the outbreak of war in 1975. When the war broke out, he felt compelled to add some comments relating the past to the tragic present, and speculating about the fate of the Lebanese values of generosity, honour, courage, and tolerance he had cherished in his pages. Reading his work, it is clear that his central purpose in writing it was to preserve for posterity the stories and scenes he had witnessed and heard about during his life, because he felt that if they went unrecorded they may be lost, and lost with them would be the values they relate. The war brought this fear to life as his beloved country plunged into hatred and violence, becoming a place virtually unrecognizable to him. When he expresses his dismay at the war's inhumanity, one takes some solace in the fact that he did not have to witness the gruesome events of some of its later stages.

Did he have a premonition that Lebanon was about to undergo such violent upheaval and transformation? Did that drive him to such lengths to preserve the memory of the Lebanon he knew? Perhaps, but as he laments in his second introduction, he had already seen those values eroding around him before the war, giving way to a new culture of materialism. He did not have to anticipate the catastrophe to recognize the necessity of memorializing the world he had known.

Today his three sons Ghassan, Khalil and Nadim all live with their families in the southern suburbs of Flint, Michigan, maintaining the close family ties they had forged in their father's home in another time and place. His eldest son Ghassan had immigrated to Flint in the 1960s, joining relatives who had been there as early as the 1920s. Like his father, Ghassan was a graduate of the American University of Beirut. He joined a Flint-based construction firm as an engineer in 1966 and went on to become its president. His brother Khalil joined him in Michigan in the 1970s, followed by his brother Nadim and his mother Najla in the 1980s.[1] The author's only daughter, Nada, is married to Walid Kamil Abushakra, and they divide their time between the Middle East and the United States.

I was only three and my brother only five when Jiddo Mahmoud died, but we had already forged an intimate bond with him. Today I can still remember him sitting the two of us down at either side of him at the table and feeding us pomegranates. I can also remember walking into the office of his home in Choueifat and seeing him sitting at his desk with his reading glasses on, poring over the recollected details of a noteworthy life or a memorable event.

Stories and Scenes from Mount Lebanon stands as a testament to the people of Lebanon and their rich culture, to the values and faith of the Druze, and to the pride and heritage of the Arabs. As a man of community, Jiddo Mahmoud felt a strong sense of belonging to all three of these groups, and to humanity itself. The collection is also a testament to the human spirit and its capacity for joy and pain, for laughter and sorrow, for honour and strength, and for courage and compassion. But

---

1. Ghassan was both the magnet that drew the rest of the family to Michigan and the conduit that made the immigration possible. His accomplishments in his professional and personal life have touched many people, from his business success to his philanthropic work to the role he has played in the lives of his family members. He has been the driving force behind the effort to translate his father's book into English, if only for the benefit of his many family members in America for whom the Arabic original is inaccessible. He deserves all the credit for bringing this translation to fruition. In fact, the book itself was Ghassan's idea. He used to read his father's writings and tell him he should write a book. In 2002, Ghassan Saab was named the American Druze Society's Man of the Year. The recognition was nice and well deserved, but for his family, no award can adequately express our appreciation of him.

most of all it stands as a testament to the author himself. Even from his grave, Jiddo Mahmoud is still reminding us how much better we all can be.

Preface

by Dr Jabbour Abdelnour

Some years ago my friend Youssef al-Sha'ir came to me and handed me excerpts from the manuscript of Mahmoud Khalil Saab so that I might read them and write a preface if the manuscript were to be published. I did not imagine then that these few pages were but a tasty appetizer that would lure the reader to a literary and intellectual feast. In its modest presentation, the text revealed an elegant style of composition and a novel outlook on life in the narrowness of its individuality and the breadth of its humanity. By the time the book was completed, after a period of painful suffering in an environment of national strife, its author had bid the world farewell, leaving us a precious legacy to tell of himself, just as he had revealed Lebanese traits rarely found in the writings of others.

***

The book in its present form is not a work of objective or theoretical research. It does not aim for scientific, proven, and accepted conclusions. Instead it represents an appealing simplicity where the university graduate's attention to investigation and accuracy encounters the grace of an eloquent observer who sometimes departs from the strictness of methodology in order to colour his words with the pleasantness of wit and the strangeness of legend and myth.

In shaping the general framework of his stories, the author sometimes relies on the seminal sources and draws on the work of established experts on Lebanese history such as Amir Haidar Chehab, Tanious al-Shidiaq,

15

Churchill Beik, Ibrahim al-Aswad, Suleiman Abu 'Ezzeddine, and Youssef Khattar Abu Shaqra. But he consciously avoids falling into the monotony of their writings and wandering into their historical labyrinths. He takes from their offerings just what serves his needs.

In most of his stories, he sets aside the written sources and resorts to the original source of their flow, taking his material from the memories of those who had either witnessed the narrated incidents or heard of them from their predecessors. He would listen to them and then assess what he heard, investigating the reported stories and selecting the conclusions supported by the consensus of the various narrators. He designates these conclusions as rational and sound, alerting the reader to the issues of the fallibility of memory and the distortions of prejudices and partisan biases that might have affected these stories. He refers, when necessary, to the names of the persons he received the accounts from to relieve his conscience of the burden of intentional or unintentional errors.

Through his thrift in drawing upon the historians and his cautious confidence in the accounts of the living who had either lived the events themselves or learned of them from their forefathers, he creates a unique free-flowing style, and retains the freedom to take his reader from a report of a surprising event to an ethical, national, or humanitarian theme. In following a method free of any artificial constraints except those he believed captured the reality of life as Lebanon knew it at a particular time, he makes it easy for the methodological historians who follow him to use his material, with its warm, vivid accounts of reality, as a building brick in their own compositions.

***

I did not have the opportunity to meet the author, and I do not exaggerate when I say that I read a part of his manuscript some years ago while I was ignorant of his name and lineage. His name is of no concern to me, except in relation to what he says in his words and writes in his pages – the issues he raises, the positions he chooses, and the goals he seeks to achieve through his writing. From this perspective only, I set forth what has occurred to me in the way of opinion, trying to the extent possible, briefly and within the limits of my capabilities, to form a mental picture of him through his prose. This impression may be deficient and far from the precise reality and it may contradict in some respects what is commonly known of him in his environment. However, it is, in its broad outline, derived from the hopes he expressed in his writings and the comments he offered on his stories.

The man I envision through this book is an instigator who seeks to do more than just amuse and entertain the reader and aims for more than the mere writing of distinct accounts of historical occurrences. Above all else, consciously or unconsciously, his book revolves, even in its simplest accounts, around three basic axes: Druze achievements, sectarian conciliation, and Lebanese pride. These three themes constitute the impetus that motivated his pen and instilled in him the will to collect over long years the threads from which he wove his book, *Stories and Scenes from Mount Lebanon.*

As for the first axis, even if it dominates the book in terms of volume, it works in unusual coordination with the other two axes to arrive together, after a long journey, at one conclusion. The author believes that the Druze faith creates closeness and purity, and that its teachings are filled with fine lessons and the pursuit of virtue. He states: 'The Tawhid has its basic beliefs and its spiritual philosophy, and it has its rituals, which are based on promoting the knowledge and enlightenment of the complete mind. Alongside this, the faith prescribes a strict and precise programme for conduct in society and in life.'

The author does not dwell on settled views or theories. He rarely pauses to offer general judgements because the basis of the methodology he chooses and adheres to is to lead the reader, through his entertaining accounts with their varied content, to the underlying moral or theme. Through these accounts we are able to see the decisive stages through which the Muwahhidin (or Druze) passed, and the important tasks they accomplished in the life of Lebanon, causing the names of their leading families to emerge prominently and actively in the making of its history.

In order to realize this end, the author touches upon the pride of each Druze family, and traces the names of those who performed noble deeds or heroic acts. He specifically mentions the names of those who 'performed miraculous feats of strength, courage, generosity, loyalty, forgiveness, understanding, perception, and other good traits'. In explaining these noble deeds, he elaborates on the incidents that illustrate his descriptions. In particular, he revisits wars and battles such as the Battle of Wadi Baka in the district of Rashayya against Ibrahim Pasha of Egypt in the year 1838. He describes Druze history as 'a series of battles and wars that have cost many lives but have also included heroic feats and honourable stands rarely matched in the histories of nations and peoples, ancient or modern'.

As for sectarian reconciliation, he devotes fewer pages to it. Nonetheless, the author is taken with the notion of purity within the constituent communities of Lebanese society. He traces, in some of his efforts, all that reflects the close systematic ties between them, ancient and recent. To this end, he describes a number of Christian families and their connections to Druze families. He describes their partisanship and their stances in times of crisis according to their political and party affiliations. He demonstrates this through reference to known historical incidents and the narration of occurrences that reveal the sense of fraternal bonds and the strife of adversities and conflicts. He sees national divisions as a novel phenomenon that began to appear in the reign of Amir Bashir II due to external influences that turned brother against brother and neighbour against neighbour. This broke the bonds of friendship and intimacy and planted the seeds of hatred in the people's souls to seize Lebanon's independence.

The author investigates in his pages the acts of chivalry and the accomplishments of strength, generosity, and loyalty among the Christians and stresses that these attributes are common to all. He supports his view of a sense of citizenship among Lebanon's sects with accounts of specific incidents. He describes how Jirjis al-Dibs, Ibrahim Pasha's guide at the Battle of Wadi al-Taym, would inform the Druze of the Egyptian army's movements so they could avoid its perils, and details how Minister Youssef of Bhamdoun saved Bashir Abu al-Mona from the wrath of the feudalist Youssef Beik Abdel-Malik.

He narrates other incidents that support this proposition, and leads the reader with him to a quasi-general principle that conciliation among Lebanon's various sects is a natural matter, socially, historically, and politically. What afflicted this organic unity was therefore a mere temporary impediment that ultimately must yield to the inevitability of history. Lurking in his conscience is his awareness of his own Chouiefat biases. Thus he writes, 'The harmony that existed, and still does exist, between Choueifat's Druze and its Christians withstood the hurricanes of hatred, enmity, and intrigue that swept Lebanon in that era.' In another place, he says, 'When the sons of Chouiefat meet, there are no Christians or Druze.'

Here the third axis appears, namely the author's pride in his Lebanese identity – the basic but distant background to the entire book. He rarely mentions it explicitly, but instead contents himself with the occasional, brief, eloquent insinuation. He is a great admirer of Amir Fakhreddine al-Ma'ni II, 'the builder of national unity in Lebanon', and the 'hero of independence and liberation', who 'laid the foundations for development, prosperity, and civilization, aided by the knowledge he had gained from the West'. The author also sees in Fakhreddine a symbol of the aspirations of the Lebanese people in the realization of their national aims, and the translation of those aspirations into the establishment of a political entity all communities participate in shaping. He writes, 'Lebanon belongs to all of us, and the Druze have contributed a great deal to its development.'

The author takes a contrary view of Amir Bashir II, tracing the errors he committed in the second phase of his rule. He illustrates the prevalence of conspiracy, treachery, torture, injustice, ambushes, the dismantling of ranks, the creation of divisions, and the fragmentation of unity among the sects under his rule, all of which served the purposes of the foreign occupier, Ibrahim Pasha of Egypt.

I am convinced that Mahmoud Khalil Saab lived his darkest hours in the final days before his death in 1976. He witnessed his 'small and beautiful country' destroying itself in an insane suicidal project, and watched the national traits he had so frequently lauded turn into vicious brutality. This astonished him and challenged the cherished notions he had held dear throughout his life. Lebanon's political and economic collapse followed its human failure. The country lost itself because it had abandoned its moral foundation. I imagine that the author was astounded by what he saw, heard, and read of the massacres that stabbed at the very heart of the Lebanese values of which he had written. He writes, 'In 1860 the Lebanese fighters would cease fire if women got between the fighting ranks, but in 1975 the snipers would hunt women on the roads and bridges and fire bullets at anyone trying to aid them.' It may have crossed his mind then that the love, conciliation, and noble traits he had collected together to stand as a lesson for the nation's youth were but a dream torn apart by the nightmare of reality with its terrible events.

* * *

Apart from offering fascinating anecdotes, little-known stories, and precious pieces from the fabric of Lebanese society and the life of its people, with the diversity of its various social classes and religious sects, and raising existential issues of national concern, the author sometimes transports us to folkloric scenes that existed in the past. Among them are rock throwing, equestrian games, wedding traditions, weightlifting, sparring with swords and shields, *zajal*[1] circles, dancing monkeys, donkeys, and goats, wrestling bears, and other amusements of old Lebanese society. These are scattered throughout the pages of his book. He sometimes provides us with topographical information about villages, squares, police stations, and roads as he knew them in his early life. He narrates the stories and unusual experiences of those with whom he shared close bonds, especially within his family and among the powerful well-known families. He articulates all he has drawn from others or witnessed himself in a gracious and simple manner, avoiding hurting people's feelings or provoking anger. If his stories include material that might be damaging to someone's reputation, he omits the person's name and simply gives an account of the incident.

***

I should like to make one final, sincere remark. If I were given one wish after reading this book, it would be that sections of it reach the hands of the youth in our schools to serve as a living testament of love, forgiveness, national loyalty, and proper civic upbringing. Their need for such a lesson has never been greater, and perhaps in this endeavour lies the realization of some of Mahmoud Khalil Saab's hopes in authoring the book *Stories and Scenes from Mount Lebanon.*

---

1. *Zajal* is the preeminent form of folk poetry throughout Lebanon. It is in slang and mostly extols strength. Two *zajjala* usually spar over a topic and take turns forming verses to the same rhyme.

Author's Introduction

This book contains a collection of Lebanese stories and scenes. Its protagonists are actual people who lived, laboured, and died; some of them are still alive. These events took place, and these scenes occurred, at specific times and in particular places in this small and beautiful country.

The stories and scenes contain no trace of fantasy, nor is there any place in them for invention or authorship. Instead they contain simple narration and free description. For that reason, I am nothing in them but a narrator. I drew the accounts from those who experienced these events or from other narrators who in turn had received them from their predecessors or contemporaries. It was of course left to me to determine the linguistic style and organize the narration. Thus the stories are naturally subject, although to varying degrees, to the limitations of sight, sound, perception, memory, and narrative techniques, and to the inevitable errors, changes, defects, or distortions.

That is why my first step in this introduction is to acknowledge the inevitable presence of some mistakes here and there in the narration. Some of the stories were exposed, over the passage of years and generations, to the fallibility of memory, and the tendencies of narrators to fill gaps, to assert what is deemed appropriate, and to dismiss what may be considered vile by both speaker and listener. These factors are inevitable and beyond an author's control.

However, I spared no time or effort when ascertaining the facts. I would seek out all the sources of a story, listen to each one, and then I would compare, contrast, and derive a conclusion. I have included what most of the sources agreed upon, and omitted what does not accord with logic. I have also omitted what does not accord with the general course of history and well-established facts.

***

For the reader's benefit, I have placed the majority of these stories in their historical, social, and religious context. To this end, I have relied on the accepted sources of Lebanese history and on what I know of the principles of social relations and religious beliefs in the society in which I grew up and lived.

***

I believe in the connection of the past to the present, and the present to the future, in the lives of individuals as well as in the lives of peoples and nations. This book is a modest attempt to record a selection of stories and scenes that contain fragments of our heritage and reveal some of our national virtues. I have attempted to record this heritage and these virtues for I fear they might be lost in the scheme of our contemporary concerns or swept away by the currents of materialism and opportunism that are presently overpowering moral values.

And God guides the endeavour.

Mahmoud Khalil Saab
Chouiefat, Lebanon

Second Introduction

On 18 August 1975 I submitted the typescript of this book to the publisher. However, the security situation soon regressed once again (to use the phrase of Shareef al-Akhawi, the broadcaster who has become well-known for his humanitarianism), so the printing was halted and the printers were forced to close.

With the end of the civil war in Lebanon in late January 1976, the printers, having remained safe from fire and destruction, started work again and we resumed printing the book. However, I saw that the circumstances called for a second introduction since the events that took place in Lebanon during the difficult months of the calamity are organically related to the ends for which the book was written.

***

I chose the stories and scenes contained in this book for what they reflect of the traits and morals by which the Lebanese abided, and by whose light they were guided, in their behaviour with their friends and foes, without regard for personal gain or loss. There was a great need for the dissemination of these virtues of generosity, bravery, decency, integrity, righteousness, and sacrifice, and for the reassertion of these traits in the face of the current supremacy of materialism over moral values in people's relations.

We sensed the deviation from our daily morals and we witnessed the corruption in our political life. We assumed our society would be able to hold together despite this deviation and this corruption if the foundations for its remedy and reform were in place. However, the events of the civil war soon revealed how wrong we were in these assumptions, for before Lebanon's political and economic collapse came its moral collapse.

The latest civil war in Lebanon was characterized by treachery, the killing of innocent civilians, the maltreatment of women, children, and the elderly, torture, and pillage. Where does all this stand with respect to our history? In 1860 the Lebanese fighters would cease fire if women got between the fighting ranks, but in 1975 the snipers would hunt women on the roads and bridges and fire bullets at anyone trying to aid them. How low they have stooped.

A Word of Thanks

Duty dictates that I commend those who made the writing of this book and its publication possible. Thus I thank the faithful narrators from whom I drew, mentioning in particular the revered men of religion:

Abu Taufiq Mahmoud Abd al-Khaliq – Majd al-Ba'na
Abu Nou'man Hussein Hamzeh – Shanay
Abu Amer Muhammad al-Ayyash – Ba'werta
Abu Amin Hussein Daw – Bshatfeen
Abu Fayez Fakhreddine Abu Khozam – Kfar Heem
Abu Milhem Hamad al-Faqih – Aley
Abu Hassan Ali Abd al-Khaliq – Majd al-Ba'na
Abu Jamil Taufiq al-Qontar – al-Mtein
Abu Fouad Nimr Khalil al-Jurdi – Choueifat

Then:
Youssef Mishrik al-Haddad – Bhamdoun
Elias Jirji al-Jureidini – Choueifat
Fayez Abd al-Khaliq – Shanay
Shaykh Sami Muhammad Atallah – Ain Dara
Nadim Hassan al-Khishin – Choueifat
Fayez Abd al-Khaliq – Shanay
Nayef 'Ezzeddine Chehayeb – Aley
Khalil Rashid Hassan – Atrin
Rashid al-Qadi – Baysour
Fouad Mahmoud Ataya – Abey
Sa'eed Hussein al-Jurdi – Choueifat

Chafiq Mansour al-Jurdi – Choueifat
Victor Khalaf – Souk al-Gharb
Sha'ya al-Nakouzi – al-Mrouj
Fouad Abu Ghanem – Kfar Nabrakh
Kamel Raydan – Ain 'Inoub
Hassan Qaed Bey – Ain 'Inoub
Fares Abu al-Mona – Shanay
Dr Fouad Ifram al-Bustani – Dayr al-Qamar
Colonel Nou'man Abu Shaqra (Retd) – Amatour
Lieutenant Kamel Abu Shaqra (Retd) – Amatour
Dr Farid Badoura – Dayr al-Qamar
Ma'rouf Rashid Nou'man – Choueifat
Najib Milhem Salman – Choueifat
Shaykh Salim al-Khazen – Faraya
Salim Diab Hobeika – Rishmaya
Sharif Abu Rislan – Ras al-Matn
Raja Fayez Qaed Bey – Ain 'Inoub
Dr Sami Makarem – Aytat
Kamel Mansour al-Souqi – Choueifat
Aref Saeed al-Qadi al-Jurdi – Choueifat

I shall not mention the narrators from the Saab family for they are my partners in this book and in thanking those who helped me with it.

I should also like to thank Kamal Fouad Abu Ghanem, who read the entire manuscript and offered much guidance in the realm of linguistic style and expression.

Rulers and Battles

Shaykh Bashir Jumblatt and Shaykh Sej'aan al-Khazen

The al-Khazen *mashayekh*[1] were originally Qaysis, but when the Jumblatt–Yazbaki rivalry occurred they became Jumblattis. Thus their relationship with the Jumblatt family was one of intimacy and friendship.

***

It is said that Shaykh Bashir Jumblatt enjoyed close relations with most of the guardians (feudal lords) of the al-Khazen family, among them Shaykh Sej'aan ibn Abboud Ken'aan al-Khazen, the guardian of Kfar Thibian and its surroundings in the Kisrwan area. The two leaders exchanged letters and gifts.

One year, on the occasion of the al-Adha holiday, Shaykh Sej'aan sent a gift of Adeni (Yemeni) coffee to Shaykh Bashir with a letter of felicitation. The messenger was advanced in age and the journey exhausted him, so he arrived in Mukhtara in a miserable state. When he came before Shaykh Bashir, the Shaykh asked his name. The man answered proudly, 'Maroon'. Shaykh Bashir responded, 'If you are Maroon, what shame on the Maronites.' Some days later, Maroon returned to Kfar Thibian carrying the letter printed below to Shaykh Sej'aan and reported Shaykh Bashir's wisecrack to him. Shaykh Sej'aan committed the incident to memory.

---

1. The word *mashayekh* (sing. *shaykh*) is an honorific title used to refer either to an aristocratic social rank, especially in pre-twentieth century Lebanon, or to the clergy of the Druze faith. [Translator]

Just before Christmas, Shaykh Bashir sent Shaykh Sej'aan a gift of pine nuts and a message of holiday greeting with a messenger of comparable standard and appearance to Maroon. The first thing that Shaykh Sej'aan did was ask the messenger's name. He answered, 'Fakhr al-Din' (pride of the faith). The Shaykh responded, 'If you are Fakhreddine – may God burn this *din* (faith).'

The letter Shaykh Bashir Jumblatt sent to Shaykh Sej'aan al-Khazen reads:

> *Your Honour, our brother, the respectful Shaykh Sej'aan, may God protect him:*
> *We are gratified to see you in the best of health and well-being, and in the best of times. Your letter arrived, and we were pleased by your news. You have asked about us. With thanks to the Almighty, at the present time we are in full health, wishing your continued enjoyment of the same. May your holiday wishes be returned upon you, and please continue to give us your pleasant news.*
> *Your brother,*
> *Bashir Jumblatt.*
> *And the ten pounds of coffee you sent have arrived.*
> *God bless you and your good kindness.*

Al-Sit[1] Hbous Arslan

Al-Sit Hbous – this is how I came to know her when I began to attend the gatherings of the prominent members of society where they discussed the events of the time and the deeds of the great and the heroic. This was in the early 1920s in Choueifat. The Druze–Syrian revolution had yet to erupt, Amir Adel Arslan had yet to become known as the Amir of the Sword and the Pen, and Amir Shakib had yet to take his place among the prominent Arab and Islamic leaders. People in the Gharb area, the western part of Mount Lebanon, were still talking admiringly about al-Sit Hbous Arslan and her son Amir Amin, labelling him 'the Great', and about her grandson, Amir Mustafa al-Amin.

They would say that al-Sit Hbous was endowed with political skill and boldness, but was better known as a cruel, unjust, and tyrannical executioner of people – fair in some instances but more often oppressive and unjust. Amir Mustafa was no less tyrannical, but he is a man and a man's tyranny is more palatable than that of a woman. For these reasons, al-Sit Hbous was not loved by the people.

It was said that she would imprison people, confiscate their money and property, and mercilessly persecute those who crossed her. She would order executions, and there is a place in Bshamoun where she is said to have erected a gallows for the execution of those she had sentenced to death. I have seen nothing that proves she really ordered executions, nor anything that proves she did not. We do know that the imposition of the death sentence was beyond the authority of the feudal rulers, and that al-

---

1. *Al-sit*, meaning madam or lady, is an Arabic term used to refer to women of high status or advanced age. [Translator]

Sit Hbous did not rule from Bshamoun but from Choueifat. She built a castle in Bshamoun and resided there in the last year or two of her life, but that was after the reins of power had passed to the hands of her son Ahmad.

As legend has it, the Ottoman authorities finally lost patience with her and she decided to disappear. She disguised herself as a bedouin and began herding goats in the mountains. The disguise required her to go barefoot, as all the shepherds did, and her soft white feet caught the attention of a soldier. Becoming suspicious, he arrested her and turned her in. She was executed for mistreating her subjects. Women who heard the story would respond by saying, *Allah la y'qayyimha'* (May God never revive her).

So who was this powerful, tyrannical ruler, and what was her role in Lebanese history?

***

Hbous was the daughter of Amir Bashir ibn Muhammad ibn Haidar ibn Suleiman ibn Fakhreddine ibn Yehya ibn Muhammad[1] ibn Mazhaj ibn Jamaleddine Ahmad. It is said that she fought alongside the Ottoman ruler Sultan Salim against Qansou al-Ghouri at the Battle of Marj Dabiq. There is now a new theory, however, according to which Jamaleddine Ahmad did not take part in the battle at all and only sided with Sultan Salim after the Sultan's victory, following the popular saying, *Abaqash badha, qoumou ta n-hanni'* (The outcome is clear, let's go and congratulate the winner).

Al-Sit Hbous was born in Choueifat in 1768 and married Amir Abbas ibn Fakhreddine ibn Haidar ibn Suleiman, etc. (thus he was her father's first cousin and seventeen years her senior). Abbas and Hbous are the two pillars of the Arslan family's modern history. All of the Arslanis alive today are their descendants except for al-Sit May and al-Sit Nazimah, the daughters of Amir Shakib, who is related to Amir Younis ibn Fakhreddine, the brother of Amir Abbas. With the death of their brother Ghalib some years ago, the male lineage of that household came to an end.

---

1. Muhammad's name has been left out of Ibrahim al-Aswad's book, probably inadvertently since the Arslani document mentions it.

It seems that al-Sit Hbous's talents emerged before her husband's death 'obliged' her to rule on behalf of her young children. Her husband had 'good looks and manners, was intelligent, clever, benevolent, just, eloquent, gentle, and witty'.[1] He was also brave. 'He witnessed the Battle of al-Jazzar in the year 1206 Hijra (AD 1791), and his bravery was revealed in the battle.'[2] Nonetheless, al-Sit Hbous used to interfere in matters of government during his lifetime, as the following story reveals:

'In 1807 Amir Mousa Mansour Chehab died in the town of al-Hadath. Amir Abbas and his wife al-Sit Hbous attended the funeral, accompanied by some relatives and others from Choueifat. The sons of Choueifat and the sons of Baabda and al-Hadath disagreed about who would take the camel litter and the *terza rima* horses, and the disagreement developed into a physical confrontation between the people of the coast and the Choueifatis. The Choueifatis retreated to the road and fired some shots to intimidate their adversaries. Amir Milhem Chehab was injured when a stone struck his head. The people of the coast fled and the Choueifatis withdrew. When they reached the place called al-Warwar, they met Amir Hassan Chehab coming from Wadi Shahrour to the funeral with his servants. Al-Sit Hbous ordered her men to chase them and a fight broke out which ended in defeat for Amir Hassan with his servants.'[3] We see from this story that even with her husband present it was al-Sit Hbous who gave the order to the men of Choueifat to attack Amir Hassan's followers, and therefore it was she whom Amir Bashir II would punish.

Amir Abbas died in 1809 at the age of 58. Amir Bashir II appointed Abbas's wife, al-Sit Hbous, as ruler because her children were still young and she was known to be intelligent, eloquent, and brave. Amir Bashir was angry with her and her husband Amir Abbas over the incident described above, so he sent a force to burn down the house of her relative, Amir Ahmad Arslan. Eventually his anger subsided and he ordered the persecution and punishment to cease because of al-Shaykh Bashir Jumblatt's intercession on behalf of al-Sit Hbous.

Here we must pause to address the issue of her children's ages. Al-Sit Hbous gave birth to six sons – Ahmad (the first), As'ad, Haidar, Mansour, Ahmad (the second), and Amin. Ahmad (the first) and As'ad died young and unmarried in the plague of 1794. Thus in 1809 Amir Amin

---

1. Tanious al-Shidiaq, *Akhbar al-A'yan fi Tarikh Lubnan* [Eyewitness Reports on the History of Lebanon], p. 519, Beirut, 1970.
2. Ibrahim al-Aswad, *Zhakhaer Lubnan*, p. 194, Baabda, 1896.
3. Al-Shidiaq, p. 519.

was still a baby of 2, Ahmad (the second) was 13 years old, and Haidar 19. I have not been able to determine Amir Mansour's date of birth.

Amir Haidar, at the age of 19, was not considered young by the standards of that era. In truth, al-Sit Hbous assumed power because of her own ambition, strength, and self-confidence to the point of conceit, and because of people's recognition of these qualities. She was not really forced to take power because her children were young.

Let us consider what historians have to say about her. According to Tanious al-Shidiaq, 'She ruled over her subjects in a beneficent manner and was known for her good qualities, and she became an authority and source of aid for the people.'[1] Ibrahim al-Aswad says, 'She enjoyed an evenness of opinion, acuteness of intellect, clarity of perception, strength of resolve, and benevolence of hand and soul. She married Amir Abbas ibn Fakhreddine and frequently sat in company with men, overwhelming them with her eloquence and enlightening them with her ideas. She was zealous in her support of those who resorted to her, helping them address their concerns, and was not hesitant to spend money if the situation called for it. As for those who opposed or sided against her, she was excessive in taking revenge through the favour she held with the powerful, eventually depriving her antagonists of all their rights.'[2]

Amir Haidar Ahmad Chehab does not mention al-Sit Hbous at all. Perhaps her death at the hands of his relatives caused him to exclude her from his history despite his inclusion of the stories of individuals of lesser account.

As for the English historian Colonel Churchill (Sharshar Beik), he describes the prominent status women hold in Druze society and their participation with men in the work in the home, the council, and the battlefield: 'One of the Muwahhidin women who reflected (this prominence) was al-Sit Hbous, wife of Amir Abbas Arslan, who exercised over her husband the type of control to which the normal mind not only succumbs but accommodates with deep understanding. Her intellectual abilities were widely recognized, and she boldly asserted herself until finally, and with implicit acceptance, she took the reins of power into her own hands. She attained power through merit and diligence despite the presence of a number of Amirs within her family with the necessary qualifications of lineage and ability. All the people of the lower Gharb

---

1. Al-Shidiaq, p. 519.
2. Al-Aswad, p. 197.

area, including the plains of Beirut, acknowledged her as their *za'im* (leader or representative).

'Her residence in Choueifat became a meeting place for many of the prominent leaders of the mountain. Making use of her opinions, they discussed all the critical matters of the day. She also ruled on civil and criminal judicial cases. Seekers of justice from all classes and places were allowed to stand freely before her, within the strictures of the Druze moral code about meetings between men and women.

'The parties would gather in the grand council and present their cases to a specific number of scribes who chaired the proceedings and acted as a court of appeal. But observers could not help noticing that the speakers' eyes were directed at a strange curtain hanging in a corner of the room. Every now and then from behind the curtain a voice would be heard interrupting, questioning, suggesting, and ruling according to the particular facts of the case. The tone of voice was that of an authority accustomed to receiving compliance and obedience from others.

'The people in attendance would acknowledge this unseen presence with respect and awe, as though it were some sort of revelation. This was al-Sit Hbous Arslan, a woman of extraordinarily liberated mind, free of the normal deficiencies of human nature. This mental ability, along with her abusive authority, often caused her to exaggerate her own significance in the balance of public affairs. This was most obvious when she would claim that the powerful Jumblatt family was under her complete will and control.'[1]

Next Colonel Churchill discusses al-Sit Hbous's position in the eyes of Amir Bashir II, which was based on her friendship with his ally Shaykh Bashir Jumblatt.

***

As for the story of her death, both the time and the manner of it are shrouded in mystery.

Tanious al-Shidiaq says, 'When Amir Bashir 'Omar II returned from Egypt as a ruler, Amir Ahmad (Arslan) met him and handed him over to the ruler of his district (the lower Gharb). His mother (al-Sit Hbous) moved with her two sons (Haidar and Ahmad, as Mansour had died that

---

1. Colonel Churchill, *Mount Lebanon*, Vol. 3, p. 237, London.

same year, 1823) to Bshamoun. The aforementioned Amir sought to collect money from her and sent Amir Bashir Milhem (Chehab) with his men to seize it. They harassed her, so her sons went to Ain Traz to ask al-Shaykh Mansour al-Dahdah, the Amir's administrator, to persuade the Amir to accept whatever she was able to pay.

'In the meantime she died. When her sons learned of her death they returned to Bshamoun and held a funeral for her. She was buried in the dome of Amir Najm (Arslan). Then Amir Ahmad agreed with his brothers to leave for Akkar, where Ali Pasha Mir'ib al-As'ad lived, because they enjoyed an old friendship with Ali Pasha. He greeted them with warmth and generosity.'[1]

The first thing I would like to point out here is that al-Shidiaq places this entire account in his narration of the events of 1822. Perhaps he began recounting the incident and completed it despite the fact that the story ends in 1824. Al-Aswad states that al-Sit Hbous died in 1824.[2] It is also known that Amir Bashir II returned from Egypt in October 1823.

I would also note that al-Shidiaq says nothing of why Amir Ahmad changed his mind and sought refuge at al-As'ad's. However, if we consider that Tanious al-Shidiaq was one of the Chehabs' men and fought alongside them in the civil wars of the 1840s, we uncover the secret behind his ambiguous narration of the incident and his attempt to conceal the way al-Sit Hbous really died.

As for Ibrahim al-Aswad, he narrates the story of the confiscation of their money as follows: 'The aforementioned Amir Bashir ordered Amir Bashir Qassem to confiscate her money. Bashir Qassem treated her severely, and she soon died amid some intrigue. She was 58 (lunar) years old and was buried in Bshamoun.'[3] What is meant by the use of the word 'intrigue' without identifying the individual(s) responsible is clear.

Hussein Ghadban Abu Shaqra, the narrator of the story *al-Harakat fi Lubnan* [Movements in Lebanon], also addressed the subject. The story was written and drafted on his behalf by the lawyer Youssef Khattar Abu Shaqra, and was published after being edited, with footnotes, bibliography, appendices, and introduction, by Afif Youssef Abu Shaqra. Abu Shaqra finally spills the beans.[4] He says, 'In that era, the Arslani al-Sit Hbous ruled over the far *Gharb* (West) district entrusted to her after

---

1. Al-Shidiaq, p. 520.
2. Al-Aswad, p. 197.
3. Al-Aswad, p. 197.
4. The Arabic original uses the phrase '*yabiq al-bouhsa*', an Arabic saying literally meaning, 'to spit the pebble'. [Translator]

the death of her husband, the Arslani Amir Abbas. The Chehab and Arslan families were in constant disagreement over some villages and small towns along the border between their respective territories. The two sides followed the rule of *man 'azz bazz, wa man ghalab salab* (the triumphant robs, and the conqueror loots). At that particular time the disputed villages were under the control of the Chehabs. Al-Sit Hbous's personality, extensive authority, and Druze pride drove her to take over the farm of Wadi al-Dulab, which the Chehabs had previously taken from her predecessors during the reign of Amir Bashir al-Malti. This provoked Amir Bashir's anger to the point that he ordered his followers to set up an ambush for her on certain roads. They ambushed al-Sit Hbous, opened fire, and killed her.'[1]

This story accords with the general belief among narrators that al-Sit Hbous was killed in an ambush. One of them reports that she was killed at 'Kharnubat al-Gharb' in Hay al-Oumara in Choueifat. The same narrator claims that the person who fired the deadly shots was Suleiman Ahmad Abu Hassan of Choueifat, accompanied by others.

Assassination and treachery were among the habits and traits of Amir Bashir II. No Lebanese Amir before or after him practised this deadly art form as he did. He showed no mercy to kin and no pity to friends, and spared neither supporter nor ally. He invited the Nakad family to his house and slaughtered them. He summoned Jirjis Baz to his court and murdered him, and sent someone to kill his brother Abd al-Ahad Baz the same day. He gouged out the eyes of Amir Youssef Chehab's sons and prohibited them from marrying. Then came the turn of al-Sit Hbous. And after her he turned his attention to his ardent ally and supporter Bashir Jumblatt, employing deceit at times and coercion at others, until he finally brought about Bashir's death by strangulation in Akka (Acre) prison. He then cut out the tongues of Amirs Abbas, Fares, and Suleiman Chehab and gouged out their eyes.[2]

Amir Bashir perpetrated all this and more in the way of persecution, severe punishment, and injustice just to keep Lebanon under his iron fist. There is no doubt that he was extremely intelligent, brave and respected. In his fifty-two years of rule, with some interruptions, he secured his subjects' lives and money from others. But none were safe in their person and property from his whims because he had committed himself to

---

1. Abu Shaqra, pp. 35–36.
2. To learn more about Amir Bashir's horrible deeds, see Abu Shaqra's book, cited above.

gaining the favour of his masters, first the Turks and then the Egyptians, by offering them money and men, further burdening the people of the mountain.

Some violate the integrity of reality and history by placing Amir Bashir II on an equal footing with Amir Fakhreddine, as though he continued the endeavours initiated by the great Ma'ni. There are major differences between the two men in this respect. Fakhreddine was the builder of national unity in Lebanon while Bashir led Lebanon into war and schism. Fakhreddine was the hero of the independence and liberation he fought for, while Bashir only fought to support one Turkish Pasha over another, and later to support the Egyptians against the Turks. (We cannot forget one of his proud moments when he led the people of the mountain to subjugate the Arabs in the fortress of Sanour in favour of the Turks.) Fakhreddine came a few generations before Bashir and laid the foundations for development, prosperity, and civilization, aided by the knowledge he had gained from the West. Amir Bashir, on the other hand, accomplished nothing during his long reign other than the construction of some bridges and the plan to bring water to his castle in Beiteddine. He accomplished this by dredging, following the recommendation of Akhwat Shanay (the madman of Shanay). Apart from all these differences, there is the large discrepancy between the territorial outline of Fakhreddine's Lebanon and that of Bashir.

***

Returning to the story of al-Sit Hbous, her husband and brother-in-law supported Amir Bashir in his confrontation with al-Jazzar. 'In 1800 al-Jazzar led about 10,000 soldiers in a surprise raid on Choueifat, seeking to transfer power to the hands of Amir Youssef Chehab's sons (the enemies of Amir Bashir). They were met by Amir Abbas and his brother Amir Younis (Arslan) with their men, aided by Amir Hassan 'Omar Chehab. A battle erupted between the two sides; the soldiers were defeated and dispersed.[1]

'When Amir Bashir, his brother Amir Hussein, and Bashir Jumblatt entered Ahmad Pasha al-Jazzar's prison in Akka, (al-Sit Hbous) gave money to Amir Bashir, spent generously on his household, and did

---

1. Al-Shidiaq, p. 519.

38

everything within her power to gather support for him among the people. When Abdallah Pasha appointed Amir Hassan and Amir Salman of the Chehab family rulers over the mountain, after extracting a promise from them to increase taxes in the mountain, she left with Amir Bashir and Shaykh Bashir (Jumblatt) to Hawran. She conferred with them about the state of the country. It is said that she quarrelled with the Arab bedouin for their transgressions against the Druze of Hawran, overcoming them.'[1]

She also felt some goodwill towards Amir Bashir because of the services she rendered to him. 'In 1813 Amir Bashir sent some men to punish the al-Shidiaq family, accusing them of siding with relatives of theirs who had beaten two of his servants. Fares fled with his son Antoun to Choueifat, seeking the protection of the Arslani al-Sit Hbous, and Youssef and his sons Tanious and Mansour fled to Qannoubine seeking the protection of Patriarch Hanna al-Hilou. Fares and Youssef's other sons sought out some Chehab Amirs. When the Amir learned of their flight, he ordered his men to burn down the houses of their relatives who had committed the offence. Al-Sit Hbous and Patriarch Hanna interceded on their behalf. They succeeded in softening the Amir's heart, and the al-Shidiaqs were allowed to return to their homes. Fares and his brother, Youssef, returned to the service of the Amir as they had before.'[2] But none of this gained al-Sit Hbous enough sympathy with the Amir for him to spare her. What caused him to turn against her and kill her?

Al-Shidiaq and al-Aswad agree that Amir Bashir demanded a sum of money from al-Sit Hbous that she was apparently unable to pay. This infuriated him, and I believe that herein lies the secret. When Amir Bashir sought refuge in Egypt, Muhammad Ali Pasha received him well, anticipating the need for Amir Bashir's aid in Muhammad Ali's attempt to conquer Syria, for which he was already making preparations. During his stay, Amir Bashir was able to win approval for Abdallah Pasha to rule the district in question. Muhammad Ali's same decree required Abdallah Pasha to make a payment of 50,000 bags of gold to the state treasury at Istanbul.[3] Once Amir Bashir returned to power in Mount Lebanon, it was of course incumbent upon him to assist his patron and ally in collecting this large sum.

Amir Bashir took advantage of the situation, for he held a double-edged sword. On the one hand, he was exacting in collecting the money,

---

1. Al-Shidiaq, p. 118.
2. Al-Aswad, p. 197.
3. Churchill, *Jabal Lubnan*, Vol. 3, p. 354.

securing his position by gaining the favour of Abdallah Pasha. At the same time, he was able to demand impossible sums from certain people as a way to squeeze them and punish them. Thus he advised Abdallah to impose on Shaykh Bashir Jumblatt the sum of 1,000 bags of gold. The Shaykh managed to raise half the sum,[1] but that did not satisfy Amir Bashir, who continued to harass and antagonize him until he finally eliminated him, clearing the way for himself to rule Lebanon unopposed.

We may surmise that the same happened with al-Sit Hbous. Amir Bashir demanded payment from her when he returned from Egypt, and when she could not pay he had her murdered. This would explain why her sons fled after her death and later fought alongside Shaykh Bashir Jumblatt against Amir Bashir.

Now, a century and a half after her death and in the days of radio and television, no one mentions al-Sit Hbous's name in public meetings. Part of her legacy is a name she gave to a site in Choueifat, the area called al-Qasr (the Castle), situated on a small promontory north of al-Nahr al-Yabis (the Parched River) on the town's coast. It was named al-Qasr because al-Sit Hbous built a castle there where she would spend part of the summer. Nothing remains of the castle today.

There is one eternal, living remnant of al-Sit Hbous. We know that the Choueifat families of al-Jurdi and al-Khishin are sister families. The credit for that goes to al-Sit Hbous. The two families had a long disagreement that developed into a heated rivalry. Al-Sit Hbous intervened and repaired the hostile relations between the two families. She encouraged them to intermarry until they became like one family.

* * *

This is what I have been able to discover about the life of al-Sit Hbous Arslan. There are other figures like her in Druze history. There is a great similarity between her and al-Sit Nazira Jumblatt, for example, despite the differences in time and political systems. Al-Sit Nazira waits for someone to write her story before the details are lost and all those who knew her personally are gone.

Even more deserving of attention is al-Sit Nassab, the mother of Amir Fakhreddine al-Ma'ni. Al-Sit Hbous Arslan and al-Sit Nazira Jumblatt

---

1. Churchill, *Jabal Lubnan*, Vol. 3, p. 354.

were both gifted individuals who enjoyed success on the local level, but al-Sit Nassab was an advisor to her great son on all levels, including the international front.

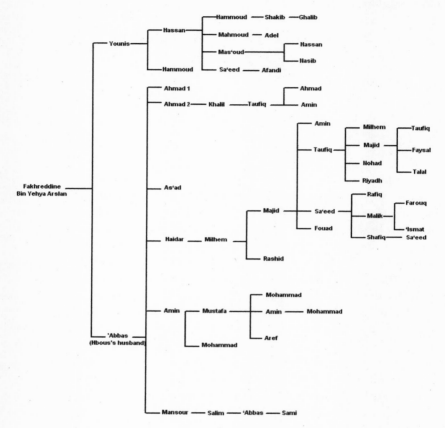

Arslan Family Tree

The Battle of Wadi Baka

Druze history consists of a series of battles and wars that have cost many lives but have also included heroic feats and honourable stands rarely matched in the histories of nations and peoples, ancient or modern. I do not make this claim out of pride but simply mention it in the course of narrating historical facts as they actually occurred, without embellishment or understatement. What would a historian say of a small minority that revolted against the Egyptian Ibrahim Pasha, conqueror of the Ottoman Empire, wearing out his forces and killing a number of them before finally succumbing? When the Ottomans treated the Druze unjustly, the Druze waged war against them more than once, despite the fact that the Ottomans held the Caliphate and were masters of the Islamic world. And when France failed to take the Druze seriously after its defeat of Germany and Austria, they ignited the flames of war against the French and stretched their troops to their limit. The revolt soon spread to become a full-fledged Syrian revolution.

Many fierce and glorious battles took place during these and other wars, but none has impressed me more than that between the Druze and Ibrahim Pasha in late June or early July of 1838 in Wadi Baka near Yanta in the Rashayya district (Qada). There are many reasons for this bias, some personal and others general, as explained below.

My paternal grandmother is from the S'eifan[1] family from Beit Lahya near Rashayya. She often told me during my childhood about Wadi al-Taym and the wars of Ibrahim Pasha. Her father and paternal uncles

---

1.   The al-S'eifans were part of the Saab famiy in Choueifat, but none of them survive today.

fought with Shibley Agha al-'Iryan against the Egyptians. One of her uncles was especially agile and active, and was a member of the contingent that used to climb Jabal al-Shaykh and light a fire at its peak. The Druze of the mountain would see the fire and respond by lighting a fire on top of Jabal Kleib in Jabal al-Druze. This was the fire of war.

Wadi al-Taym was the first residence of the Tawhid faith and what took place (and still takes place) within it evokes special feelings among the Druze. The battles in Wadi al-Taym against the armies of Ibrahim Pasha, including the Battle of Wadi Baka, represented the highest levels of courage and devotion. They occurred after the Egyptians were able to subjugate the Jabal al-Druze and Druze hopes of victory were lost. Confronting them in Wadi al-Taym was the pinnacle of pride and honour. It represented a choice of death over surrender and submission.

History has immortalized the Battle of Thermopylae in Greece, where 300 of Sparta's men stood in the face of the huge Persian army. But the Battle of Wadi Baka was a greater marvel than the Battle of Thermopylae. In Wadi Baka the Druze were able to resist for a longer period of time and kill a larger number of their enemies. Some even managed to survive the jaws of death. Forty pairs of brothers died at the Battle of Wadi Baka. The Druze still refer to it as the 'Battle of the Brothers'. This alone is enough to stir feelings and emotions.

In all the battles of Wadi al-Taym we find noble efforts on the part of both the Druze and the Christians to avoid fighting among themselves. Amir Bashir was not willing to disobey the orders of Muhammad Ali Pasha, so he began to recruit Christians to support the Egyptians against the Druze. He sent his son, Amir Khalil, at the helm of a force to Wadi al-Taym to accomplish this task. But despite this prevailing criminality, Jirjis al-Dibs, Ibrahim Pasha's guide at the Battle of Wadi al-Taym, would keep the Druze apprised of the Egyptian army's movements.[1] The Druze showed concern for the safety of every Lebanese that fell into their hands, simply disarming him and setting him free. The story of how they were able to distinguish between the Lebanese and the Egyptians through their different pronunciation of the Arabic letter '*jeem*' is well known.

***

---

1. Kamal Salibi, *Tareekh Lubnan al-Hadeeth* [The Modern History of Lebanon], p. 67.

Ibrahim Pasha invaded all of Syria and part of Anatolia in 1831 and 1832. Syria submitted to his rule, and some saw him as a saviour from the unjust and corrupt rule of the Ottomans. Ibrahim Pasha introduced some useful administrative, economic, and judicial reforms, but also overburdened the people with taxes, confiscated their weapons, and imposed conscription on their young men. Movements and revolts against him soon materialized in different places, the most famous being the Druze revolution in Hawran and Wadi al-Taym (October 1837–August 1838).

While the Druze war against Ibrahim Pasha was mainly a result of his efforts to disarm and conscript them, there were two other reasons. First, the Druze did not support the Egyptians against the Ottomans. Second, Ibrahim Pasha wanted to subjugate the Druze of Hawran because Jabal Hawran and al-Lajat at that time were a sanctuary for those who feared the tyranny of the sovereign or revolted against the government.[1]

The fact that the Druze did not welcome the Egyptians into Syria to begin with is worth noting because it reveals two things: first, the foresight of the Lebanese Druze *mashayekh* (religious leaders) and their love of freedom and independence, and, second, Amir Bashir II's rejection of these patriotic considerations for the sake of his personal advantage. It is obvious to those with some knowledge of the political affairs of that era that Ottoman rule in Mount Lebanon did not extend beyond nominal control and the collection of *amiri* taxes. The Egyptian system, on the other hand, meant colonialism in its fullest form, including disarmament and conscription.[2]

Amir Bashir put himself and his principality at the service of Ibrahim Pasha and behaved towards Muhammad Ali Pasha as a 'humble slave'.[3] The Druze went along with him at first but soon began to defect to the Ottomans' side. Ibrahim Pasha resorted to force and trickery to subjugate the Lebanese. He sent 4,000 Egyptian soldiers to Beiteddine and was able to disarm some of the Druze and recruit others. He did not spare the Christians and soon disarmed them too. (When the Druze revolted against him, he ordered that the Christians be recruited to fight the Druze.)

---

1. Suleiman Abu 'Izzeddine, *Ibrahim Pasha fi Sourya* [Ibrahim Pasha in Syria], p. 198.
2. See Charles Henry Churchill, *Mount Lebanon*, Vol. 3, p. 397.
3. Literally. See his correspondence with Muhammad Ali in the book by As'ad Rustom: *Bashir beina al-Sultan wa al-Aziz* [Bashir between the Sultan and al-Aziz].

Ibrahim Pasha was able to carry out his designs on Lebanon, but when he insisted on applying them in Jabal Hawran the Druze revolted against him. A number of major battles and confrontations broke out between the two sides and the Egyptians lost about 10,000 men (some even put the number of Egyptians killed at 15,000). All this despite the fact that the Druze of Hawran numbered no more than 1,600 fighters, in addition to about 400 fighters from among the bedouin Arabs.[1]

Ultimately, the Druze did not have enough men and equipment to continue the fight, and the Egyptian army was able to overcome the armies of the Sultan, especially since Ibrahim Pasha devoted himself to pursuing them and employed a variety of tactics and schemes to defeat them. They began to retreat, and the end of the revolution appeared imminent. Then Shibley Agha al-'Iryan returned from Hawran with 200 fighters and opened a front in Wadi al-Taym to take some pressure off the Druze of Hawran. About 700 men from Wadi al-Taym joined Shibley, as did some 700 fighters from the Druze of Mount Lebanon under the leadership of Shaykh Hassan Jumblatt and Shaykh Nassereddine al-'Imad.[2]

The Druze set out to attack the Egyptian garrisons and kill their troops. War erupted in Wadi al-Taym, creating a problem for the Egyptians, so Ibrahim Pasha confronted them himself, leading 4,000 Arnaout fighters. Muhammad Ali Pasha had sent his son Ibrahim to fight the Druze. They were also joined by 2,000 Lebanese fighters under the leadership of Amir Khalil, the son of Amir Bashir Chehab.[3]

That was the first time the Druze and Christians had fought. Amir Bashir had forced the Christians to fight the Druze under the orders of Muhammad Ali Pasha in a war in which they had no stake or interest other than Amir Bashir's aim of winning the favour of Muhammad Ali Pasha.

Some fighting took place on the plains of Jabal al-Shaykh without any gains on either side. Then Ibrahim Pasha resorted to trickery. He sent for a caravan of provisions from Damascus and saw that the Druze received word of it indirectly. Shaykh Nassereddine al-'Imad, accompanied by 300 horsemen, set out to intercept the caravan. He seized it easily but fell into an ambush. When dawn broke, Mustafa Pasha, leading an Arnaout army,

---

1. Abu 'Izzeddine, p. 197.
2. Abu 'Izzeddine, p. 214.
3. Al-Shidiaq, p. 445.

met them from the north, and after a few hours Ibrahim Pasha and his regular army closed in on them from the other end of the valley.

When Shaykh Nassereddine saw the first soldiers of the army in the morning, he ordered his men to chase away the camels they had taken from the battleground. They led the camels away until they reached a fountain in the wadi from which they drank and quenched their horses' thirst. Then they set out to attack the Arnaout forces. Launching one raid after another, they disrupted their lines and forced them to retreat to one of the mountain plains.

We should note a psychological factor that had a great deal to do with how the battle unfolded. After the battles between the Druze and Ibrahim Pasha in the mountain in which the Druze defeated one army after the other, the Egyptians were somewhat in awe of the Druze and began to have serious doubts about confronting them.

Returning to the course of the battle, what emerges from the accounts of historians and narrators is that when the regular army headed by Ibrahim Pasha arrived, the Druze launched a fierce attack, causing the soldiers to retreat and in some cases even attempt to flee. Ibrahim Pasha then ordered his commanders to dismount from their horses and lead their soldiers on foot to force them to return to combat. This measure apparently proved insufficient as Ibrahim Pasha was forced to dismount from his own horse, draw his sword, and rush in front of the army to lead them back into battle. From this sequence of events stems the Druze conviction that had it not been for Ibrahim Pasha, the surrounded Druze would have been able to escape the siege imposed upon them. Of course, this would not have influenced the outcome of the war since the rebels had reached the limits of their resources in men and machinery.

Shaykh Hassan Jumblatt rose to the aid of Shaykh Nassereddine, leading a fighting force of 450 men to the scene of the battle, but he lost 130 men without managing to breach the sea of forces assembled against him. He retreated in order to spare the lives of his remaining men. The sun was about to set. The horses were tired, the men were fatigued, and the Druze munitions were exhausted. With 200 of his men dead, there was nothing left for Shaykh Nassereddine to do but surrender or die with his remaining horsemen. But Shaykh Nassereddine al-'Imad did not accept defeat or surrender. He is the man Tanious al-Shidiaq called 'the most courageous of people of his time'. He delivered the following final order to his remaining men: 'Attack the enemy with your knives and swords.'[1]

The remaining fighters included a substantial number of Druze clergymen. When they were in no doubt as to their fate, they gathered in small groups and read the *fatiha*,[2] holding each other's shoulders and bending their heads to God. When they had finished reading the *fatiha*, they raised their heads, expanded their chests, drew their swords, daggers, and other weapons, and attacked the surrounding army. One fact that is difficult to explain is how some of these proud men, aided by nightfall, were able to break through the surrounding lines and escape unscathed. It is said that some of them passed under the bellies of horses. Historians disagree on the exact number of survivors. Some put the number at fifty, others around thirty, and still others say even fewer.

As for Shaykh Nassereddine al-'Imad, he drew his sword and proceeded to 'cut to pieces all those who reached him until he was killed himself'.[3] The site of Shaykh Nassereddine and his men's demise was called Qal'at al-Qatla (The Fortress of the Dead), a well-known place near Yanta. Among those killed at the Battle of Wadi Baka were forty pairs of brothers. That is why, as mentioned above, it is known as the 'Battle of the Brothers'.

The revolution did not endure long after this extraordinary battle. The number of soldiers amassed against the insurgents increased and the Druze were forced to lay down their weapons. Shibley Agha al-'Iryan surrendered to Ibrahim Pasha and was treated with all due consideration and respect.

One important question remains. How many Egyptians were killed at the Battle of Wadi Baka? The historians only say that the Druze killed a large number of them. Druze estimates are around 1,700 Egyptians killed.[4]

---

1. Al-Shidiaq, p. 457.
2. The *fatiha* is a *surah*, or verse, from the Qur'an recited on many fateful occasions, both happy and tragic, to signify belief in, and devotion to, God. On this occasion, it was used as an opening to martyrdom in battle. [Translator]
3. Al-Shidiaq, p. 456.
4. The first adjutant in the Lebanese army, Yehya Ammar, is working on a military history of the Battle of Wadi Baka. He is qualified to do so because he is from Yanta. He grew up on the land on which the battle took place, and heard and recalled what the elders told their successors among the region's people. Moreover, he is a soldier and knows how to study and scrutinize military stories and discern the truth. I have relied on him for some of what is narrated above.

***

We should add a brief note about Shaykh Nassereddine al-'Imad – a man for whom Tanious al-Shidiaq abandons his usual reserve to describe as the bravest of his time. Shaykh Tanious was a contemporary of Shaykh Nassereddine and knew him as he knew all men of politics and war of that era. It can truly be said that the al-'Imads are masters of courage because of the number of first-class horsemen they produced. Their valour in war reached extremes of recklessness, with a lack of concern for their safety and a total disregard of the consequences. Their pride was so great that, as their master in courage in our days, Shaykh Farhan, says, not one of them acknowledged the superiority of another.

Shaykh Nassereddine, the hero of the Battle of Wadi Baka, was the son of Shaykh Abu al-Nasr, and it appears he was his only son. His date of birth is not known, but he makes his first appearance in history as the leader of a vanguard, just as he left this world as the leader of a vanguard. He was the first of the group sent by Amir Bashir to kill Abd al-Ahad Baz and seize the children of Amir Youssef to enter Abd al-Ahad's house in Jbeil. Shaykh Nassereddine followed Abd al-Ahad to his house, and there they exchanged fire. Shaykh Nassereddine was wounded but continued to pursue his adversary. This forced Abd al-Ahad to jump from a high window and fall to the ground, only to be killed by the Amir's men.

We next find Shaykh Nassereddine in revolt with the rest of the 'Imads against Amir Bashir II. No battle took place between Amir Bashir and his enemies without Shaykh Nassereddine on the front line – fighting with a determination and bravery that have rarely been matched. To illustrate his bravery and boldness, we recount the following story told by Colonel Churchill in his book about Mount Lebanon.

On 26 May 1821 Amir Bashir attacked Damascus under the orders of Abdallah Pasha, the ruler of Akka, in support of the latter's struggle against Darwish Pasha, the ruler of Damascus. Amir Bashir was helped by the element of surprise and by superior numbers. After a fierce battle the city's defenders, including Shaykh Nassereddine al-'Imad, retreated to its interior. When they reached the palace, Darwish Pasha received them with scorn, blame, and insults, attributing his fall to treason among the defenders' ranks. Shaykh Nassereddine stood before him pointing to his torn and blood-soaked clothes and shouted, 'Are these wounds evidence of treason?' Indeed, Shaykh Nasser's actions that day ensured fame and glory for his name and that of his family. He took on so many opposing men, led so many raids, and swung his sword so often that the blood dried on his hand and his fingers became rigid and cramped, requiring him to soak his hand in warm water to ease the stiffness.

His pride prevented him from spending another hour in the service of a man who rewarded his efforts in this manner, even if he was the Pasha of Damascus, so he cleaned his wounds with '*araq*[1] and left Damascus. He headed north to join Mustafa Pasha's camp and fight on his side against Abdallah Pasha and Amir Bashir.[2]

In 1831 Amir Bashir pardoned his enemies and allowed Shaykh Nassereddine to return to al-Arqoub. His settled lifestyle did not last long, however, as he soon returned to battle until he met his extraordinary heroic demise in Wadi Baka.

---

1. *Araq* is an alcoholic beverage made from fermented grape juice and anise seeds. [Translator]
2. Churchill, *Mount Lebanon*, Vol. 3, p. 336.

Shaykh Youssef Abd al-Malik and Abu al-Mona Bashir Abu al-Mona

In the 1840s Shanay, with all its lands and homes, was still owned by the *mashayekh* of Abd al-Malik. The people of Shanay worked as farmers on the land in return for a share of the crops. The feudal *mashayekh* were still the actual rulers, each in his fief, despite the heavy blows dealt them by Amir Bashir II. Employing force in some instances and conspiracy in others, the Amir went to great lengths to kill them, force them into exile, and seize their property. This weakened them to varying degrees. But as soon as Amir Bashir fell and Egyptian rule over the country was broken and routed, the feudal families returned to power in the Chouf area, perhaps not with the same position and authority they had previously enjoyed, but with a considerable level of power, wealth, and sovereignty nonetheless.

Despite the establishment of the *qa'emmaqamiyyatain* system,[1] 'each prominent family governed its territory with complete independence ... The Druze *qa'emmaqam* sufficed with receiving nominal allegiance from the *mashayekh*, because he lacked the power to garner their genuine respect of his authority ... They continued to exercise their freedom without restraint. They were entrusted to collect the *amiri* taxes, and they spent them according to their whims. This was how they built houses,

---

1. After continuing civil strife between the Maronites and the Druze of Mount Lebanon, the European powers and the Ottoman Empire agreed to divide the area of the mountain into two self-governing cantons, one for the Maronites and the other for the Druze, each headed by a member of his sect. The system lasted until the civil war of 1860. [Translator]

51

bought lands, exploited government property, and gained ownership of thoroughbred horses.'[1]

This was quite natural since it was the *mashayekh* themselves who had introduced the *qa'emmaqam* system in the first place. When the system was announced in 1842, representatives of the Druze feudal families met at Dayr al-Sheer near Aley to agree on a *qa'emmaqam*. What took place at that meeting replicated the events of a similar occasion in 1712. In that year, the Tanoukhi Shaykh Qabalan al-Qadi, the most prominent of the Chouf *mashayekh*, died without a male heir, so the *mashayekh* agreed that his son-in-law, Ali Rabah Jumblatt, be his successor. Similarly, in 1842 it became apparent to the *mashayekh* at the Dayr al-Sheer meeting that they could not tolerate any one of them becoming *qa'emmaqam* and ruling over the others. Shaykh Hussein Talhouq therefore suggested that they appoint Amir Ahmad Abbas Arslan to the position of *qa'emmaqam*.

Amir Ahmad took over the *qa'emmaqamiyya* on the first day of 1843. His brother, Amir Amin, succeeded him in 1844, and then the latter's son, Amir Ahmad, succeeded him in 1859. After the events of 1860, a new political system was devised for Lebanon and the *mutasarrifiyya* era began. The new order officially abolished the feudal system, but the sons of the big families, aided by their traditional authority, took over the jobs in public service. It was as if nothing had changed, except that economic and agricultural feudalism had been eliminated.

***

Returning to our story in Shanay, we mentioned that all the town's lands belonged to the *mashayekh*, except for one tract of land that had somehow come into the ownership of Abu al-Mona Bashir Abu al-Mona. The property did not exceed 0.4 hectares in size.

The most prominent member of the Abd al-Malik family at that time was Youssef Beik Shibley. When he learned that Abu al-Mona privately owned a piece of land in Shanay, he ordered his *fellahin* (sing. *fellah*) (yeomen in his service) to farm the property with the rest of his feudal lands. One morning someone came to Abu al-Mona and informed him that Youssef Beik's *fellah* was plowing his land. This provoked his ire, so

---

1.   Charles Henry Churchill, p. 110; Kamal Salibi, p. 112.

he went to the *fellah*, untied the ox from the plow, and threw the *fellah* off the land.

God's blessings then deserted Abu al-Mona, and were replaced by the vengeance of Youssef Beik. In the early afternoon of the same day, news of the incident reached Btater (where Youssef Beik resided). Youssef Beik immediately rode to Shanay with some men and a slave he owned. He lodged at the homes of the village shaykhs, Abu Hussein Shibley Abu al-Mona and Abu Youssef Hamdan Abu al-Mona.[1]

Abu al-Mona was brought forth and Youssef asked him how he dared expel the *fellah* from the land. Abu al-Mona answered him saying, 'May you live long, Beik. We live by your charity. But this land is my property and I wish to use it to better my family's condition.' Youssef Beik got angry and ordered him to sign a deed acknowledging that he did not own the land. Abu al-Mona refused. Youssef Beik gestured to his slave, who quickly responded by assaulting Abu al-Mona with blows and kicks. He then firmly tied Abu al-Mona's arms behind his back, and upon his master's order, carried him to the roof and tied him to a roof roller (dirt leveller). Then he returned and stood at the door awaiting further orders.

The *mashayekhs*' attempts to intercede were unsuccessful, and their pleas were futile. The sun set, and a bitter cold spread through the village's alleys. Stoves were lit and Youssef Beik was offered the obligations of hospitality in the hope that his mood would soften and he would order that Abu al-Mona be untied and brought down from the roof, but to no avail.

From behind the walls and windows, Abu al-Mona's wife saw and heard what was taking place, and sorrow began eating at her heart. When night fell and Youssef Beik continued to be stubborn, she put on her clothes, covered her face, and took the rural route to Bhamdoun. She knew that Father Youssef was in excellent standing with Youssef Beik, and that the latter would not refuse any request from the minister. She went to his house in Bhamdoun and asked for his help. The minister mounted his horse and quickly headed to Shanay while the woman returned through the fields and pastures as she had come.

When the minister appeared before the council of *mashayekh*, Youssef Beik shouted, 'I know why you have come. Your pleasure is precious to us.' He gestured to his slave standing at the door. The slave climbed up

---

1. The two shaykhs were greatly endowed with righteousness, abstemiousness, and devotion. Shaykh Abu Hussein Shibley was the third *shaykh al-'aqil* at that time. His half-brother (by his mother) Abu Youssef Hamdan is the writer of the famous letter to Queen Victoria.

to the roof and untied Abu al-Mona. Some of his relatives, not knowing whether he was dead or alive, brought him down. But Abu al-Mona regained consciousness after they had covered him with clothes, seated him by the fire, and given him a hot drink.

Abu al-Mona was bedridden for one month after the incident because of the severe combination of cold weather and physical punishment he had suffered. When he returned to health, he was informed that Youssef Beik had ordered his exile from Shanay, so he took his children and some of his personal belongings and left the village.

Abu al-Mona went to al-Mukhtara and sought out Saeed Beik Jumblatt. Saeed Beik gave him shelter and he remained there for one full year. After the year had passed, Abu al-Mona returned to Shanay carrying a letter from Saeed Beik Jumblatt to Youssef Beik Abd al-Malik. The letter, of course, was a request that finally persuaded Youssef Beik to end his persecution of Abu al-Mona. The tract of land that caused this incident remains in the hands of Abu al-Mona Bashir Abu al-Mona's descendants to this day.

Fouad Abu Ghanem at al-Mokhallis Monastery

The centre of the Chouf's *qa'emmaqamiyya*[1] moved to Aley during the First World War. The *qa'emmaqam* was Amir Adel Arslan. Amin Beik Talie' was responsible for administering the *qa'emmaqamiyya*'s money. At the beginning of 1917, a committee was established under the order of the financial administrator to survey the number of Arabs, bedouin, and their cattle in the Chouf area. The aim was to establish a basis for the *mal al-'onouq* (poll tax) on the men and *al-'idad* (tax on equipment/material) on the cattle. The committee was made up of Muhammad Afandi Abbas Abd al-Samad from Amatour as president, Fouad Afandi Suleiman Abu Ghanem[2] as secretary, and Salem Shdid Abu Hassan from Ba'tharan and Youssef Rafe' Abd al-Samad from Amatour.

In the course of its work, the committee reached the Joon area next to Saida on a rainy day. When the day was over, the committee chairman, Muhammad Afandi Abbas Abd al-Samad, went to the house of Ayyoub al-Shami, the mayor of Joon, and became his guest. The three other committee members had no friends in the area, so they had to seek shelter for the night at al-Mokhallis Monastery.

They reached the monastery after dark and knocked on its big outer door. It was a time of robbery and lawlessness, so the door was not opened immediately. Instead a guard appeared at a high window and asked, 'Who is knocking?' The committee members tried to explain that

---

1. The *mutasarrifiyya* left the *qa'emmaqamiyya* system intact but deprived the *qa'emmaqams* of their autonomy. [Translator]
2. Fouad Abu Ghanem is the glorious writer, the eloquent poet, the scrutinizing narrator, and the refined conversationalist. He is now 85 years old and still enjoys these qualities and traits despite the weakness of his body.

they were state employees who had been overtaken by nightfall and the rain and needed to spend the night at the monastery. The man was not convinced. The discussion between them continued until the guard recognized the voice of Fouad Afandi Abu Ghanem. He then quickly came down to open the door and let them in. All that Fouad remembers about the guard is that he was called Abu Aziz and was married to a woman from the al-Ashi family from al-Mukhtara, and that he and his wife met in the house of Jumblatt in al-Mukhtara.

Abu Aziz invited the guests into a warm room where they stood next to the fire, drying their rain-soaked clothes. Abu Aziz left and soon returned with another of Fouad's friends, Brother Youssef Raad (the ecclesiastical name of Saeed Raad from Kfar Nabrakh, the home town of Fouad Abu Ghanem). Fouad and Brother Youssef not only shared bonds of citizenship and friendship but also those of partisanship, since both were ardent Jumblattis. Once the guests had rested and dried their clothes, Brother Youssef said, 'Now I wish to inform the monastery director (high priest) of your arrival.' He left them and went out of the room.

After some time Brother Youssef returned with the monastery's director, who was walking with difficulty because of his great age. However, he greeted his guests warmly and asked, 'Which of you is the grandson of Wehbeh Abu Ghanem?' Fouad answered, 'It is me, master. Pray, I hope it is good.' The director answered, 'Good, and all the good. You, my son, are entitled to invite 100 guests to this monastery, even in these difficult days.' Fouad answered, 'May God grant you long life and may He protect this monastery. You are known for your compassion, generosity, and benevolence. But may I ask why you granted me the privilege of such a warm welcome?' The director said, 'Let us go and have dinner and I'll tell you the tale of this monastery and our story with Wehbeh Abu Ghanem.'

At the dining table, the director narrated the following story to his guests: 'After the events of 1860, a new land survey was carried out in Lebanon. The committee responsible for surveying this area severed a piece of the monastery's land and annexed it to the lands of the Islamic *awqaf* (Islamic religious endowments) in Saida. The value of the piece of land at that time was not less than 10,000 gold liras (pounds). The transfer of ownership was accomplished by moving the boundaries of the lands from one brook to another. After obtaining the consent of the Catholic Patriarch in Beirut, the monastery filed a suit before the court of Jizzine, but we lost and the decision came out in favour of the Islamic *awqaf.* His Eminence the Patriarch directed us to appeal against the decision to the Grand Administrative Council, since it was a lawsuit and the Council had the authority to review the decision in its appellate capacity.'

The high priest continued: 'I was at that time a simple monk. When our master sensed that the Grand Administrative Council was not sympathetic to our rights, he sent me to Beirut to inform His Eminence the Patriarch and abide by his orders in the matter. I went to Beirut and reported the news to His Eminence. He said to me, "I have a friend on the Administrative Council and his name is Wehbeh Abu Ghanem. He is a powerful man whose voice is heard and he is a champion of rights. He is now in the village of Kfar Nabrakh. Go to him, convey my regards, and give him a detailed account of our case. I think he will be helpful." I returned to the monastery and informed the master of the Patriarch's orders. The master asked me to go to Kfar Nabrakh and do as His Eminence had directed.

'On the morning of the following day I rode a mule, accompanied by a muleteer, and we went to Kfar Nabrakh. We arrived there just after midday and I went to the home of Wehbeh Abu Ghanem.'

The high priest paused briefly because talking had tired him and then returned to his narration of the story: 'After he had offered us food and we had eaten, your grandfather received me in a hall that overlooked some villages, small towns, and farms that ran along the shoulders of the valley. He spoke to me first about a variety of topics, impressing me with his calmness and solemnity. I was also taken with the breadth of his knowledge and understanding. He then asked me why I had come. I relayed the Patriarch's greetings and narrated our case in detail. When I had finished speaking he just said, "Give my greetings to His Eminence the Patriarch, and God willing everything will be fine." I thanked him and left.

'The date arrived for the Council's inquiry into our case in Beiteddine, and I was present. The Council's chairman, Eid Abu Hatem, read aloud the decision of the Jizzine court ordering that the land be given to the Saida *awqaf.* He then asked if any of the Council members had any objection to the ruling. They all remained silent and the chairman stood ready to announce that the Council affirmed the Jizzine court's decision until Wehbeh Abu Ghanem raised his hand and said, "I have something to say on the matter."

'Wehbeh Abu Ghanem spoke words that were great in both form and meaning. He examined the case documents and discussed the witnesses on both sides, explaining their motives and dispositions. He set forth arguments and evidence in support of the monastery's position that had not even occurred to us, the owners of the right. He then suggested that the Jizzine court decision be reversed. The members of the Council agreed unanimously and the land returned to the monastery.'

The high priest concluded by saying, 'Is it too much for us, then, to open the monastery's doors to the grandson of Wehbeh Abu Ghanem and his companions, even if they were 100 people?'

***

The next day was stormy and rainy, so Fouad and his companions did not leave the monastery. Instead the high priest sent someone to invite the committee chairman, Muhammad Afandi Abbas Abd al-Samad, to the monastery for lunch. At lunch the group gathered around a lamb that had been slaughtered and prepared for the occasion.

***

Abu Hassan Wehbeh Abu Ghanem (1818–1879) was one of Lebanon's builders, and one of the men who bore the responsibilities of government and administration during the tense, unstable period that followed the events of 1860. He was elected to membership of the Grand Administrative Council three consecutive times. He was renowned for his understanding, perception, tolerance, sobriety, and courage. He enjoyed the people's confidence and support. Rustom Pasha, the most prominent of Mount Lebanon's *mutasarrifs*, showed Wehbeh special favour. Rustom Pasha was known for his keen judgement of men's characters and his astute evaluation and appreciation of the qualities they possessed.

Fouad Abu Ghanem keeps a hunting rifle (double-barrelled shotgun) given by Rustom Pasha to his grandfather Wehbeh as a gift. The gun has beautiful carvings inlaid with silver and an engraved image of a lion. Rustom Pasha gave similar rifles as gifts to Ali Beik Hamadeh from Baaqline and another to Suleiman Ahmad Abd al-Samad from Amatour, but those two rifles have been lost.

Amir Mustafa Arslan

When I returned to live in Choueifat in 1925, twenty-three years had passed since the end of Amir Mustafa Arslan's rule of the Chouf district and eleven years had passed since his death. Yet his name remained on people's tongues as they spoke of him with appreciation and admiration, not only in Choueifat but also in all of the Chouf's villages. Though Amir Taufiq Arslan and Amir Shakib Arslan had assumed power after him, neither was able to steal his limelight.

In that era, the primary measure of men's worth was their courage, and Amir Mustafa was greatly endowed with dignity, charisma, and boldness. In days of old, Easterners liked and accepted tyrants if they were just, and Amir Mustafa was a just tyrant. He did not climb the ladder of public office beyond the position of *qa'emmaqam* of the Chouf (which included both the present-day Chouf and Aley districts). He was one of seven *qa'emmaqams* under the command of the *mutasarrif* of Mount Lebanon, as the protocol of 1864 provided. However, his resolve, determination, and pride made him an outstanding figure in Lebanon's history.

It was indeed an ironic twist that Amir Mustafa's appointment as *qa'emmaqam* of the Chouf came about as a result of an argument between Archbishop Boutrous al-Bustani and al-Sit Baderman, the widow of Saeed Beik Jumblatt. Both wished to get rid of Amir Milhem Arslan, who held the position of the Chouf's *qa'emmaqam* from 1861 until the time of Franco Pasha's death in 1873. They persuaded his successor Rustom Pasha to oust him and replace him with the young Amir Mustafa because they thought the latter lacked experience and would be ineffectual. But once he assumed power it quickly became clear to the

Archbishop and al-Sit Baderman that they had made a mistake. The young Amir proved to be 'energetic, keenly intelligent, eloquent, wilful, bold, and stern'.[1]

Al-Sit Baderman was not happy with her son Nassib Beik Jumblatt at first, but Nassib Beik soon took a greater interest in government and public affairs and entered the political domain. Thus began the competition between him and Amir Mustafa, a rivalry that marked the Chouf's history between 1873 and 1907 as the people split into those who supported Nassib Beik Jumblatt and those who supported Amir Mustafa Arslan. Each of the two held the *qa'emmaqamiyya* twice following changes of the *mutasarrif*.

Amir Mustafa had a strong supporter in Istanbul in 'Izzat Pasha al-Abed of Damascus. 'Izzat Pasha secured for Amir Mustafa from the Sultanate the title of *bala*, a rank only one level below that of a minister. Amir Mustafa became known for his proud, self-aggrandizing character. Modesty was not among his qualities and contentment was not one of his traits. When he appeared to congratulate Na'oum Pasha on the occasion of Eid al-Julous al-Hamidi[2] on the first of September every year, an army detachment with drawn swords would march ahead of his carriage. The Amir assumed this illegal privilege and no one took issue with it because of the favour he enjoyed with the *mutasarrif*.[3]

Amir Mustafa understood that his power rested with the Druze and so he affiliated himself with them and took pride in their heritage. He did not ignore them or violate their traditions. He revered the *ajaweed* (the Druze men of religion) and relied on the brave. He was brave, resolute, dignified, and stern, but not unjust or treacherous. He imposed peace and security on the area, preserving people's property, and organized its operations and transactions. He himself was a large landowner who loved property and land. Through his diligence he gained extensive holdings and was loath to let go of a piece of real estate. He appointed brave and trustworthy watchmen and rural wardens so that transgressions ceased and people felt that they and their property were safe. Amir Mustafa mingled and interacted with the people. He held intimate gatherings at which he would set aside his sternness and listen to people's anecdotes.

---

1. As'ad Rustom, *Lubnan fi 'Ahd al-Mutasarrifiyya* [Lebanon during the Mutasarrifiyya], p. 162.
2. The anniversary of Sultan Abdel Hamid's assumption of the Ottoman throne. [Translator]
3. Bechara al-Khouri, *Haqa'iq Lubnaniyya* [Lebanese Facts], p. 13.

He also had amusing stories of his own concerning people whom we shall meet in other sections of the book.

***

In 1898 Emperor Wilhelm II of Germany visited the East and travelled through Beirut and Damascus. The *mutasarrif* of Mount Lebanon at the time was Na'oum Pasha, and he invited the Emperor to a luncheon in Aley. The *mutasarrif* mobilized the Lebanese from all sides to welcome the Emperor upon his arrival in Aley by rail. Since the area was Amir Mustafa's, it was, of course, he who organized the reception.

On the morning of the designated day, people came from all parts of the mountain to Aley until the town's square became overcrowded. Amir Mustafa began to distribute the attendees among the various parts of the square. He directed the Druze men of religion, with their *'ama'im*[1] to occupy the foot of the mountain overlooking the square. They gathered there until the area looked as if it was covered with snow. He organized the young men in the square, and all were prepared to play their part.

The *mutasarrif* and his wife, Amir Mustafa and the high-ranking officials stood awaiting the train. The Amir, donning his *bala* scarf and carrying his sword, stood in full glory. The train arrived and the doors of the royal car opened to the cheers and applause of the crowd. The *mutasarrif* approached the steps of the carriage, took the hand of the Emperor, and kissed it. He then introduced his wife and the Emperor bent down and kissed her hand. As for Amir Mustafa, he remained in his place, two steps away from the train. He assumed a challenging posture, placing his hand on his sword, holding his head up high, and thrusting his chest out. The Emperor looked at him and people held their breath. Who was going to walk towards the other?

The Emperor, faced with Amir Mustafa's solemn, dignified bearing, felt compelled to approach the Amir himself. Amir Mustafa extended his arm and shook the Emperor's hand as one would his equal. He then pointed to the mountain and told the Emperor through a translator, 'Those are the Druze men of religion.' Then he turned to the square and told him, 'And those are the Druze youth.' Responding to the Amir's signal, four young men, appearing like eagles in their traditional

---

1. Special white turbans worn by the pious. [Translator]

embroidered Lebanese attire, emerged from the crowd, each of them carrying two swords. They began to sway and dance as they displayed their deft handling of the swords in time with the music of the horns and the beat of the drums.

The Emperor was engrossed in watching the swordplay. He stood for some time with Amir Mustafa by his side and the *mutasarrif* and the rest of the group behind them. And after some time, the Emperor and the important people in attendance were invited to a large pavilion prepared for their reception.

***

Amir Mustafa visited Europe and carried out some official tasks in its various capitals. The European states had some say in Lebanon's administration, especially in the choice of *mutasarrif*. Amir Mustafa also visited Istanbul, accompanied by his son Amir Muhammad, who enjoyed a lofty position in the Ottoman capital. There they met Sultan Abdel Hamid. It is said that Amir Mustafa behaved freely in the presence of the Sultan and did not abide by the rules of protocol that his son Amir Muhammad called to his attention.

***

After he left the *qa'emmaqamiyya*, Amir Mustafa continued to enjoy considerable influence in Lebanon. He did not end his involvement in politics or abandon his interest in the nation's public affairs. In 1909 he participated with Amir Shakib Arslan, Habib Pasha al-Saad, Nassib Beik Jumblatt, Shaykh Ken'aan al-Daher, Rashid Beik Nakhle, and others whose names have not come down to us, in the campaign to force the *mutasarrif* Youssef Franco Pasha to abide by the new Ottoman constitution. The new constitution was declared after the coup led by the Party of Unity and Progress in Istanbul, in collaboration with high-ranking army officers from among the members of the Young Turks.

These Lebanese leaders were able to organize a popular march on the *mutasarrifiyya*'s summer headquarters in Beiteddine. They forced the *mutasarrif* to pledge loyalty and allegiance to the constitution, and to dismiss Amir Qabalan Abu Alameh from chairmanship of the Administrative Council and appoint Salim Beik Ammoun in his place. They also made him remove Amir Taufiq Majid Arslan and appoint Amir Shakib in his place as *qa'emmaqam* of the Chouf.[1]

Amir Mustafa maintained his respected position and influence until the last years of his life. In 1913 a dispute arose between the residents of Baysour and the residents of Souq al-Gharb as a result of an individual incident. The towns' learned men of religion were able to settle the matter peacefully, but the state decided to open an investigation into the incident. It appointed the head of the criminal court at that time, Ahmad al-Husseini, and the judicial assistant Aref Beik Nakad to look into the matter.

Among those called for questioning was Shaykh Rashid al-Qadi,[2] and a verbal altercation broke out between him and Ahmad al-Husseini. Shaykh Rashid's nephew, Shaykh Amin al-Qadi, heard the noise and became very angry. He stormed into the interrogation room and assaulted the head of the court, causing a delay in the investigation. The al-Qadis were very concerned about the case since Ahmad al-Husseini was both their adversary and the arbiter in the proceedings. The court date was set and a verdict issued declaring Shaykh Amin's innocence. Shaykh Rashid al-Qadi had asked Amir Mustafa to intercede with Ahmad al-Husseini, so al-Husseini set aside his personal right, as well as that of the public, in favour of Amir Mustafa.

***

Amir Mustafa died on 17 July 1914 in Souq al-Gharb and was buried the following day in Beirut. On 23 July, one week after his death, a memorial occasion was held for him in Ain 'Inoub. The number of those attending was estimated at 10,000. The people of Ain 'Inoub prepared a feast for the mourners consisting of 14 sheep, 60 kg of fat, 500 kg of bread, 250 kg of tomatoes, and 250 kg of every other vegetable of the season.

---

1. Bechara al-Khouri, p. 58.
2. He is the grandfather of the writer Shaykh Rashid al-Qadi, the former member of the religious council.

***

One last statement must be made. There is no doubt that recording these scenes concerning Amir Mustafa Arslan amounts to praise of his memory. I know that many people will not agree with me in this respect since the Amir, no matter how good his qualities or how great his favours, was still a feudal tyrant of the first order. And this is true. But we must remember that Amir Mustafa's time was different from our own. We must also acknowledge that the man was honest with himself and with the people. He did not hide his reality behind a mask of democracy and equality. Moreover, I am merely recording prominent scenes, some of which may not accord with our dispositions and preferences.

Amir Shakib Arslan and Fares Alameh

The political division that prevailed in the Chouf district for over thirty years, pitting Amir Mustafa Arslan against Nassib Beik Jumblatt, finally ended with the two leaders' reconciliation at the beginning of the twentieth century. But the shuffling of the deck gave rise to a new coalition countering this reconciliation. The Thalouth (or Tripartite Coalition) Party emerged, so named in reference to its three principals, Amir Taufiq Arslan, Mustafa Beik al-'Imad, and Isber Afandi Shqeir.

The new party rose to prominence during the reign of the *mutasarrif* Muzaffar Pasha, who was known for his frequent dismissals and appointments of his administration's employees and whose period of rule was unstable.[1] At the time of his death, Amir Taufiq Arslan was the *qa'emmaqam* of the Chouf and Mustafa Beik al-'Imad was the Chief of the Penal Department in Baabda. Youssef Franco Pasha, the brother of Na'oum Pasha's wife, then came to power, encouraging the hopes of his brother-in-law's friends such as Amir Mustafa Arslan and Shaykh Khalil al-Khouri, among others. However, he soon dashed their hopes by aligning himself with the party of the previous *mutasarrif*.[2]

Youssef Franco Pasha (1907–1912) is considered the weakest *mutasarrif* to have ruled Lebanon under the 1861 system, and as luck would have it, significant political events took place during his reign. Early in the summer of 1908, the Ottoman coup led by the Party of Unity and Progress took place in Istanbul, carried out in collaboration with high-ranking army officers from among the Young Turks. The coup

---

1. Bechara al-Khouri, *Haqaiq Lubnaniyya* [Lebanese Facts], p. 50.
2. Bechara al-Khouri, p. 52.

resulted in the enactment of a new constitution and Sultan Abdel Hamid's abdication.

It was natural for Lebanon, despite its independence, to be affected by this coup, especially after Beirut witnessed a coup of its own. The Turkish army officers forced Beirut's *wali* (governor) to withdraw and made changes in government positions, installing 'free men' in the place of 'reactionaries' and 'Hamidis' (i.e. loyalists of the Sultan).[1] The unrest reached the *mutasarrifiyya* of Mount Lebanon. Voices rose demanding reform, with the ousted government officials carrying the banners of opposition. They organized a march on Beiteddine, the summer residence of the *qa'emmaqamiyya*.

On 31 August 1908 a delegation arrived at Beiteddine headed by Amir Mustafa Arslan, Amir Shakib Arslan, Habib Pasha al-Saad, Nassib Beik Jumblatt, Shaykh Ken'aan al-Daher and Rashid Beik Nakhle. The *mutasarrif* met with the leaders of the delegation, who demanded that he implement the new constitution, except in matters related to Lebanon's distinct system and characteristics.[2] The *mutasarrif* refused. However, when thousands of people gathered the second day, besieging Beiteddine, the *mutasarrif* grudgingly conceded.

'Freedom' thus triumphed by granting entry to those on the outside and expelling those on the inside. The most important changes were Salim Beik Ammoun's replacement of Amir Qabalan Abu al-Lame' as head of the Administrative Council and the appointment of Amir Shakib Arslan as *qa'emmaqam* in place of Amir Taufiq.[3]

***

Because the *mutasarrif* Youssef Franco Pasha's appointment of Amir Shakib Arslan as the Chouf's *qa'emmaqam* had been made under duress, and against the will of the ascendant Thalouth Party, his position as *qa'emmaqam* was awkward. Along with his intelligence, broad education in science and literature, and keen memory, Amir Shakib, especially in his youth, had an impulsive, hot-tempered nature. His impulsiveness drove

1. Bechara al-Khouri, p. 56.
2. Lahd Khater, *Ahd al-Mutasarrifeen fi Lubnan* [The *Mutasarrifeen* Era in Lebanon], p. 179.
3. Bechara al-Khouri, p. 58.

him to commit an error that led to his dismissal from the *qa'emmaqamiyya*. This was called 'the mistake of the clever'.

***

One day in 1911, Fares al-Lame' Sha'ban sat and gambled with Masoud Haidar al-Khishin in Saeed Habib's coffee-house in Hay al-Oumara in Choueifat. Fares had luck on his side and won 40 Majidi liras from Masoud. The sum was a fortune in those days. Once the euphoria of gambling had subsided, Masoud felt the gravity of his loss and became anxious. He went to the government palace and aired his grievance to Amir Shakib. The Amir appreciated the significance of the man's loss and he sent after Fares. When Fares came, the Amir asked him to return the money to Masoud. He refused, saying, 'If Masoud had won this sum of money from me, he would not have returned it.' The Amir invoked the law, since gambling was forbidden, but Fares persisted in his refusal. Fares's defiance angered the Amir, so he slapped Fares, took the money from him and returned it to Masoud, and jailed Fares for two days. This slap would enter history because of the consequences that ensued.

The *mutasarrif*, the three leaders of the Thalouth Party, and other opponents and agitators were waiting for an opportunity to bring down Shakib. After the Amir's incident with Fares, they immediately attempted to take advantage of the situation. They held a meeting at Amir Taufiq's house in Khalde and agreed on a plan of operation. They had Khattar Beik Ali Daher Saab[1] bring Fares to Khalde. They persuaded Fares to file suit against Amir Shakib and appointed a lawyer for him. Then, with the *mutasarrif*'s assistance, they waged a publicity campaign against the *qa'emmaqam*, focusing on his dispute with Fares and his harassment of a poor man who makes his living selling *ka'k* (round puff bread).

The lawsuit reached Istanbul, where each party had its supporters. Amir Mustafa intervened and tried to assist Amir Shakib through his friends in the Turkish capital. It was not deemed appropriate for Amir Shakib's adversary to be a commoner, so others saw to it that Fares Alameh was given the title of *beik*. This became the subject of jokes and

---

1. Khattar Saab was a wise, perceptive, and knowledgeable man. He sided with Amir Taufiq, who later procured the title of *beik* for him. He devoted himself to politics and neglected his land. He later had to sell it all and died a poor man.

some amusement, for what was Fares Alameh doing with the title of *beik* when he was a simple *ka'k* seller? He grew tired of people's jokes, however, and insisted that he should no longer be addressed by that title. The case was finally resolved in accordance with the *mutasarrif*'s inclination to remove Amir Shakib from the *qa'emmaqamiyya*.

***

Choueifat's administrator, Farid Beik al-'Imad, had been appointed to his position by Amir Shakib, but he turned against the Amir and supported his own maternal uncle, Mustafa Beik al-'Imad. The Choueifat police force was under the leadership of Commander Hassan Rafe' Fakhr. Ali Hammoud Saab, Ali Fares Saab, Mahmoud Masoud Reeman Saab, and Salim Shakib al-Jurdi were all among the rank-and-file, and their allegiance was to Amir Shakib. Ali Mahmoud was the administrator's secretary, responsible for receiving and reviewing the administrator's mail and presenting it to him.

On the day that word of Amir Shakib's removal got around, Ali Mahmoud received a letter from the Amir in Baaqline. In the letter, the Amir informed him that Nassib Beik Jumblatt was to be the new *qa'emmaqam* and asked him to commemorate the occasion in Choueifat, since he was in agreement with Nassib Beik, and 'one hand had yielded to its sister'. Ali folded the letter and put it in his pocket. Before noon, the administrator, Farid Beik al-'Imad, left government house and headed for Khalde. After that another letter arrived addressed to him. Ali opened it and found that it was from Amir Taufiq asking the director to organize celebrations and demonstrations in the town on the occasion of the fall of Amir Shakib and informing him that he, meaning Amir Taufiq, would be appointed *qa'emmaqam*. Ali folded the letter and put it in his pocket with the letter from Amir Shakib. He then closed the office and headed to Hay al-Oumara to consult with his relatives about the series of events and the conflicting reports.

In Baabda, the police leadership learned of Amir Shakib's removal. Their leader, Milhem al-Khouri from Bkasin, knew the extent of political dissension in Choueifat. He saw that it was his duty to anticipate potential unrest, so he wrote a letter to Choueifat's administrator warning him of possible riots and challenges to authority during the celebrations and urging the necessity of using the police force to prevent such disturbances. He then entrusted a mounted policeman, Saeed Hussein al-Jurdi,[1] to carry the letter to Choueifat's administrator.

When Saeed al-Jurdi arrived in Choueifat that afternoon, he did not find anyone in the administrator's office. He went to the administrator's home (he lived on the estate of Fares Mhana al-Jureidini) but did not find him there either. As he proceeded through Hay al-Amrousiyya, he sensed the ongoing preparation of decorations and banners for that night and heard threats to burn down Amir Shakib's house. He crossed to Hay al-Oumara, left his horse at his house, and went to the house of Amir Shakib. There he found Ali Mahmoud and they exchanged information. They were both in the same party, so they agreed that each of them would mobilize his relatives in preparation for what might happen that night.

The sun set, darkness fell, and the celebrations began. Fires were lit on rooftops, and then the gatherings began and shots were fired from rifles, pistols, and revolvers. According to Ibn al-Wardi, 'Half the people are opposed to him who rules – and that's only if he is just.' Such was the case with Amir Shakib. He governed and enforced the law, and many people who were considered his supporters consequently distanced themselves from him. He banned trading in arms, so many of the avid adventurers who made their living selling arms, such as Salim Masoud Sharafeddine Abu N'eim, Khalil Mahmoud Wahab, and Salim Shibley Saab, turned against him. They all rejoiced at his ouster from the *qa'emmaqamiyya*.

Politics then, just as today, had the ability to violate the sanctity of kinship and divide households, separating fathers from sons and brothers from brothers. One of that night's strangest occurrences was when Salim Abu N'eim climbed the roof of his house to light a fire in celebration. His brother Nasib, a member of Amir Shakib's party, followed him to the roof to prevent him from lighting the fire on the grounds that the house belonged to them both and Salim did not have the right to decorate it.

Hundreds of armed men gathered in the government palace square and received orders to march to Hay al-Oumara by way of Ain 'Inoub to attack Amir Shakib's house and burn it down. The crowd moved, announced by the blare of gunshots.

Meanwhile, in Hay al-Oumara, about thirty men of the Saab, Jurdi, Musharrafiyya, and Khishin families gathered in front of Amir Shakib's

---

1. He was one of Choueifat's strong, brave men and one of the national warriors. He fought with Sultan Pasha al-Atrash in the First World War and entered Damascus with him. He also fought with his two brothers Abd al-Halim and Shafiq in the Druze–Syrian revolution and they were among its listed heroes. Abd al-Halim and Shafiq were both martyred in the battle.

house. Among them were Shaykh Salim Qassem Saab and his brothers Abd al-Halim and Khalil, Hamad Mahmoud, Ramez Khalil Reeman, Fad'a Abdallah Ahmad, Fandi Hussein Hamad, Hussein Ali Khattar, Hamed Amin Daher and his brother Aref, Saeed Wehbeh Suleiman and his brothers Wadie' and Abd al-Halim, Qassem Ibrahim Qassem and his brother Saeed. From the Musharrafiyya family there was Ibrahim As'ad, Nassib Fares and his brother Khalil, and Dawoud Milhem Fahd. From the Jurdi family there were Nassib Fahd and his brother Muhammad and Salim Shahin. From the Khishin family there were Saeed Ahmad, Hamad Khza'i, Muhammad Nimr, and Hamad As'ad and others whose names I do not know.

The demonstrators' motives were partly serious and partly frivolous, since some of them had no political inclinations and simply walked with the crowd to jump on the bandwagon. But the defenders were serious in their resolve that no one would reach the house of Amir Shakib. To let the crowd know what they were up against, Fad'a Abdallah Saab called his relative Hamed Amin (who was neutral) and told him, 'Go to the protesters and tell them we are here.' And Hamed went.

Some of the young men of Bani Saab did not wait for the demonstration to arrive but set out to intercept it. When they peered over the rim of Wadi Ain al-Bir, they began to fire shots in the direction of Hay al-Amrousiyya. At that point, the mob's leaders understood the reality of the situation, so they stopped at the turn of Amrousiyya's spring and redirected the crowd towards the upper part of the neighbourhood. And Choueifat was saved from a massacre.

***

Hassan Rafe' Fakhr and Ali Mahmoud Saab prepared a report on the night's events and sent it by night to the police leadership in Baabda with the two policemen, Masoud Muhammad Reeman Saab and Salim Shahin al-Jurdi. They were told that the leadership was awaiting the return of Saeed Hussein al-Jurdi so he could present a detailed oral report of the events in Choueifat that day.

In the morning, Saeed Hussein went to the government house square in Hay al-Amrousiyya and saw that everything was normal. Carriages, ready for travel to Beirut, stood awaiting their passengers, their owners standing next to them. He saw Daher Saeed Fares Abd al-Khaliq, the sons of Salim Mefas al-Souqi, and other known carriage owners. Saeed asked about the administrator and was told that he was on the roof of government house with Khalil Najib al-Khouri al-Juraidini and Youssef Ali Hammoud Nassereddine. Saeed went to the rooftop, gave the administrator the official salute, and handed him the letter from the police leadership.

Farid Beik took the letter and read it. He then turned to Saeed, cursed Amir Shakib and said, 'Tell your master Milhem al-Khouri that Amir Shakib is gone with the wind, and he, meaning Milhem, will soon follow.' Saeed could not accept Amir Shakib's being insulted in this way, so he returned Farid Beik's greeting with a better one. Farid jumped, wanting to enter government house, but Saeed threatened him with worse. Then he mounted his horse and rode to Baabda.

Once in Baabda, Saeed wrote a detailed report, with the help and guidance of police chief Amir Fayez Chehab, about all that had taken place in Choueifat. He supplemented the report with a complaint against the administrator, Farid Beik al-'Imad, accusing him of defaming all of the responsible officials, and the papers were presented to the *mutasarrif*. Nassib Beik Jumblatt was appointed the Chouf's *qa'emmaqam* and Farid Beik al-'Imad was transferred to Ain Zhalta.

Choueifat Enters the First World War

Towards the end of September 1918, the Turkish–German front collapsed in Syria before the advance of the British, approaching from Palestine under the leadership of General Allenby, and the Arabs, approaching from eastern Jordan under the leadership of Amir Faysal ibn al-Hussein. The Turks stopped fighting and retreated north towards their country. As a consequence of Turkey's defeat, everyone working in the political domain in Lebanon set out to restore their livelihoods and redirect their efforts to fall in line with the new situation and its requirements. The British and the French were now at the doorstep.

Amir Shakib Arslan had cooperated with the Turks throughout the war. He extended a squadron of Druze volunteers to the Turkish army when the Turks attacked the Suez Canal in an attempt to enter Egypt but retreated in defeat.[1] As soon as Turkey was defeated, he left the country and settled in Switzerland. Amir Nasib remained in his home reading and writing. Amir Adel, their younger brother, was the *qa'emmaqam* of the Chouf district. When the *mutasarrif* of Mount Lebanon fled with the entire contents of the *mutasarrifiyya*'s coffers, Amir Adel, along with Amir Malik Chehab, took over the administration of the *mutasarrifiyya*'s affairs. They handled the task competently and diligently for a full week before the French entered the country and took over all functions of civil and military administration. At that point Amir Adel went to Damascus.

Amir Taufiq Majid Arslan had returned from exile on 26 March 1918. To the French his exile represented a certificate of good conduct, so he

---

1. Among those who volunteered in this campaign and survived the two plagues – the plague of killing and the plague of hunger – were two of us: Mustafa Qassem Hussein Saab and Salim Fandi Hussein Hamad Saab.

had nothing to fear. As for Amir Amin Mustafa Arslan, he was in Lebanon, and as soon as he saw the change in the political wind he began inciting civilians in the Gharb area to attack the defeated Turkish army. He arrived in Choueifat on the evening of 1 October and went around its neighbourhoods inviting people to a meeting in the government palace square in Hay al-Amrousiyya that evening.

After dusk fell, a large number of Choueifatis gathered in the square, and lanterns and torches were lit. Amir Amin stood before the crowd and began inciting them to intercept the path of the Turks, withdrawing from Palestine individually or in scattered groups under the leadership of Aref Beik al-Hassan. He told them they could overcome the defeated soldiers with canes and clubs alone.

A telegram had arrived from Damascus that morning, addressed to the people of Choueifat and signed by Amir Saeed al-Jazairi,[1] asking them to revolt against the Turks and informing them that the Arab armies had overrun the Syrian plains. The director of Choueifat's telegraph and mail centre was a Turk called Na'el Afandi. He did not disclose the telegram's contents but went to Shafiq Mansour al-Jurdi and showed it to him, asking him not to publicize it until after he had left Choueifat. Shafiq purchased all of Na'el's belongings for 3 Majidi liras, and once the Turkish employee had left town, Shafiq al-Jurdi announced the news of the telegram. After the telegram and Amir Amin's speech, the youth were roused and Choueifat declared war on Turkey.

***

During the early years of the war, Turkish forces had dug trenches along the high grounds of Choueifat's grapevines and in Jamhour and elsewhere, anticipating retreat before the Allies. Amir Amin chose al-Jamhour as the place to intercept the Turks as they withdrew. He ordered the people of Choueifat to follow him north and walked in front of them carrying a military rifle he had borrowed from Amin Hanna Mer'ei al-Jureidini. He sent two braves ahead of him, Khalil Muhammad Wahab and Ali Mahmoud Saab, to act as scouts.

---

1. He was the grandson of Amir Abd al-Qadir al-Jazairi I and the brother of Amir Abd al-Qadir al-Jazairi II. He took power in Damascus when its Turkish administration fell. He sent telegrams to all the areas of Lebanon and Syria to announce the establishment of Arab rule.

When the crowd reached the bend under the church of Hay al-Amrousiyya, Kamel Salim Nou'man Saab came to them from the west and told them that there was a small group of Turkish soldiers with camels, mules, and guns near Hamid Shahin al-Rishani's vault (outbuilding). Without waiting for the order to attack, the people swept along the road and through the fields towards Saida. They closed upon the Turkish soldiers from all sides. The soldiers numbered no more than thirty, so they surrendered without any resistance. Thus the Choueifatis won the first battle without firing a single shot and those who arrived first made away with the spoils, leaving the soldiers with nothing but the clothes on their bodies.

Amir Amin was not impressed with the battle and its spoils, however. He said to the people, 'I want you for something greater – follow me,' and began marching towards Kfar Shima and Baabda. But the Choueifatis had other ideas. Those who had secured camels, mules, guns, or bags of food returned home to deposit their spoils and possibly not return to battle. Also, most of the men preferred to fight on their own land and not to go to Baabda and al-Jamhour, leaving their homes and kin unguarded between themselves and the soldiers coming from the west by way of Khalde. They defied the leadership's orders and began deserting one after the other. By the time Amir Amin reached the bridge of Kfar Shima, his army had been reduced to eight men.

Yet he insisted on continuing the march, and they reached Sibneih at midnight. Hunger and fatigue had set in, so they stopped. Amir Amin went to the house of Shaykh Saeed Hamdan, the Druze denomination's magistrate at the time, and returned with bread and cheese. They ate and resumed their march until they reached al-Jamhour and took positions for themselves in its trenches.

Amir Amin stood on the Beirut–Damascus road seeking news. He saw a horseman coming from the direction of Beirut and approached him. After conversing with the horseman, the Amir immediately returned to his men and said he had just learned that a Turkish squadron had set up camp in the Hadath area, and that he had decided to attack it.

At that point Khalil Wehbeh, Ali Mahmoud Saab, and Nasib Fahd al-Jurdi decided to give up the wild adventure, so they apologized to Amir Amin. The rest of the group did the same and they all returned to Choueifat. They arrived there at dawn to find that the battle was raging on the southern front, so they walked towards Khalde. As for Amir Amin, he went from Jamhour down to Beirut.

***

The people of Choueifat had not slept that night – 'Its world was turned upside down.' After four years of trials, deprivation, scarcity, and hunger, God had opened the doors of sustenance at the expense of those who had caused these calamities. Men and boys rose up and started attacking the Turkish soldiers, seizing their livestock, clothes and tents, guns, and supplies. Everything had some value and satisfied some need. They would stop the soldiers and take their guns and goods, and intercept the wagons and undo the animals' reins and saddles. One would take the mule, another would take the saddle and harness, and they would share the cargo.

The assault continued until morning, which was easy since the soldiers were retreating individually or in small, unorganized groups. Still, some of them resisted their assailants, and several clashes took place, some of which were bloody. It was said that Nasib Fahd al-Jurdi killed a Turkish soldier, and Jamil Khza'i al-Khishin killed another.

It seems that some of the soldiers who suffered attacks went back towards the south and told their leaders what had happened. Aref Beik al-Hassan reorganized and regrouped his forces, and by morning everything had changed. The Choueifatis were now confronting an organized army with a full complement of weapons and abundant ammunition. As the confrontations began, Khalil Muhsin Saab was wounded in the leg near the Parched River, and Saeed Ahmad al-Khishin was killed. As the Turks approached, the Choueifatis went up the hills overlooking the road, and violent clashes took place between them and the army.

But what can a few rifles, hunting guns, and revolvers do against a fully equipped and organized army? The Choueifatis' ammunition was exhausted within an hour, so they retreated inwards towards Dayr Qoubel. In Choueifat, the houses near the road were evacuated, although the soldiers did not attack the houses but continued on their way towards Beirut.

***

As for the leader of the scouting mission to al-Jamhour, he returned very quickly. Khalil Wahab, known for his bravery and adventurousness, had many friends in Beirut. He had not gone very far towards Khalde when he encountered three men of the al-'Itani family from Beirut. They had been conscripted by the Turks and were surrounded by some of the sons of Choueifat. He rescued them and returned with them to his house. Once things had settled down, he took them to Beirut. As for Ali Mahmoud, he acquired a military rifle, but one of his relatives took it from him and did not return it, so he settled for an exchange.

A few days later, new shoes began to appear in Choueifat made of saddle leather. When the olive harvest season came, camels and mules appeared on the road of the Choueifat desert. These were among the spoils of war.

***

In Aley, Sofar, and Riyaq no one took the initiative in confronting the soldiers as the people of Choueifat did. They would wait for the troops to pass and then attack the warehouses. In Aley the citizens seized a huge cache of weapons and supplies. However, the arms warehouses were in Sofar. As soon as the Turks passed through the area, the people of Jurd and Qobbei' raided the warehouses. A Turkish guard named Muhammad Amin stood at its door. We do not know why this soldier stayed at his post after the army had retreated. This brave man insisted on performing his duty, so the people killed him and grabbed the guns, bullets, and gunpowder.

Some people from al-Jurd used gunpowder to light fires for a long time after this raid. Rifles became so abundant that shepherds started carrying carbines instead of canes. But al-Jurd's citizens remain regretful to this day about one missed opportunity: they went for the weapons and missed out on the mules, which were very valuable. Zahle's citizens ended up with most of the mules, along with what they captured in the way of weapons and ammunition. Whatever goods eluded the people of Choueifat, Aley, al-Jurd, and Zahle fell into the laps of the people of Riyaq and its surrounding areas. Milhem Qassem and his people from the Beqaa exhibited great skill and creativity in this effort.

***

What the people of Choueifat gained from the Turks in 1918 they lost to the ally France many times over in 1923 and 1926. In 1923 a breach occurred in Mount Lebanon's security and a number of murders took place. Some were motivated by sectarian considerations, but most were individual acts of retribution and robbery and had nothing to do with sectarianism. Although all the incidents occurred in the mountain, Shaykh Salim Qassem Saab, Choueifat's *shaykh solh*,[1] met with the concerned parties and discussed the general state of affairs. The meeting went well because those in attendance, who were from different sects, pledged to cooperate to keep the coastal area free of such dreaded incidents.

But those defying authority had a different opinion. A number of them entered Choueifat surreptitiously on a moonlit night and obstructed the Saida–Beirut road at the place known as Sakour, which lies between Choueifat and the Parched River. They stopped a large number of cars passing in both directions and took all of the money and jewellery their passengers carried. Then they went back to the hills and mountains.

The (French) authorities quickly imposed a fine on the Chouf requiring each man to hand over a military rifle. Whoever did not have a rifle bought one and handed it in. Once the collection of weapons was complete, Amir Shafiq Arslan, the administrator of Choueifat, summoned some of the town's notables to a meeting at his home to discuss the matter. What had taken place was done and could not be undone, so the meeting focused on how to prevent a recurrence of the incident. The parties decided to support the authorities in their security efforts. They elected two of Choueifat's bravest men, Ramez Khalil Reeman Saab and Saeed Hussein Ali Mansour al-Jurdi, to guard the roads around the town. Nothing happened after that to disrupt Choueifat's security until the outbreak of the Druze revolution in 1925.

***

The Great Druze Revolution against the French began on 25 July 1925 and was joined soon thereafter by nationalist elements in Damascus and other parts of Syria. It was natural, as has been the case over the course of generations and even centuries, that Lebanon was influenced by events

---

1. *Shaykh solh* is a term used frequently in this book. It means a village notable who is designated by the public to act as a peacemaker in village disputes.

in Syria. A large number of the sons of the Chouf, Matn, Wadi al-Taym, and Baabda joined the revolution. Many of the revolutionaries would go to the battlefields in Jabal al-Druze, al-Ghouta, or al-Iqlim and return covertly to Lebanon for rest, medication, and supplies, and to see their families. The country's security was disrupted once again and there were some isolated incidents.

A policeman was killed in Khalde. Khalde was within the municipal jurisdiction of Choueifat, so the authorities quickly imposed a monetary fine on Choueifat to the amount of 1,000 gold liras and 50 rifles. The people of Choueifat initially refused to pay because the punitive fine was unjust and oppressive. Amir Shafiq Arslan urged them to pay since he was still Choueifat's administrator, but they refused. Twelve of the town's prominent men were arrested and placed in Baabda prison as hostages. The detainees were: Fouad Jad'oun al-Jureidini, Kamel Mansour al-Souqi, Badi' Youssef al-Jureidini, Ma'rouf Rashid Salman, the *mukhtar* (village chief) Amin Elias al-Jureidini, Jibran Ne'meh Hanna, Nakhle Ne'meh Hanna, Amin al-Shoueiri, Amin Suleiman al-Musharrafiyya, Hamed Adnan al-Musharrafiyya, Muhammad Isma'il Saab, and Salim Shahin Hammoud Haidar. They were treated well in Baabda.

Intercessions and communications then began, and finally Shaykh Abu Kamal Mansour al-Souqi, Salim Masoud Sharafeddine Abu N'eim, and Najib Milhem Shahin Suleiman went to Mukhtara, where al-Sit Nazira Jumblatt gave them a letter of request to the French military governor in Beiteddine. Although the meeting was not a success, the matter was resolved with the fine being reduced to 500 gold liras and 12 rifles. The money and rifles were collected and submitted and the detainees were released after spending twenty-seven days in prison.

The War between France and the al-B'eini Clan

At the beginning of 1919, Amin Qassem al-B'eini was killed on his way back from Saida to his home town of Mazra'at al-Chouf (or al-Mazra'a). Though the location of the crime was known and the identity of those with prior records in the area was not a secret, the authorities announced that Amin had been killed under mysterious circumstances and that the investigation had not uncovered the identity of the killer or killers. This outcome did not sit well with the al-B'einis. They felt sure that they were the victims of wilful neglect on the part of those in power. It pained them that their relative's blood had been shed with impunity. But the incident did not end there, and the case was not closed. It was not long before Amin Qassem al-B'eini's killing was avenged.

This time the people were astounded by the authorities' hasty response. Not even three days had passed since the act of vengeance when formal charges were brought against five of the al-B'eini men: Hassan Shahin, Youssef Alameddine, Nasrallah Youssef, Muhammad Hussein Salman, and Hussein Fares. The police leadership in Beiteddine directed the *mukhtar* of al-Mazra'a, Muhammad Hamad Abu Karroum, to ask the five men to turn themselves in. They all refused.

At that point a police force headed to al-Mazra'a and overtook the town by surprise from the north and the south. The al-B'eini men retreated to the mountains, where they spent a quiet night, and then returned to their homes at the break of dawn thinking that the force had withdrawn from the town. But within less than an hour noise erupted and screams arose. The police had actually feigned withdrawal and hidden in some abandoned houses and fields on the town's outskirts. When they were certain that the al-B'eini men had returned to the town, they gathered and began their approach towards their houses.

The police had committed an error of judgement, however. They thought the al-B'eini men's retreat to the mountains was an act of fear and weakness. In reality it was only avoiding a confrontation with the authorities. But now the encounter was forced upon them, and a confrontation was inevitable.

The first of the al-B'eini men the policemen met was Hassan Shahin, whose name was at the top of the wanted list. When they ordered him to surrender, he complied. But then he began to converse with them and retreated backwards until he led them into the square known as Sahat al-Ain. And there they 'fell into their laps'. They were closed on from all sides, not only by the sons of al-B'eini but by the daughters of al-B'eini as well. Hand-to-hand fighting ensued, resulting in the police being disarmed and then set free. The banner from the battle was given to Zahia al-B'eini, Hassan Shahin's ex-wife, as she had done deeds of which not even men were capable.

It is well known that our al-B'eini sisters are no less powerful or violent than our al-B'eini brothers. They have a glorious history in this respect. There are many of them about whom stories and tales, seemingly woven from fantasy, are still told.

***

It was natural for the police leadership to repeat its raid against the rebels. The leadership sent a bigger force than the first, including both infantry and horsemen, and devised a careful military plan to seize the sons of al-B'eini. Some members of the force appeared on the roads. A large contingent of them climbed the mountains west of al-Mazra'a and from there approached the edge of the village. But their movements were not concealed from the sons of al-B'eini, who were not fooled. Before the soldiers could take their positions in the fortresses, shots rained down on them from all directions, and they were forced to retreat after losing two horses and some arms. Youssef Alameddine al-B'eini and Nassralleh Youssef al-B'eini returned to town with the *qali'a*.[1]

---

1. *Qali'a* is a colloquial term meaning a horse taken as part of the spoils of war. Its
   (continued...)

At noon the same day, the police attempted to attack the town once again. They clashed with the town's defenders. The al-B'einis were able to take five more rifles and the police retreated, realizing that if the sons of al-B'eini had intended to strike their targets, many of the authorities' men would have been killed or wounded. They returned to Beiteddine after the failure of their mission.

Lebanon at that time was still under the control of the British and French forces, but civil authority was in the hands of the French. When the second police assault on Mazra'at al-Chouf met the same fate as the first, the French became angry and sent soldiers into the area. That night a number of relatives and friends of the al-B'einis came to Mazra'at al-Chouf and warned them that the French had moved heavy weaponry and a great assembly of soldiers towards the Chouf. The al-B'eini war council held an emergency meeting to study the situation and lay plans for all possible contingencies.

On the morning of the following day, the news was confirmed as cannon, machine guns, and cars were seen approaching al-Mazra'a from the north and west. At that point the al-B'einis became convinced they stood no chance before the military campaign directed against them, and their only options were surrender or flight. Resistance would have exposed the elderly, women, and children to death. But the al-B'einis preferred emigration to surrender. They did not fear prosecution or imprisonment, but worried about being subjected to humiliation and insults at the hands of the military authorities after all they had done the previous three days.

The horn sounded and the call for departure was made. Saddles were fastened to the backs of beasts, animals were loaded, cattle were gathered, and men, women, and children departed from the town on horseback, on foot, and in cars, all heading south-west on the rugged mountain roads. Not one of the al-B'einis stayed in al-Mazra'a. They all took the rural route to Jabal al-Druze except for one old man, Shaykh Abu Hussein Mahmoud al-B'eini, who did not have the strength to travel because of his age. He went to Bater with his children and became the guest of his friend, Shaykh Abu Ahmad Amin Awdeh.

The French army entered al-Mazra'a like conquerors, and commands were issued ordering the burning of the al-B'einis' houses. Not one of

---

(...continued)

origin might be the verb *qala'a* (to pluck), referring to the plucking of the rider from the horse's back. In *zajal*, the adventure's hero is referred to as the 'taker of the *qali'a*'.

their houses was spared, and the houses of the *mukhtar* Shahin Abu Karroum and Younis Hamed Abu Karroum were burned on the pretext that shots had been fired on the police from the two houses. The *mukhtar*'s mother and wife were al-B'einis, so a price was paid for this kinship. And thus France, after its victory over Austria, Turkey, Bulgaria, and Germany, defeated the al-B'einis, exiled them from their homes, and turned their houses into firewood.

***

In Jabal al-Druze, the al-B'eini clan received a warm welcome and settled with ease as the doors of houses and guest rooms were opened for them. Leading the welcome was al-Amir Sultan al-Atrash, then still in his youth. The new arrivals suffered no harm and lacked for nothing.

After some time, conciliatory moves were made and Amir Amin Mustafa Arslan mediated between the French authorities and the al-B'einis. His efforts bore fruit and the emigrants were allowed to return to their town and rebuild their houses. They were also paid some compensation for their losses. But many of the al-B'einis had established businesses in Suwaida so they chose to stay there, and they prospered and multiplied. Today the number of al-B'einis in Suwaida is not less than that in Mazra'at al-Chouf.

Fouad Beik Hamzeh (1901–1952)

One spring morning in 1933, the royal convoy left Mecca al-Mukarrama for Jeddah. His Majesty, King Abdulaziz ibn Abd al-Rahman al-Faysal Al Saud, ruler, founder, and builder of the Kingdom of Saudi Arabia, had just performed the Hajj, as was his habit every year. While there he received the leaders of delegations and other prominent worshippers coming from all parts of the Kingdom and from outside. Since representatives of Christian countries, including commissioned ministers and counsellors, could not enter Mecca, His Majesty would go to Jeddah where they would come to greet him.

A group of Jeddah's nobles and notables, led by Amir Faysal ibn Abdulaziz, the King's deputy in Hijaz, travelled for half an hour outside the city's walls to greet His Majesty. Among those present were: Abdulaziz ibn Mou'ammar, the Amir of Jeddah; Shaykh Abdallah al-Fadl, President of the *al-Shura* Council; the *'alim* (religious scholar) Shaykh Muhammad Nassif; Hajj Abdallah Ali Rida; Shaykh Ahmad Bonajeh; Shaykh Abd al-Qader Qabel and his brother Shaykh Suleiman Qabel; Shaykh Muhammad Hazzazi; Shaykh Ali Ammari; Shaykh Muhammad al-Tawil, and a number of other nobles, gentlemen, and high-ranking employees of the administration in Jeddah.

The King's car, a grand Mercedes, appeared. His Majesty sat in the middle, with pillows and cushions around him and beneath his hands. On each of the car's running boards, to right and left of the driver, stood a slave carrying a rifle in one hand and hanging on to the car with the other. Tens of cars of different models trailed His Majesty's car carrying guards, attendants, amirs, and companions.

The convoy stopped and the welcomers stepped forward and greeted the King one after the other as he sat in his car. One would kiss his hand, another his head, and another his nose, each in his own way. Among the welcomers was a man of angular appearance and fair complexion with a wide brow, no older than 33. He stood a few steps from the royal car. Once the group had finished greeting the King, this man stepped towards the car, opened the door, entered, sat on the seat facing His Majesty, and shook his hand. The two slaves remounted the car's running boards, and the driver turned on the engine and drove towards al-Kindara Palace in the suburbs of Jeddah. The group of companions and welcomers followed in their cars.

This young man in whose mind, sound judgement, and good counsel King Abdulaziz confided, on whose loyalty, devotion, and sacrifice he relied, and of whose integrity and good character he was assured, was Fouad, son of Amin Ali Hamzeh from Abey in the Aley district of Mount Lebanon.

***

Fouad Beik Hamzeh attained the greatest heights a Lebanese can reach outside Lebanon. Salim Pasha Malhama and Suleiman Beik al-Bustani in Istanbul, Saeed Pasha Shqeir in Sudan, and Rustom Beik Haidar in Iraq all achieved the rank of minister or its equivalent. But none was able to exceed it since this rank was never usually surpassed. But with a ruler such as Abdulaziz ibn Saud, a man whose like history sees only once every few hundred years, it is up to a man and his ambition to become one of his close advisors or ministers.

***

Fouad Hamzeh reached adolescence in an era that produced the great fateful events of the Arabs' modern history. The First World War ended, as did the Ottoman expansion into the lands of the Arabs. Europe returned to the Arab East and entered through a wide door – the door of military victory – and then divided the region and stood over it in contravention of pledges and treaties. Britain and France brought with them many of the leisure pursuits and vices of modern civilization and part of the Arab youth fell under their spell, especially in Lebanon.

But Fouad's heart only yearned for glory and achievement and his soul only found joy in freedom and independence, so he dedicated himself to work and struggle. It was natural, given his character, that the countries that had fallen under foreign rule could not tolerate him. His progress and fate led him to the Arabian peninsula, where Ibn Saud was establishing a kingdom and building a state. He entered the King's service and remained his counsellor for as long as life allowed them to be together. Fouad held the offices of ministry general secretary, minister of state, vice-minister, and ambassador. But these titles were merely for outside appearances. The important point is that he stood at the King's side and was considered a part of *ahl al-bayt* (the people of the house).

***

Fouad's companionship with Ibn Saud endured for a full quarter of a century. Over the course of that time, the state went from tribalism and nomadism to organization and civilization. It also left behind the days of scarcity and poverty as a result of the discovery of oil within its territory. Likewise the Arab region witnessed monumental events, most significantly the Palestinian cause, which was Fouad's eternal concern as he represented Ibn Saud at most conferences on the issue.

***

Just as Fouad moved quickly on the path of life and reached the heights of prestige and glory at an early age, he was also quick to complete the course and died while still only 51 years of age. His Majesty King Abdulaziz sent a brief telegram to his family that read, 'His loss to us is as it is to you. We are from God, and to Him we return.' The King remained behind closed doors and refused to receive anybody for an entire day.

Two weeks after Fouad's death, the two brother Amirs, Sultan ibn Abdulaziz, the Amir of Riyadh (and the current minister of defence) and Fahd ibn Abdulaziz (the current king) came to Beirut and visited Fouad's home to offer their condolences. Samir, Fouad's eldest son, and I received them. After shaking hands, Amir Sultan looked around and said, 'Praise God, Uncle Fouad is no more?' (meaning, 'He no longer exists?').

***

We have not written this chapter to record Fouad Hamzeh's biography, for that would require an entire volume. He participated in the building of a state and in Arab and international events of great consequence. However, in keeping with this book's purpose, I felt it appropriate to record some scenes and anecdotes from his life that would not be found in what others have written or will write about him from a greater distance.

***

When Fouad intensified his political activities against the French in the early 1920s, the authorities sought to arrest him and he disappeared from sight. They seized his father, Shaykh Abu Saeed Amin Ali Hamzeh, and detained him for several days. After he was released and the cloud had lifted, he blamed Fouad bitterly. Fouad packed his belongings, bid his family farewell, and told his father, 'If I become the man I wish to become, I will return to you. Otherwise my absence will be very long.' And he left Lebanon.

Ten years later he returned to his country, but not to be chased away by French and Senegalese soldiers. He was to receive a visit from the French High Commissioner's Secretary and an invitation to a tea party, attended by the elite officers of the Commissariat, in honour of 'Sir' Fouad Beik Hamzeh, Under-Secretary at the Saudi Ministry of Foreign Affairs. That was in 1930.

***

As for how Fouad Hamzeh reached Hijaz and entered the service of the master of the Arabian peninsula, that is an exciting story. When the fires of the Druze–Syrian revolution against the French ignited in 1925, Fouad was working in Jerusalem as a teacher at al-Rashidiyya High School and studying law at night. He also worked to support the revolution and gather aid for it. He would often go from Jerusalem to east of the Jordan River by night to transport money, weapons, and provisions for the rebels.

When the intensity of the fighting subsided, Shukri Beik al-Quwatli, a member of the National Front in Syria (and later President of the Republic), set off on a trip through the Arab world. He wanted to garner support and aid from the Arabs to enable Syria to continue its struggle against the mandate. Then he came to Jerusalem. Since Fouad lived in a house while the other members of the Committee for the Support of the Revolution stayed in hotels, Shukri Beik became Fouad's guest for the month he spent in Jerusalem and other parts of Palestine before going on to Hijaz. His stay in Jerusalem allowed him to get to know Fouad Hamzeh well, observe his activities, and understand his dedication to the Arabs' national causes.

When cooperation between France and Britain resumed, the British authorities began to tighten the noose around the necks of pro-Syrian activists in Palestine and the Eastern Jordan, almost all of them Druze. This forced them, under the leadership of Sultan Pasha al-Atrash, to leave al-Azraq and seek refuge in Wadi al-Sirhan in the Kingdom of Saudi Arabia. The British also began close surveillance of the activities of the revolution's political leaders.

One day Ajaj Nouweihed came to Fouad and told him he had learned that a warrant had been issued for his arrest. So Fouad left Palestine for Egypt where he became an exile, forbidden to enter the countries under French and British mandate. He wrote for *al-Ahram*, not knowing when or how God would bring him deliverance. It was not long before deliverance came from the Holy Lands in the form of a telegram from Abdulaziz inviting Fouad to Hijaz to meet him. Fouad did not hesitate, for he was adventurous, courageous, and bold. He went by sea to Jeddah, and from there to Mecca. In Mecca he was informed that His Majesty the King had gone to visit al-Madina al-Munawwara, so he followed him there. After a brief interview, the King appointed him Assistant Director of Foreign Affairs. Among the many things for which Abdulaziz ibn Saud was known were his discerning judgement and quickness in gaining a knowledge and understanding of men.

***

What had happened was that Shukri Beik al-Quwatli had arrived in Hijaz and become a guest of His Majesty the King. Dr Abdallah al-Damlouji, the King's Director of Foreign Affairs, was in Iraq. In a private session, Shukri Beik asked the King about Abdallah al-Damlouji. Abdulaziz replied, 'He's not bad, but he does not speak any foreign languages. Moreover, today he is in a dispute with his people in Iraq and needs to be reconciled with them. I would like to find a young Arab man who is educated and suitable to administer our foreign affairs.' Shukri Beik said to him in a confident tone, 'Your Majesty, I have just the right man for you.' He told him about Fouad and what he had seen of his work in Jerusalem. The King ordered the sending of the above-mentioned telegram and Fouad went to Hijaz.

Three years later, Dr Abdallah al-Damlouji left Hijaz and returned to his own country. Fouad Hamzeh took over the administration of foreign affairs in the government of 'Hijaz, Najd, and its dependencies', as it was then called.

***

After Fouad settled in Hijaz he decided to marry, so they engaged Elmaz, the daughter of Khalil Saab, to be his wife.[1] By an odd twist of fate, Fouad had tried to get a death sentence issued against Khalil Saab in 1925. When the Druze defeated the French at the Battle of al-Mazra'a, thwarting General Michaud's campaign, they advanced towards Damascus, occupied the al-Joulan (Golan) region, and entered Hasbayya. The French called on the Lebanese to resist the rebels and opened their doors to volunteers. Hundreds of adventurous young men came forward, took up weapons, and headed to the front. The gathering point was in Marj'ioun.

Then the rebels burned Kawkaba. The Druze leaders in Lebanon, led by Amir Fouad Arslan, saw that the rebels' entrance into Lebanon would

---

1. Elmaz is the author's sister.

provoke sectarian disturbances. Amir Fouad wrote a letter to the rebel leader in the region, Zeid Beik al-Atrash, apprising him of the situation in Lebanon and appealing to him to halt the Druze advance. He chose two of the community's sons to carry the letter to the rebels: the well-known writer Abdallah al-Najjar and the young police commissioner Khalil Saab.

Abdallah and Khalil agreed to carry out the mission in order to prevent bloodshed and ward evil away from Lebanon. As if the dangers of crossing the firing line were not enough, the two men faced the possibility of being murdered at the hands of either of the two sides – the side of the revolution or the side of its enemies. Khalil took along one of his relatives, Nimr Muhammad Saab, a strong young man familiar with the people and affairs of Jabal al-Druze.

In Marj'ioun, Khalil al-Jizzini and a group of volunteers ambushed them. Khalil Saab was about to engage them in an uneven fight when the police interfered and moved Khalil al-Jizzini off the road. When the car carrying them reached the plain, shots rained down on them from the hills surrounding Ibl al-Saqi. No one was hurt, and they went on to Hasbayya and did what they had gone there to do.

When Fouad Hamzeh and other young men of the Committee for the Support of the Revolution in Jerusalem learned of the two men's mission, they plotted to have them killed. They devised a plan to have Shakib Wahab or another rebel kill Khalil Saab and Abdallah al-Najjar for their attempt to halt the rebels' march and prevent their occupation of Lebanon. The young men's initiative did not receive adequate support, so they abandoned their suggestion. And Fouad Hamzeh went on to become the son-in-law of the man he had wanted to have killed.

Fouad wanted to celebrate the announcement of his engagement so he invited some of his brethren to a party at his house in Mecca al-Mukarrama. Once all the invited guests were present, he announced the news to them. Al-Hajj Hussein al-'Oueini asked, 'Who is the bride?' Fouad replied, 'She is Khalil Saab's daughter.' When al-Hajj Hussein heard Khalil Saab's name he jumped from his seat in a state of alarm and shouted, 'Khalil Saab's daughter?' Fouad and those present were astonished by al-Hajj Hussein's anger and Fouad held his breath as thoughts rushed through his mind. What did Hussein al-'Oueini know about Khalil Saab and his family that he and his brothers who had chosen this family and this relationship for him did not know? He asked,

'Hussein, tell me what is wrong with Khalil Saab that caused this news to disturb you so much.' Hussein replied, 'He once gave me a beating.' The tension lifted from Fouad's chest and he said jokingly, 'I wish he had beaten you to death.'

As for al-Hajj Hussein's story with Khalil Saab, it goes back to the early 1920s when As'ad Beik Khorsheid, Director of the Ministry of Interior in Beirut and brother of 'Izzat Beik Khorsheid, was killed. The authorities accused several Beirut youths of plotting to kill him on the pretext that he was cooperating with the French. Orders were issued directing that the men be arrested and treated harshly. One of the men was Hajj Hussein, and when Khalil tried to arrest him and he refused to surrender, what happened happened.

Although Hussein was exonerated and released, he found life in Beirut difficult after the incident and went to Hijaz to work in commerce. However, he did not discontinue his patriotic activities. In 1925 he played an important role in mediating between King Ali ibn al-Hussein and Sultan Abdulaziz ibn Saud over the siege of Jeddah. Finally he returned to Lebanon and became a deputy, then a minister, and then Prime Minister a number of times. He was known for his integrity, loyalty, objectivity, and diplomatic skills.

***

One point requires clarification. Fouad Beik Hamzeh, Shaykh Youssef Yassin, sons and relatives of the King, and other Arab men all participated in the establishment and construction of the Kingdom of Saudi Arabia, the organization of its internal affairs, and the shaping of its foreign policy. But the primary and greatest credit belongs to King Abdulaziz himself. He was the shining sun and the others revolved around him. He was a giant of keen intelligence, quick wit, and foresight, and a great man in his morals and personal traits.

***

Fouad Hamzeh was the envy of many of those who fell short of the heights he reached. They would write to the King warning him against

Fouad. They had no avenue other than Fouad's religion, as if Ibn Saud was not aware of it. He would forward the letters to Fouad, especially those from people Fouad had previously helped and on whose behalf he had interceded with the King.[1] Fouad feared nothing – he had no family, party, or supporter in the Kingdom of Saudi Arabia but his morals and his work. And he excelled in both.

After the Second World War, the extraction of petroleum in huge quantities got under way and signs of the economic boom that continues to flourish today began to appear. Arabs started coming by the thousands to work in the Kingdom. In 1947 I agreed with the gentlemen of the Hamadeh and al-Bizri families, owners of the Sypes paint factory, to become their agent in the Kingdom. I would not have gone without consulting Fouad. When he came to Lebanon I asked him, but he did not consent. He said to me, 'The majority of large construction and development projects in the Kingdom are carried out by the government. It is therefore inevitable that you would work with some of its departments. Some would expedite your transactions to show favour to your relative Fouad Hamzeh. That is not my custom, nor do I want it to become so.' I apologized to the brothers for my inability to accept the agency. Such are true statesmen, and that is how kingdoms are built.

---

1. I have the names of some of them and they include feudalists from Lebanon.

Strength and Virility

Ali Hassan al-Hajj

Nicholas Raad of Kfar Nabrakh was leading his donkey up the winding mountain road from Kfar Nabrakh's 'crater' above the river flowing towards the town, his donkey's back loaded with mulberry tree branches. When he neared Khalwat al-Roueiseh, the donkey veered to the right side of the road to avoid falling into a ditch on the left. The load on the donkey's back hit the wall and the impact sent the animal falling to its left. It hit the ground, rolled over twice, and collapsed on its side in an embankment 5 metres below the level of the road.

Nicholas quickly ran down after the donkey and turned it over to examine it. He then took its reins and started pulling on them, using the various expressions and sounds of donkey drivers to urge the animal to return to its feet. But the donkey would not budge. Nicholas's heart raced and he feared his donkey had been injured. He shouted to anyone who heard to come to his aid. A shepherd herding his goats in Malzaq Ain al-'Iqdeh, a land on the adjacent mountain owned by the al-Doueik family, heard his call. He rushed to where Nicholas and his donkey were.

Nicholas asked the shepherd to help him untie the ropes around the branches, thinking the donkey would be able to stand if relieved of the load on his back. But the shepherd had another plan to save the donkey and the load. He asked Nicholas to help him move the donkey, and Nicholas did so until they got the animal to the edge of the embankment with its feet extending outward. Then the shepherd descended to a lower embankment and stood with his back to the wall that the donkey was leaning on. He bent forward slightly, extended his arms above his shoulders and held the donkey's front feet. He had Nicholas push the load towards him, then quickly and forcefully pulled the donkey's feet so that it rolled along the wall on to the shepherd's back, but horizontally. He walked with the donkey to where the embankment met the road, and there he lowered it on to its feet. After the men made sure the donkey was not hurt, Nicholas took it into the town and the shepherd returned to his herd on the adjacent mountain.

That shepherd was Ali Hassan of the al-Hajj family in Kfar Nabrakh. They were originally Shi'a, as their name suggests, but converted to the Druze faith a long time ago. However, the family have since died out, and no one living today carries their name. Ali Hassan al-Hajj was poor and owned nothing of this earth's possessions but a simple dwelling and a herd of about thirty or forty goats. His home consisted of a cellar in which he kept his goats and an attic above it where he slept, ate, drank, and received his guests. But despite his poverty and modest lifestyle, his name was famous. He was not just the strongest man in Kfar Nabrakh but in the whole area. Moreover, he was a man of courage and integrity, always willing to help others, and never bullying or wicked. As for Ali's adventures and deeds, they seem like miracles beyond the capacity of men. He lived in the early part of the nineteenth century.

***

Shaykh Abbas al-'Imad died early one evening in Kfar Nabrakh. People gathered, death notices were written and young men came forward to deliver them, except for those meant for the al-Qadis, Abu Harmoushs, and al-'Iqaylis in al-Simqaniyya, and the Taqieddines and Hamadehs in Baaqlin. No one volunteered to carry these because the road to al-Simqaniyya passed through Masqifeh, an area of trees, bushes, rocks, and caves inhabited by wolves, hyenas, and tigers. No one dared cross Masqifeh at night. An elder of the al-'Imad family recognized that men were reluctant to go to al-Simqaniyya. He said, 'This job can only be done by Ali Hassan al-Hajj.' Ali gladly agreed to do what was asked of him. They suggested he take along one or more men from the town, but he refused and swore that he would only go alone.

Ali got ready. He put his gown on over his trousers of dyed cloth, tied his belt around his waist above the gown, carried his cane, and left the town. Ten minutes later he entered the dangerous land of Masqifeh. He went through without incident and was about to pass the area and had reached the well of al-Zayyat[1] when he sensed a movement at the side of the road. He turned to see two glowing eyes and quickly realized it was a hyena.[2]

No one and nothing scared Ali. He continued to walk with calm, confidence, and assurance. He shouted to the hyena, 'Welcome, Abu Fares.[3] By God, I need a companion on this lonely path and you have come to keep me company, isn't that so?' But the hyena had come to eat Ali, not to keep him company. It trailed him momentarily, then attacked him from behind and went between his legs. Ali spread his legs and sat on the hyena, clasped his iron hands around its neck, and held it by its rough fur so that it was unable to move. He squeezed harder, and the hyena began to moan and groan from the pain. The animal was humbled and softened, and became the prisoner of what it had thought was its prey.

Ali loosened his arms and legs a little and the hyena started to stretch and strain until it was able to move only in the direction Ali allowed it to. It walked towards al-Simqaniyya with Ali on its back, sometimes raising his feet and sometimes dragging them along the ground so as not to fall off Abu Fares's back. Ali did not forget to thank the hyena for its good deed. He said, 'You knew I had tired of walking and came to carry me.' When the hyena bucked or swayed, Ali would say, 'Come now. Have you become upset with me so quickly? Don't you like my company?'[4]

Finally, Ali reached Simqaniyya on his hyena's back. As he went between the town's houses and alleys, all hell broke loose. Livestock, including cows, sheep, and goats, picked up the hyena's scent and escaped from their pens, running in all directions. The townspeople awoke and the men went out to the square to find Ali on the hyena. Of course, they knew

---

1. It is said that this well is Phoenician. To this day it is surrounded by stone tombs.
2. The people of the mountain believe that hyenas and cats are the only animals whose eyes shine at night.
3. This is a popular nickname for hyenas. The Arabs of old called hyenas 'Um Amir'.
4. The elders say that some hyenas in the past were much bigger than those today. Could this be true? They also say that a hyena *yasba'* a person, that is, causes the man to freeze in terror, unable to move or talk. It is very possible for fear and awe to tie a man's tongue and make him unable to speak. It is also plausible that he becomes very weak from fear and unable to move.

   It is also among the hyena's characteristics and hunting habits to carry a man to where it can eat him. I have heard from my grandmother that a man from Wadi al-Taym was walking in the snow when a hyena attacked him from behind. It went between the man's legs and carried him off, but the man was brave and did not panic. Instead he drew his dagger, grabbed the hyena, and began to stab it, leading it to the town while still on its back. Once he got the hyena to town he killed it. This is similar to the story of Ali al-Hajj.

him, so they stood by and watched, mesmerized by the scene. Ali told them, 'May God compensate you with your own safety. Shaykh Abbas al-'Imad has died.' He gave them the letters and asked them to take the Baaqlin notices to their intended recipients. He then turned the hyena's head back towards Kfar Nabrakh and started prodding it.

The trip back to Kfar Nabrakh took a long time and they did not get there until dawn. What had happened in Simqaniyya happened again in Kfar Nabrakh as the cattle escaped and ran in fear and horror when the hyena passed between the houses. Ali led the hyena to a large old mulberry tree and tethered it. After the people of Kfar Nabrakh had looked at the animal, he killed it by beating and punching it with his bare hands.

***

One year the rains stopped early. When summer came, the vegetation was sparse and dry in the pastures. So Ali started herding his goats in the early afternoon and then setting them loose in the vineyards to feed on the leaves of the vines and oak trees and on acorns.

Ali had a maternal cousin named Youssef al-Dilghan, also from the al-Hajj family, who held the rank of sergeant in the police force of Amir Bashir II. However, this Youssef hated Ali and wished him dead. This was because Ali the shepherd was stronger than he was, and had it not been for Ali, Youssef would have enjoyed the glory of supremacy in physical strength in the area. This was reprehensible jealousy.

Youssef al-Dilghan owned a piece of land on the mountain shoulder over the Safa River containing vines, fruit trees, and wild trees. The plot is still known to this day as Na'sit al-Dilghan. Ali tended the land and let his goats graze on it. But the goats did more than just eat the branches: they demolished some of the embankment walls. This forced the warden to send word to Youssef of his cousin's transgressions on his land.

When Youssef got word of the matter, he asked for his supervisor's permission and went to Kfar Nabrakh. He stopped to see the damage for himself. Coincidentally, Ali happened to be grazing his herd on Youssef's land. Youssef looked around and saw Ali's goats all over his land, eating the leaves of the trees and the vines, and Ali sitting on a rock overlooking the valley under a terebinth tree whose roots extended into the cracks of the rock. Ali was playing his oboe, oblivious to the world and all that is in it. Youssef stood thinking. He would not have dared fight Ali face to face, but now Ali was facing the vast space of the valley with his back to his rival. Youssef saw that nothing stood between him and getting rid of Ali but a strong swift push that would send Ali plunging to his death. It was the opportunity of a lifetime, and he could not pass it up.

Youssef took off his shoes so as not to make a noise as he walked – shoes in those days were reinforced with nails – and he approached cautiously and slowly until he stood behind Ali. He held him by the shoulders and pushed him towards the valley. Ali fell forwards slightly until his muscles awoke and he threw his hands back from his sides and caught hold of Youssef's legs. He dug his iron fingers into Youssef's legs and pulled so that their bodies were stuck together. Youssef realized that if his cousin fell, he would fall too, so he caught on to the hanging terebinth branches and began to pull backwards until he managed to save himself and Ali along with him. When they stood up, Ali grabbed Youssef, slapped him, and said, 'By God, if it wasn't for the sanctity of the suit you are wearing, I would have killed you.' He then gathered his goats and led them home.

Youssef returned to Beiteddine and went before Amir Bashir to complain to him about Ali Hassan al-Hajj's transgressions on his property. Amir Bashir, who knew of Youssef's strength and toughness, was astonished. He could not help but say, 'Is that your status in your town? You can't keep a shepherd off your property?' Youssef replied, 'By God, Amir, this shepherd is a demon of the jinn and could defeat a whole army.' The Amir called for the police sergeant, Mahmoud Walieeddine, and ordered him to take a group of his men to Kfar Nabrakh to seize the shepherd Ali Hassan al-Hajj and bring him to Beiteddine.

The next morning, Ali awoke to the sound of horses' hooves around his house. He got up and opened his attic door to see Mahmoud Walieeddine with ten horsemen of the police force accompanied by Kfar Nabrakh's village chief, Abu Suleiman Mahmoud Abd al-Samad. Mahmoud asked, 'Are you Ali Hassan al-Hajj?' 'Yes', Ali replied. Mahmoud said, 'You are to appear in Beiteddine by order of the Amir, so come with us.' Ali said, 'I obey the Amir's orders but I have forty head of goats. Give me time to find someone to look after them in my absence.' Mahmoud refused to give him time. Ali said, 'The goats might die of hunger if I do not find someone to look after them.' Mahmoud answered, 'I don't care if they all die. The important thing is that the Amir's orders are observed.' Ali, who was a proud man, told Mahmoud Walieeddine, 'I am not going with you, so do as you wish.' Mahmoud became very angry and jumped off his horse. He scaled the attic steps in two bounds and reached Ali who was standing at the attic door.

Mahmoud Walieeddine was a strong and powerful man. It is said that he could knock down a raging horse with a blow from his hand. When he reached Ali, he grabbed him by the chest and pulled him forcefully, but his hand bounced back. Looking down, he saw that he held a piece of cloth from Ali's robe in his fist, and Ali had not budged. Mahmoud remembered what Youssef had said about Ali and realized he was up against a true titan. He went back down the steps and ordered his men to dismount and seize Ali. They got off their horses and rushed up the stairs one after the other. When Ali saw the men rushing towards him, he retreated inside the room and stood between the door and the window. As each man entered, Ali grabbed him at the door and threw him out of the window and on to a heap of barley. Once he was through with all the men, he returned to the door and saw Mahmoud Walieeddine red with anger and the policemen shaking the dust and straw off themselves and tidying up their clothes.

The police retreated in defeat, humiliated at the hands of Ali Hassan al-Hajj. Mahmoud Walieeddine could do nothing because Amir Bashir wanted the shepherd alive, not dead, so he returned to Beiteddine. No one could lie to Amir Bashir, so Mahmoud told the Amir all that had happened. To illustrate and explain what Ali had done, he said, 'By God, sir, he'd lift each one of us like this.' He extended his hands and held Jirjis al-Hammamji, the palace's short, skinny coffee maker, raised him above his head, and then put him back down on the floor.

Amir Bashir was fond of brave, strong men. When he heard the account of what Ali Hassan al-Hajj had done, he forgot about the injustice done to Youssef al-Dilghan and decided to ignore the police sergeant's failure. All he wanted was to see the rebel who did these deeds. He sent for Shaykh Abu Qassem Hussein Abu Ghanem, a leader of his people, builder of Kfar Nabrakh's *khalwe*[1] and administrator of its *waqf* (endowment). He admonished him saying, 'How can you have a man in Kfar Nabrakh like Ali al-Hajj and not tell me about him?' Shaykh Hussein replied apologetically, 'Our ruler, the man is a shepherd and I thought he was not suitable for your service.' The Amir said, 'I want him from you today.'

Abu Qassem got on his horse and went to Kfar Nabrakh. Ali saw the Shaykh entering his house. He went up to him and asked if he could leave

---

1. The *khalwe*, or hermitage, is the religious assembly hall of the Druze. [Translator]

his goats in his barn because he wanted to go to Hawran to escape the ruler's wrath after what had happened between him and the policemen that morning. Abu Qassem said, 'I have something better than that for you. The Amir wants to see you and he admires tough men. I guarantee you his pardon.' Ali complied with what Shaykh Abu Qassem had arranged for him, in view of the Shaykh's status with the Amir and among the people. After the Shaykh had rested a little, he rode his horse and Ali walked ahead of him until they reached the palace in Beiteddine.

It is said that one of Amir Bashir's famous habits was to only allow those he approved of to kiss his hand. When he was angry with someone he would withdraw his hand and not allow the person to kiss it. When Ali Hassan al-Hajj came before him, he tried to withdraw his hand so he could not kiss it. But Ali managed to clutch the Amir's fingers in his iron grip and the Amir was not able to pull back. Ali kissed his hand and the Amir laughed at the gesture. Abu Qassem saw that things were moving towards a resolution.

The Amir asked Ali, 'How did you dare do what you did to the policemen?' Ali replied, 'By God, my lord, I did not hit any of them out of respect for your dignity.' The Amir smiled again and ordered him some food. Ali ate and the Amir noticed that he was not greedy but sufficed with little food. The Amir set aside matters of government and went out into the courtyard. He winked at Istephan Ghazal of Wadi al-Dayr, leader of the Amir's strong men. Istephan understood and he and his men brought out the palace's mortar. The mortar is still there today and weighs 43 *ratls* (over 100 kg). No one had been able to lift the mortar except a man from Zgharta, and he was only able to lift it up to his shoulders.

The ruler ordered Ali to step forward and lift the mortar. Ali tested the mortar by raising it a little off the ground. He then turned to Amir Bashir and said, 'Does Your Excellency wish me to lift it with my left hand or with my right?' The Amir, enchanted by Ali's self-confidence, said, 'Lift it with your right hand.' Ali grabbed the mortar and lifted it to his shoulders. He raised it as far as his arms extended two consecutive times and threw it to the ground. He then did the same thing with his left hand.

The Amir was amazed and the others were humbled by this awesome show of strength. The Amir turned to Istephan Ghazal once again. Istephan understood the signal and took the mortar out of the square and brought in two ropes. He tied them around Ali's wrists and asked him to intertwine his fingers, forming a single fist with his two hands. Ali did so. Istephan then gave the end of each rope to a man – one on the left and one on the right. They tried to undo Ali's grip, but were not able to. Istephan brought in two more men and now two men held each rope. The four men were also unable to loosen Ali's fingers. So Istephan placed three men at the end of each rope. They pulled, and soon blood appeared on Ali's hands where his fingers dug and his palms separated slightly. At that point the Amir ordered the men to stop.

Ali kept the ropes tied to his wrists and asked the Amir to allow him to demonstrate a game of his own. The Amir granted him permission. Ali asked three of the six men to hold the end of one of the two ropes and stand to his left, and the other three to hold the end of the other rope and stand to his right. He fully extended his arms to the left and right and told the men to hold their ground and not allow him to bring his arms into his chest. The six men stood firmly in place with all their might. He pulled back quickly and abruptly and the two groups fell towards each other, some falling to the ground and others bumping into each other.

Ali Hussein al-Hajj's fate was decided. He sold his goats and Amir Bashir added him to his entourage. He remained in the Amir's service for a long time until great events overtook the country with the arrival of the Egyptian army. When the call came, Ali went to the aid of Shaykh Nassereddine al-'Imad, with Shaykh Amin al-'Imad and Youssef Barakat Abu Ghanem, and they were all killed at the Battle of Wadi Baka.

Fares Shdid al-Jureidini

We do not know the exact dates of Fares Shdid al-Jureidini's birth and death. We do know that he was in the prime of life during the reign of Amira (Sit) Hbous Arslan. Al-Sit Hbous, as people called her, assumed the rule of the Gharb district from Amir Bashir 'Omar Chehab after the death of her husband, Amir Abbas Fakhreddine Arslan, in 1809. Her reign lasted until 1822.

Fares Shdid was a young man of good reputation with a kind heart and an abundance of courage. God had endowed him with awesome physical strength that greatly influenced the course of his life and has kept his memory alive among the people to this day. But he was poor and had no money or wealth. All he had to his name was an ox he ploughed for hire, earning the revenues off which he lived.

It happened that Fares saw 'Issa al-Kourani's daughter in church and took a liking to her. He asked her father 'Issa for her hand in marriage, but he refused. 'Issa was an intelligent, beneficent man and a capable manager with a simple lifestyle, all of which made him a lord and leader among his people. His refusal did not dissuade Fares from his love or from continuing to try to win her father's approval. He knew there was no bar to the marriage he desired since the al-Jureidini and al-Kourani families were of the same class in terms of descent and lineage. Some even say the two families were of the same origin and had both come from al-Koura to Choueifat, though not at the same time. Thus the only objection was Fares's poverty – but money comes and goes, which is why Fares set out to work with seriousness and dedication in the hope of accumulating some assets and gaining 'Issa al-Kourani's blessing. The word quickly got around about Fares and his fondness for 'Issa al-Kourani's daughter.

There is no place in the village for secrets. Its climate is wide open and revealing, as are the hearts of its people.

***

In those days a thief called Suleiman Qassem came on the scene. He lived in al-Lailakiyya near Bourj al-Barajneh, and from there he would descend to plunder the coastal villages day and night. He feared no one and bowed to no authority. He possessed strength, daring, and agility, and did not hesitate to attack one, two, or even three men, and then escape from them like a demon. His reputation spread, and his name came to fill people's hearts with fear, so much so that the rural wardens started walking in groups in case they ran into him, even though in those days the guards were chosen from among the bravest and most virile of men.

One sunny morning the three guards of al-Amrousiyya were patrolling the area of olive groves in Choueifat when they passed Fares Shdid grazing his ox on the bank of the Ghadir River. They were not far from Fares when they saw Suleiman Qassem, stealing olives and packing them in a burlap bag. They approached him and engaged him in a fight with hands and sticks. His hands proved stronger than theirs and they were not able to subdue him. They were heading back to get help when they remembered Fares and his strength, so they went to him and explained what had happened and asked for his help. He tied up his ox and rushed with them to where they had left the bandit.

Suleiman had retreated to a nearby field belonging to al-Sit Hbous and climbed one of its trees. When he saw the men returning, he shouted, 'You were three dogs and now you are four; and that changes nothing.' He descended from the tree and attacked them. However, he did not know who their fourth was. When Suleiman neared them, Fares grabbed him by his belt and shoulder and lifted him in the air, like a bird caught in the claws of a hawk. Fares then turned to the guards and said, 'This land belongs to al-Sit Hbous. Out of respect for her, I will not hit him on it.' He walked to the edge of the river and threw the thief to the other side of the water. Suleiman covered a distance of more than 3 metres before hitting the ground hard. Fares forded the water across to Suleiman and grabbed him again, but the thief was no longer in need of a beating, having sustained cuts and bruises. He humbly submitted.

The guards tied the thief's hands behind his back and led him with their canes to the government house in Hay al-Oumara. Fares returned to grazing his ox by the Ghadir River. And people began to speak more and more of his strength and virility.

***

One day there came before al-Sit Hbous a wandering wrestler who earned his living by performing feats of strength. Al-Sit Hbous was impressed. At the end of the show, the wrestler stood in the centre of the ring and challenged the men in the audience, inviting them to fight him and offering a monetary reward to anyone who could defeat him or stand his ground before him. The audience had witnessed his feats, from breaking rocks on his chest to bending iron with his arms, so they feared him, and no one came forward.

Al-Sit Hbous grew angry, refusing to believe that there was no one among her men capable of defeating the wrestler. They said to her, 'There is no match for this man but Fares Shdid,' so she sent for him. Fares was ploughing with his ox in the olive groves. When he got word that al-Sit Hbous had called for him, he left his work and went to the government house in Hay al-Oumara. She asked him to take on the wrestler, and Fares did not hesitate to obey.

The wrestler suggested they start with finger wrestling, and Fares agreed. Their fists tangled and the wrestler started pressing hard on Fares's fingers. Fares responded by doing the same. He was about to crush the wrestler's fingers when the wrestler raised his left hand, signalling he had had enough. Fares stopped and released the wrestler's hand, revealing some lacerated skin on the man's fingers. Fares had won.

Al-Sit Hbous was very pleased and, as was the custom of rulers in those times, she asked Fares to tell her how he would like her to reward him and fulfil his wishes. Those present thought that Fares's dilemma had been resolved. Surely he would ask al-Sit Hbous to make 'Issa al-Kourani grant his request and give him his daughter in marriage. But the simple and humble Fares only asked to be allowed to graze his ox among the olive trees, something forbidden for fear of damage to the trees and land.

***

Fares's reputation spread to all parts of the mountain. Physical strength enjoyed a certain status and regard. People still say that 'strength is glory', especially if placed at the service of bravery and chivalry. One of the Lebanese customs of those days (a custom that lasted until the beginning of the twentieth century) was that no bride left her village to join her husband before a weightlifting contest was held between the bride's people and the groom's people. The world 'people' here includes both relatives and the sons of the town. The bride's people would throw down a *qayma*[1] that one of them would lift. One of the groom's people would then have to lift the same weight. *Kibbeh* mortars were used for this purpose.[2] If no one among the groom's people could lift the mortar, the wedding would be postponed. Sometimes the groom's people could redeem themselves with a chicken stuffed with rice and pine nuts, but they would still have to live with the admission of failure. Because of his strength and pride, Fares Shdid became the lifter of the *qayma* for all the grooms of Choueifat.

It is said that one of Choueifat's sons became engaged to a girl from one of the villages of the Matn. When the wedding date arrived, a delegation from Choueifat went to bring the bride, and Fares went with them. Coincidentally, the Matn's champion in *qayma*-lifting was also named Fares Shdid. Each of the two Fareses had heard of the other and his accomplishments, but they had never met. The groom's delegation arrived and people met, got acquainted, and were invited to sit. The Matni Fares approached our Fares and sat next to him. He extended his hand, grabbed his thigh with his fingers, and applied pressure. The Jureidini Fares felt as if his flesh was tearing, but he remained silent and showed no sign of concern.

The people dined and enjoyed the evening, and at the end of the night each went on his way to sleep. Every house in the village received its share of guests, and our Fares was the Matni Fares's guest. The house consisted of one room with a ceiling no higher than a man's head. The ceiling rested on the house walls and a wooden beam extended from one wall to the other. At the centre of the room, a pole with two prongs at its top

---

1. *Qayma* probably comes from *qawma* (rising), which is derived from *qiyam* (rising). (It is a weighty rock, usually made of mortar. [Translator])
2. *Kibbeh* is a Lebanese dish made of crushed wheat (bulgar) and ground beef or lamb. Before the arrival of food processors, women made *kibbeh* by pounding the mixture of bulgar and meat in a basin carved from rock. *Kibbeh* mortars were notoriously heavy. [Translator]

supported the beam. As for the ceiling, it consisted of a layer of compacted dirt on wooden boards of oak and mulberry tree branches.

The Matni Fares draped a curtain along a rope in the middle of the room. He slept with his wife on one side and the Jureidini Fares slept on the other. But our Fares could not sleep. The Matni Fares had challenged and offended him, and he felt it necessary to respond to the greeting with a better one. He wanted to humble him with a single devastating blow, but he did not like to humiliate his opponents in front of others. He preferred to settle the matter privately, before morning when the people would reconvene. He thought long and hard to come up with a way to do so.

The room was illuminated only by the dim light of an oil lamp in one of its corners, but its features were still visible. Fares heard the snoring of his host and his wife, so he was sure they were asleep. He turned on to his back and looked up at the roof, the beam, and the pole until an idea came to him. He got out of bed, lifted the edge of the curtain, and took one of the Matni Fares's slippers. He then stood upright and placed his right hand under the beam of the roof. He lifted the beam and placed the slipper between the beam and the top of the pole. He lowered his hand and the beam came down on the slipper. He returned to his bed and slept soundly until the morning.

The Matni Fares awoke early and woke up his wife, and they got up to prepare breakfast for their guest. The Jureidini Fares also woke up, but he stayed in bed pretending to be asleep to see what the slipper's owner would do. His wife joined in the search, but they could not find it. He stood scratching his head, his suspicions aroused by the matter. Then he happened to glance upwards and noticed the slipper, half of it protruding from between the beam and the pole. He nodded, indicating that he understood everything. He approached the beam and tried to lift it with one hand but could not. He put both hands under the beam and motioned to his wife to grab the slipper. They strained until they grew tired, and the slipper still awaited its rescuer.

At that point the Matni Fares raised his voice and said to our Fares, 'Get up, Fares, you win.' Fares answered, 'I will return your slipper to you on condition that you announce to the people today that we competed and that you acknowledge that I am your equal in strength, and you give us the bride and we leave.' The Matni Fares agreed and the Choueifatis returned with the bride.

***

A year passed, and then another, and Fares Shdid's dilemma was still unresolved. But he remained forthright in his love, his modest life, and his good conduct, despite his glorious feats of strength.

***

It happened that 'Issa al-Kourani built an additional guest room in his house. (The house later became the site of the Protestant school in Choueifat.) Construction of the room's walls was complete, and it was now the turn of the roof. 'Issa ordered a wooden beam from Beirut to support the roof. Work on the room stopped until the beam came. One rainy day, the beam arrived from Beirut on a camel's back. When the camel reached Mahallat al-Billait at the beginning of Hay al-Amrousiyya from the direction of Beirut, the mud slowed its progress. The camel guide worried his beast might slip if he tried to push it to climb. 'Issa al-Kourani was informed of the matter. It was a Saturday.

On Sunday morning, 'Issa attended mass as usual. Afterwards he called some of the town's young men to him and told them about the beam. He asked them to help him move it to his house. The young men were enthused and they eagerly followed 'Issa to Mahallat al-Billait, but they did not find the beam. They saw its marks on the ground and noticed some human and camel footprints. 'Issa thanked the young men for their concern and returned home in a fury. How had the beam been stolen and who had stolen it? Within an hour the news had spread throughout the neighbourhood.

At noon, a man from the N'eim family came to 'Issa al-Kourani's house and told him that during the previous night, his wife had woken up to care for her child. She heard firm steps on the road and looked out of the window to see a man carrying a huge beam on his back and climbing with it towards the town. 'Issa jumped to his feet. He knew that a thief would not carry the beam towards the town, and he knew of only one man capable of carrying the beam on his back and climbing the town's steps with it. He ran to the room that was being built and saw the beam in its place – from wall to wall.

It was easy for people who knew Fares and his strength to believe that he had transported the beam from the bottom of the village to the top. But to this day, a century and a half later, they still ask, 'How was Fares able to lift the beam to its place on the walls?' Thanks to the beam, the bride moved to Fares Shdid's home, as 'Issa al-Kourani agreed to her marriage to Fares after this incident. Fares was blessed with sons and daughters, and his grandchildren and other descendants now live in Beirut.

***

Fares's strength eventually killed him. He had become an old man but still possessed strength and dignity. One day, he went to the mill to grind a sack of wheat and found it was not working because the millstone needed some chiselling and there were not enough men in the mill to move the rock. But with Fares's arrival the number was complete. Fares stepped forward and moved the rock, and after carving it, he returned it to its place with a little help from the men present. Fares did not know that the body's vessels become rigid with age, and the muscles and joints lose their flexibility with the passage of the years. After returning home he felt some internal pains and became ill, and soon thereafter he passed away. People said he was a victim of the 'evil eye'.

Shahin Abd al-Salam Abu Faraj

Water is the elixir of life. Sources of water have been the axes of human population centres since the earliest ages of mankind's existence on Earth. The great civilizations arose on the banks of rivers in China, India, Iraq, Egypt, and elsewhere. On a narrower scale, we find that villages and towns in the mountain areas develop around springs and fountains, as is the case in Lebanon. We never mention a village without reference to the spring from which it draws water for itself, its livestock, and its crops.

People have classified the various springs and fountains according to their senses. Some became known for their taste and others for being 'light on the stomach' because they helped digestion. That is what the springs of Ma'aser Beiteddine and Sofar were known for. People used to (and some still do) stop and drink from the two fountains whenever they passed by; and even when they were not thirsty, some people would carry flasks and pots to fill and keep.

Some even went as far as to claim that the kind of water a person drinks influences his traits. Based on this view, the Chouiefatis used to believe the water of the Amrousiyya fountain promoted intelligence and clarity of mind. They also claimed that the water of Ain Shibley (Alameh), which lies between Hay al-Oumara and Hay al-Qubbeh and supplies both neighbourhoods, produces hard-headedness and sturdiness of character. No doubt these beliefs are based on the large number of men from Hay al-Amrousiyya who have gained renown in the fields of literature, administration, and politics, and the men from Hay al-Oumara and Hay al-Qubbeh who are reputed to show steadfastness and perseverance.

But despite this claim, Fares Shdid al-Jureidini's successor in superior physical strength, Shahin Abd al-Salam Abu Faraj, known as Abu

110

Hamad, was also from Hay al-Amrouseyya. Shahin Abu Faraj lived in the second half of the nineteenth century and enjoyed a long life. Like Fares Shdid, he was poor. He worked as a camel guide and muleteer and served for a period of time in the cavalry of the *qa'emmaqamiyya* during the term of Amir Mustafa Arslan. Amir Mustafa liked Shahin, admired his strength, and cared about his welfare.

The story of the escaping calf and the attempt to rein it in by grabbing its ear and allowing it to escape only after its ear is torn off is widespread in Lebanon. It is told of many of those with exceptional physical strength. But the incident involving Shahin Abd al-Salam Abu Faraj is different from the other stories. Abu Hamad Shahin was able to stop the calf by facing it head-on, grabbing its ears, and forcing it into submission. After this incident, whenever someone was unable to capture an escaping calf or horse, they would offer the excuse, 'Am I Shahin Abd al-Salam?'

An eyewitness from among Shahin's relatives told me that pulling a medium-sized mulberry tree from the ground was an easy matter for Abu Hamad, assuming the ground was moist. What he is best remembered for in Choueifat is the time his camel got stuck in the archway of a house's outer entrance. He started prodding it, but the camel would not move. Shahin thought the camel was afraid to enter the house, so he pressed his shoulder to the camel's underside and pushed hard, forcing the camel forwards but destroying the archway in the process. Shahin miraculously escaped death.

***

During his time in Amir Mustafa's cavalry, Shahin's salary was insufficient for his needs, so he would ask Amir Mustafa for bonuses and the Amir would grant them. Shahin used to implore the Amir artfully with displays of strength, knowing that the Amir himself possessed a good measure of physical strength and admired strength and courage.

On one occasion, when Shahin had exhausted all his usual methods of asking the Amir for assistance, his situation became difficult. He tried to think up a new approach and came up with a ploy. He asked the farrier to put one of his horse's shoes on backwards. So the farrier placed the shoe's opening to the front and fastened it with nails – what did he care as long as he was paid? And Shahin rode his horse with the cavalry in the morning parade before the *qa'emmaqam*. Amir Mustafa noticed the

111

backwards horseshoe and yelled at Shahin, 'Shahin, why are you riding your horse with the horseshoe nailed backwards?'

Shahin jumped off his horse and pretended he was checking the horse's shoes. He clutched both its rear legs with one hand and used the other hand to hold the front legs. He pulled back his first hand and the horse fell to the ground. He pulled back his other hand and the horse was turned upside down with its legs in Shahin's hands as he pretended to examine it. The audience murmured, awed by the spectacle. Shahin let go of the horse and said to Amir Mustafa, 'My lord, the horseshoe was nailed backwards because its owner's days are backwards.' Amir Mustafa understood Shahin's meaning and gave him some money.

***

Although Shahin Abd al-Salam was strong, he was not bold. He had a cool temperament, was slow to offer help, and did not fight unless he was hit or in pain. His kin and fellow villagers knew of this weakness, so when a fight broke out they would hurt him in order to incite him. When he worked as a camel guide he would go to Saida and Sour to transport grain and hay. Other camel guides from Bourj al-Barajneh and other coastal villages joined him on these trips. They would go in caravans of three, four, or five camels to enjoy each other's company and to rely on one another to ward off transgressions and danger.

On one such trip, two camel guides from the coast accompanied Shahin. On their way back from Saida through al-Damour they came across a cultivated field lined with ripe sugar cane. Shahin's companions' mouths watered, so they left their camels with him and went in the direction of the field. Shahin knew their intention and tried to dissuade them from the theft, but they would not listen. He said, 'By God, if you get caught, I am leaving you to your fate.'

And in fact that is what happened. As soon as the camel guides entered the field and started cutting the sugar cane, some men jumped them and started beating them. Their cries were audible, but Shahin continued to walk without looking back. Then one of the camel guides told the owners of the field, 'You are beating us and letting the one who sent us leave safely with the camels.' The group of three strong men followed Shahin and started beating him. When Shahin felt the pain, he sprung up like a wounded tiger and took the three men between his arms in a bear hug.

They cowered before him as he almost broke their ribs. The two camel guides approached and helped rescue the men from Shahin. They started humouring them and the encounter ended with apologies and a reconciliation.

***

It happened once that, while Shahin was grazing his camel in the al-Qasr neighbourhood near the sea, a caravan passed along the road known as Sikket al-Sultaniyya, which extends from Beirut to the south. There was some damage to the olive trees by some of the men of the caravan. The warden rebuked them and the situation escalated into a fight. A number of Choueifat's men were in the area. They rushed to the source of the commotion and fought with the strangers. The clamour grew loud as canes rained down on heads and shoulders. The Choueifatis were outnumbered so they took a beating, all this while Shahin stood by, motionless as a statue as men rushed past him. Mahmoud Youssef Saab (the author's grandfather) was among those who witnessed the fight and did well against the opponents. But he sensed the adversaries' superiority and looked around and saw Shahin as we have described him. Knowing Shahin's temperament, Mahmoud sneaked up behind him, raised his cane, and brought it down on him, striking his left shoulder like a bolt of lightning. Shahin jumped off the ground like a madman and rushed towards the crowd like a sweeping flood, throwing men aside like toys. The Choueifatis redoubled their efforts behind him, turning the tables in the fight, and the men of the caravan fled.

***

Shahin had reached old age. One day he sat in front of his house in Hay al-Amrousiyya watching people go by when Halim Beik Shqeir happened to pass by. Halim was a strong, brave man and a daring horseman (he later became a commandant in the Lebanese police). Halim's strength was greatest in his fingers. He could hold a clay jar in his left hand and snap at it with the index finger of his right hand, and the jar would shatter and its fragments fly in all directions, as though he had struck the jar with an iron rod.

Halim greeted Shahin and wanted to joke around with him. He extended his hand and asked Shahin to finger wrestle with him. Shahin said, 'Forget it, Halim.' But Halim insisted, so Shahin extended his hand and their fingers tangled. It only took a moment for Halim to ask Shahin to release his hand – he had almost crushed it.

Salim Qassem Saab

After Fares Shahin al-Jureidini and Shahin Abd al-Salam Faraj, supremacy in physical strength in Choueifat moved from Hay al-Amrousiyya to Hay al-Oumara, and the emirate's mortar-lifting title was bestowed upon Salim Qassem Saab. Salim was born in 1861 to a well-to-do household and never did any work that required physical strength. His participation in contests of strength was out of youthful exuberance and the desire to show manhood and heroism. He grew up at a time when men still competed and took pride in weightlifting, horseback riding, fencing, rock and javelin throwing, and target shooting.

By the age of 20, Salim was among the masters of the square in mortar lifting and the equestrians of the field in horseback riding and fighting. He was also endowed with a good measure of bravery and boldness. More importantly, from an early age he showed signs of intelligence, understanding, nobility, dignity, and good character. The custom of lifting the *qayma* at weddings was still common, so Salim Qassem became the hero not just of the Saab family but of all Choueifat. His reputation spread and his name became known.

***

Salim's big test came during the wedding of Nassib Beik Jumblatt in Dar al-Mukhtara. The Saab family's delegation to the wedding was large. It included Abu Ali Mansour Ahmad, Ali Daher and his brother Amin,

Ta'an Qassem and his brother Zattam, Ali Khattar, and the young Salim Qassem.

Lebanese weddings were huge events. They were the merriest of social occasions and the pinnacles of happiness. People would save money, provisions, and equipment so that they could spend freely when a wedding came. The celebrations sometimes lasted a week or two as people moved from one feast to the next and from one celebration to the next, interrupted by contests in fencing, riding thoroughbreds, and reciting *zajal.* Each day would end with song and dance until the drafting and signing of the marriage contract and the return with the bride. Then life would return to its usual routine and state of calm.

It was only natural for the wedding of Nassib Beik Jumblatt, the son of Saeed Beik and grandson of Shaykh Bashir, the pillar of the heavens, to be the most magnificent of celebrations and the grandest of occasions. The Chouf, including the near Gharb and far Gharb districts, has never known such glory as that of al-Mukhtara in the shadow of the Jumblatts. It is true that the Jumblatt family had not come to Lebanon, as the Arslanis, Tanukhis, and Ma'nis (all originally Tanukhis) did, with multitudes of kinfolk and wealth, but the Jumblatts were descended from ancestry and glory equal to that of the Tanukhis. They were aided by a keen instinct for self-preservation, so they thrived where they were strangers and wealth became theirs when they had not previously been rich.

They were well qualified for leadership and wealth and their generosity became exemplary in Mount Lebanon. The palace of al-Mukhtara kept its doors open to guests in whatever number they came until the last days of Sit Nazira Jumblatt. Sit Nazira's income from the private property she had inherited from her father exceeded 1,000 gold liras a year. She spent it on the kitchen to keep the palace's table hospitable and to prevent people from accusing her of squandering the inheritance of her children, Linda and Kamal, from their father Fouad Beik in order to strengthen her position.

Returning to Nasib Beik's wedding, people came to al-Mukhtara from all parts of the mountain. Sheep were slaughtered, storage rooms containing provisions were thrown open, feasts were prepared, and all sorts of contests and competitions were held. Horsemen and swordsmen appeared in the field and the *zajal* poets declaimed their words and praised the glories of the house with strong foundations.

When the time for the weightlifting arrived, people brought out a big mortar and hammered a handle into it. They threw it in the square and the crowd formed a large circle around it. Nasib Beik descended from the palace with the *muqaddam*[1] Rashid Mizher, himself a recreational weightlifter of notable physical ability. The strong men sized up the mortar, its size discouraging them from coming forward, until a tall, broad-shouldered, full-bodied man stepped forward from among them. He held the mortar with his hand and shook it a few times. Then he lifted it off the ground and over his head, fully extended his arm, and threw it to the ground. The crowd applauded and Nasib Beik asked, 'Who is the young man?' They said, 'He is Saeed al-Najjar from al-'Ibadiyya.'

The crowd waited for another competitor to step forward, and the wait dragged on for some time. Nasib Beik turned and his eyes met the gaze of Khattar Saab, who winked at him and pointed to Salim Qassem. Nasib Beik called Salim forward to lift the mortar. His cover blown, Salim stepped forward and pulled his shirtsleeve above his right forearm. He took the mortar, raised it to his shoulder, extended his arm twice, and threw it to the ground. Sounds of approval arose until someone pointed out that Salim had not lifted the mortar in one motion as Saeed Najjar had, but instead first took it up to his shoulder and then lifted it higher from there. The *muqaddam* Rashid Mizher intervened. He liked Salim and was confident in his strength, so he told the crowd, 'I have something better for you.' He called three of the palace's men and asked them to bring down the palace's coffee mortar.

It should be pointed out that Salim Qassem always lifted the mortar in two motions to avoid relying on his fingers, whose strength did not match that of his arms and body. Moreover, they were short and did not completely cover the mortar's handle. Lifting the mortar directly from the ground over the head requires reliance on the fingers. When the coffee mortar was introduced it was obvious to everyone that it was larger than the first mortar. Salim approached and examined it. He was not sure of the strength of the handle, so he asked his relative Ta'an Qassem to have a look at it. Ta'an brought another handle and firmly fastened it to the middle of the mortar. (Ta'an Qassem was also a champion weightlifter.)

Grasping the handle, Salim raised the mortar to his shoulder in one quick motion. But when the mortar reached his shoulder, its weight bent back his wrist. The mortar swayed and its edge came to rest on his wrist. The onlookers' hearts were in their mouths and Nasib Beik yelled, 'Throw the mortar, Salim.' However, Salim did not throw the mortar.

---

1. In the class society of the nineteenth century, *muqaddam* was a rank below that of shaykh or *beik* but higher than that of commoner. [Translator]

Instead he used his hand and shoulder to move it forward with visible force until the mortar straightened. Blood flowed from Salim's wrist, but he was mindful of nothing because he was boiling like a cauldron. He raised the mortar as far as his arm extended, lowered it to his shoulder, walked to where Saeed al-Najjar was standing, and threw it down in front of him. Saeed al-Najjar came forward, but he stepped over the mortar, approached Salim Qassem, and kissed him between the eyes.

***

In those days, fighting and combat were unavoidable. But to avoid bloodshed and killing, people would clash for hours without resorting to guns. It was the limited combat of hands, sticks, and stones. In one such 'encounter', the onlookers witnessed an amusing scene. Salim Qassem was beating a man when another man attacked him. He held the first man under his arm in a headlock and ran after the second until he had caught him and beaten him to the ground. Then he returned to the first, having freed himself to deal with him properly.

There were many incidents outside Choueifat that demonstrated Salim Qassem's strength, although that was not his calling in life. He worked in commerce and then took to dealing with public affairs, both administrative and political, so his other talents surfaced. His resolution of local and national issues revealed intelligence, wisdom, patience, and faithfulness. The people of Choueifat promoted him to the position of mayor. They later elected him Chief Negotiator on 10 April 1921, a position he held until the *mutasarrifiyya* was abolished in 1927. Shaykh Salim Qassem Daher Saab died in 1941.

Shaykh Nasif Nakad and Elias al-Haddad

The Nakad family comes originally from Hijaz. The Arab conquests carried them to Egypt and then to Morocco. They lived in Marrakesh for some time before moving to Lebanon. When Amir Ma'n al-Ayyoubi came to the Chouf in 1120, they joined his ranks and remained among them until the al-Ma'n family line expired in 1696.[1]

When Amir Haidar Chehab assumed control of the emirate of Mount Lebanon in 1706, the Nakads tried to develop close relations with him but he antagonized them. The situation remained in a state of flux until the days of Bashir II. The Nakads were in charge of the Manasif district and lived in Dayr al-Qamar.

When Amir Bashir resolved to crush the feudal *mashayekh*, especially the Druze among them, he began with the Nakads in 1779. He conspired with his namesake Shaykh Bashir Jumblatt and other feudalists and invited the Nakads of Bani Kleib to his palace, where he killed them all.[2] He then closed in on their money and property and confiscated it. Their women fled to Damascus with the only two remaining males, Shaykh Nasif ibn Bashir and Shaykh Hammoud ibn Qassem, accompanied by Shaykh Salman. After a series of incidents whose details we need not recount, Shaykh Hammoud and Shaykh Nasif returned and Amir Bashir's wrath subsided. The two men went on to take part in many significant events and to enjoy a positive influence on the course of affairs in Mount Lebanon in that era.

---

1. Al-Shidiaq, p. 166.
2. It is said that nine men of the Nakad family were killed in this massacre. However, Youssef Khattar Abu Shaqra says the number of victims was eleven.

119

***

The Nakads were known to be men of the sword, and many among them became heroes, warriors, and conquerors. What is beyond doubt is that among those Nakads known to us, none had as great an impact as Shaykh Nasif ibn Bashir (1792–1854). He was well versed in war and endured it throughout his life. He was a valiant hero, a daring horseman, a wise leader, and a skilled planner. He had an abundance of reason and was tolerant, venerable, dignified, and endowed with great physical strength. The stories told of him seem as if woven from the imagination. It is said that when he visited the zoo in Cairo and passed by the lion, the lion averted its gaze in awe. People did not find the story to be an exaggeration, but rather believed it and still retell it. They say he used to strike a horse with his sword and sever it, including the saddle and its cover. What is true beyond doubt is that more than once he severed a man's body with a single blow from his sword.

***

One day, Shaykh Nasif's horse lost one of its shoes, so he went to the farrier in Dayr al-Qamar named Elias al-Haddad. The farrier knew Shaykh Nasif and welcomed him. The Shaykh asked him to shoe the horse. Elias took a horseshoe and was about to nail it to the horse's foot but the Shaykh asked to see the horseshoe first. (He wanted to play a trick on the farrier.) He took the horseshoe in his palm and without much effort he pressed on it with his iron fingers and bent it out of shape. He returned it to Elias saying, 'This one is no good. You see how it bent?' Elias calmly replied, 'Maybe this one is better, Shaykh Nasif,' and handed him another horseshoe. The Shaykh did the same as he had done to the first and returned it to Elias. Elias threw it out and gave him a third shoe. The Shaykh took it and pretended to try to bend it. He said, 'This one is not bad.' Elias took it and shoed the horse.

The Shaykh asked the farrier his fee and he said, 'One Majidi riyal,' the price of one horseshoe and the service of nailing it on. The Shaykh gave him a riyal. Elias took the riyal, and ran his fingers over it, wiping off the inscription. He told the Shaykh, 'This riyal's inscription has been wiped off, Shaykh Nasif.' The Shaykh took the riyal and saw the effects of Elias's rubbing. He threw it away and gave Elias another. Elias did the same to the second riyal as he had done to the first. The Shaykh gave him a third riyal, and Elias said, 'This one is all right. May God grant you good fortune, Shaykh Nạsif.' Shaykh Nạsif extended his hand, shook the farrier's hand, and said, 'Elias, you have from me a pledge of brotherhood.'

Fatima

In 1874 Salim Abu Ghanem from Kfar Nabrakh became engaged to a woman from the al-Kaukab family of Kfar Matta. When the wedding day arrived, a delegation went from Kfar Nabrakh to Kfar Matta to execute the marriage contract and receive the bride. The delegation included about ten elderly men and a similar number of women. The road was long and rough, so the young men stayed in Kfar Nabrakh and celebrated with the groom.

Heading the delegation was Shaykh Mustafa al-Dweik. It is said that the attributes and meanings of manhood never came together in a person as they did in Mustafa al-Dweik. He combined handsome features with an upright stature and powerful build, and complemented comprehension and intelligence with eloquence and fluency. He was also generous, proud, and brave. But above all, he embraced his faith at an early age and sought religious purity with passion, understanding, and knowledge. He became one of the *'ulema* of the faith and donned the white *qumbaz* (garment) and striped *'aba* and put on the white turban, increasing his dignity and completing his venerable status.

The journey through Kfar Qatra, Jisr al-Qadi, al-Shahhar, Qabrshmoun, and finally to Kfar Matta took most of the day. The delegation travelled on horses, mules, and donkeys. They slept in Kfar Matta, and after breakfast the following morning they prepared to leave. The bride came out after an emotional farewell and a horse was prepared to carry her to the town of her partner for life.

Then a young man from the Gharib clan threw down a mortar and yelled, 'Honourable gentlemen, may all your days be merry, and may the single among you and yours follow.' He reached for the mortar, raised it above his head, and threw it to the ground, and then called for one of 'the groom's people' to step forward and lift the mortar, as was the custom at weddings. The men from Kfar Nabrakh were taken by surprise. They had not thought of bringing young men with them in anticipation of this matter. Mustafa al-Dweik spoke up and said to the young man, 'Son, you see that we are all old men and no young men have accompanied us. For that reason we ask that you forgive us for not lifting the *qayma* this time.' But the young man insisted and said, 'How can the town that produced Milhem Beik al-'Imad, Wehbeh Abu Ghanem, and Mustafa al-Dweik allow itself to take a bride without lifting her *qayma*?'

The young man's challenge angered Mustafa al-Dweik and despite his religious attire he almost approached the mortar to lift it himself. But then he remembered something and called one of his companions, As'ad Isma'il Nasr, and said to him, 'As'ad, go and call Fatima.' The people were surprised by Shaykh Mustafa's unexpected request as they did not see what Fatima had to do with a matter that only concerned men. As'ad Nasr returned with a woman of full body, tall stature, and sturdy build. She wore a white veil that covered her entire face but for one eye. She bade the men good morning and wished them everlasting joy, all with evident timidity and shyness, and then waited to hear what Shaykh Mustafa al-Dweik wanted of her.

The Shaykh told her, 'Fatima, step forward and lift this mortar.' The woman was embarrassed and said, 'My lord, how can I lift the mortar when I am but a weak woman?' Shaykh Mustafa insisted, but she said, 'My lord, I am afraid that the *ajaweed* (Druze clergy) will excommunicate me.' The Shaykh said, 'Fatima, I am the religion and I am the *ajaweed*, so who is going to excommunicate you? Now step forward.' So Fatima stepped forward, tightening her veil around her head. She then raised the ends of her outer garment, tucked them under her belt, and grabbed the mortar, saying, 'With the aid of God.' She lifted the mortar without much trouble or strain. She then threw it to the ground and quickly went to rejoin the women. Shaykh Mustafa turned to the young man, who stood in astonishment at the bashful woman's feat, and said, 'Son, a *qayma* like this one we leave to the women.'

***

As for our heroine, she was Fatima Hussameddine, wife of Hassan Hammoud Abd of Kfar Nabrakh, and she was known for two things: her religious devotion and sincere faith, and her formidable build and strong muscles. No other information about her has reached me.

Shaykh Muhammad Atallah

Lebanese emigration is a saga whose chapters began in the mid-nineteenth century and have yet to be concluded. Rarely does one find a Lebanese village or town without a number of sons who have migrated to some corner of the globe. Lebanese emigrants and their descendants in their places of emigration have come to outnumber those residing in Lebanon.

***

Among those who emigrated in the late nineteenth century was a group of *mashayekh* from the Atallah family of Ain Dara. They settled in Buenos Aires, the Argentine capital. Argentina was in chaos at the time. The government had no authority over its subjects, and the security forces were not up to their task. Gangs would rob, steal, and kill, even in the heart of the capital.

It happened that a number of Atallah young men went to one of the capital's neighbourhoods seeking a living and fell into an ambush set up by one of the gangs. A fight ensued, resulting in the death of two of them – the brothers Saeed and Hussein Youssef Atallah. By the time the news reached Ain Dara, it was 1904. The family's tempers were inflamed and the men gathered to discuss the matter. Khalil Youssef Atallah, the brother of the two victims, refused to hold a funeral for them before avenging their deaths. He surprised his relatives by announcing his intention of travelling to Argentina for that purpose. The young Muhammad Mustafa Atallah agreed and accompanied him.

The mission sounded impossible. But the determination of men, especially those of the Atallah family, does not admit of impossibility. And so the two men set out on their mission. Upon arriving in Buenos Aires, they contacted their relatives and verified the truth of the matter and the details of the incident. Then they set about learning the language and studying the country's landmarks. Two months after their arrival, the plan of action was in place.

First the Atallahs contacted the local authorities and secured their consent. Then they equipped themselves and set out, accompanied by a number of the Lebanese present there. They attacked the headquarters of the gang that had killed Saeed and Hussein and clashed with its members in a bloody battle, resulting in the death of four of the gangsters and the dispersal of the rest. Some of the Lebanese sustained non-fatal injuries.

News of the incident spread among the Lebanese emigrants and the country's own people, and Shaykh Muhammad Atallah, the campaign's heroic leader, gained renown. The chief of police called to congratulate him on his accomplishment and asked him to work with the Buenos Aires police. Shaykh Muhammad refused, explaining that he had only come to avenge his cousin's death; having completed the mission, he intended to return to Lebanon. The police chief proposed that Shaykh Muhammad carry out just one more mission: to apprehend the outlaw Juan Cordova, who was terrorizing the city's districts by his robberies and murders. Shaykh Muhammad protested, 'But Juan has a large gang.' The police chief replied, 'I'll prepare a group of policemen to work under your command.'

There was a bounty on Juan's head. Adventure and the prospect of a quick gain whetted Shaykh Muhammad Atallah's appetite, so he accepted the mission. However, Shaykh Khalil Atallah was incensed because he wanted to return quickly to Lebanon to complete his duty by holding the funeral for his two brothers. He tried to talk Shaykh Muhammad out if it, but to no avail.

The necessary arrangements were made, and Muhammad Atallah, son of Ain Dara in Lebanon's Jurd, set out, leading a force of the Buenos Aires police in the most distant country in the Americas, and attacked the bastion of Juan Cordova, the most notorious and dangerous of Argentina's gangsters. The battle between the two sides went on for six hours, with many falling dead or wounded before both sides ran out of ammunition. The gang members began to flee and the policemen started to retreat because no one wished to engage in hand-to-hand combat except Muhammad Atallah and Juan Cordova, who decided to settle the matter with a duel. Each of them took a dagger and attacked the other. They clashed, and soon Muhammad's dagger went through Juan's chest. He fell forward with his dagger in his hand and hit Muhammad's leg, causing a slight wound.

The Argentine government gave Muhammad Atallah the cash reward and all of Juan Cordova's loot, including clothes, weapons, and horses. He divided the horses and weapons among his relatives but kept the reward and the clothes and returned with them to Lebanon, accompanied by his cousin Khalil. After their return, the Atallah family *mashayekh* held a funeral for their two fallen men, Saeed and Hussein.

The most valuable of Juan Cordova's possessions that Shaykh Muhammad won was a thick belt inlaid with silver coins, with pockets for weapons, bullets, and money. The belt remained in Ain Dara until Shaykh Muhammad presented it as a gift to Sultan Pasha al-Atrash, leader of the Druze–Syrian revolution.

***

Shaykh Muhammad Atallah was no stranger to bravery, pride, and chivalry – they were noted qualities of his father and uncles. His father Shaykh Mustafa and his maternal uncle Shaykh Ali Abu Hamzeh were both valiant heroes with famous achievements to their names. Shaykh Muhammad was tall and broad-shouldered, with great physical strength and a voice that boomed like thunder when he spoke. After his return from Argentina, Shaykh Muhammad joined the Lebanese mounted police, remaining in the service of Fouad Beik Jumblatt for eleven years. Fouad Beik was at that time the governor of the two Choufs (upper and lower) and lived in al-Mukhtara.

Fouad Beik was daring and brave, so Dar al-Mukhtara during his reign was as it had been in the days of his fathers and forefathers – the meeting place of the brave, the domain of horsemen, and the arena of games of strength and excellence. Hunting trips would carry him with his entourage to parts of Wadi al-Taym and the western Beqaa, usually joined by Nasib Beik Dawoud,[1] Taufiq Agha al-'Iryan,[2] and Muhammad

---

1. The son of Muhammad Beik al-Dawoud and the father of the (parliamentary) deputy, Salim Beik al-Dawoud.
2. The father of Shibley Agha al-'Iryan, the former deputy.

Jamal from al-Mhaydthe, nicknamed Sultan Hassan for his abundant generosity.

As for the Mukhtara exhibitions, they included equestrian games, sword and shield contests, mortar lifting, and target shooting. Common scenes included dancing bears, monkeys, donkeys and goats paraded by strangers who travelled around the villages with their animals and lived off what they received from the spectators. Such shows were prevalent until the early 1920s and entertained adults and children alike. Bear dancing was the most impressive of these games. The bear's owner would hold it by a ring through its nose and make it dance to the music of a tambourine or drum. He would control the bear with a thick stick, using it to threaten and sometimes strike the animal. This is the origin of the popular saying, 'A stick can teach a bear to dance,' referring to the benefits of the use of force.

On the margins of the bear-dancing scene developed another exquisite spectacle: men wrestling against bears. Brave and strong young men would take on the bears in free-style fighting, including everything but biting, as a muzzle would be placed over the bear's mouth. The man would try to throw the bear to the ground. As for the bear, it could do anything. It might strike the man with its claws, break his limbs, or fall on him and crush his bones.

One day someone brought a huge white bear with a bad temper into Dar al-Mukhtara. Fouad Beik Jumblatt and his entourage were in the field when they saw the bear dancing. Those present were astonished by the bear's size and did not think anyone would step forward to fight it. Fouad Beik sensed the men's whispers and their reluctance to take on the bear, so he turned to Muhammad Atallah and asked him to go before the animal and fight it. Shaykh Muhammad entered the square, and the bear's owner stepped aside. The bear stood on its hind legs and raised its paws. It looked like a giant, awesome and threatening. Shaykh Muhammad realized he had to do something before the bear lowered its claws on to his shoulders. He sprang forward and stepped firmly on one of the bear's feet. He then raised his hand and swung at its face. The bear lost its balance and fell back to the ground. The owner returned to his bear, but neither kindness nor blows from his stick could get the animal to get back on its feet. The man asked Shaykh Muhammad to leave the bear's sight, so he went into the castle. The bear then got up and walked behind its owner, and they left al-Mukhtara.

People say that a bear comprehends the meaning of fighting with a man and senses victory and defeat. It often happens that a bear, after

The author

خبايا ايفتاك انبه سبها زالحلم حفظا رتبك

ليدم يزيدك الله شوليغ الو ما هذا نم في كل خير وافيه في احسن وقت وعلى مكنويم سرنا اخبار صنكم وما بين هنا بجمل قدّ وقت نجا ويجد يجهد اصل الصم نزوم تكونو بدلها وما يدينا يياد عليكم يا خير ولا نفظهر اخباركم المره عشان

*A photocopy of the letter Shaykh Bashir Jumblatt
sent to Shaykh Sej'aan al-Khazen.*

Fouad Suleiman Abu Ghanem

Amir Mustafa Arslan

Sa'eed Hussein al-Jurdi

Amir Shakib Arslan

The commissioner in the Lebanese police Khalil Mahmoud Saab (1885–1943)

Abdallah al-Najjar

Nimr Muhammad Sharafeddine Saab

The English mediated between the Saudis and the Hashemites. The meeting of King Abdulaziz Al Saud with King Faysal the first, the King of 'Iraq, on board an English ship in the Fao bay in 1930. In the picture, the king Abdulaziz and to his left Sir Percy Cox, Great Britain's representative, then Fouad Beik Hamzeh, and to the far right Shaykh Youssef Yassin.

Sir Fouad Beik Hamzeh (1901–1952)

Salim Qassem Saab (1861–1941)

Shaykh Muhammad Atallah in the clothes of the criminal he killed in Argentina (1883–1956)

Khalil Mahmoud Saab in police clothes during the days of the Turks

The Hobeish Station troop in 1921. Commissioner Khalil Sa'ab, and policemen around him, from right to left: As'ad Nou'man, Shaykh Salim al-Khazen, Abdel Rauf Bekdash, Sa'eed Jihjah Saab, Omar Sabri and Saadeddine al-Labban

Shaykh Abu Fayez Sharafeddine Abu Khozam (108 years old)

Shaykh Abu Hassan Hani Ali Raydan (1884–1970)

being defeated and thrown to the ground by a man, revolts until its owner is able to subdue it with his stick. But the strangest thing I have heard is the story of one of our forefathers, Reeman Insaf Saab, who fought a ferocious bear and struck it down. The bear was enraged, but its owner was able to control it and leave Choueifat with it. When the bear reached Kfar Shima, it dropped dead from the ignominy and anguish.

***

In 1917 Shaykh Muhammad was transferred from al-Mukhtara to Baabda. The police chief at the time, Fouad Beik Shqeir al-Arsuni, charged him with enforcing security in the Jurd area and the road between Aley and Dahr al-Baidar. It happened that Jamal Pasha[1] visited the area that summer, and one day he went on a leisurely outing from Sofar to Dahr al-Baidar, accompanied by Amir Shakib Arslan. The carriage was escorted by a number of horsemen from the police force, under the leadership of Shaykh Muhammad Atallah.

In Dahr al-Baidar, the convoy stopped at the water fountain to rest and drink. There was nowhere to sit except for some rocks, so Shaykh Muhammad started taking the square-shaped rocks and moving them closer to the fountain for the guests to sit on. Jamal Pasha looked on in astonishment, unable to conceal his amazement at Shaykh Muhammad's unusual strength. As a result of that visit, the fountain was named after Jamal Pasha, and it is still known by that name today. Then, in the spring of 1918, an order was issued assigning Shaykh Muhammad Atallah the task of leading the company in charge of purchasing wheat for the military authorities from the plains of Hawran and al-Iqlim. The order

---

1. Jamal Pasha was the fourth leader of the Turkish army and the military ruler of Lebanon and Syria during the First World War (1914–1918). He was the butcher who erected the scaffolds for the Free Arabs. Despite that, Amir Shakib and many other men of the country's different religious sects preferred to support the Turks, believing it was better for the Arabs to align themselves with the Turks than to fall under the authority of the Allies, especially the British. When al-Hussein and the Arabs revolted against the Turks, Amir Shakib sent an open letter to Amir Sharif Ali ibn al-Hussein admonishing him for his alliance with the British. Amir Shakib anticipated all that would happen in Palestine at the hands of the British, and his predictions were correct. (The letter was published in the Syrian Official Gazette and it was also reported by Lutf Allah Nahra al-Bakasini in his book, *Waqai' al-Harb al-Kawniyya* [The Events of the World War], p. 512.)

came from Jamal Pasha himself, who had not forgotten Shaykh Muhammad and the amusement of Dahr al-Baidar.

After Shaykh Muhammad had completed his assigned mission, he resigned from the police force and settled in Ain Dara to look after his property and raise his children. But it was not for a man of his ilk to leave public life. He endeavoured to settle disagreements between people and was a voice of peace and goodwill in his area, remaining a social and political pillar of society.

Taqtaq

'Taqtaq' is a nickname for two brothers from the people of Dayr al-Qamar, Abu Iskandar Youssef Z'aiter and Salim Z'aiter, part of the Abu Nader family. The people of Dayr al-Qamar distinguish one from the other by calling Abu Iskandar 'Taqtaq al-Kabir' (Taqtaq the Elder) and Suleiman, who was a bachelor, 'Taqtaq al-Saghir' (Taqtaq the Younger). No one knows the reason for this nomenclature or its origin. The things Abu Iskandar was known for were very different from those Salim was known for and distinguished by, so the name does not indicate any common trait.

Taqtaq al-Kabir had many pursuits but few successes. Finally he settled on the business of making *safiha* (a type of meat pastry). He would carry his merchandise on a platter and call out, 'They are swimming in lard and fat, they are floating.' In those days people craved lard and fat. Fat signified fulfilment and well-being, and a big belly was called *kirsh al-wajaha* ('the status belly'). People did not know about cholesterol in those days, and a butcher would ration the amount of sheep fat he sold to each customer to keep them all happy.

Abu Iskandar's *safiha* was tasty and popular, but that is not the reason this chapter is dedicated to him. Taqtaq al-Kabir was the most skilful and precise swordsman I have ever heard of. In this domain, he performed miracles. It is worth mentioning that Abu Iskandar lived in the beginning of the last century, and that I learned of the stories I narrate about him from people who are still alive and witnessed them in person.

Abu Iskandar would stand a bottle at one end of a table, and another at the other end, and balance a green or dry staff on top of them. He would then strike the staff with his sword and break it without shaking the bottles. On one occasion the staff remained straight and in place. The audience assumed Abu Iskandar had missed it until one of them touched it and it broke into two pieces. Abu Iskandar would also throw a silk handkerchief into the air and strike it with his sword, cutting it as precisely as with a pair of scissors.

One story about him truly inspires awe. There was a boy who was related to Abu Iskandar and hung around him, and Abu Iskandar was fond of the boy and generous to him. He would feed him from his *safiha* and use him in his games and sword tricks. He would place a cigarette paper on the boy's bare shoulder. Then he would bring down his sword and tear the paper without even grazing the boy's skin. Once Abu Iskandar brought a watermelon, cut off its top, and set it on the boy's head. Then he swung his sword and sliced it in half while the boy remained calm and secure and the audience's hearts were in their mouths. The show was over.

It is said that Taqtaq al-Kabir was sagacious, upstanding, quick-witted, engaging, and a friend to all people. One of his childhood friends was Ghosteen Deeb, also from Dayr al-Qamar. But Ghosteen's path in life, his achievements, and his work were different from those of Abu Iskandar. Ghosteen studied and advanced and then travelled to Egypt and returned with his name changed to August Pasha Adeeb. On 25 March 1930 he became the Lebanese Prime Minister.

Taqtaq al-Kabir was still selling *safiha*, but he moved from Dayr al-Qamar to Beirut seeking prosperity and hoping for greater profits. In Beirut he committed a crime, which cannot be discussed here, and was sent to prison in the old government house. (It was at the northern end of Martyrs' Square and has since been demolished and replaced by a parking lot.) The prison had a small window overlooking the stairs leading to the Prime Minister's office.

When Taqtaq's stay in prison became prolonged, it occurred to him to seek the help of his childhood friend. One day he stood at the small window, and when the Prime Minister passed he shouted to him, 'Oh Pasha, oh Pasha.' But the Pasha did not answer, as if he heard nothing. Taqtaq tried the same thing the next day, calling out in a louder voice, 'Oh Pasha, oh Pasha.' But the Pasha did not turn around. On the third day, Taqtaq stuck his face through the metal bars and looked towards the steps of the government house. When the Prime Minister passed he called to him, 'Oh Ghosteen, oh Ghosteen,' and the Pasha turned around and saw Taqtaq at the window of the prison. He came up to him and asked about his situation. When August Pasha learned that the reason for Taqtaq's imprisonment was a domestic dispute, he ordered his release.

***

As for Taqtaq al-Saghir — Salim Z'aeter Abu Nader — he was a photographer and watch repair man and worked in a shop above the pharmacy in Dayr al-Qamar's square. (It was recently demolished to expand the square in front of Amir Fakhreddine al-Ma'ni's palace.)

Like his brother, Salim possessed a good character, was light-hearted, and had an ever-ready wit. The people of Dayr al-Qamar recall one of his noble deeds. In the days of the First World War, poverty held the country in its grip, and the number of vagrants, especially children, increased in the streets of the villages and cities. Locusts came and ate all the crops, whether green or dry, and vegetation became scarce, so the livestock was slaughtered for lack of feed. Salim would go around Dayr al-Qamar's butchers at the end of each day and collect the leftover meat and bones. He would then cook them and feed the poor children in the town.

As for his jokes, I have learned of two of them, one by him and one played on him. Dr Ifram al-Bustani's grandmother had a watch that was of sentimental value to her but it did not work properly because time had overtaken it. She would constantly send it to Taqtaq al-Saghir for repair, but then it would soon stop again and so she would send it back to Taqtaq. Finally, he got tired of it and told the maid who brought the watch, 'Return it to your mistress and tell her that this watch has become like her and me — it is no longer suitable for and cannot benefit from repair.' And that was the watch's last time.

As for the other joke, which is better known, it took place with a respectable lady from Dayr al-Qamar named 'Thalja' (meaning literally one snowfall). It is said that Thalja had a beautiful face, a graceful figure, and a good measure of intelligence and boldness. It happened one year that the weather became very cold in February, and Taqtaq saw Thalja coming down the street. He went out on to the balcony of his shop and stood there until she approached. Pretending that he was talking to the shopkeeper across from him, he said in a loud voice, 'February will not leave us without throwing *thalja*.' So Thalja said in an audible voice to no one in particular, 'Because of the extreme cold, the sole of my shoe

133

taqtaq,' using the slang word for dried and broken up. Thalja lived to be 106.

Manly Escapades

Amshe al-Qontar

Before the Islamic conquests, Arabs would come to Syria to trade and settle there, entering it from the south. But after the conquests and the fall of Persian Iraq to the Arabs, the route of the Fertile Crescent was open to them. Their caravans followed the trail of water and vegetation, so they travelled along the Shatt al-Arab and then along the Euphrates River into northern Syria. From northern Syria the tribes would head either towards Damascus and its fertile oasis or the Beqaa valley. The Beqaa had appealed to the Arabs since the earliest times, and Arab tribes had lived there since before the coming of Islam. This was because its natural environment and land were hospitable to the nomadic lifestyle the Arabs had enjoyed in the Arabian peninsula. The Beqaa contains pastures and plains suitable for agriculture. This facilitated the transition from nomadic to sedentary life – from herding livestock to planting seeds and trees.

The Arabs who came by the Fertile Crescent route did not come in a single wave. The migration continued over a long period of time. The travellers may have settled for tens or even hundreds of years in some areas along the way before reaching their permanent homeland and ending their wandering. This was how the vast majority of the Arab tribes and clans that later embraced the Druze religion first came to Lebanon. Almost all of us passed through Aleppo, almost all of us are Arabs, and this is beyond doubt. History has acknowledged this, and it calls things by their names. But some are uncomfortable with this reality, so they complicate matters and pretend to know the philosophy of history.

All the historical sources agree that the Tanukhis, including the Arslans, Buhturis, Ma'nis, and Lam'is, came with their tribes to these

137

mountains when they were almost completely uninhabited, settled in them, and built on them. Amin Abu 'Izzeddine calls the standard version of Lebanese history 'lame,' meaning that it stands on one leg. And this is correct. All that has been written to date was written from a single point of view. The matter will not be corrected until the other point of view emerges and the facts are placed under the microscope of objective and scientific study. Lebanon belongs to all of us, and the Druze have contributed a great deal, indeed a very great deal, to its development.

***

Spread among scores of villages in Lebanon and Jabal al-Druze are parts of the Halabi clan. Most of these families were so named in reference to Aleppo (Halab) from which they came at different intervals in history. Most were fleeing the injustice and persecution they suffered for their affiliation with the Muwahhidin. The last great migration was in 1811 when the Druze of al-Jabal al-A'la (the Higher Mountain) near Aleppo appealed to Amir Bashir II for help. He sent them Fares al-Shidiaq with a group of supporters. Shaykh Bashir Jumblatt also sent a Druze named Hassoun Ward with a group of backers. The Druze came with them, numbering 400 households, so the Amir gave them 100,000 piastres and they distributed them in the Druze areas.[1]

***

We do not know when the al-Qontar clan came, but it is known that they came from Aleppo to the Beqaa and settled there with many other Druze families. But the political and social events of the nineteenth century, and the loss of security and comfort they entailed, drove these Druze families to ascend into the mountains to the east and west. Some remained, but they changed their disposition, way of life, belief, and faith, and assimilated with the majority of people in the environment they inhabited.

Let us look at a few comparisons. Of the Masri clan, there are Druze in al-Mreijat, Salima, and al-Qal'a, and Shi'a in Brital and Hawr Ta'la.

---

1. Al-Shidiaq, p. 392.

Of the Munthir clan, there are Shi'a in Niha in the Beqaa and Druze in Broummana. Of the Qaq clan, there are Shi'a in Brital and Druze in Jirnaya, which lies in the Damascus oasis. Of the Zeineddine clan, there are Shi'a in al-Ain and al-Qasr and Druze in al-Khreibeh in the northern Matn. And of the Abu Isma'il clan, there are Shi'a in Brital and Druze in Dayr Baba and B'aklin. There are many others. However, the Shi'a clans are bigger and more extended than their Druze counterparts. We believe that the reason for this lies in the practice of polygamy among our cousins.

***

Let us return to the al-Qontar clan. They settled in Ali al-Nahri, Hawsh al-Ghanam, Kfar Zabad, Chtaura, Zahle, Timnin, Hoshmoush, and elsewhere. They were and still are of the toughest mettle, and took part in a number of famous wars and battles. The people of Zahle say they fought a battle with the al-Qontars and were victorious. And that is fine. Whoever goes to the market buys and sells, and the courage of the people of Zahle is widely acknowledged. But the point is that the Qontars had the strength and numbers to take on the people of a town considered one of the biggest in Mount Lebanon.

There remains no one in the Beqaa today who carries the Qontar name. A group of them moved to Hammana and from there went on to al-Mtein. Others went to Kanaker, Milh, and Dameh in Jabal al-Druze. There is also a group of them in Dayr al-Ashaer and its vicinity. No doubt some of them remained in the Beqaa and assimilated with the majority of its residents. I have heard it said that the religious leaders of al-Nabi Sheet were originally from the al-Qontar. They had many strong men. Among them were Hussein al-Qontar, who gained fame in the days of Bashir Chehab, and Ahmad al-Qontar who migrated to Brazil, where something took place to make him a target of the authorities. He was a thorn in their side for a long time until finally the Brazilian army killed him treacherously.

And then there was Amshe. Despite my efforts, I have not been able to ascertain the basic facts of Amshe's life. When was she born? When did she die? Where was she born? Where exactly did she live? We know she lived in Zahle and Hawsh al-Ghanam, and her 'military operations' extended to Wadi al-Qarn, where she would ambush and rob passers-by

on the road to Damascus. She is from the Beqaa, and her stories are with
the people of the Beqaa from Baalbeck to Wadi al-Taym.

Amshe al-Qontaria, as the people of Wadi al-Taym call her, was
known for her strength, bravery, haughtiness, and violence. These traits
distinguished her not only from members of her own gender, but from
men too. Her haughtiness was so pronounced that it led some to question
her femininity. She never married. Others say she was a lesbian. But the
consensus is that she was a woman, as she claimed to be. History has
known others like her.

Amshe used to carry (all at once or separately) a pistol, a bayonet, and
a whip. Her reliance on the bayonet indicates that she enjoyed superior
physical strength. In Rashayya, they say she used to carry her bayonet in
her *shaqaban*.[1] In Hawsh al-Ghanam, they say she used to place her whip
near the water fountain and no one would dare approach the water until
she allowed them to.

The people of Zahle, who stand tall as the sky in heroic deeds and
embellish them with their popular exaggerations, say that Amshe used to
enter shops in Zahle and take what she needed by force without paying
for it. They say that when she was angry, she would put her foot on one
of the two scales of the weighing machine and order the shopkeeper to
equal the weight in wheat, barley, or any other grain. They also say she
used to pass through the streets on the back of her beast, and one of her
shoes would fall to the ground. She would ask the first man she saw to
pick it up and put it back on her foot, and he would do so ...

In al-Mtein they tell this story: Abu Najem Moussa Azar, of al-Mtein,
went to Zahle to purchase supplies and ran into Amshe. She knew him,
and since he was from al-Matn where her relatives lived she wished to
honour him. She took him around the shops and dressed him in expensive
clothes, without either of them paying for anything.

The Qontars say they came to al-Mtein in 1850. If this is correct, then
it may be inferred that Amshe was still in her 'prime' around the middle
of the nineteenth century.

In al-Mtein and Ras al-Matn they related the following story: Hussein
Abu Rislan from Ras al-Matn, As'ad Birjas Daw from al-Qrayya, and
Abu Hussein Rashid from Beit Miri worked as guards along the
'Diligence' line between Beirut and Damascus (a regular wagon passenger

---

1. The *shaqaban* is the tail of the *'aba* which one folds behind one's back and uses
   to carry things in. Gypsy women carry their children in their *shaqaban*.

line). These three well-known, strong, and heroic men were responsible
for the stretch of road extending from Chtaura to Damascus.

Hussein Abu Rislan was conducting his patrol through Wadi al-Harir
one dark night when suddenly a masked person shouted at him from the
side of the road and ordered him to dismount from his horse. Hussein
recognized the voice, but he pretended not to. He dismounted, put his
hands up, and approached the person. When he neared her he wrapped
his strong arms around her chest and held her. She recognized him and
shouted, 'Hussein – aren't you ashamed of picking on a woman?' Hussein
let go of her and laughingly said, 'And you Amshe, aren't you ashamed of
committing highway robbery?' Assuming this story is true, it means that
Amshe was still alive until at least 1863, the year that the wagons of the
'Diligence' first travelled between Beirut and Damascus.

***

All the sources agree that Amshe was murdered. This is quite natural in
view of the life she lived. The Qontars say that the Kurds killed her near
Qatna, and that her death led to a battle for revenge in which seventeen
men died.

***

When my grandmother came from Wadi al-Taym around 1879, Amshe's
fame had spread throughout the length and breadth of the country. To
this day, when a woman possesses strength and forcefulness, they give her
the title 'Amshe'. She is the Antar of women.[1]

---

1. Antar is a famous figure from pre-Islamic Arab history, renowned for his strength
   and his successes in battle as well as for his poetry. [Translator]

Khattar Beik al-'Imad and Ali Nou'man Abu Shaqra

Never in its ancient or modern history has Lebanon attained the geographic limits it enjoyed during the reign of Amir Fakhreddine al-Ma'ni. It traditionally consisted of what we know today as the districts of the Chouf, Aley, the northern and southern Matn, and Kiserwan, with the cities of Beirut and Baalbeck and the Beqaa valley being added for short periods of time. Lebanon's Amirs always looked to Beirut as a port and an outlet from the mountains to the sea, and to the Beqaa valley for the abundance of its crops, and the mountain people's need for those crops. But for most of the days of Ottoman rule, Beirut belonged to the *vilayet* of Saida and the Beqaa to the *vilayet* of Damascus.

Thus it was a great blessing for Lebanon when As'ad Pasha al-Azm, governor of the *vilayet* of Damascus, ceded control of Baalbeck and the Beqaa valley to Amir Milhem Chehab, the ruler of Mount Lebanon, in 1748.[1] Amir Milhem immediately relinquished the villages and plains of the Beqaa to the mountain *zu'ama* (leaders) of the Jumblatt, 'Imad, Nakad, Abu 'Ilwan, 'Eid, Atallah, Talhouq, and other clans to exploit under the feudal system that prevailed at that time. Amir Milhem did this to distract them from undertaking political manoeuvrings that could destabilize and disrupt his rule. Although As'ad Pasha later regretted his concession and Damascus regained control of the Beqaa, the Druze *mashayekh* maintained their position as feudal lords of the Beqaa valley until 1860.

---

1. Colonel Charles Henry Churchill, *Mount Lebanon*, Vol. 3, pp. 41–42.

Our story takes place around 1848. Hussein Ghadban Abu Shaqra[1] was Saeed Beik Jumblatt's appointed agent in the village of Saghbin in the Beqaa. He came to Mukhtara one day and told Saeed Beik that Khattar Beik al-'Imad[2] had passed through the village of Sultan Ya'qoub, part of the Jumblatts' feudal estate. Khattar Beik ordered the villagers not to thresh the harvest unless he was present because he wanted to take one-fourth of it in accordance with the prevailing feudal system.[3]

Saeed Beik Jumblatt did not wish to enter into open conflict with Khattar Beik al-'Imad and drag the Druze into a schism and possible strife. But on the other hand he could not tolerate Khattar al-'Imad's transgression against his family's property. He sent for Ali Nou'man Abu Shaqra from Amatour. Ali was among the country's famous strongmen and heroes, and an adroit and knowledgeable man. When Ali came before Saeed Beik, Saeed said to him, 'Ali, Khattar al-'Imad is riding through the Beqaa with his horsemen, terrifying the *fellahin* (peasants) and he is not afraid of violating our rights. He went into Sultan Ya'qoub and prohibited them from dividing the crops unless he is present so he can take our share. I am in a quandary over this matter. I do not want to court sedition, but I cannot overlook the violation of our properties.'

Ali said, 'My lord, do you think that Khattar Beik al-'Imad, with all his might and valour, seeks battle and conflict with you?' Saeed Beik replied, 'I do not know.' Ali said, 'Love death, and others will loathe it. Leave the matter to me and I will take care of it.' Ali returned to Amatour, took up his weapons, and mounted his horse. He rode towards the Beqaa and reached Sultan Ya'qoub in less than five hours. There he called on the *fellahin* and asked them to prepare to thresh the corn harvest the following morning. The work began early the next morning. Ali Nou'man Abu Shaqra, bearing his arms, stood by and supervised the process. His horse was near him, and he had saddled it and prepared it for flight.

---

1. Hussein Ghadban Abu Shaqra, Abu Abbas, is the famous storyteller who dictated to the lawyer Youssef Khattar Abu Shaqra the transcript published by his son, Aref, under the title *al-Harakat fi Lubnan* [Movements in Lebanon].
2. Khattar Beik al-'Imad was one of the bravest men of his time. He led the campaign on Zahle in 1860. He was the son of Ali Beik al-'Imad, the greatest adventurer and horseman of his time.
3. The English historian Churchill (*Mount·Lebanon*, Vol. 3, p. 339) said that the robbing of the Beqaa was a 'suitable and hereditary vocation for the al-'Imads.' What he meant, of course, is the taking of the governor's share, whether he was in Damascus or Dayr al-Qamar.

It seems that Khattar al-'Imad had eyes and spies in the area. It was not yet midday when he arrived in Sultan Ya'qoub with twelve of his horsemen and advanced towards the threshing grounds. When Ali Abu Shaqra saw them approaching he mounted his horse and rode it towards them. He went before them, greeted Khattar Beik, and said, 'I am Ali Nou'man Abu Shaqra from Amatour, and I have ordered the *fellahin* to thresh the corn upon the order of Saeed Beik Jumblatt. I know that you want to seize the share of the Jumblatt family, and you are certainly capable of doing so. But I have given my word that I will not relinquish this share as long as I am alive. I am not unaware of your valour and strength, and I know that I could not overcome you. So if you would kindly leave the share to its owners, you would be giving me my life. Otherwise my fate is in God's hands.'

Khattar al-'Imad was listening and thinking. Considering his own overwhelming power, he found this man's willingness to stand before him this way compelling and extraordinary. Moreover, he did not want a conflict with Saeed Beik Jumblatt, the Druze's leading *za'im*. And the killing of one of the Abu Shaqra clan was a dangerous matter, deserving of much thought and deliberation. He was convinced that Ali was resolute in his position and admired his manhood.

One of Khattar's men spoke up before him and rebuked Ali, saying, 'You dog – you dare stand before Khattar Beik?' Khattar Beik turned to his man and said, 'A man whose legs carry him from the Chouf to the Beqaa to stand in the face of Khattar al-'Imad is not a dog. He is a lion among men.' He then turned to Ali and said, 'We have granted you your life, and left the share of the crops for your sake.' He turned his horse's head around and rode away, followed by his men.

Najmeh of the Heroes

Najmeh, daughter of Fayyad al-Jurdi, was from Choueifat. Her brother was Faraj. She was born around 1820, and by the time she was sixteen she was known for her threefold beauty: beauty of appearance, completeness of mind, and kind disposition. Any mother who met her wanted her as a bride for her son, and any sister who heard of her wished her as a wife for her brother. Her suitors were many. Her parents used to discuss each request with her, in view of her keen understanding and awareness.

Najmeh finally agreed to marry Hamad As'ad al-Khishin. Her father told her, 'By God, my daughter, you have chosen the best of young men and the epitome of bravery. But I warn you, Najmeh, Hamad is a man of war and adventure, and his life will be one of struggle and peril.' Najmeh said, 'I know that, my father, but he treasures the glory of heroism, be it long- or short-lived. Besides, all lives are in the hands of God.'

Fayyad al-Jurdi was proven right. The country soon saw episodes of war and strife, and Hamad As'ad acquitted himself well in these events. His reputation spread and his status increased, but he soon met his end and was killed as a result of his zeal and courage.

***

Hamad As'ad al-Khishin's most famous adventure was his journey with Amir Abbas Arslan to Baghdad and Istanbul in 1843. The journey would make a good subject for an epic poem because of the struggles, dangers, and travails it entailed and the battles and confrontations that took place along the way in which alertness, courage, boldness, and perseverance were displayed.

The Turkish authorities had accused Amir Amin of aiding the Druze in their war with 'Omar Pasha, so he fled Choueifat with ten of the Gharb's strong men.[1] First he went to the Beqaa and met up with Shibley Agha al-'Iryan, who had been defeated in his war with the Turks. They all went to Iqlim al-Ballan, and Shibley Pasha went on to Damascus and surrendered. Amir Amin refused to do so and went with many of the Druze to Hawran. The translator of the British consulate in Damascus came to them and asked them to surrender, promising to ensure their safety. They all agreed except for Amir Amin. He separated from the group and went off with his men, taking the desert road and passing through Wa'ra Saeeda and the Hayth road. When they ran out of supplies, they entered the area of Dayr al-Zour and bought what they needed as the bedouin Arabs chased them. Many times, they struck and fled their pursuers like wild lions until they finally got to the Euphrates valley. They also had many surprise encounters and tough battles with the tribes of the Euphrates until they managed to cross the river near 'Ana' and enter Baghdad without suffering any casualties.[2]

The *wali* (governor) of Baghdad, Najib Pasha, aided them and allowed them to travel on to Istanbul after giving them letters of commendation to his sons there. The journey from Baghdad to Istanbul was no less exciting than the trip across the desert between Syria and Iraq. But they reached Istanbul, and there Amir Amin was declared innocent of the charge of inciting the Druze against the state. He returned with his men to Lebanon, having been away for seven and a half months, two in Istanbul and the rest en route. Shortly thereafter he was appointed the Druze *qa'emmaqam* in place of his brother Amir Ahmad. He held the office until 1858, when he passed away in the Ouza'i area and was buried there. Hamad As'ad returned safely to his wife and two sons, As'ad and

---

1. Tanious al-Shidiaq and Ibrahim al-Aswad say there were eleven men with Amir Amin. Youssef Khattar Abu Shaqra says there were nineteen horsemen. But I have heard Amir Shakib Arslan (the most knowledgeable source) mention the journey. He said there were ten men. Among them were Mansour al-Fahd al-Jurdi (he received the title of *qadi*), Hanna Mireh al-Jureidini, Hamad As'ad al-Khishin, Suleiman al-Musharrafiyya (he received the title of *agha*), and Abbas Abu Ibrahim (he received the title of *beik*). Amir Shakib said there was among them a son of the Abu Suleiman family from Ain 'Inoub and one of the Saab family of Choueifat (from the house of Hussein Ali Jaber). I have not been able to obtain the names of the others.
2. See al-Shidiaq, p. 525, and Abu Shaqra, p. 64.

Khza'i. He would tell his guests how he had prayed with the faithful in the mosques of Istanbul.

In 1845 fighting broke out again between Druze and Christians in the mountain. It happened one day that the Druze of Choueifat raided Baabda, igniting the flames of war between themselves and its inhabitants. The exchange of fire went on for a long time but to no avail. Hamad As'ad was on the front line, and he grew impatient with the situation. He loaded his two pistols and rode his horse towards the enemy line until he almost penetrated it. He fired his pistols and rushed back towards his own side. But as he reached the middle of the square separating the two sides, a deadly bullet struck him and he fell to the ground. His horse returned to the Chouiefatis without its rider. The exchange of fire intensified and the smell of gunpowder filled the air. A cloud of smoke formed in the middle of the battlefield, above the corpse of the fallen hero.

Dusk was falling, and the air had yet to clear. How could the warriors return and leave the body of Hamad As'ad, their vanguard horseman, lying out in the open? Pride was uppermost in Youssef Hamad Saab's[1] mind and he told his comrades, 'Keep the enemy occupied and distracted.' He got on his horse and rode it to where Hamad lay. He dismounted and lifted Hamad on to the horse's back, and then led the horse through a barrage of gunfire back to the Choueifati lines. They say that when some of the fighters went to tell Amir Amin the outcome of the day's fighting, they said, 'No one was killed on our side except Hamad As'ad.' The Amir replied, 'I wish he had survived and 100 others had fallen.'

***

After the death of Hamad As'ad al-Khishin, his widow Najmeh entered the house of grief while still only 25 years old. The house of grief for Druze women is like a dark, bleak prison. A woman who loses her husband wears black and remains in the house for one year, two years, three years, or even longer. And when she does return to society, her outings are limited to attending funerals and offering condolences. Then she graduates to visiting and attending to the sick. Even though the Druze

---

1. The author's great-grandfather.

religion does not require any of this, this dark mourning is still prevalent among most of us.

***

Yet Najmeh's light still shone through the darkness and sadness of mourning. Her beauty blossomed, sorrow burnished her soul, and life's events heightened her understanding and perseverance. Hardly two years had passed since the death of her husband Hamad before suitors began to request her hand in marriage, using friends and relatives as intermediaries with her parents. Her parents encouraged her to marry again. The Druze saying asks, 'What did the free woman do?' and answers, 'She got married.'

When Najmeh agreed to marry again, her father asked her to choose from among her suitors. She said, 'If I must marry, I accept the one who picked up Hamad As'ad from the field of battle.' Youssef Hamad Saab was one of her suitors. Her father said, 'I warned you the first time and told you that the life of the brave is rigorous, and they view their lives as expendable. You saw for yourself the truth of my words when tragedy befell you. Yet I see this has changed nothing in your soul.' Najmeh remained silent, and her father continued: 'Youssef Karam is a man of kind traits and good character, but like Hamad As'ad he is a warrior of tough mettle and is not reluctant to throw himself into dangerous situations.'

Najmeh said to her father, 'Does life last for ever for anyone, father? But the glory of courage and the honour of heroism remain. And if I go through struggles, it is God's will.' Najmeh was married to Youssef Hamad Saab. He was a faithful and loving husband, and she was a good wife. They were blessed with three children – two boys, Hassan and Mahmoud, and one daughter, Husn.

***

Najmeh thought she had had her share of grief and did not know what fate had in store for her. She remembered the calamity of her first experience, but did not know the coming one was greater. Her father's

148

intuition proved correct once again, but in a way that no one could have expected. Youssef Hamad witnessed many battles in which he fought with typical courage, but he emerged from each battle safe and sound. He was killed inside his own home, near his wife and children, because of his lack of caution.

Youssef Hamad used to make and trade in gunpowder. One night, after his wife and three children had gone to sleep, he entered his gunpowder storeroom with an old oil lantern in his hand. There were two barrels of black gunpowder in the room, and a spark flew from the lantern and landed in one of the barrels, setting fire to the gunpowder and causing an explosion.

The people of Choueifat never knew, either before or after the incident, an explosion of such force. They say that it slammed shut every open window in all of Choueifat's three neighbourhoods, and forced every closed window open or sent its wooden frames flying. The town's people were awakened, cries arose, and men rushed to the source of the noise in Hay al-Oumara. Youssef's house stood where Ma'rouf Ali Fares Hamad Saab's house stands today.

Youssef Hamad's brothers and cousins arrived, and in place of the house they found a hollow pit. Youssef was lying on the road below the house, where the explosion had thrown him. He was badly injured and burned but still alive. They heard moaning under the roof, which now lay on the ground. Strong arms stretched and lifted the rubble to find Najmeh and her three children unharmed. This was the result of an amazing miracle that the mind cannot conceive or comprehend.

The house was built on a cliff, and its eastern wall leaned up against a mountain. The room in which Najmeh and her children slept had a *youk*[1] built into its eastern wall. When the gunpowder exploded, it brought down the room's other three walls and the roof fell in one piece, but the part of the ceiling that ran along the eastern wall fell on the side of the *youk* and did not reach Najmeh and her children sleeping on the floor.

Najmeh had withstood the jarring force of the explosion, the terror of destruction, and the fear of being buried beneath the rubble. Once they had rescued her from the pile of rubble, she immediately rose to her feet and yelled, 'Where is my husband?' ... and then she found him – his brother Hussein had lain him on his chest as he sat near the wall of

---

1. The *youk* is an opening in the wall used to store mattresses in the daytime.

Qassem Ibrahim Salim's house. Najmeh screamed from the depths of her soul, 'Oh God ...mercy...'

Before Najmeh closed her eyes earlier that evening she had seen her husband, radiant, solemn, tall, and broad-shouldered, circling around her and her children, with tenderness shining in his eyes and loving words issuing from his mouth. She awoke less than an hour later and found him like a charred pillar of coal, broken and smashed. But Youssef suddenly opened his eyes, as if he had heard her voice. He saw her and their children, and on his face was an expression of relief. Then he breathed his last and gave up his soul. Najmeh could bear it no longer, since patience has its limits; she felt as if her back had been broken. The women carried her to one of the nearby houses.

***

This is how the beautiful, faithful, gentle, intelligent, and courageous Najmeh became a widow twice and the mother of five orphans before reaching the age of 40. Hamad As'ad al-Khishin and Youssef Hamad Saab had retired from life's struggles and tragedies, and she remained broken-winged, enduring misery and grief, confronting sorrow, and suffering life's troubles and worries alone. Then ill health overcame her and she died, but death did not defeat her. It was enough for her to have only lived with heroes, as she wished and chose to do. It was enough for her to have brought together three families in the best and most virtuous of kinship. And her descendants today number tens of men and women. She was certainly worthy of this loving mention.

Amir Milhem Arslan and Mansour Ahmad Saab

Amir Milhem Haidar Arslan was the first *qa'emmaqam* of the Chouf district in the era of the *mutasarrifiyya*. He held the position throughout the terms of the first two *mutasarrifs*, Dawoud Pasha and Franco Nasri Pasha, from 1861 until 1873. There is no doubt that Amir Milhem had to be very able and competent to maintain his rule over the turbulent Chouf district for all this time. He was wealthy and generous, but he had a short temper and a sternness in his nature that caused him problems with people, even those closest to him.

Among those very close to him was Mansour Ahmad Saab. Abu Ali Mansour was an adventurous hero and renowned horseman who had made his way through wars and calamities and whose courage and influence men acknowledged. He was also known for his wise advice and good counsel. The Amir used to depend on him in dealing with issues and rely on his counsel in conducting his affairs.

***

It was a common practice then (and one that is still followed in Lebanon's villages today) for the authorities to abide by the will of the landowners in appointing the rural and village wardens. The warden was of great importance in the past. People's fortunes were their properties since other resources were scarce. People also valued integrity and sought to select wardens from those who possessed strength, principles, and rectitude.

151

Choueifat was Amir Milhem's home town and the seat of his government in the winter. He was also one of its largest landowners, and for that reason he would chair the annual meeting of landowners to agree on the naming of new wardens. And that is what happened in 1868. Abu Ali Mansour, however, missed the meeting because he was out of town. When he learned of the appointment of new wardens without his participation he became angry. He went to Amir Milhem and complained. It appears that the *qa'emmaqam* did not respond favourably, which only made Mansour Ahmad more angry. He said to the Amir, 'I do not acknowledge your wardens, and I shall hire a private warden to look after my own estates.'

Abu Ali Mansour was not a large landowner, but he was one of the town's influential people. He refused to consent to a measure taken without his participation, so he appointed a relative of his as warden of his estates in the area of al-Bahsasa. He equipped his warden with a stick, and defied anyone who did not approve of his action. The challenge was of course directed against the *qa'emmaqam*, who could not bear to acknowledge Mansour's importance. Instead, when told of what Mansour had done, the Amir said to those in his court, 'And who does Mansour Ahmad think he is?'

Less than an hour later, someone told Abu Ali what Amir Milhem had said. Abu Ali was enraged. He took up his weapons, his son Ali followed him, and they attacked the house of Amir Milhem. At the outside gate, a slave named Khaled confronted them. Ali grabbed the slave and slew him, and they opened fire on the house. The Amir sent a few of his men out by the back door to enlist the support of the strong men of Choueifat's other families, but none of the other families would come to his aid against the Saab clan. The Amir sneaked out of his home and left Choueifat.

The clan council convened, and they concluded with certainty that the police would descend on Choueifat the next morning in search of Mansour, his son, and anyone from the Saab family who was supporting them. Abu Ali decided to leave town. He departed with his two sons Ali and Abdallah, and they became guests of his friend Mansour Daher al-Rishani in the province of Beirut where Amir Milhem's hand could not reach them. Mansour al-Rishani owned a plot of land in Ras Beirut called Jal al-Nakhel, extending from the area now known as Qouraytem to the seashore to the west. On it he had built himself a house. He had a close relationship with the French consulate in Beirut and enjoyed some measure of immunity, so Mansour Ahmad stayed with him for sixteen days, secure from prosecution.

When Abu Ali realized his absence from Choueifat would be prolonged, he moved to al-Lwaizeh and rented a house in its northern sector – the part under the jurisdiction of the *qa'emmaqamiyya* of al-Matn. His wife and other children followed. Abu Ali had old friendships and associations in Beit Miri, Broummana, and the other Matn villages, and he kept himself occupied with these. Then he arranged his son Abdallah's engagement to Hind Maqsad from Broummana. The wedding was held in Lwaizeh. Abdallah was 40 years old.

Three years had passed since Mansour Saab and his children's migration from Choueifat, and the town missed them. Abu Ali had remained in constant touch with the family in Choueifat, and the whole family had attended the wedding of his son Abdallah in 1870. But he was now 69; he had grown weary of his state of exile, and was vexed by his distance from Choueifat. Nor did he wish to bequeath the predicament to his sons to deal with after his death. He therefore decided to resolve the matter himself in his own way. Either it would end in peace and reconciliation with Amir Milhem or it would escalate and explode. At any rate, it was all in God's hands.

Once Abu Ali had made his decision, he put his faith in God and set out. He took up his weapons, his sons did the same, and they headed for Choueifat. They reached Choueifat in the evening and Abu Ali sent out his sons to tell the men of the family what he was up to. He went to the high square in Hay al-Oumara and started walking in front of Amir Milhem's house. A man coming to spend the evening at the *qa'emmaqam*'s court saw Abu Ali and told the Amir, 'Mansour Ahmad is walking in the square, and he is fully armed.' Amir Milhem looked around and saw that none of the Saab men were present. They were in their homes, awaiting the results of Abu Ali Mansour's initiative.

***

The three years that had passed since the incident had had an effect on the two men. Both were kind people whose souls did not bear hatred and did not easily forget love and friendship. And Amir Milhem had spent the three years of Mansour Ahmad's exile from himself and from Choueifat in a state of discomfort, both within Choueifat and outside of it. In Choueifat, Amir Milhem could not count on the support of the Saab family as long as Abu Ali Mansour was in exile. He also knew that if some harm befell Abu Ali while he was in exile, his family would not tolerate it. On the other hand, outsiders blamed him for the behaviour that had caused him to lose an ally and supporter of Mansour Ahmad's importance.

***

They say it was Amir Milhem's custom to order coffee to be presented to his guests twice – once upon their arrival and once when he wanted them to leave. When he was told that Mansour was walking outside his house, he ordered the second round of coffee for his guests. They drank it and left. The last man to exit informed Abu Ali that Amir Milhem was now alone, so Abu Ali entered.

The two men greeted one another with apparent reserve and coldness, but each could see the signs of relief on the other's face. Amir Milhem said, 'Abu Ali, couldn't we have done without everything that happened?' Mansour answered, 'Amir, maybe we could have done without it, but who started it?' Amir Milhem said, 'And now, with what intent have you come?' Mansour replied, 'That is up to you.' Amir Milhem took a long look at him and said, 'Welcome home, Abu Ali.' Mansour Ahmad returned to Choueifat with his children, and on the day of his arrival Amir Milhem sent him a valuable *aba*.

***

Two years after Mansour Ahmad Saab's return to Choueifat, Franco Pasha's term of office ended and he was replaced by Rustom Pasha. Archbishop Boutrous al-Bustani, President of the Conference of Bishops of Saida and Sour, and al-Sit Baderman, the widow of Saeed Beik Jumblatt, began their campaign to oust Amir Milhem from the *qa'emmaqamiyya* and replace him with his cousin, Amir Mustafa al-Amin. People came to Ain 'Inoub for that purpose.

Mansour Ahmad was invited, so he went to Ain 'Inoub. Amir Mustafa asked him to sign a petition. Abu Ali said, 'This would mean that I support you against Amir Milhem, right?' Amir Mustafa answered in the affirmative. Abu Ali said, 'I will not sign anything against Amir Milhem.' And he walked off without looking back. The loyalty of Mansour Ahmad and his children and grandchildren to Amir Milhem and his descendants lasted until the beginning of the 1930s, by which time all of the circumstances and individuals had changed.

***

Abu Ali Mansour's friendship with his namesake Mansour Daher al-Rishani also endured, and a chance arose for Abu Ali to return the favour. In 1875 Mansour al-Rishani wanted to build some shops on his land in Hay al-Amrousiyya (which later became Government Square). His neighbours rushed to prevent him from doing so because the building would obstruct their view of the sea and the olive groves. When Mansour Ahmad heard the news, he went to Hay al-Amrousiyya and asked a friend of his to call the workers and begin work. Abu Ali stood over them to supervise the work, and all opposition ceased.[1]

***

The life of Mansour Ahmad Saab is an affirmation of the timeless expression that courage does not hasten death and cowardice does not prevent it. Abu Ali Mansour was on the front lines of scores of battles and wars. He suffered countless wounds, and a number of bullets lodged in his body. Yet he lived to the age of 96 and died in his bed in 1898. 'May sleep abandon the eyes of cowards.'

---

1. The building Mansour al-Rishani erected is the one that became the coffee-house of Saeed Habeeb Hanna, and later was rented by Salim Zaka. In the middle of the twentieth century, the municipality expropriated it from Nadim, Mansour al-Rishani's grandson, and annexed it to Government Square.

The Three Musketeers

In the days of the *mutasarrifiyya*, respect for government authority in Lebanon rose and fell according to the respect a particular ruler wielded, his resolve, and his abilities. This was also the case in all the other Ottoman districts. But rural areas remained subject to tribal order to a great extent, and to acts of robbery, pillage, and banditry. Transport was difficult and moving soldiers and equipment to maintain security was ineffective, especially in response to individual acts of violence.

Adventurers, fugitives, and those with vendettas would travel to the far corners of the country, set up ambushes on highways, and rob and sometimes kill passers-by. The great trap between Lebanon and Syria was the Wadi al-Qarn pass, because of its location and topography. It is a long way from any outpost of civilization, and is surrounded by mountains on both sides. Travellers had no way of escape once the road was blocked off ahead of them and behind them. As for the villains who robbed the travellers, they would retreat into the mountains to immediate safety, beyond the authorities' reach. That was why the villains chose it for their operations and Wadi al-Qarn became a proverbial metaphor for fear and terror. Travellers to and from Damascus could not avoid passing through Wadi al-Qarn, and the journey through it became an adventurous feat attempted only by the brave. When they wanted to honour a bride, the women would sing to her:

Your husband, beautiful one, went to Syria alone.

Your husband, beautiful one, is Abu Zaid al-Hilali.[1]

***

But the pursuit of sustenance used to, and still does, lead people to risk their lives and withstand strain and strife. The traffic of travellers, traders, and others did not cease. They would organize themselves in caravans in order to cooperate and assist each other in case of danger. However, there were always some individuals and traders who could not manage to join a caravan, so they would entrust their lives and fortunes to God and walk with His blessings.

One such travelling trader was a man who used to take oil from Hasbayya and sell it in the villages of the Iqlim (Golan). Then he would use the money to buy wheat and barley that he would bring back to Lebanon. Finally, he went on one of his journeys and did not return. His kin learned that the men of one of the Aghas[2] in the Golan had killed him and taken his goods. They were also informed that the incident had been mentioned in the Agha's court, and that some of those present had warned him of the consequences. They told the Agha that the Druze were known to be exacting when it came to revenge, especially since they included the likes of Nasib Beik Jumblatt and Amir Mustafa Arslan. But the Agha cursed the Druze, cursed Nasib Beik, cursed Amir Mustafa, and showed a lack of regard for them.

The victim's family relayed the entire story to Nasib Beik, the Chouf's *qa'emmaqam* at the time. The news disturbed him deeply. He thought the matter over and saw that justice could not be achieved through the authorities and the law, since the governor of Damascus did not care about the death of a Druze and the Agha in question was a powerful man. But the matter was a serious one. It was an insult to the dignity of the Druze community, and failure to act could jeopardize the lives of others. Nasib Beik decided to leave the matter to his political rival and equal in the leadership of the Druze community, Amir Mustafa Arslan. He wrote him a letter apprising him of the incident and asking him to handle matters in his own way. Nasib Beik promised to support him with all that he owned or was able to provide. He sent the letter with one of his attendants.

---

1. Al-Hilali is a mythic figure known for his strength and prowess. [Translator]
2. *Agha* is a Turkish title of nobility. We have omitted mention of this Agha's name.

The messenger delivered the letter to Amir Mustafa in Ain 'Inoub. The Amir read it and said to the messenger, 'Is this what my brother Abu Muhammad wishes? Give him my regards and tell him we will take care of the matter and there is no need for him to worry.'

***

Word of the incident spread among the people. Amir Mustafa verified the details, making sure they were in accordance with the account he had received from Nasib Beik. Retaliation and revenge became inevitable. And since insult to a proud spirit is more serious than murder, retribution was due from the Agha himself.

Amir Mustafa opened his quiver of braves and chose three men known for their strength, prowess, common sense, pride, and preservation of the clan's dignity and status. They were Shaykh Mustafa Atallah[1] from Ain Dara, Hamad Muhsin al-Ayyash[2] from Ba'werta, and Muhammad Hassan Abu Khozam[3] from Kfar Heem. He called them to his court and conferred with them, explaining the situation, and they immediately understood what was meant and what needed to be done. They pledged to kill the Agha on his own land and in his own home. They agreed to meet the following night at Shaykh Mustafa's home in Ain Dara, and then set out early the next morning so as not to draw attention to their movements.

In Ain Dara, Shaykh Mustafa introduced them to Shaykh Hassan Mirzi. Shaykh Hassan was a dear friend of Muhammad Beik al-Dawoud and had spent many days at his home, so he knew the area of Rashayya and Majdel Shams very well. They received adequate and sufficient information from him. They learned that their adversary the Agha had a partner in sheep trading named Jirjis Malek of Rashayya, and that Jirjis would know precisely the Agha's movements in the coming seasons,

---

1. Shaykh Mustafa is the father of Shaykh Muhammad Atallah, to whom we have devoted a chapter of this book. He is also the grandfather of Shaykhs Sami and Aref.
2. We have mentioned elsewhere in the book that Hamad did not have any children.
3. Muhammad Hassan Abu Khozam is the famous horseman and runner, the father of Mustafa Abu Khozam, who was also a man of strength and boldness, and was killed in the events of the Druze–Syrian revolution of 1925–1926, and the grandfather of Muhammad Abu Khozam, the former mayor of Kfar Heem.

months, and days. The three horsemen agreed to leave Ain Dara one at a time at half-hourly intervals, and then meet at a designated point in the Beqaa valley. They prepared and equipped themselves and set out on horseback before dawn, in accordance with the agreed plan.

They reached Rashayya after nightfall and went straight to the house of Jirjis Malek and knocked on the door. He opened it, and they entered before he invited them in. Jirjis was a leader of his clan and had knowledge of events, so their issue and their intent were not unknown to him. He assured them of where he stood and told them that his partnership with the Agha in sheep trading was seasonal and not permanent, adding that what bound him to them was stronger than what tied him to the Agha. They asked two things of him. First, that he keep the matter a secret and to keep their horses at his home. Second, to tell them about the Agha's way of life and how he spent the day when at his ranch. He responded positively to all their requests and invited them to spend the night at his home. They left Rashayya on foot before the break of dawn and followed the roads and trails he had directed them to until they reached their intended destination.

After hearing what they heard from Jirjis Malek, they agreed that the most suitable place to carry out what they had come to do was a small fountain at the bottom of a hill near the Agha's ranch. The Agha usually spent the afternoon hours near the fountain accompanied by only one or two men. When they reached the site of the fountain, they took up positions among the rocks above the surrounding hills. They spent two days suffering the cold of night and the heat of day without catching sight of their target. But God rewarded them. On the third day the Agha appeared, accompanied by a huge slave carrying his weapons. They closed in on them from all sides and killed them both. They severed the Agha's head and returned with it to Rashayya. They got there before dawn and woke Jirjis from his sleep. They showed him the head, and he confirmed that it was the head they had sought. They had recognized their target by his attire and appearance.

They saddled their horses and rode them out of Rashayya one at a time. They reached Ain Dara in the evening, overcome by exhaustion and lack of sleep, so they spent the night at Shaykh Mustafa Atallah's house. The next morning, Hamad al-Ayyash and Muhammad Abu Khozam left Ain Dara. Muhammad went to Kfar Heem. As for Hamad, he passed through Ain 'Inoub, handed Amir Mustafa a securely tied bundle, and continued on his way to Ba'werta.

Hamad Muhsin al-Ayyash and Saeed Muhammad Daw

Hamad Muhsin al-Ayyash was known for his courage, boldness, and strength. He was from Ba'werta but spent most of his days and some of his nights in Abey, where he worked for Qassem Beik Abu Nakad, president of the criminal department in the *mutasarrifiyya*'s Supreme Judicial Council. Along with Muhammad, there was a group of strong men that included Mahmoud 'Izzeddine al-Shareiqi, Mikhael Abu Tahtah, Shahin Mar'i, and Murad Abboud al-Khouri, who, in addition to his valour, was known for his understanding and good counsel.

On the other side of the mountain – in Bshatfeen in the Manasif area – another man was gaining renown for his strength and courage. He was Saeed Muhammad Daw. His reputation spread quickly once he had rented the Jisr al-Qadi[1] property from the Hamdan clan and opened a shop in it. He was able to safeguard it against all the villains who had been corrupting the area long before his arrival.

***

---

1. This is the bridge on the al-Damour River connecting the Manasif to the Shahhar. It was called Jisr al-Qadi because it was built by the judge (*qadi*) of Ain Ksour, Amir Zeineddine al-Tanukhi of the Baysour branch in the Gharb. It is said that what drove him to build the bridge was that while he was supervising the work in a mill on the river side, he saw a woman crossing the river. She lifted up her skirt and her legs were revealed. He stopped construction of the mill and began building the bridge.

One day Saeed Muhammad Daw went to Beirut, as he did once a month, to buy the goods he needed for his shop. He made his purchases early in the day and then went to the khan (inn for muleteers) of Mahmoud Ahmad Abu Salman from Ain 'Inoub to rent donkeys to carry his goods to Jisr al-Qadi. Mahmoud Ahmad's khan was a station for men of the Gharb and other mountain people going to Beirut. They would lodge there and tie up their donkeys, and then gather there once again to leave Beirut together in caravans and groups. (When cars replaced donkeys, the khan became a garage. Then the garage was destroyed and replaced by a new building where the Roxy Cinema now stands in Martyrs' Square.)

Hamad al-Ayyash happened to go to Beirut on the same day. He too tied up his horse at the khan of Mahmoud Ahmad. He went and conducted some business, and then returned to the khan at the same time that Saeed Daw was preparing to transport his goods to Jisr al-Qadi. A quarrel broke out between the two men over some now-forgotten issue. They were both enraged and attacked each other, but the other men in the khan at the time came between them and neither was able to reach the other with a punch or a blow. The caravans dispersed in all directions.

The matter weighed heavily on Hamad al-Ayyash. He was older and more influential than Saeed Daw. How did this youth dare stand up to him? Hamad felt wronged, and he was never one to take such an offence lightly. He resolved to kill Saeed Daw, or at least to discipline him severely. He prodded his horse and it raced towards Ba'werta. When he got there, he took up his weapons and headed to Qabrshmoun, where Saeed would pass on his way to Jisr al-Qadi from Beirut. From there he walked towards Aytat and found a suitable spot in the area known as Fashkhet al-Arous, where the German Hotel now stands. He hid behind a rock overlooking the road waiting for Saeed to pass. About two hours after sunset, he heard the beating of hooves approaching from the direction of Aynab. He stood ready.

***

From the time Saeed Daw left Beirut with the muleteers until they got to Aynab, they spoke of many subjects but no one mentioned that morning's incident between Hamad and Saeed. This was in keeping with a wise village custom: when an incident takes place, people do not speak of it until after the anger has had time to subside and tempers have had time to cool.

When the muleteers ascended Aynab's steps and walked through the plain towards Qabrshmoun, they had completed the difficult part of their trek, and also felt that sufficient time had passed for them to talk about the incident. This was a strange coincidence because the caravan was now close enough for Hamad al-Ayyash to hear the men's voices. Someone said to Saeed, 'You are the burning fire of al-Manasif, and you drove the villains away from Jisr al-Qadi. How could Hamad al-Ayyash escape your hands?'

Hamad al-Ayyash heard what the muleteer had said loud and clear, since it was the muleteers' habit to talk loudly so their voices could be heard over the sound of their donkeys' hooves. Also, voices carry at night. Hamad's curiosity was aroused and he listened eagerly for the answer. Saeed's response could be used as justification for Hamad's attack. Saeed spoke up and said, 'My brothers, it would be more appropriate for you to ask me how I managed to escape the hands of Hamad al-Ayyash. By God, I am not Hamad's equal. He is the master of men and I am not fit to be more than his servant.'

Saeed had barely finished speaking when Hamad jumped into the middle of the road and shouted, 'Listen, Saeed. I am Hamad al-Ayyash, and I came here to meet you and kill you. But I heard your words and I now recognize your good nature and sweet disposition. A man who acknowledges his opponent as you just did is the best of men and a leader of heroes. What you have said about me is reciprocated, and I should be your servant.' Hamad threw down his weapons, Saeed got off his horse, and they embraced.

Khalil Mahmoud Saab and Misbah al-Marakibji

The protocol of 1864 exempted the Lebanese from service in the Turkish military. However, Beirut, Saida, Tripoli, the Beqaa, and Wadi al-Taym were not part of the *mutasarrifiyya* of Mount Lebanon. When the Turks entered the war in 1914, they came to conscript the sons of these towns and provinces and lead them to the battlefields. Many of the young men would flee and hide in the towns or in the mountains. The police and the gendarmerie were not serious about apprehending these fugitives from military service unless higher authorities gave them direct orders to do so. It was therefore easy for the youths to hide in the abandoned houses, quarries, and caverns surrounding Beirut where no one could intimidate them, as long as the matter remained unknown to the Turkish military authorities.

One of these young men was Misbah al-Marakibji, who was called up for service but fled to the area of Nahr Abu Shahin, now known as Saqiat al-Janzir. Misbah was known to be a parasitic monster. He had a huge body, a strong build, and was agile, daring, and courageous. He was also savvy and crafty and could handle situations well. He extracted his living from the people of the neighbourhoods around his home. He would take goods and supplies from them, with their consent if they gave it, or otherwise by threats, coercion, and robbery. No one dared complain to the authorities for fear of Misbah's retribution.

***

In those days – 1917 to be exact – the police station of Ras Beirut was situated at the north-west corner of the triangle now occupied by the new building facing the mission of the French embassy on Clemenceau Street. Next to the station was the hospital of Dr Nicholas Rbeiz, Beirut's best-known surgeon in the twenties and thirties. One of the station's officers was Khalil Mahmoud Saab from Choueifat.[1] Khalil knew of Misbah al-Marakibji's presence in the area of Nahr Abu Shahin, within the jurisdiction of the Ras Beirut police. But neither he nor any of the other police officers made any effort to apprehend Misbah for evading the draft.

One afternoon, Khalil Saab went to run an errand in the area of Nahr Abu Shahin. Afterwards he paid a visit to his friend Ali Abdallah Younis, one of the area's homeowners and residents. At Ali's house, he noticed that Ali and his wife were trying to keep their children away from him. Finally one child got through the door, despite his parent's efforts to keep him out, and told Khalil that Misbah al-Marakibji had broken into their home the night before and tried to steal their cow. When they felt his presence, he left the cow behind and ran off. Khalil realized that Ali and his wife had tried to keep the matter from him to avoid trouble, since they knew of Misbah's power. He remained quiet and pretended he had heard nothing, and after completing his visit he left.

But Khalil was not prepared to let the matter go. Ali Abdallah was his friend, and he did not wish his person or his property to be harmed. Moreover, the people of the area knew of his friendship with Ali, so any transgression against Ali would reflect on him too and cause him to lose face for abandoning his friend. As soon as he was out of Ali Abdallah's sight he went through a garden and headed towards the shore to an old house where Misbah al-Marakibji was hiding out.

Khalil had never seen Misbah in person, but he knew of his strength, courage, and violence. He could have gone back to the police station and brought one or more of his colleagues to help him arrest Misbah, but he would never have thought of such a thing because he was himself a prodigy of strength, courage, boldness, and perseverance. He feared no man and never relied on anyone else in the areas of confrontation and battle.

Khalil reached the house after passing through an open area bordered by a wall of medium height. He entered an empty room that led him into an open area within the house. He looked and saw a man sitting on a chair, which was completely obscured by his body, and near him was a

---

1. The author's father.

woman preparing food on a stove made of stones. There was no doubt it was Misbah. His huge physique gave him away.

Khalil asked, 'Are you Misbah al-Marakibji?' The man answered in a whisper, 'You want Misbah? We will lead you to him.' He then turned to his companion and said, 'Get up and show him Misbah's place.' But Misbah's trick did not work on Khalil since his unique physical features left no chance of mistaken identity. Khalil drew his gun and said, 'Get up and walk in front of me or I'll blow your brains all over these walls.' Misbah got up and walked in front of him without resistance or protest. They walked along the outside wall.

Here Khalil committed a mistake that almost proved fatal. He was lulled by Misbah's submissive cooperation, so he let his guard down and slid his gun back into its holster. Police officers in those days carried their guns openly, tucked into the front (just right of the middle) of a belt of reinforced leather worn over the jacket. Misbah glanced back and saw that the gun was no longer pointed at his back but had returned to its holster. He turned with the agility of a tiger and attacked Khalil, grabbing him by the belt with both hands and throwing him against the wall, almost smashing his bones. Then he extended his hand towards the gun and tried to grab it. Khalil reacted and both his hands went towards the gun. Soon the woman got in on the fight as well and all six hands were bending and tangling around the gun.

The fight escalated into a tug of war. Khalil Saab was tall and broad-shouldered, with a prominent chest and strong limbs, but from this introduction to Misbah he realized that his antagonist, in addition to being taller and bigger than himself, was also stronger. He tried to get rid of the woman first so he could then devote himself to Misbah. He started kicking her knees so that she would react by bending her legs back, but she would not let go of the belt and the gun.

Misbah knew that Khalil was tiring from the way that he was gasping for air. He felt triumphant and said, 'By God, I'm going to kill you with the gun you threatened me with.' At that point Khalil realized the fight was no longer a struggle between a policeman and a draft dodger but a fight between two men for life itself. The realization did not weaken his resolve or reduce his awareness and perception but instead boosted his intensity and pain threshold, and he resumed the pushing and shoving with renewed vigour and ferocity. Khalil Saab always espoused courage. He would say, 'What does one know of life and death until he has grasped the first and feared the second?'

As Khalil thought of a way to rescue himself from the situation he remembered something. In the right-hand pocket of his trousers he had a knife of the kind called *um sit takkaat* (the mother of six clicks), so named for the noise it makes when it is opened. He bent his head forward and began hitting it against Misbah's face to conceal what he was doing. He freed his right hand, extended it towards his pocket, and took out the knife, but was unable to get it to open completely. The woman saw what he was doing and shouted a warning to her companion, but Khalil was quick to press the knife against Misbah's shoulder and push it in the direction that opens it up completely.

When she saw the blood on Misbah's shoulder, the woman withdrew from the action and ran off. This left Khalil's left flank free. He raised his knife and aimed for his antagonist's neck. He brought it down with all of his remaining strength, and Misbah saw death coming his way. He threw himself backwards, avoiding the stab of the knife, but then fell hard to the ground ... Khalil took his gun from his waist and started firing one bullet after another into Misbah's body. Misbah writhed and screamed until the gun was empty, and then his body lay still.

Khalil remembered the woman and her role in the attempt on his life, so he reloaded his gun and followed her into the house. He took her by the hair, put the gun to her side, and fired one shot. She let out a cry and fell on to a pile of hay. Khalil left her there and went out into the courtyard. He adjusted his clothing and tried to catch his breath. After he had rested, he went out to where he had left Misbah dead but did not find him, or so he claimed. He ran around the house but saw no trace of Misbah. He entered the house through the back door and checked the rooms, but again found nothing. He then went back to where he had left the woman dead, as he thought, but did not find her either.

Khalil Saab stood, checking his body and its extremities. He asked himself, 'Am I alive or dead? Am I awake or in a dream?' He heard voices outside and rushed to where they were coming from, clutching his gun in his hand. He saw two officers of the beach police who had been on patrol along the sea road when they heard the gunshots and rushed towards the house. The three men had examined the place where Misbah al-Marakibji had fallen and seen red spots. They followed the trail of blood to the wall and over into an adjacent property, but there was no one there. Misbah al-Marakibji and his companion had disappeared without a trace.

One of the two officers went to the police station and came back with a large contingent of policemen. They split into three groups and made searches of all the homes in which Misbah might have sought shelter. The search went on all night, but they found no trace or clue that could lead them to Misbah. Khalil asked the policemen to return to their station. As for him, he headed to al-Rawshe and down to the shores of Shawran. He remembered he had heard that Misbah's female companion was friendly with the wife of a certain fisherman. He went to the fisherman's shack.

When he arrived, he called for its owner and his wife appeared. He asked if they had anyone with them and she said her sister was sleeping on the upper level of the shack. He climbed the stairs, disregarding the woman's protests, and pulled the covers off the sleeping woman. It was Misbah's companion. She was startled and quickly sat up, trembling in fear. He asked what had happened to her when he shot her and she said it had only caused a superficial wound. He insisted on seeing the wound … she uncovered her back to reveal that the bullet had only grazed her skin, searing it from one side to the other.

He asked her about Misbah and she swore she had not seen him since the incident. Then he asked her about places he might be hiding out in, and she mentioned the names of some people whose houses had already been checked. He left her and went, thanking God that she had not been killed. The investigation continued for some time but produced no result, and the case was closed. Misbah al-Marakibji had vanished.

***

One morning in 1922, a police officer came into the office of the new police deputy of Beirut Seaport, Khalil Mahmoud Saab, and told him that a man wanted to see him. He ordered the officer to ask the man his name and his mission. The police officer left and then came back in and said, 'The man is called Misbah al-Marakibji, and he wants to kiss your hand.' Khalil said, 'Show him in.' He came in, and Khalil extended his hand and Misbah kissed it. Khalil then stood up and shook Misbah's hand and invited him to sit down.

Without waiting to be asked, Misbah started telling his story. He said, 'The six shots you fired at me all hit me, but none were fatal or broke any bones.' He took his fez off his head and moved his hair to reveal a scar from an external wound. He returned to his story: 'I did not lose consciousness. When you stopped shooting I remained still and pretended to be dead. When you went into the house I got up and ran into the fields. I went to the house of a friend you did not know about. He brought me

167

a doctor who treated my wounds, and I stayed there for three months until I regained my previous health and strength. I had sworn not to stay in Beirut as long as you were in it, so I went to Nabatiyya and lived there.' Khalil asked him what he was going to do next. He replied that he was travelling to America, and it had occurred to him to bid Khalil farewell since he knew that men do not hold grudges. Khalil wished him luck, and Misbah al-Marakibji departed, never to be heard from again.

Hobeish Police Station in Beirut

All of Beirut's police stations carry the names of their locales except for the police station of Ras Beirut, which is called Hobeish police station in reference to Shaykh Youssef Hobeish. Behind the name lies a violent, but touching story.

In 1920 the British and French occupying armies were still in Lebanon, but matters of civil administration were the domain of the French under the famous Sykes–Picot agreement. A fight took place in one of Beirut's coffee-shops between a British soldier and three young men from the family of Da'boul. They riddled the soldier's body with cuts from their daggers, but miraculously he survived. Some time passed before the perpetrators were brought to justice. The British military leadership sent a strongly worded memorandum about the incident to the French authorities, so the French encouraged the police department to move on the matter.

The police commissioner at the time was the famous poet Elias Fayyad, the brother of the young literary figure and public speaker Nicholas Fayyad. Elias Fayyad summoned the deputies Khalil Mahmoud Saab and Shaykh Youssef Hobeish and teamed them with four other tough officers. He told them not to return until they had apprehended the three Da'boul youths. The force set out after sunset in the direction of Ras Beirut, where the fugitives lived. The security men were lucky and they captured the three Da'boul sons and headed back to the police station on foot.

Shaykh Youssef Hobeish was pleased with the success of the mission and began to joke, chatter, and sing with his companions. Whenever they passed a coffee-house he would stop and buy them soda. Khalil was uncomfortable with the delay and urged Youssef to move along more quickly, but to no avail. Shaykh Youssef Hobeish had a date with death, but he could not have known that his delay was to avoid being early or late for the terrifying appointment.

Around midnight, they reached the crossroads that still exists today where it did then, north-east of the Sanaye' garden near the Union building. Shaykh Youssef looked down the road leading south and saw a group of people coming towards the crossroads. He said to Khalil, 'We must see who these people are.' Khalil Saab replied, 'Leave them alone, Youssef, and walk with us to complete our mission.' But Youssef insisted, so Khalil said, 'Fine, I will see who they are.' He drew his gun and walked towards the group. He was afraid that they might be innocent civilians or that there might be women among them so he hid his hand with the gun behind his back. But he quickly realized that the group was suspicious. They were five men dragging a sheep, and as Khalil approached them they spread out in an organized fashion. He called out to them, 'Who are you, young men?' Their guns answered him in unison. He threw himself to the side of the road until the gunfire subsided. He then got up and attacked them while firing his gun and his assault forced them to retreat. But Khalil noticed that there were now only four of them. Where was the fifth?

He did not have to wait long for an answer: he heard the sound of three shots being fired behind him, followed immediately by the sound of Shaykh Youssef Hobeish crying for help and screaming in pain. Khalil could not turn his back on the four suspects confronting him, but he put more pressure on them. He then heard the voice of his relative, the police officer Saeed Jihjah Saab, so he knew that what was behind him was fiercer than what was in front of him and he ran back towards his comrades with the speed of lightning.

To understand what had happened on the rear front, we have to go back to the beginning of the battle. When the villains' bullets flew, the men were still in a single group, so two of the detained and one of the policemen were slightly wounded and the entire group fled except for the deputy Shaykh Youssef Hobeish and the policeman Saeed Jihjah Saab. But the two men, though not lacking in courage, were not seasoned in battle like Khalil. Each of them had drawn his gun and emptied it in a single flurry of gunfire and then stood still, having run out of ammunition.

The strange thing is that the gang leader behaved just as Khalil Saab did. He too was an experienced fighter, and he moved out of the way of the first round of bullets and took shelter in the ditch on the side of the road until Khalil went after the four criminals and Youssef Hobeish and Saeed Saab ran out of bullets. Then he quietly aimed his gun at Shaykh Youssef and fired three shots. Shaykh Youssef fell to the ground in a pool of blood. He then moved towards Saeed Saab, but Saeed gave him no chance. He leaped on him like a tiger and gripped his right wrist. They struggled mightily until their fists untangled and each of them fell backwards to the ground. They got back up at the same time, but the criminal was pointing his gun and saying, 'Take it from the hand of ...' But he did not complete the sentence. Khalil arrived at that moment and quickly understood the situation, so he treated the suspect to a bullet in the head. The suspect spun around three times and then dropped dead. Khalil took his gun and told Saeed, 'Take care of Youssef.' He returned to where he had left the four suspects but they were no longer there. He fired some more shots in the direction in which they had retreated and then returned to Youssef and Saeed. Before noon the next day, Shaykh Youssef Hobeish died from his wounds.

Three days after Shaykh Youssef's funeral, Deputy Khalil Saab entered the Ras Beirut police station to find a man kneeling in front of his room. A police officer told Khalil the man was Shaykh Youssef's father. Khalil helped the man to his feet and hugged him, both of them in tears. The father did not live long after his son's death. He died from grief. The government honoured Deputy Khalil Saab with a cash reward and a medal, and named the Ras Beirut police station 'Hobeish police station'.

***

But Khalil's struggle did not end there. The suspects whose leader he had killed swore revenge. They also continued to cause trouble, some of them committing horrible crimes. A year and a half passed without incident. Then one cold evening in February, Fawzi Ramadan, who had succeeded Elias Fayyad as police commissioner, summoned Deputy Khalil Saab and told him that one of his informants had reported that the group of suspects was hiding out in an old room near al-Ramla al-Baida. The commissioner assigned Khalil to head a force of deputies and other officers to bring them in dead or alive.

The force went to the place in question and surrounded it. Khalil circled around the room and saw that it had a window in the back. He brought three police officers and stationed them under the window to cut off the suspects' escape route and then went back to continue instructing his men. Suddenly he heard the sound of gunshots behind the room. He ran to the back, and the police officers told him that one of the suspects had opened the window and jumped over their heads and run while shooting at them, so they returned fire.

Khalil left them, but instead of returning to complete the siege of the room he drew his gun and approached the room door and kicked it in, forcing it off its hinges. He uprooted it from both sides and the door fell to the ground. He walked over the door into the jaws of the unknown. A shot was fired at him from the right side but it missed. He aimed his gun at the head of the suspect in the corner of the room and fired, and the man fell to the ground.

None of the police deputies or other officers reacted except for Deputy Dawoud Abu Shaqra. When he heard the shots he shouted to those around him, 'Khalil has gone in by himself.' He ran to Khalil's side and saw an apparition approaching from the left corner of the room. He shot at him and hit him in the belly, but the criminal kept coming towards Khalil Saab. Khalil fired another shot at him and he fell as if thrown against the wall. Khalil and Dawoud felt around the room but only found the two slain suspects.

***

As for the criminal who escaped through the window, he benefited from a general pardon after some time. But he was accused of participating in an act of murder known as 'the crisis of Bir al-Takhikh', so he was arrested and imprisoned, and died in jail.[1] The identity of the fifth person present on the night that Deputy Youssef Hobeish was killed remains unknown.

---

1. The names of the gang leader and the three criminals are known, but there is nothing to be gained from mention of their names here.

Sharafeddine Abu Khozam and Najib Halloum

Mount Lebanon, with its abundant yields of fruits and vegetables, does not produce enough wheat and other grains to satisfy the needs of its inhabitants. That is why throughout the ages the Lebanese would buy wheat from the plains surrounding the mountain. They would travel to the south, the Beqaa, and Syria to buy this essential foodstuff. In the past, such journeys were not safe. Bandits and highway robbers would cut off the mountain passageways and bottlenecks and rob the passers-by of their money and lives. That is why the traders would form caravans and travel in groups in order to assist one another in the event of an attack. But there were always some adventurers who would travel alone, relying on their strength or good fortune.

One such adventurer was Sharafeddine Abu Khozam from Kfar Heem. He travelled frequently to Syria and escaped more than once from the criminals and thieves. He would go once a year to the eastern Beqaa or to the south to purchase his home supply of wheat. In July of 1920, he went to Saida and purchased the freight of three donkeys in wheat. Since the weather was hot, Sharafeddine preferred to travel by night, so he stayed in the khan of Saida until the sun set and then set out, relying on the grace of God. Sharafeddine noticed that a caravan consisting of five camels carrying forage and wheat had set out ahead of him towards Beirut.

Sharafeddine walked behind his donkeys without coming across anyone until he got to the cape just south of the town of al-Jiyya, where the electricity station is today. There a man came at him from the side of the road wielding a dagger. He attacked him and stood between him and his donkeys and shouted at him to hand over what he had. But Sharafeddine had nothing. His donkeys and their loads were all that he

173

owned, and he was separated from them now. He drew his dagger with his right hand and used his left to defend himself with his cane. He was defending himself and retreating at the same time. He announced his name and the name of his town, thinking his antagonist would be terrified, but to no avail. Then another man emerged from the side of the road and shouted at the first, 'Haven't you killed him yet?'

Sharafeddine recognized the danger of the situation and saw that if he maintained his defensive posture the two men would overcome him. He recited to himself the famous Druze saying, '*abaqash badda*',[1] and attacked the first man with his knife, cutting him from one side to the other. He let out a harsh cry and fell to the ground. He approached the other man and shouted at him threateningly, and the man cleared out of his way. Sharafeddine left him and went after his donkeys. He found them walking among five camels and saw three men leading them. Sharafeddine realized it was the caravan that had started out ahead of him from the khan of Saida. They were the ones who had set up the ambush.

Sharafeddine felt that his moment of truth was at hand. He attacked the group of men, his dagger gleaming in his hand. The men dispersed and ran some distance from him and began pelting him with stones. Soon the fourth appeared behind them, carrying his friend. A battle of movements led by camels and donkeys ensued between him and the group. He followed them into the town of al-Jiyya, where they stopped and started shouting to wake those who were asleep. Sharafeddine understood that they were from al-Jiyya, and they had not attacked him and endangered themselves because they knew he would fall into their hands once they reached their home town.

Nothing could spare Sharafeddine but flight, if he could find a way. He looked around and saw the side street leading to the shrine of the prophet Younis. He went up the path, having lost all hope of regaining his donkeys and settled for preserving his life. He ascended the mountain, hearing the cries of men and women, as if the whole town had awakened. At the top of the hill, Sharafeddine left the road and walked into the wilderness out of fear that the men might catch up with him. The walking and fighting had sapped his strength and his pace was now slower. He was hungry and thirsty. Most of the night had passed and he still had a long and difficult road ahead of him to get to Kfar Heem.

---

1. 'Enough is enough.' [Translator]

He walked towards Dahr al-Meghara, a farm that lies between al-Saadiyyat and al-Jiyya. He arrived by dawn and went to a specific house and knocked on the door. The door opened and a middle-aged woman appeared. Sharafeddine asked, Are you from the family of Shibley Dagher?' She answered, 'Yes. And who are you?' He replied, 'I am Sharafeddine Abu Khozam from Kfar Heem.' He did not enter but instead sat on a rock in the garden and asked her for a drink of water. She brought him a jug and went back into the house. Then she brought him a bowl of water to wash his face and hands and went back in again. She soon returned with a tray of food, and he ate and thanked her. Having regained his energy, he resumed his journey and reached Kfar Heem. He went home and slept for the rest of the day and through the night.

The next morning he sat at the entrance of a relative's store on the town's main street waiting for news. Dr Khalil al-Masfi, the district's doctor, passed by on his horse. Sharafeddine intercepted him, greeted him, and invited him to sit down. Dr al-Masfi told him that one of Kfar Heem's sons had stabbed a man in al-Jiyya, and the local authorities had summoned him to attend to the victim. Sharafeddine showed concern and told him he would wait for the doctor's return that evening to learn the seriousness of the victim's condition, since the perpetrator was from Kfar Heem.

Dr al-Masfi returned the same evening and told Sharafeddine that the stab had torn the man's skin from one side to the other but had done no harm to his vital organs. But because of the bleeding and lack of medical care the victim would be in a critical condition for a whole week. The doctor then smiled and said, 'How many Sharafeddines are there in Kfar Heem?' and he nudged his horse and headed towards B'aklin.

On the third day, a gendarmerie force led by Officer Fuad al-Mughabghab raided Kfar Heem, but Sharafeddine was not to be found. On the fourth day, a delegation from the Abu Khozam clan went down to al-Damour and received Sharafeddine's three donkeys from the al-Damour police station, along with some reassurance about the condition of the wounded. One week after the incident, Sharafeddine turned himself in to the authorities and was put in the prison of Ma'aser Beiteddine, where he remained locked up for three months until the trial.

The trial took place in October before the great judge, writer, and poet Shaykh Ahmad Taqieddine. He asked the parties to seek a reconciliation, and they reached a settlement out of court whereby Sharafeddine Abu Khozam paid his antagonist Najib Halloum the sum of 70 Egyptian liras and Najib dropped the case.

Most of the day had passed, so Sharafeddine said to Najib, 'Najib, you are carrying 70 Egyptian liras and the way to al-Jiyya at night is full of danger.' Najib replied, 'That's true, but what can I do?' Sharafeddine said, 'Accept my invitation and come with me to Kfar Heem and spend the night at my house, and then go to al-Jiyya in the morning.' Najib hesitated before answering. Shaykh Ahmad Taqieddine, who was following the conversation, said to Najib, 'Najib, you have experienced the courage of Sharafeddine. Why don't you try his generosity?' Najib accepted the invitation. Sharafeddine honoured him and prepared dinner for him, and Najib slept at his antagonist's house. In the morning he bid him farewell and went down to al-Jiyya.

***

Shaykh Abu Fayez Sharafeddine Abu Khozam is still alive today and has reached 108 years of age with his mind, memory, and health intact. He is probably one of the oldest people in Lebanon. He does not eat much but is always moving, his energy always apparent. He continuously travels across the country carrying out religious and social duties. He is a witty and engaging conversationalist who enjoys the company of people and whose company is enjoyed by others, *ajaweed* and *juhhaal*[1] alike.

---

1. As opposed to the *ajaweed*, or clergy, the *juhhaal* are the Druze laity who have not chosen the rigorous and demanding life of abstemiousness and religious devotion. [Translator]

Knowledge, Principles and Moral Deeds

Bechara al-Khouri, the Jurist

The house of al-Khouri in Rishmayya and the house of al-Saad in Ain Traz have a common origin – both are of the lineage of Parson Saleh, who went from Kiserwan to Rishmayya in 1700 and took up residence there. They were called al-Khouri (Parson) because of the large number of clergymen among them.

In 1711 Khouri Abdallah participated in the Battle of Ain Dara and captured two Amirs from the Yemeniyya.[1] Amir Haidar Chehab rewarded him by granting him Rishmayya. When Amir Youssef took power in 1771, Saad ibn Ghandour grew close to him and became a manager in his service. The Amir bestowed on him the status of shaykh (by addressing him in writing as 'Dear Brother'). Shaykh Saad had two sons – Ghandour, who is the forefather of the Saad house, and Saleh who is the forefather of the al-Khouri house.[2]

Our subject is Shaykh Bechara ibn al-Khouri Antoun ibn Saleh (the grandfather of Shaykh Bechara Khalil al-Khouri, the former President of the Lebanese Republic). Shaykh Bechara Antoun is considered Lebanon's most capable judge of his era.[3] He did not study law, as there was no law school in the Ottoman Empire at that time except in Istanbul, but he educated himself, and his intelligence and excellence became evident. In

---

1. As mentioned earlier in the book, the Druze of the seventeenth century were divided into two competing partisan blocs, the Qaysis and the Yemenis, divisions that date back to the days of the original Arab settlement of the Eastern Mediterranean. [Translator]
2. Al-Shidiaq, p. 86.
3. As'ad Rustom, *Lubnan fi Ahd al-Mutasarrifiyya* [Lebanon in the *Mutasarrifiyya* Era], p. 180.

1838 Amir Bashir II sent him and Habib al-Khouri al-Btaddini to Tripoli, where they studied Islamic jurisprudence. After Shaykh Bechara returned, Amir Bashir appointed him a judge in his court, charged with deciding cases.[1] Shaykh Bechara was distinguished not only by his education, vast knowledge, and perceptiveness, but also by his vigilant enforcement of justice, his integrity in deciding cases, and his freedom from bias or prejudice.

A few months after his appointment, an important case was brought before him in which one of the parties was among those close to Amir Bashir. The Amir summoned Shaykh Bechara and commended the man to him. Despite Amir Bashir's commendation, Shaykh Bechara ruled against the man favoured by the Amir. The Amir was angry. He summoned Shaykh Bechara and admonished him for his action. The judge said, 'Justice, my lord, is on the other side. Do you wish that I rule against justice?' The Amir answered, 'Fine, but I do not want to see your face for a month.'

When Amir Bashir II fell from power and Amir Bashir III succeeded him, he appointed Shaykh Bechara as a judge in his consultative council. Shaykh Bechara had a maternal uncle from the Risha family of Rishmayya. There was a dispute between the Shaykh's uncle and a son of the Khair family over a plot of land with a small shop. The plot straddled the two men's respective properties. The dispute had exhausted the mediators and Rishmayya's notables were not able to settle it, so the contending parties resorted to a court of law, and the case came before Shaykh Bechara in Beiteddine.

The public followed the lawsuit with keen interest. The disagreement was no longer strictly material but had taken on ethical and moral dimensions, bearing on the parties' dignity and status. Everyone wondered, 'Can Shaykh Bechara rule against his uncle, whatever the facts of the case may be, after matters have come to this?'

The date of the announcement of the court's decision arrived, and the courtroom overflowed with men from the Risha and Khair families and others from the town of Rishmayya. Judge Bechara al-Khouri addressed the crowd and ruled against his uncle, finding that the shop and the land belonged to the man from the Khair family. But before the parties had had a chance to consider the ruling, Shaykh Bechara summoned his uncle to

---

1. This appointment evidences two matters worthy of attention and concern: first, the extent of Lebanon's internal autonomy; and second, the absence of sectarian partisanship at that time.

his chambers and asked him if he would agree to sell the shop. His uncle consented and asked for 20 gold liras. The judge gave him 30 gold liras and brought the prolonged dispute to an end.

***

In 1844 Shaykh Bechara was appointed judge for the Maronites in the consultative council that was established by Shakib Afandi for the Druze *qa'emmaqam*, Amir Amin Abbas Arslan of Choueifat.

Shahin Salman

Shahin Salman Abu Faraj was born in Choueifat in 1819. In those days, there were no schools in this town, but Shahin was intelligent and perceptive, and taught himself how to read and write during his childhood. His father, Shaykh Salman Abu Faraj, was a pious and virtuous man, held in high regard by the town's powerful and notable people. He would bring his son Shahin along to attend public gatherings, and Shahin would listen, observe, memorize, and learn. Soon he was taking part in life's struggles and in public affairs. His talents were revealed and his virtues came to light. Amir Ahmad Arslan, who ruled over the Gharb area, made Shahin his confidant and later made him his secretary and treasurer, entrusting him with his secrets and fortunes.

When Amir Ahmad became the Druze *qa'emmaqam*, Shahin continued to serve as his secretary, remaining at his side until the Amir's death in 1847. At that time Shahin collected all he had of Amir Ahmad's papers and assets and delivered them to his brother, Amir Amin. Amir Amin was impressed with Shahin's integrity and honour and asked him to remain in his company as he had with his brother. Shahin accepted and stayed with him until Amir Amin's death in 1858. When Amir Muhammad, Amir Amin's son, assumed the *qa'emmaqamiyya*, Shahin continued his work until Amir Muhammad retired from government in 1860.

The time Shahin spent in rulers' circles of power and private councils exposed his traits and talents. He undertook tasks and assignments that brought his literacy, eloquence, intelligence, perceptiveness, and administrative skill to the surface. He also demonstrated a commitment to justice and perseverance in the face of hardship. He was known for his patience and gentleness, the likes of which people had only known from the stories of holy men and saints. People loved and respected him, though a few hated him out of envy or spite. Some would intentionally hurt his pride, but he would frustrate their efforts with mercy and tolerance.

It happened once that a social gathering brought him together with Khza'i Hamad al-Khishin, and the conversation developed into a debate that Shahin won. Khza'i was a strong man, so a number of those who envied Shahin and disliked him incited Khza'i against him, and Khza'i was determined to insult him. The next morning Khza'i walked to Shahin's house and entered it by force. He went straight to where the horse was tethered, saddled it, untied its tether, and was about to leave with it when he heard Shahin calling out to him, 'Abu Salim, Abu Salim, the rider of this thoroughbred should carry this sword.' He handed him a sword plated with gold and silver. Khza'i froze, not knowing what to say or do. After a short silence he returned the horse and apologized to Shahin saying, 'By God, you cannot be beaten.'

On one occasion, the Amir sent him with Hanna Mer'i al-Jureidini on a mission to the Beirut coast. When they reached the intended place, Shahin dismounted from his horse and tethred it to a ring in the wall. Hanna tied his horse to the trunk of a fig tree in front of the house, and the two men entered the house to carry out what they had come to do. After some time, Hanna was looking out of the window and saw his horse gnawing the trunk of the fig tree. He quietly went out of the house and switched the horses' places, leaving Shahin's tied to the chafed tree.

A short time later the owner came by and saw that her tree was chafed, so she seethed with anger and started cursing the horse's owner and hitting the horse with a stick. The men looked out from the house and Shahin instantly realized what had happened, recalling Hanna's exit during the meeting. He put on a smile and went out to the woman and started apologizing to her, but she would not relent or calm down until he gave her a handful of silver coins. When the woman left, Hanna spoke up and told those present the truth of the matter.

The third story that has reached us about Shahin Salman's patience and generous heart took place after he became Choueifat's *shaykh solh*. He passed a group of the town's men sitting in front of a shop and one of them began to curse him loudly. The other men tried to restrain him, but he continued to curse Shaykh Shahin. As for Shahin, he greeted the others and walked on calmly, as though he neither heard nor saw the cursing fool. Shaykh Shahin's son Amin heard about the incident and rushed home and took up his weapon. He was about to go out when his father

183

stopped him and said, 'Son, I have a more potent medicine for him than fighting. Go back home now and you will see.'

The Shaykh called his servant and gave him a sack of flour and ordered him to deliver it to the man's house. The Shaykh knew that the man was poor, and that someone had probably given him a few coins to do what he had done. The man was not at home, so his wife took the flour, kneaded it, and sent it to the bakery. She ate and fed her children and prepared lunch for her husband. When he came home, she fed him and told him of the Shaykh's gift. The next day the man was going from one place to the next in Hay al-Amrousiyya thanking and praising Shaykh Shahin Salman.

***

Let us return to the course of Shaykh Shahin's life. We have mentioned that he retired from public service and then stayed at home. When the events of 1860 occurred, there was fighting near Dayr al-Qamar. Shahin remembered two friends of his, Khalil al-Jawish and his brother Habib, between whom there was mutual admiration and respect. He went to Dayr al-Qamar and brought the two men and their families back with him to Choueifat and put them up at his house. They lived with him until the storm cleared and security was restored.

***

Choueifat remained free of any disturbance. The harmony that existed, and still does exist, between Choueifat's Druze and its Christians withstood the hurricanes of hatred, enmity, and intrigue that swept Lebanon in that era. But many of Choueifat's sons took part in the battles throughout the Gharb, and they would follow with interest the measures taken by the authorities. Inevitably, the events had an effect on Choueifat's political and social environment, and it was also incumbent on the town to play the role required of it by its history and circumstances. That is why the Choueifatis elected Shahin Salman to be their *shaykh solh* and to confront the serious issues raised by the events of the day.

184

It did not take long for the Choueifatis to reap the benefits of their fine choice. A French battalion entered Choueifat and set up camp just west of Hay al-Oumara. It was known that the French were biased and had caused many of the incidents of murder, robbery, and pillage. As soon as they came to Choueifat, security was disrupted, and Shaykh Shahin was out of town. When he returned he hurried to meet with the battalion commander, accompanied by the young and precocious Isber Shqeir, who acted as interpreter. When Shaykh Shahin asked the commander why his forces had entered Choueifat, he answered that he had come to take back all the goods and livestock stolen from Baabda or al-Hadath. The Shaykh promised to return all that the people of Choueifat had taken of the goods and livestock on condition that the commander and his soldiers withdraw from the town. The commander agreed and withdrew to the forest of Beirut, and the Shaykh kept his promise.

When Dawoud Pasha, the *mutasarrif* of Mount Lebanon, decided to make an official assessment of the population and area of northern Lebanon, he agreed with the *qa'emmaqam* Amir Milhem Arslan that Shaykh Shahin Salman should be appointed foreman for the land survey on behalf of the Druze, and Nasr Afandi Nasr al-Sarraf on behalf of the Christians. A short time later, Habib Beik Karam replaced Nasr Afandi. The Shaykh carried out his assigned task with a competence and dedication that caught the attention of rulers and commoners alike. Patriarch Boutrous Mas'ad invited him to lunch at the seat of the Patriarchate and lauded his dedication, his principles, and his fine work. He also wrote the *mutasarrif* a personal letter praising Shaykh Shahin and commending him to the *mutasarrif*. After the work on the land survey was done, Shaykh Shahin went back home and henceforth declined to accept any other position or assignment.

However, he did continue to work on resolving problems between people and arbitrating in their disagreements and controversies. His most famous achievement in this regard was his settlement of the disagreement between Shaykh Nassif Talhouq and his nephew Shaykh Hussein Mahmoud Talhouq over a number of estates and a water fountain near al-Kahhaleh. The dispute perplexed the conciliators and exhausted the courts because it had taken on a political character. Shaykh Nassif's supporters would testify in his favour, and Shaykh Hussein's supporters would testify in his, and the court could no longer ascertain the truth. Amir Milhem Arslan, the Chouf's *qa'emmaqam*, directed Shaykh Shahin to take the matter on personally. He went first to Aley and then to al-Kahhaleh, spending enough time in each place to see the lands and water and to talk in a calm, even-handed manner with those who had knowledge of the situation. In this way, he was able to determine the identity of the rightful owner. He returned to the two adversaries and persuaded them to settle the matter based on the facts he had learned. The parties were convinced and they were reconciled in the courtroom.

Nine male and three female children were born to Shaykh Shahin Salman. He educated them all at elite schools, by the standards of the day, and not one of them was illiterate. Perhaps this was his greatest achievement. He died in Choueifat in 1876 at the age of 60.

As for Shaykh Shahin Salman's children, they were Hamad, Abdallah, Amin, Aref, Masoud, Rashid, Milhem, Salim, and Shahin (who was born four months after his father's death and was therefore named after him), Islah, Hasna, and Najla. In those days it was not customary to mention the family name when referring to someone. Instead people would mention the name of the father and grandfather. That was one factor. Another was that the status and fame Shaykh Shahin Salman attained led his name to eclipse that of the family. The new name stuck and Shahin Salman's descendants became known as the Salman clan (Al Salman). But the historical reality is that (Al) Shahin is a branch of (Al) Faraj.

According to the family's writer and historian Shaykh Mer'i Shahin Salman, his grandfather Salman was the son of 'Izzeddine ibn Ibrahim ibn 'Izzeddine ibn Ibrahim ibn Shdid ibn Mahmoud ibn Shahin ibn Aqil, the last of the Abu Faraj forefathers to reside in the town of Choueifat. The first forefather of this family to move to Choueifat came from Aley, when the first forefathers settled in it around 650 Hijra/AD 1252, in the era of the Tanoukhi Amirs.[1]

---

1. The reader will note some lack of clarity in the phrases 'last of the Abu Faraj forefathers' and 'the first forefather'. I have taken this text verbatim from a document in the possession of the Salman family. Shaykh Mer'i Shahin Salman dictated the text to his son Halim, who wrote it by hand.

Hassan Zeineddine Abd al-Khaliq and Milhem Ali Hassan

When Lebanon's silk season came to an end, the merchants and manufacturers' agents collected the cocoons from the farmers, the season's debts were settled, and its profits were computed. Summer was here, and people were free to rest and enjoy their time, embarking on both long and distant social visits.

Hassan Zeineddine Abd al-Khaliq from Majdel Ba'na was an agent for the owner of the silk factory in al-Qrayyeh near Bhamdoun. The position made him wealthy by the standards of the time. He also commanded a good measure of bravery and generosity. It is therefore no surprise that he attained a prominent social status and had friends and associates in all the various areas of the mountain.

One of his friends was Milhem Ali Hassan from Atrin. Like Hassan, Milhem was a fine, upstanding young man, and the two men enjoyed a bond of brotherhood and goodwill. Hassan decided to start his summer visits by checking on his brother Milhem. One day, after he had eaten, he got on his horse and rode towards the Chouf, arriving in Atrin in the afternoon. He went to his brother Milhem's house and knocked on the door. A veiled woman appeared and he asked her about Abu Saeed Milhem. She said he was not at home. He asked if Milhem would be returning soon and she said she did not know. He asked who she was and she informed him that she was Um Saeed, Milhem's wife. He introduced himself as Hassan Zeineddine Abd al-Khaliq from Majdel Ba'na. She said she was pleased to meet him but did not invite him in. Hassan said, 'Give my regards to my brother Abu Saeed, and tell him that I came to visit him but did not find him at home. Tell him also that the mare he has does not suit him. He should sell her and come to Majdel Ba'na, and I will get him a better one.' He then turned his horse around and went back to where he had come from.

When Milhem Ali Hassan returned home that evening, his wife Khawla told him of Hassan Zeineddine's visit, naively and innocently recounting the details of Hassan's words. Once Abu Saeed figured out the whole conversation and understood exactly what had happened, he said to her, 'Prepare yourself to return to your father's house. You are divorced from me.'

***

Shirking the duties of hospitality was among the most serious of matters for a proud man, equalled only by fear or cowardice in the hour of hardship and battle. Here the question poses itself: What is a woman to do, especially a Druze woman for whom the veil was required, in the event of her husband's absence from the house, as happened with Khawla, the wife of Milhem Ali Hassan?

The answer to this question requires some clarification. First, Druze society does not include, and has never included, the institution known as the 'harem', where women are secluded from society, denied access to sunlight and air, and limited to bearing children. The Druze faith forbade polygamy because it saw that a man could never treat his wives equally. The religion gave the woman equal status and made her man's partner in life, through good and bad. Second, the Druze religion emphasized the importance of good morals for both men and women, so the need for hiding and isolation in bedrooms was reduced. We should note here that the moral standards that apply to men are as stringent as those for women. The Druze have exaggerated these mores lately, but to no one's benefit. (No one doubts that the Druze community has always been first in preserving the lives and honour of its enemies' women in war and conflict.) Third, the Druze way of life required cooperation between men and women. The Druze are a minority, yet their wars were numerous and great, demanding the energies of men as well as women. In times of peace, the Druze till the rough, rocky terrain of their mountain stronghold to extract their livelihood. This too required the labour of all working hands. For all these reasons, Druze women enjoyed a certain social status in times of war and in times of peace.

When a woman finds herself in a position like that of Khawla, Milhem Hassan's wife, she is supposed to invite the guest in and give him the impression that her husband will be home soon. Then she should call on one or more of her relatives to keep the man company, and she should offer him some suitable food. After he has eaten, she is supposed to tell him where her husband is, and the guest is then expected to do the normal and acceptable thing by either leaving the town or being received by some of the house owner's relatives.

When a Druze errs and suffers adverse consequences, it is said that it was an 'hour of forsaking' (*sa'at takhalli*), meaning that God forsook him in that hour and he fell into error. In Khawla's case, the entire day was a 'day of forsaking'. She failed to fulfil her duties of hospitality towards her husband's guest out of naivety and innocence. Even though she was from a proud and generous family – the Fayyad clan from Bshatfeen – and had given Milhem two sons, Saeed and Rashid, and even though she was a good woman, he divorced her and she returned to her parents' household.

***

A few days later, Milhem Hassan went to Majdel Ba'na and became the guest of his friend Hassan Abd al-Khaliq. He told Hassan that, upon his suggestion, he had divorced his wife and was now waiting for his friend to find him a suitable new wife. Hassan Abd al-Khaliq felt responsible for what had happened. He told Milhem that he had only meant what he said as a joke and had not imagined that the matter would lead to that outcome. But what was done was done, and there was no way to undo it. Hassan felt he was now obligated to find his brother Milhem a suitable new bride, and he promised he would do so.

Through his work and status, Hassan Abd al-Khaliq knew most people in al-Jurd and al-Matn. He began to search fervently for a bride for Milhem and solicited the help of some of his friends in the endeavour. They met with fortune in Ras al-Matn. Hassan was guided through the help of his friend Hamad al-Ma'ari to a suitable bride for Milhem Hassan, and they engaged Badr Makarem on Milhem's behalf. The wedding date arrived, and Hassan decided to hold a grand celebration for his brother Milhem. He invited the area's notables, and when the Hassan family delegation appeared, Hassan accompanied them in a large convoy to Ras al-Matn.

On the first day, the marriage contract was written. On the second day, the people prepared for the wedding. It was expected, as was customary, that the people of Ras al-Matn would throw down a *qayma* to be lifted by the groom's relatives or friends. And among the group from Atrin and 'Einbal there were young men who were worthy of the challenge. But the people of Ras al-Matn surprised the groom's people with a *qayma* of a different kind. They suspended an egg from a tree using twine and required that the cord be cut by firing bullets on condition that it was done with the first or second shot. Hussein Zeineddine Abd al-Khaliq stepped forward carrying a loaded double-barrelled hunting rifle. Once the target was in place, he took his rifle, cocked it, inserted the bullets, rested his left arm on the shoulder of a man from Ras al-Matn, aimed, and fired. The cord was severed and the egg fell to the ground, settling the matter.

The bride came out. They seated her on a white horse, and the convoy set off on its journey home. In Hammana, the people lined both sides of the street and threw rice and candy over the bride. Hassan Abd al-Khaliq dipped his hand into his pack-saddle, which he had filled with coins of silver and copper, and began to throw one fistful of coins after the other into the crowd. In al-Modayrij, the convoy split up. Those from al-Jurd and al-Matn returned to their villages and the people of Atrin proceeded with the bride towards the Chouf, accompanied by Hassan Abd al-Khaliq. In Atrin, the festivities and feasts went on for three consecutive days. When they were over, Hassan Abd al-Khaliq returned to Majdel Ba'na relaxed, assured, and content.

***

The Druze have a number of expressions of congratulations on wedding occasions. Among the most exquisite of these is the prayer that the marriage will 'meet the needs of time'. What is meant by this is the hope that the marriage will endure and that neither partner will be forced to marry again because of divorce or the death of the other. And when the formalities are over, the Druze employ a phrase which entails some humour and teasing. They pray that the bride and groom will 'tear each other apart', meaning that they will use up their clothes and shoes in merriment.

On the day that Milhem married Badr Makarem, many expressed to him their hopes and prayers that the marriage would 'meet the needs of time', but it did not last long. After Badr Makarem had given birth to his third son, Mustafa, he divorced her and she returned to her parents' home in Ras al-Matn. No details about the reasons for this divorce have reached us, but Milhem earned the reputation of being 'a marrying man', which shows that Badr's divorce, like Khawla's before her, was not for any genuine reason recognized by the standards of today.

After Badr Makarem, Milhem married one of his relatives, Khazmeh, the daughter of Amin Hassan and the sister of the famous hero Khza'i Amin Hassan, and he was blessed with four sons by her – Khattar, Qassem, Ali, and Salim. Milhem Ali Hassan was blessed with a long life, and his seven sons grew up and became men while he was still healthy and active. He would go out to attend functions surrounded by all his sons, eight men walking out of a single gate. That was a scene of power, prestige, and glory.[1]

---

1. Among the fascinatig things that happened in the telling of this story is that I first heard it from Shaykh Hassan Ali Abd al-Khaliq (96 years old), the son of Hassan Zeineddine Abd al-Khaliq. Then I went back to collect the details from the Hassan side. I met with Khalil Hassan, an employee in the Ministry of Labour and Social Affairs and the grandson of Milhem Hassan, and he knew the general outlines of the story. Khalil went to Atrin and gathered details, notes, and names, and kindly related them to me. But in the course of his investigation, Khalil discovered that Khawla, the wronged woman Hassan Zeineddine Abd al-Khaliq had divorced, was his grandmother, the mother of his father Rashid.

'Izzeddine Najem Shehayyeb and Ibrahim Shayya

'Izzeddine Najem Shehayyeb from Aley worked as a travelling salesmen. He would buy goods from Beirut's stores, load them on to the back of a pack animal, and sell them in the mountain villages. Of course, he was never absent from the market in his home town of Aley, always keeping abreast of the latest news about buyers and sellers, supply and demand, and fluctuations in prices.

One day, he met Ibrahim Shayya from Badghan in the shop of one of his relatives. They became acquainted and talked for a while, and each felt comfortable in the other's company. Both men were *ajaweed*; both were tellers of funny and strange anecdotes, and both were *zajal* poets. Ibrahim was on his way to Beirut, so 'Izzeddine invited him to stop by and visit on his way back. Ibrahim accepted the invitation.

Ibrahim returned from Beirut the following evening and visited 'Izzeddine. 'Izzeddine showed him the warmest generosity, and they spent an enjoyable evening together exchanging kind words, reciting poetry, and trading stories and news. The next morning, at the end of Ibrahim's visit, he insisted that 'Izzeddine return the visit in Badghan. 'Izzeddine promised he would visit Ibrahim in Badghan on his next trading trip. When Ibrahim returned home, he told his wife all that had happened with 'Izzeddine, and that he awaited his visit. He instructed her to carry out her duties of hospitality to the fullest extent if 'Izzeddine happened to come while he was out.

***

192

After some time, 'Izzeddine Shehayyeb left Aley on his usual trading route and stopped in Badghan to visit his friend Ibrahim Shayya. When he found the house, he knocked on the door with his stick and Ibrahim's wife appeared. She quickly recognized 'Izzeddine by his loaded mule, so she welcomed him and invited him in. She called one of her sons, and he opened the living-room door. 'Izzeddine entered after Ibrahim's wife had told him that her husband was out but would return soon.

The truth was that Ibrahim's wife did not know when her husband would return. But she left nothing to chance. She quickly began to carry out her husband's instructions, preparing an assortment of food for the guest from what was available in the house. She brought the food in to 'Izzeddine on a tray and invited him to eat. Abu Mahmoud 'Izzeddine was hungry, so he started to eat. As he was reaching for the food, Ibrahim's wife remembered something. She did not know her husband's guest's *gharadiyya*.[1] Were the Shehayyebs Jumblattis like the Shayya family, or were they Yazbakis? She asked 'Izzeddine, 'Shaykh, I know that you are Abu Mahmoud Shehayyeb from Aley, but I want to ask you, is the food you are eating *halal* for you, or is it *haram*?'[2] Abu Mahmoud understood what she meant and said, 'If you want the truth, it is completely *haram*.' The woman turned away and said, 'Then let *haram* befall you if you take even one bite,' and walked out quickly and abruptly.

We have mentioned that Abu Mahmoud was hungry, but Ibrahim's wife had cast the *haram* upon him if he 'took even one bite'. He thought of a way round this prohibition, and an answer quickly occurred to him. He took a loaf of bread, rolled it, and held it in his left hand, and took the spoon in his right. He started taking bites from the loaf, as we would with a sandwich today, and then followed the bread with a spoonful of stew.

Ibrahim Shayya returned. When he saw his friend, he began to shout, 'Welcome, welcome.' Abu Mahmoud answered, 'Welcome to you, Ibrahim, *hirmat al-aysh*,' and continued eating in the way we have described. The custom was, and still is, that those seated to eat do not rise to greet someone entering the room out of respect for *hirmat al-aysh* (the sanctity of food). But once they have finished and have washed their

---

1. *Gharadhiyya* literally means partisanship. In those days, partisanship divided the Jumblattis from the Yazbakis, two groups allied to the two seats of Druze political power, the Jumblatts and the Arslans. [Translator]
2. *Halal* and *haram* are expressions relating to whether or not a commodity, be it food or money, is obtained piously or according to religiously sanctioned norms. Ibrahim's wife was apparently under the impression that if 'Izzeddine Shehayyeb was a Jumblatti like her husband, his food would be *halal*. [Translator]

hands and chin, they will greet the person properly and ask about their health, family, friends, and affairs. But the anomaly that was not lost on Ibrahim was the manner of eating. He had shared food with 'Izzeddine before in Aley and his friend had eaten food one bite at a time, as proper table manners required, so he could not help but ask him why he was eating that way. Abu Mahmoud said that he was very hungry, but Ibrahim was not convinced. He went to his wife and asked her if she had done anything to make 'Izzeddine eat in that unusual manner. She claimed not to know the reason.

'Izzeddine finished eating the hot food and dishes of fig and other fruit preserves were brought in. He took the porcupine quill in his hand and ate his fill of sweets. He then thanked God and got up and shook hands with his host, and they sat down to talk. After they had talked, 'Izzeddine got up to go and sell his goods. Ibrahim insisted that his guest stay at his house, saying he would invite the town's people, and they would come and buy what they needed from him. Abu Mahmoud apologized and asked permission to leave.

At that point Ibrahim returned to the subject that had disturbed him and occupied his mind. He said to Abu Mahmoud, 'Listen, my friend. The way you ate your food was not normal, and I am sure there is a reason for it. No doubt my wife said or did something that made you behave that way. Tell me the truth and I promise you I will not direct any bad words towards her about it.' So Abu Mahmoud told him what his wife had done.

Ibrahim stood up calmly and called one of his cousins and sent him to bring his wife's parents. They came promptly. He then ordered her father to carry his daughter's chest, and her mother to carry her mattress and declared, 'Your daughter shall never eat in my house again.' 'Izzeddine got up, demanding that Ibrahim keep his promise not to 'direct any bad words' at his wife. Ibrahim answered, 'I kept my promise. I directed my words at her parents.' And that was how Ibrahim Shayya divorced his wife.

The Raydan Clan

Never have so many virtues been found together in such a small group of people as in the Raydan clan of Ain 'Inoub. Throughout the nineteenth century, the number of men among them never exceeded the number of fingers on one hand. Yet despite their small numbers, they became known for a number of qualities and traits which are 'feared and desired in men'. They were known for the sword, the guest, and the treacherous nights, as much as for goodness, piety, scholarship, and knowledge. They carried these and other pleasant traits with modesty in their souls, tenderness in their nature, and an easy smile on their faces.

They were originally known as the Abdallah clan and resided in the upper Gharb before they settled in Ain 'Inoub. Among them was Shaykh Zahreddine Abdallah, who rests in a shrine atop the heights of the village of Fisaqin. He was well versed in religion and passed his knowledge on to Amir Jamaleddine Abdallah al-Tanoukhi (Sayyid Abdallah). It is no way to the detriment of Shaykh Zahreddine to say that the student surpassed his teacher. Also among them was Arefeh, the wife of Shaykh Hammoud Makarem, who attained a level of devotion and worship that earned her the title 'al-Sit Arefeh', and whose grave is a well-known landmark in Aytat. Another was Abed, who was renowned for his generosity and grace. He built the fountain in Ain 'Inoub that bears his name to this day, inscribed above its arch. The clan also included those mentioned in the following discussion.

***

All living members of the Abdallah clan are descendants of Fares Abd al-Wahab Saeed Abdallah. Fares, who was nicknamed Abu Raafi'. He lived in the mid-eighteenth century and was the Shaykh of Ain 'Inoub. He had two sons, Raydan (Abu Ali) and 'Izzeddine. 'Izzeddine died childless. As for Raydan, he had three sons, Fares, Ahmad, and Ali. His name eclipsed that of the family, and today they are all his descendants. To be more specific, all the remaining Raydans are descended from his son Ali, since Fares and Ahmad had no sons.

Thus they were five men in the first half of the nineteenth century. They owned vast properties, so they were able to do without work and devote their efforts and their fortunes to the pursuit of praise and glory. They collected thoroughbreds and swords, and excelled in horsemanship and the use of instruments of war. They built houses and opened them to guests, completing the circle of 'bravery and generosity'. They did not forsake the traditions of the home and adhered to their religion and faith.

They lived in days of caution and concern. The security, stability, and national unity the Lebanese had enjoyed under the Ma'nis and the early Chehabs was gone, replaced in the days of Bashir II with conspiracies, plots, murders of individuals and groups, torture, and confiscation. The fires of sectarianism were also starting to be fuelled. Then the Egyptians entered Syria, and Amir Bashir tied his fate to theirs. The situation worsened and revolutions erupted, the Druze revolution being the most fervent and the most consequential among them, beginning in Jabal al-Druze in Syria and then extending to Wadi al-Taym. Some 1,000 Druze young men went from Lebanon to join the faction of Shibley Agha al-'Iryan.

Three young men went from Ain 'Inoub. 'Izzeddine Abdallah and his nephew Fares Raydan Abdallah were two of them. Sources differ as to the identity of the third. Some say he was from the Qaed Bey family while others say he was from the Qamand family. In our discussion of the Battle of Wadi Baka in a previous chapter, we mentioned that the Druze called it the Battle of the Brothers because forty pairs of brothers perished in it.

This phenomenon – the phenomenon of brothers and relatives going into battle together – deserves attention and requires analysis because it is contrary to the practice and custom of other communities, and also contravenes modern standards. The custom of other peoples was not to allow all the men of a particular house to go to war and face the risk of death. Some would stay at home to raise the children and carry on the family name. But the Druze do not take these matters into consideration because they believe in the certainty of fate and the transient nature of life. They say that 'a child of ten does not die at nine'. He whose death is written for a certain hour cannot hasten it by recklessness or delay it by caution. That is why a brother goes with his brother, and a son with his father, to the battlefield. In companionship there is intimacy and cooperation, and nothing can change the predetermined fate of each man.

When the Druze of the Chouf were called upon to aid their brothers in Wadi al-Taym in the spring of 1838, Ahmad and Ali Raydan were still children and Fares was on the threshold of adulthood. 'Izzeddine was younger than his brother Raydan, so Fares and his uncle 'Izzeddine were close in age. They took up their weapons and whatever money and provisions they could and rode their horses to the Arqoub, and from there to Wadi al-Taym. It was their destiny to accompany the master of horsemen Shaykh Nassereddine al-'Imad into the Battle of Wadi Baka. 'Izzeddine died a glorious death and Fares was among the few survivors who were able to escape the hellfire of that battle. However, he sustained an injury to his left hand and was to suffer its effects for the rest of his life.

When the war ended, Fares returned to Ain 'Inoub, and the other survivors returned to their villages. As the people learned who had survived and who had not, funerals were held throughout the land. The worst of the tragedies was in Majdel Ba'na, as seven pairs of brothers from the Abd al-Khaliq family fell at the Battle of Wadi Baka.

***

We will not address the events of the 1840s and those of the year 1860. Suffice it to say that the Raydan clan had their share of them. Ahmad Raydan was killed, and since his father Abu Ali had also died, only Fares and Ali remained alive. If the great events gained Fares fame in the areas of courage and chivalry, they also heightened his devotion to his religion and faith, elevating his status among clergymen and laymen alike. Like his grandfather, Fares too was nicknamed Abu Raafi'. He pledged himself to remain chaste, choosing not to marry, as an extreme expression of asceticism, devotion, and self-denial.

The house grew in status, and its doors were open to men of religion as well as commoners. After the events of 1860, al-Sit Naifa, the widow of Shaykh Amin Shams and sister of Saeed Beik Jumblatt, had to disappear from view. She became a guest of the Raydans and stayed with them for forty days.

Despite the injury to his left hand, Fares remained a master of the battlefield and a teacher of strikers and slayers. One of his students in this domain was Amir Mustafa Arslan. Amir Amin, called 'al-Kabir' (the Great) in view of his courage and strong resolve, and to distinguish him from his grandson, Amir Amin Mustafa, entrusted Abu Raafi' with the task of teaching Amir Mustafa horsemanship. He trained the young Amir in swordplay, horse riding, javelin pitching, and shooting until he excelled in all of them. They say that in the last lesson in horsemanship, Abu Raafi' and Amir Mustafa mounted their horses, and Abu Raafi' placed a spear on his head and Amir Mustafa laid a sword on its side on his. They roamed the field for about half an hour with the spear and the sword remaining in place. The sword did deviate slightly from its place on the head of Amir Mustafa, but the teacher was satisfied and announced the 'graduation' of his pupil.

Ali married Karima Baz from Ba'tharan. The memory of the Battle of Wadi Baka remained in the house, for Ali's wife was the cousin of Youssef Baz. Youssef was with Shibley Agha al-'Iryan in Wadi al-Taym. On the day of the Battle of Wadi Baka, Shibley led 200 horsemen in an attack on one of the flanks of the Egyptian army in an attempt to alleviate the pressure on Shaykh Nassereddine al-'Imad and his 300 surrounded Druze men. Shibley fell into a dangerous quagmire. He was returning from an attack on the enemy's line, his weapon empty of ammunition, when one of the Arnaout horsemen chased him. He placed his spear between Shibley's shoulders and was about to kill him when Youssef Baz jumped from the side of the line of pursuit on to the Arnaout horsemen, threw him off his horse, and killed him.

***

In 1873 Amir Mustafa became *qa'emmaqam* of the Chouf, and remained so until 1883. Nassib Beik Jumblatt succeeded him as *qa'emmaqam* until 1892, when Amir Mustafa returned and ruled for another ten years. The seat of the *qa'emmaqamiyya* during the two reigns of Amir Mustafa was in Baaqlin during the summer and in Ain 'Inoub during the other seasons. During the reigns of Nassib Beik Jumblatt, it was in Baaqlin in the summer and in Choueifat in the winter.

The reign of Amir Mustafa Arslan was the golden age for the Raydans, not because of any reward they received or position they held, but because it gave them the opportunity to give of themselves and their money, and they 'purchased praise at a profitable price'. During Amir Mustafa's time as *qa'emmaqam*, Ain 'Inoub became the regional capital. Rules were issued from it and about it, and men came to it from all parts of the *qa'emmaqamiyya*, which included what today comprises the two districts of Aley and the Chouf. There was an almost constant movement of delegations coming into the town on official and social occasions.

The modes of transportation available in those days did not allow people to travel to or from distant places in a single day. There were no hotels, so guest-houses played that role. Ain 'Inoub withstood the pressure of its visitors with acceptance and appreciation, in a society that valued (and still does) value, courage, and generosity above all other virtues except the preservation of honour and dignity.

What Ain 'Inoub experienced during the reigns of Amir Mustafa, Baaqlin and Choueifat had seen for longer periods of time during the days of the Ma'nis, Jumblattis, and Arslanis. From here springs the widespread but inaccurate accusation that the people of Baaqlin and Choueifat are mean. But men sometimes become bored, demand sometimes exceeds that which is offered, and needs sometimes exceed capabilities. The Raydans never became bored or apathetic, however, and they performed miracles in the realms of hospitality and generosity.

I was once talking with one of Baysour's *mashayekh* and we mentioned the house of Raydan. The Shaykh said, 'They are the owners of the ninety-nine beds.' There were not really ninety-nine beds, but as a story is circulated and retold, exaggerations creep in. In fact, there were thirty-seven beds. One stormy winter night, thirty-seven guests dined and slept at the Raydan house in Ain 'Inoub. All that was left for Ali Raydan that night was a *'aba*, so he wrapped himself in it and slept in a corner of the house. It was a huge occasion, and all of Ain 'Inoub's people received their share of guests, each according to his abilities.

One day, a group of people from Jabal al-Druze, headed by the Syrian Druze Mufti Shaykh Ahmad al-Hajari, came to Amir Mustafa. At the end of the visit, the Amir 'invited' them to eat at the house of Ali Raydan. There were thirty-two men, and Suleiman Jumblatt Abu Hassan led them to the house. None of the men were at home, so Um Muhammad, Ali's wife, welcomed them and went to prepare their food. Shaykh Ahmad called her and swore on behalf of himself and his companions that they would not eat anything cooked over fire. Because of lack of time, they would settle for whatever cheese, yogurt, olives, and bread was available.

It is known that when the *ajaweed* have decided something, there is no chance of persuading them to change their mind.

A short time later the guests were invited to eat, and the table was set with uncooked food. But the table's four edges were lined with thirty-two plates, each containing two raw eggs. The guests were puzzled, but their questions were answered when they sat down and the servants turned over the dishes and poured boiling margarine over them. The eggs were cooked without being put over fire, and the *ajaweed* accepted the solution. When the skies cleared and the guests tried to ease their burden, the Raydans set up a stand on the side of the road stacked with loaves of bread rolled with cheese and *labneh* (strained yogurt). They invited the travellers to take all they needed to eat and as provisions for the road.

***

We have previously alluded to the level of devotion, worship, and jurisprudence attained by Shaykh Abu Raafi' Fares Raydan. Amir Mustafa Arslan would not attend any religious council other than that of Shaykh Abu Raafi'. Of course, Amir Mustafa would not participate in the prayers. He was among the ranks of the *juhhaal* (laymen). However, it is a Druze custom that the *ajaweed* devote the first half of the blessed Adha night to preaching, guidance, and the recitation of religious poems, and the *juhhaal* are allowed to participate. Amir Mustafa would take part in this celebration and listen to the counsel of Shaykh Abu Raafi'. We should also mention that Shaykh Abu Raafi' was his teacher in horsemanship and the use of weapons of war.

When Shaykh Abu Raafi' died, Amir Mustafa was deeply saddened and abandoned his usual arrogance and aloofness. He cried for the Shaykh, eulogized him, and called him 'master of masters, my master'. It is a Druze custom that when an individual attains a high level of virtue and devotion, and a distinguished status in worship, jurisprudence, and knowledge, people refer to him as (my) master. In the case of a woman they refer to her as (my) mistress.

***

After wars, visits, and meetings, some unspent resources and energies usually remained. The Raydans would devote these to reconciling people and settling disputes. Some still remember the two close friends Ali Abu Ali Raydan from Ain 'Inoub and Hussein Youssef from Dayr Qoubel, who would look into individual disputes and expend effort and money to settle conflicts between adversaries.[1]

A generation passed, and another came. Fares, Ahmad, and Ali passed away, and Muhammad, Ahmad, and Hani arrived. Times and circumstances changed, but the spirit of the Raydans and their traditions and morals remained the same. Muhammad excelled in handwriting and composition and became a clerk in the Chouf's court. He did not need the work, but he took it out of dedication and for the prestige of a position in the *mutasarrifiyya*. But fate did not allow him to reach full bloom, and he died young and childless. Ahmad also died without descendants.

Only Shaykh Abu Hassan Hani and Ibrahim remained. The house was not harmed and they embodied all of its fine habits. Faith and honesty remained, and the tradition of giving and generosity endured. The days of war and horsemanship passed, and the courage of righteousness and ethics was apparent in them. The flow of visiting delegations to Ain Inoub ceased, and guests became scarce.

Hani lived the last days of horsemanship and learned and perfected the craft to become the most skilful of riders. (The skill lost its significance soon thereafter with the arrival of cars, planes, and tanks.) He then devoted himself to study, education, religion, and jurisprudence. He studied morphology, grammar, rhetoric, metrics, and then read all of the modern and ancient poetry and prose. Soon his talent for gentle yet strong poetry emerged. He delved into religion and became a point of reference for others. He was austere, modest, and shy, and was a good conversationalist. Those attending his council never had enough of his conversation.

On the day of Shaykh Abu Hassan's funeral, some writers were about to eulogize him when Shaykh Muhammad Abu Shaqra, the Druze Mufti, said to them, 'The purpose of a eulogy is to make the deceased and his traits known to people. Is there any one among us who is ignorant of Shaykh Abu Hassan and his lofty status?'

---

1. In our times we saw a similar pair of men – Wadi' al-Haddad from Ain 'Inoub, a resident of Souk al-Gharb, and Shakir Hamed Abu Hassan from Choueifat. They took it upon themselves to mediate between people to resolve disputes and reconcile antagonists. Both have since passed away.

Ali 'Izzeddine Abd al-Khaliq, Jibrail Mishrik al-Haddad, and Muhammad Mahmoud

Shaykh Abu Hussein Ali 'Izzeddine Abd al-Khaliq from Majdel Ba'na was the father of Shaykh Abu Fares Mahmoud Abd al-Khaliq, who went far in the study of religion, and was renowned for his devotion and piety. There is a shrine devoted to him in Majdel Ba'na, and people visit it for blessings. He was also the grandfather of Shaykh Abu Mahmoud Suleiman. Shaykh Abu Hussein's was one of Majdel Ba'na's most recognizable faces in the nineteenth century, and he lived to be 90 (1810 –1900).

In his youth, Ali became known for his strength, fortitude, and succour. It is said that one day while ploughing his land he heard shouts and a commotion coming from a nearby field. He left his plough and ran to where the sounds were coming from to find a *shibi*[1] attacking a group of people. It had harmed one person and some livestock. Ali wrapped his *'aba* around his left wrist and approached the *shibi*, which immediately lunged at him with its mouth open and its molars exposed. Ali thrust his wrist between its jaws and grabbed its upper jaw with his right hand and pulled on it until it broke. He then threw the *shibi* to the ground and finished it off with some rocks.

As Ali approached old age, he took up religion and donned the *'amaama* and *al-jubba al-khashina*.[2] But he maintained his interest and

---

1. The *shibi* is the offspring of the hyena and the wolf, and it is among the fiercest of animals.
2. The *'amaama* is a special turban worn by the very pious and learned of the Druze clergymen. *Al-jubba al-khashina* is a gown of coarse material worn by such clergy
(continued...)

activity in public affairs. His house was always open to guests and visitors, and he established strong bonds of friendship with the people of the area, especially those from Bhamdoun, where the young men called him 'grandfather', both to endear themselves to him and out of respect. One of those young men was Jibrail Mishrik al-Haddad.[1] Jibrail was a farrier with a shop in the Bhamdoun market-place. But during harvest days, he would carry his instruments and wander round the villages like a travelling doctor. When night fell, he would sleep at a friend's house. In Majdel Ba'na, he would stay with his 'grandfather', Shaykh Abu Hussein. People knew Jibrail for his mild temper, moral rectitude, dedication, and love of others.

***

In 1885 spring came early and the snow cleared from the mountains, except for what had settled on Mount Baarouk. The warmth of life filled the land and regenerated the green grass, embroidered with blue, red, and yellow flowers, and the trees were heavy with leaves. People returned to activity, movement, and labour after the stagnancy of winter and its cold days and long nights. The farmers pruned their vines and fruit trees and then began plowing the land. Some obtained shacks to breed silkworms, and money was exchanged to purchase cows, sheep, and other livestock. Loans were dispensed and debts were incurred, with payment expected after the silk-harvesting season.

One day that spring, Muhammad Mahmoud from al-Baarouk came to Majdel Ba'na to purchase a milk-producing cow. He carried for that purpose the sum of 15 gold liras, which he had put in his belt, as was the custom in those days. Muhammad did not find what he was looking for, and decided to spend the night in Majdel Ba'na. He stayed as the guest of Shaykh Abu Hussein Ali 'Izzeddine Abd al-Khaliq.

Jibrail Mishrik al-Haddad also happened to be in Majdel Ba'na that day. Since it was the ploughing season and the oxen needed shoeing, his

---

(...continued)
    to show asceticism and self-denial. [Translator]
1. Jibrail had five sons (Youssef, Mikhael, Mishrik, Abdallah, and Ibrahim) and numerous grandsons. They reside in Bhamdoun, though some of them are overseas. The name of Youssef Mishrik al-Haddad was included in the list of members of the Municipal Council of Bhamdoun in 1903.

workload was heavy and night fell while he was still in Majdel Ba'na. He therefore resorted to the hospitality of his 'grandfather', Abu Hussein. After dinner, some of the Shaykh's relatives came and stayed up late with the family's guests. Once the relatives had left, two mattresses were laid out in the living room for the guests and they slept.

***

At sunrise the next morning, Shaykh Abu Hussein brought his guests their morning coffee. He saw Muhammad putting on his clothes with obvious anxiety and haste, but no trace of Jibrail. When he asked about him, Muhammad replied, 'I woke up a little while ago and did not find him.' Then he was quiet. Abu Hussein was puzzled, and Muhammad continued, 'Anyway, he had finished his work.' Abu Hussein asked him what he meant, and Muhammad said, 'Jibrail is gone, and so is my belt, together with the 15 gold liras.' Shaykh Abu Hussein was shocked and said, 'How dare you, Muhammad! Are you sure of what you are saying? I have known Jibrail since he was a boy and he is an honest man.' Muhammad answered, 'Abu Hussein, you know that I came to buy a cow and I had the money, and no one else entered the room, so where is the belt?'

Abu Hussein recognized that accusing Jibrail of theft was a very delicate and serious matter. But he also saw that Muhammad was his guest, and he was responsible for him and his money. The case was clear. All the evidence pointed to Jibrail, and it was necessary for Shaykh Abu Hussein to settle the issue. He told his wife what had happened and asked her to prepare breakfast for Muhammad Mahmoud, and then got on his donkey and headed for Bhamdoun. They say that had Shaykh Abu Hussein's donkey not known the way to Bhamdoun, Abu Hussein would have lost the way because of his worry and confusion. He was trying to think of a way to bring the matter up with Jibrail. He even considered turning back, but his stubbornness and determination to find the truth prevented him.

Abu Hussein reached Bhamdoun and found Jibrail in his shop, immersed in his work, with his usual enthusiasm and spirit. Jibrail hastened to say, 'Grandfather, you did not tell me you were coming to Bhamdoun today.' Abu Hussein answered, 'And you did not tell me that you were leaving for Bhamdoun before sunrise.' Jibrail replied, 'You know, grandfather, that this is the season of work, as you see.' Abu Hussein remained silent for a moment, and so did Jibrail, but then he sensed Abu Hussein's confusion and asked him why he had come to Bhamdoun.

Shaykh Abu Hussein summoned all his strength and said to Jibrail in an agony of torment, 'Jibrail, Muhammad Mahmoud lost his belt last night, and it contained 15 gold liras. No one entered the room but me and you ...' Jibrail bowed his head for a moment. Then he looked up again, suddenly appearing as though he had aged ten years, and said, 'Grandfather, the soul counsels evil, and greed lured me in, so I fell into this deed. I will return the money to you, but in the name of friendship and affection, I ask you to conceal this deed. Now wait for me here, and I will bring you the money.' Jibrail absented himself for a short while and then returned to give Abu Hussein the 15 gold liras. When Abu Hussein asked him about the belt, Jibrail said he had got rid of it on the way.

***

On the way back to Majdel Ba'na, Abu Hussein was deep in thought and shook his head in disappointment and disbelief. Had Jibrail Mishrik really committed theft? No doubt it was the 'end of days', and the final day of judgement was near. The donkey walked into Majdel Ba'na and Abu Hussein approached his house to find his wife waiting anxiously by the door. When he neared her, she shouted to him, 'What have you done, Abu Hussein?' He said, 'I have found the money.' She answered, 'How did you find the money when it was never lost and is now in the hands of its owner?'

What had happened was as follows: Muhammad Mahmoud had got up at night to relieve himself and taken the belt with him as a precautionary measure. He had hung it on a tree at the end of the outer square and then left it there and gone back to sleep. He did not remember this the next morning, but after Abu Hussein went to Bhamdoun, the children saw the belt and returned it to Muhammad.

When Abu Hussein heard the story, he chided Muhammad severely and turned back towards Bhamdoun. His extreme agitation and anger made it feel as if the world was closing in on him. When he reached the Bhamdoun market he found Jibrail's shop closed, so he went to his house. Jibrail was pacing back and forth through the house with an expression of pain and sorrow on his face, yet he still greeted Abu Hussein warmly and managed a smile. The Shaykh shouted at him saying, 'What have you done, Jibrail? The belt and money have been found. How could you take responsibility for theft?'

Jibrail felt refreshed and he awoke from his amazement. And how beautiful is redemption after distress! He said to Abu Hussein, 'Grandfather, if I had denied knowledge of where the money was, there would have been a dispute over the matter, the news would have spread among the people, and you and I would both have been subjected to suspicion. That was why I thought it better to buy my dignity and yours with money and keep the matter between us.' Abu Hussein asked, 'Where did you get the money from?' Jibrail answered, 'I borrowed it from Michael 'Issa Matta.' Michael 'Issa was one of the area's notables at the time, and a man of opinion and grace. Abu Hussein said to Jibrail, 'Let us go and visit this gentleman, Michael, and return his money and tell him about your gallantry.'

Nasib Beik al-Atrash, Fad'a Saab and Najib Beik Trad

In the summer of 1909 Nasib Beik al-Atrash, the Shaykh of Salkhad, went to visit the village of Shennaira[1] and stayed as the honoured guest of his business manager, Abu Daher Youssef al-Saadi.[2] In keeping with the people's customs, Abu Daher invited all the men of Shennaira to dinner at his guest-house in honour of Nasib Beik. After dinner, the guests stayed to chat and enjoy the evening.

One of the guests was Fad'a Abdallah Ahmad Saab from Choueifat. Nasib Beik singled him out in the conversation and started asking him specific questions about Lebanon and its men. The discussion moved from politics to history to the seasons to popular literature. Nasib was surprised by the breadth of Fad'a's knowledge and understanding, eloquence, and quick-wittedness. When the guests left, he spoke to Daher Youssef about his great admiration for his guest from the Chouf and said, 'If that man is in need of any political or economic support, I am ready to assist him.' Abu Daher replied, 'He is our relative and in-law, and he is not in need of any of the things you mentioned. He is a merchant and has a store here in Shennaira.' Nasib Beik was taken aback. He slapped his right hand against his left and said, 'What are you saying, Abu Daher? Is this man a merchant? What a waste!'

Such was people's view, especially clan leaders, of merchants and commerce. It is said that Amir Mustafa Arslan had a commercial agent in Damascus who was a man of wealth and owned a grand home there, but

1. Shaykh Nasib Beik al-Atrash was one of the heroes and martyrs of the Druze–Syrian revolution of 1925. Salkhad and Shennaira are in Jabal al-Druze.
2. Some of the members of the Saadi family are in Dmit and Kfar Nabrakh, and others are in Brih and in Shennaira.

Amir Mustafa would not stay as his guest when he was in Damascus. Instead he would lodge with the sons of some of the 'political' families, even if their home was rough and below standard, to avoid being regarded as the equal of a merchant, whom people call a 'salesman'.

After Nasib Beik al-Atrash had left Shennaira, Abu Daher told Abu Ma'rouf Fad'a what Nasib Beik had said. Fad'a composed a *zajal* poem of about 300 lines, expressing many of the morals and lessons of life, and insisting on virtue no matter what the circumstances or the endeavour. He sent it to Nasib Beik al-Atrash.[1] Nasib Beik tried to appease Fad'a by inviting him to his home in Salkhad, but Fad'a did not accept his invitation.

***

Fad'a Abdallah Ahmad was one of the Saab family's most outstanding men, combining charm with elegance and eloquence. Like his father, he was a *zajal* poet of the first order, and was blessed with the spontaneous, improvised education that distinguishes 'people of intelligence' (that was the expression used to describe popular poets). Fad'a travelled to Jabal al-Druze with his cousin Ali Mahmoud Saab, but Ali left work shortly thereafter, and their store became Fad'a's alone. Fad'a then returned to live in Choueifat, but continued to maintain his business in Shennaira, travelling back and forth whenever work required.

***

In Choueifat it happened once in 1915 that Fad'a's wife had prepared a *ghammeh*[2] for the family's lunch. After they had eaten, she cleared the table, threw the leftover food and bones out of the window into the street, and went into the kitchen. Fad'a sat by the window, resting after lunch, while his son Mazen, who was 4 years old, went to play in the room.

---

1. There is a photocopy of this poem in the memoirs of the owner of the two crafts, the educator and writer William Najib Saab, the proprietor of the magazine *al-Baidar*.
2. *Ghammeh* is an old Lebanese dish consisting of a sheep's head, tongue, and intestines stuffed with rice and nuts. [Translator]

Mazen glanced at his father and saw him looking towards the street and crying. He ran up to him to see why and saw that a number of children had gathered where his mother had thrown the bones, and they were snatching whatever meat was left on them.

It was the time of the famine during the First World War, and it had intensified and spread. Fad'a immediately made a decision. He called his wife and said to her, 'Gather the house's goods. We are travelling to Hawran tomorrow.' Before she could ask the reason behind his sudden decision, he took her by the hand and led her towards the window to show her the sad scene outside. He said, 'No one knows what people's fate will be. And our property is in Jabal al-Druze. What would happen to us if transport was cut between us and the mountain?' And with that, the preparations for departure began.

Fad'a got dressed and went to Hay al-Amrousiyya to visit Najib Beik Trad,[1] with whom he shared a close bond of friendship. Fad'a told Najib Beik of his decision to leave and asked him to lend him 100 gold liras so he could use it to revitalize his trade in the mountain. Najib Beik Trad gave him what he asked for and refused to take any receipt for the amount.

Fad'a lived comfortably, but was not able to collect the money to repay his debt to Najib Beik Trad until 1919, when he came to Chouiefat and went straight to Najib Beik's house. After they had exchanged greetings and expressions of affection, Fad'a took a bundle of money from his pocket, counted out 100 gold liras, and handed them to his friend. Najib Beik said, 'Abu Ma'rouf, it seems you have not heard of the new law that allows repayment of debts from the days of the war on the basis of 1 Lebanese lira for every gold lira. Even the rich and prominent have benefited from this law.' Fad'a was indignant. He put his hand to his fez and said, 'Yes, I know of this law. But I would not take advantage of the law to return your money to you incomplete. I abide only by the law of honour.' Najib Beik Trad enjoyed telling the story of what Fad'a Saab said and did whenever the glories of virtue were mentioned.

***

---

1. Najib Beik Trad was one of the prominent faces of Chouiefat. His father Fares Beik Trad came and settled in Chouiefat and the family grew. Emilia Trad, the sister of Najib Beik, and the founder of the Lebanese High School, was famous for her knowledge, culture, high morals, and virtue. The school is now run by Victor Beik Trad, the son of Najib Beik Trad.

Fad'a died in Shennaira in 1921 at the age of 55 and was buried there. His family remained in Jabal al-Druze. When Sultan Pasha al-Atrash revolted against the French for the first time because of the assassination of his guest Adham Khanjar, who had sought refuge with the Sultan, Ma'rouf, the eldest of Fad'a's sons (aged 23 at the time), joined Sultan Pasha al-Atrash and took up a rifle. But the pardon that was issued after Sultan Pasha's reconciliation with the French did not extend to Ma'rouf and the other Lebanese Druze. The group went to Amman and remained idle until war broke out between Sultan Abdulaziz ibn Saud and al-Hussein ibn Ali, King of Hijaz, and they went to Hijaz and joined the Hashemites. The group included the heroes Shakib Wahab and Khattar Abu Harmoush.

The contingent of Druze horsemen, who participated in a number of the clashes and battles in that conflict, was in Jeddah when the Wahhabis surrounded it. But when Sultan Pasha al-Atrash initiated his great second revolution against the French, the Druze fighters obtained King Ali ibn al-Hussein's permission and returned to Jabal al-Druze to join the revolutionaries. Ma'rouf was still with them, and he did not lay down his weapons until the revolution had ended. At that point, Fad'a's family returned with all of its members to live in Choueifat.

***

There was another young man of the Saab family who joined the Druze–Syrian revolution: Saeed Nayef Mahmoud. He fought with Amir Adel Arslan, and Amir Adel always commended Ma'rouf and Saeed for their courage. Amir Adel once told me a story about Saeed Nayef that led to his admiration but also made him laugh at the same time whenever he told it. In the final days of the revolution, Amir Adel was crossing a plain in al-Lijat with a group of men, including Saeed, when bullets rained down on them from the slope of a nearby mountain. Amir Adel ordered his men to dismount and take cover behind the rocks scattered throughout the plain. The battle ignited and the horses remained in the open, so several of them were hit by gunfire, including Saeed's horse. Saeed came out from behind the rock and ran to his fallen horse. The Amir shouted at him to return, but he would not heed the order. He threw himself on to the horse, took off its saddle and harness, and returned with them under a hail of shells and bullets. When he returned to his place near Amir Adel, the Amir chided him, 'Saeed, how can you throw yourself in the way of death for the sake of a saddle?' Saeed answered, 'Come on, Amir. Is death merely drowsiness?' This idiom is usually said of someone who fears death because of a slight illness or trivial incident.

Also among Sultan Pasha al-Atrash's supporters in the revolution was As'ad Khalil Jaber Saab, a resident of Theebin in Jabal al-Druze. As'ad was a friend of Sultan Pasha's and his partner in several commercial ventures. When swords and rifles were legalized, Abu Ma'rouf As'ad was made the head of the machinery and explosives department in view of his precise knowledge of mechanics.

Father Tanious Saad

Father Tanious Saad is the greatest educator in Choueifat's history, and one of the pillars of Lebanon's educational renaissance of the late nineteenth and early twentieth centuries. He educated three generations. He was a teacher when my father was a student at his school, and by the time I was a student he was its President. When my children began their education at the National College in Choueifat, Father Tanious Saad was still its counsellor and advisor. He resigned as President in 1942, when he was 84 years old, and his son Charles picked up the reins. But he did not retire from work and become idle until poor health forced him to do so. He died at the age of 95, and his mental faculties remained undiminished until his death.

Tanious Khalil Saad was born in 1858 in Hadath, Beirut. His father, a builder, had moved from Ras al-Matn, the family's origin, to al-Hadath in pursuit of a livelihood. Their home was near the Protestant church, and Tanious, when still a child, would take advantage of this proximity and attend mass there. He was impressed with the religious service and its simplicity and order. When his father sent him to the American Missionary School in Abey, which later became the Syrian Evangelical College and then the American University of Beirut, he found his way in the denomination he had chosen for himself. He attended the theological school affiliated with the American Missionary School in Beirut. When he graduated from the theological school, he was appointed Minister of the Protestant church in Choueifat and was asked to supervise its two missionary schools. That was in 1882. He brought a child named Khalil

Thabet[1] with him from al-Hadath and enrolled him in the school and oversaw his education.

In 1884 an Irish woman by the name of Louisa Proctor came to Lebanon and lived in Choueifat. She was a missionary and had dedicated herself to the service of humanity and proselytizing for the Christian faith. She began organizing the women into associations and symposiums and training them in healthy and scientific methods of childcare.

Father Tanious Saad was known to be inquisitive, interfering in what concerned him and what might have not concerned him. But his inquisitiveness was an endearing quality. He would not interfere in order to discover people's issues and secrets, but rather to help with advice or action. He would offer his services, and people appreciated his involvement because they would gain the benefit of his sound advice and wise opinions, or at least his sincere and heartfelt sympathy. His heart was open to all human emotions except hatred. He liked many people, indulged others, and found some unbearable. He praised, thanked, criticized, admonished, blamed, disciplined, and punished, but no one ever said that Father Tanious Saad hated anybody.

One day he asked Louisa Proctor about her work and goals, and she told him. He suggested that she open a boarding school for girls to make her work more effective and comprehensive. She liked the idea, but said she could not do it for economic reasons. Her father used to send her 100 English pounds a year to live on and she could not spare any of it without sacrificing one of her meals or her afternoon tea and biscuits. The Minister left her to her work.

He returned to her some time later and asked if she would agree to work as a teacher. She said, 'But where is the school?' He answered, 'You and I will teach without salaries. The mission will close its girls' school and transfer two of its teachers to us and pay their salaries. That leaves only the home rent, and that is not much. The tuition fees will cover the students' room-and-board expenses, and you will continue to have three meals a day and afternoon tea and biscuits.' She agreed. In 1886 the school opened with twelve boarding students and sixteen day students.

---

1. Khalil Pasha Thabet was born in Dayr al-Qamar. He went to Sudan, where he published the newspaper *al-Khartoum*. From there he went on to Egypt, where he became a member of the Council of Notables and took over the management of the *al-Muqattam* newspaper. He was born a Maronite but later embraced the Protestant faith. He returned to Lebanon in 1952, and soon thereafter he lost his sight and then passed away.

There were two silk factories in the higher reaches of Hay al-Amrousiyya that belonged to one of the al-Bakhash sons. One of the two factories burned down and Fares Beik Trad[1] bought the property. Father Tanious bought the other, which had not burned down, and sold its machinery and equipment. The sale brought him more money than he had paid al-Bakhash, and the school now had a building.

The first graduation ceremony was held in 1890. The class consisted of four girls: Zahia Kourani, who became a teacher; Eugenie Jureidini, the daughter of Amin Beik Nassour al-Jureidini, who also became a teacher, married Father Tanious in 1895, and later became the school's headmistress; Youmna Malek, who opened a school and became its headmistress and later left it in the custody of her nephew Pierre Ivanov; and Emilia Trad, who also opened a school and became its headmistress. That school is now in the custody of her nephew, Victor Beik Trad.

Father Tanious's school grew and the demand for education increased, so he opened a school for boys in 1896. He constructed a building for it that still stands today and contains the home of his son, Charles Saad.

In 1904 the Syrian Evangelical School sent a committee consisting of the teachers Jaber Doumit, Mansour Jirdaq, Boulous Khouli, and two American teachers to examine the Choueifat school's graduating students. Salim Constantine and Suleiman Nicholas Saad passed and entered the college. After that, graduates of the Choueifat school were accepted at the college without entrance examinations.

There were times of prosperity but also of hardship, and the school experienced progress as well as stagnation, but it always withstood the test of time and the changing circumstances. A transition came about in 1942, when Father Tanious Saad handed over directorship of the school to his son Charles, a graduate of the American University of Beirut. He had inherited a love of education and teaching from his parents. The Choueifat school continued on the road of progress until it became one of the country's leading high schools.

Even becoming a member of parliament did not distract Charles from his educational mission, as he gave the latter priority over the former. Throughout all his time in parliament, from 1960 to 1969, he served as Chairman of the school's Educational Committee. He left political life as he had entered it, clean and uncorrupted. But the credit for the Choueifat school's phenomenal success does not go to Charles alone. Just as God

---

1. Fares Beik Trad was the father of Najib Beik Trad and the grandfather of Fares and Victor.

had given his father a good wife and devoted educator who helped him manage and develop the school, He also blessed Charles with a good wife and headmistress for the school with a high degree of education and culture. Charles married Leila Baddoura (whose mother was Lora Saad), who too had dedicated herself to work in the school with incomparable seriousness, energy, and eagerness. Charles and Leila did not have any children, so there was only the wonderful trio: Charles, Leila, and the school. The processions of girls and boys who left at the end of every school year would spread the national message of the Choueifat school throughout Lebanon and other Arab countries. And this beneficence continues to flow today.

***

Minister Tanious Saad was a tall man of sturdy build. He was a man of keen vision, dignified, solemn, resolute, bold in the name of justice, faithful, and assured. He was intelligent, discerning, and entertaining. It was impossible to be bored in his company. He studied the holy book and the stories of famous men. His interest in people's affairs and issues made him close to them and bound him to society.

Thus the school established by Minister Tanious Saad, the foundation of the educational renaissance in Choueifat and the villages of the lower Gharb, was not the only witness to his greatness. Apart from the school, there was the unique character that made him a beacon of morality, good counsel, and the purity of love and affection. The people of Choueifat loved and respected him, and revered him generation after generation. Though he went on to become the judge of the Protestant sect in the Lebanese Republic, the title of 'Minister' still superseded his other titles and remained with him for seventy years, signifying respect, admiration, and appreciation. He died after a graceful old age in 1953.

***

So that the memory endures and the mission continues, Charles Saad and his wife Leila established an association and a board of trustees to ensure the school's continued progress after their death. Called 'The Trustees

Association of the Charles Saad Institution', it was dedicated to the memory of 'Minister Tanious Saad and Eugenie Jureidini Saad'. Scholars and educators die, but scholarship and education live on. This is the secret of human progress, a secret that was not hidden from Charles and Leila Saad, for they come from the mould of beneficent builders.

Jirjis al-Murr, Khalil Saab and Amin Zaka

The following incident took place early in the twentieth century in the city of Buenos Aires, the capital of Argentina. Lebanese emigration had expanded, and Buenos Aires boasted a large Lebanese community of different backgrounds and affiliations. At the time, Argentina was in chaos, its affairs administered by a government that was unable to preserve order and security. Its life, including life in the capital itself, was similar to that of cowboys in the United States of America in the middle and late nineteenth century.

Emigration was an arduous and perilous adventure, and the emigrants suffered many trying experiences and dangers. Sailing the high seas was an undertaking beset with hardship and peril, hence the saying that 'One entering it is lost, and one coming out of it is born.' The emigrants could afford no more than third-class fares, so they would pile on to the ship's deck when the sea was calm and gather inside its hold and interior passages when gales erupted. As for the sleeping quarters, they were the 'deck chairs' that were opened and folded as needed.

My father left some memoirs. He wrote the following passage describing one of his trips to America in 1906 (with some changes in wording and structure):

'My brother Hamad and I travelled to America in February of 1906. In March we arrived in Lisbon, the capital of Portugal, and from there we embarked on an English ship, the *Madarnes*, and the sea was rough. When the ship stopped the next day at Madeira, the passengers began to jump from the ship into the coal barges in the port to avoid travelling in the storm. I pleaded with my brother Hamad to stay on the island, but he refused and asked me to stay instead. I refused as well, so we both stayed on the ship, and it carried us to Brazil. And what a journey it was: for seven days, friends did not acknowledge one another and brothers were strangers because of the powerful storms and the raging sea. We could not tell whether the ship was still on the surface of the water or at the bottom of the ocean. The captain, crew, and passengers had all given up hope of survival, but on the seventh day, the sea became calm and the ship was stable. A few days later we reached Bara at the mouth of the Amazon River in Brazil.'

When the migrant reached America, troubles and dangers of different types awaited him. He had to find shelter, learn the language, and study the city and country's landmarks, customs, and traditions. He then had to suffer and toil as he never had in his own country. Someone who refused to carry a bag or basket in Lebanon would now carry a bundle on his back through the cities and villages selling goods. There were bandits and outlaws who would ambush and rob passers-by of their money and lives.

***

As if all this were not enough, some of the Lebanese immigrants would carry their prejudices and partisanship with them to their new home, and disagree and quarrel among themselves. One such disagreement broke out between a young Druze man and a Christian from Lebanon. They fought and then separated with mutual hatred and spite. This took place far from the heart of the capital, Buenos Aires, on a street with a number of Lebanese shop owners. News of the incident spread on both sides, and soon the shops closed as the Druze gathered on one side of the street and the Christians on the other. Each group approached the other until the two sides met.

Without resorting to discussion or admonishment, they prepared for battle. A tall, broad-shouldered individual of apparent manliness came forward from the Christian side. He stepped between the two lines with his dagger drawn and shouted in his loudest voice, 'I am Jirjis al-Murr from al-Hadath, and if anyone wants to die, let him come before me.' He had barely finished speaking when a young man aged under 20, and no less impressive than Jirjis in physical stature and boldness, emerged from the Druze side. He stepped up to Jirjis and said, And I am Khalil Saab[1] from Choueifat, and now we will see who is going to die.' He drew his dagger and stood ready to fight.

Before the two adversaries could clash, cries arose from the Christian side and a young man with a long dagger in his hand appeared, roaring like a tiger. He walked quickly into the fray and stood between Khalil and Jirjis. He turned to Jirjis and said loudly, 'Listen, Jirjis. Khalil Saab is from Choueifat, and I am Amin Zaka[2] from Choueifat, and when the sons of Choueifat meet, there are no Christians or Druze. By God, you will not get to Khalil Saab while I am alive, so step back.' The people on both sides were so surprised that they fell silent. Amin Zaka had turned the situation upside down, changing all of the standards and circumstances. The sounds of bigotry and hatred subsided, to be replaced by those of forgiveness and affection.

The silence, contemplation, and pause did not last long. From the Christian side, an older man stepped forward and addressed both sides: 'Young men, you have seen and you have heard. Do you accept that the sons of Choueifat are better than us?' An encouraging response arose from the Druze side and a contest in courtesies and conciliatory expressions commenced. The matter concluded with reconciliation and handshakes. Curiously, Amin Zaka did not know Khalil Saab and Khalil Saab did not know Amin Zaka. But the word 'Choueifat' resounded magically in their hearts.

---

1. The author's father.
2. The father of Samir and Samuel Zaka.

Youssef Karam and Mariam Saad

Youssef Jirji Saab Karam of Broummana made it a habit to spend the summer in the town of al-Mrouj, at the home of his cousin Qizhayya Sha'ya al-Nakouzi. He enjoyed the taste of its water and the purity of its air, and lived on the meats, dairy products, and fresh vegetables it produced. But he was not a rich man, so he would often put off payment for these goods until he managed to get together enough money to pay his debts.

Youssef Karam was a writer who had mastered both Arabic and French, and had contacts among Beirut's most powerful figures. In time he was offered work as a translator for the French administration in Morocco. He accepted the offer and travelled to his post at the end of the summer of 1913. He had paid off all his debts in al-Mrouj except for a debt of 1 gold lira to Mariam Saad for the milk she had brought him. He asked for some time and promised to send her 2 liras from Morocco instead of the 1 he owed her. Mariam trusted Youssef and had faith in his word and principles, so she was happy to accept his promise.

Before Mariam received anything from Morocco, the First World War broke out and all contact between Lebanon and the outside world was severed. Qizhayya al-Nakouzi offered to pay Mariam the gold lira his cousin Youssef Karam owed her, but Mariam would not accept. She told Qizhayya, 'The debt is between me and Mr Youssef. One day the war will end, and all those who are absent will return to their country, and Mr Youssef will buy me a vineyard.' Qizhayya laughed, yet he could not help but admire the kind-hearted, naive woman and her confidence in her judgement of people and their character.

The war went on for four long, harsh years that saw 10,000 Lebanese die of hunger. During this time, each person became concerned only with his own household. When the cannon fell silent in the autumn of 1918, Lebanese hearts turned to their loved ones abroad. Everyone was trying to find out who among the Lebanese emigrants had died and who had survived. Letters poured in from Lebanese emigrants in all parts of the world. They were even more anxious for news than those at home because they had heard about the death and famine in Lebanon. Among this flood of mail, a letter arrived in Hammana addressed to Mariam Saad, or her heirs if she was no longer alive. But Mariam was alive, and she received the letter to find a draft to the amount of 5 gold liras for the cost of milk, sent from Youssef Karam. Mariam was even more pleased that her judgement of Youssef had proved correct than she was with the fortune she had received. To fulfil her prophecy, she used the money to buy herself a vineyard.

***

Youssef Jirji Karam returned to his homeland of Lebanon in 1951. He lived in Broummana until he died, leaving his son, Pierre, who is still in Broummana today, and a daughter Alice who studied law and was practising in Beirut's courts in 1939. Later, she married a French officer and went with him to France.

Someone once met the previous Moroccan ambassador to Lebanon, Ahmad ibn Souda, and asked him if he knew Youssef Karam in Morocco. The ambassador answered, 'Who in Morocco does not know Youssef Karam? He was the country's official translator and wrote most of the textbooks for the state schools. Of course, he was writing for the French, which forced us to put out a special magazine we called *Sinaan al-Qalam* [The Spearhead of the Pen] just to respond to Youssef Karam.'

Shaykh Abu Nassereddine Hussein al-Faqih and the Needy Thief

Shaykh Abu Nassereddine Hussein al-Faqih is the son of Shaykh Abu Hussein Mahmoud and the father of Shaykh Abu Youssef Ali – three *ulema* of the Druze spiritual leadership. They were all distinguished by scholarship, understanding, devotion, worship, openness, forgiveness, virtue, and pure morals. This was not surprising since the al-Faqih family is among the oldest in Aley is and has always produced faithful and virtuous individuals.

The story we are concerned with took place during the First World War (1914–1918) between Germany, Austria, Hungary, Bulgaria, and Turkey on one side and Britain, France, America, Russia, and most of the world's remaining countries on the other. The Western Allies took control of the seas from the first moments because of the strength and effectiveness of the British navy – the world's strongest navy at the time – and imposed a blockade on their enemies' lands, including the Ottoman Empire. As a result, materials like sugar, rice, and other grains and essential goods were in short supply in Syria and Lebanon. And since the Turkish authorities and armed forces took priority in the purchase of agricultural products in Syria, hunger soon set in, followed by famine, and the death of tens of thousands of people from starvation.

We must mention here the widely held belief that the Turks intended to starve the people of Lebanon and Syria in order to humiliate and subjugate them. This view is wrong, not only because there are no historical facts to support it but also because there is evidence that the Turks tried to secure provisions for the inhabitants but were not able to do so. They did aggravate the conditions of scarcity and distress, however, by purchasing their grain from the threshing grounds before the people were able to satisfy their own needs. Any other sovereign authority would have behaved the same way, especially in wartime.

In those dark days, people ceased to abide by their morals. He who had never stolen now became a thief, he who had never been a criminal took up highway robbery, and he who used to warn against evil began to rob and pillage. People's hearts hardened and the spirit of mercy was gone from them.[1] Yet, by God, there was a small number of people who still had God's light in their hearts and spread His love and sympathized with the poor and the needy. And thus this story.

***

One day in the summer of 1917 the family of Shaykh Abu Nassereddine Hussein al-Faqih washed a quantity of wheat and took it to the rooftop to dry so that it could be ground. Night came and the wheat was still on the rooftop. Around midnight, Shaykh Abu Nassereddine felt some movement on the roof and was sure that he heard footsteps. Remembering the wheat, he got out of bed and quietly climbed the ladder to the roof. He saw a man there who had filled about half a sack of wheat and was trying to raise it on to his back but was not able to. Shaykh Abu Nassereddine approached him and said, 'Son, let me help you with that.'

Startled by the Shaykh's sudden appearance, the man dropped the bag and stood stock-still, tongue-tied with embarrassment. The light of the night sky was strong enough to reveal his face and identity. When he remained reluctant to move or speak, Shaykh Abu Nassereddine said, 'Listen, I know you and I know that if you had something to eat at home with your children, you would not have done this. Now if you want me to conceal your deed, all you have to do is to take this wheat from me in good faith. If you do not accept my invitation, I will expose your deed.' The Shaykh left the man no choice.[2] With the Shaykh's help, he lifted the bag on to his back, and then he descended the ladder and went on his way.

---

1. We were children then, and the stories we heard used to terrify us. They said that a woman ate the flesh of her child, and others ate the flesh of the dead.
2. I have withheld the man's name for reasons that should be obvious to the reader. But it is worth noting that he was from one of the known Druze families in the villages near Aley and resided in Aley at the time.

***

After Shaykh Abu Nassereddine Hussein al-Faqih died, the man's chest
grew heavy with the burden of his secret, and he went around telling
people what had happened to him that night in the summer of 1917, and
praising the Shaykh's grace, benevolence, and moral rectitude.

Jibrail Mishrik Haddad and his wife Sabat

Fad'a Abdallah Saab (1866–1921)

Najib Beik Trad (1865–1943)

Sa'eed Nayef Saab

The Minister Tanious Saad (1858–1953)

Charles Saad

Amin Zaka

Ahmad Abdallah Saab (1883–1948)

Ali Mahmoud Saab

Shaykh Nasib Makarem

Abu Hamad Mahmoud Youssef Saab (1854–1907)

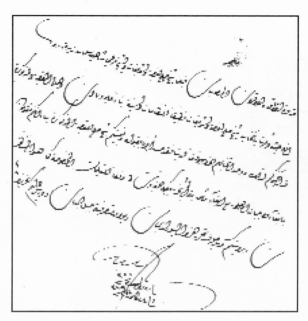

A photocopy of the executive order issued by the mutasarrif of Mount Lebanon, Muzaffar Pasha, whose stamp is on the top of the page, ordering the appointment of Shaykh Mar'i Shahin as the shaykh soloh of Choueifat.

Shaykh Mar'i Shahin Salman (1850–1932)

Suleiman Jumblatt Abu Hassan

Nasib Beik Jumblatt

The members of the Saab family in Mexico in 1926

Salim Ali Kamel Rashid (1896–1972)
'Izzat Murchid (1904–1962)
Sami Fandi Shaker Abdallah (1888–1966)
Sa'eed Mahmoud (1893–1958)
As'ad Jihjah (1885–1933)

Najib Fandi Sharif Slim (1898–1958)
Shakib Abbas (1894–1964)
Aref Hamid (1886–1956)
Hamed Abdallah (1886–1974)

Hamad Mahmoud Saab (1881–1837)

Abdel Halim Qassem Saab (1879–1951)

Labib Dawoud Saab (1920–)

Ahmad Abdallah Saab

A story captivates the reader or listener inasmuch as its events depart from what is typical and commonplace. And men gain fame through their exceptional success in one or more of the characteristics or traits of human behaviour. Excellence in virtue inspires love, appreciation, and admiration in others, and hatred and contempt surface when one only finds shortcomings and flaws.

In this book, we have presented stories and scenes of men and women from this mountain who performed miraculous feats of strength, courage, generosity, loyalty, forgiveness, understanding, perception, and other good traits. But this particular story has a hero of a different type. Though he was endowed with a good measure of these virtues, he was distinguished by another quality that is undoubtedly higher in God's estimation and more useful and beneficial to mankind. Ahmad Abdallah Saab was known for his keen desire and remarkable ability to console people, help them, and serve their legitimate interests with a wisdom, patience, and diligence rarely seen. When we consider that he was an employee in the public administration, we understand the ample opportunities he had to help others.

***

In 1938 Elias 'Eitou was working as a low-ranking employee in the company of Radio Orion in Khalde. Elias was originally Assyrian, but was a Lebanese citizen, and at one time he needed to correct the date of his birth. He went to Aley and presented his case to the head of Aley's census office, Ahmad Abdallah Saab. Ahmad told him that an age can only be corrected by means of a court order, and that Elias should present a request to the judge to schedule a hearing. Elias looked confused, and Ahmad understood, so he prepared the request for Elias and went to court with it. He returned and told Elias that his hearing was set for the following day.

Elias thanked Ahmad and asked him to direct him to a cheap hotel where he could spend the night. Ahmad said he would take him to the hotel himself after business hours. When the work day ended, Ahmad took Elias to his own house, where Elias dined and slept as an honoured guest. The next morning Elias received the order declaring his corrected date of birth and returned to the census office where Ahmad completed the paperwork. Elias bid him a grateful farewell, and Ahmad asked him how he would return to Khalde. Elias said that he was young and able to walk, so Ahmad gave him the cab fare and sent him off.

***

One day in 1943 Father Antoun al-Hilou came from Tripoli to Ahmad's house in Aley, arriving after sunset. Ahmad was ill, and when the minister found him confined to bed, he apologized profusely for coming to his home. But Ahmad welcomed him and asked what he needed. The minister said he had a quick transaction to conduct in the census office, and that he had tried to reach Aley during business hours but his car had broken down on the way, so he had not arrived in time. He had gone to the government house and asked the clerk if someone could complete the transaction for him, and the clerk had replied, 'The only person who might help you is Ahmad Saab, but he has been absent for days. If you go to his house he will definitely help you.'

Coffee was served and night fell, which only made Father Antoun more uncomfortable, not knowing what to do or say. Ahmad eased his mind and invited him to spend the night in his guest-house, but the minister apologized because he had to return to Tripoli. Ahmad rose from his bed and summoned his son Nabih and asked him to bring him his *'aba* and a candle, since it was wartime and there was a blackout. Nabih was perplexed and asked, 'Why, father?' Ahmad said, 'I want to go down to the government house and complete the Reverend's transaction.' Nabih reminded him that he was ill and that the doctor had ordered him to stay in bed. Ahmad answered, 'Son, the trip from Aley to Tripoli is a lot longer than the one from here to Aley, and if the minister's need was not urgent he would not have come at such a time.' And so Ahmad went to the government house with the minister and completed his transaction by candlelight.

***

One of Choueifat's sons was gaoled for a crime of which he was innocent.[1] Like everybody else, Ahmad knew that the man, who was poor, was innocent. Ahmad worked diligently with the *shaykh solh* until he was released. On his release, the man went to Abbas al-Souqi's restaurant in Aley to pay Abbas for the food he had sent him while he was in prison. Abbas told the man that Ahmad Sa'b had paid for all the food, so he went to Ahmad's office to thank him. It was a cold day, and Ahmad noticed that the man was shivering. He took off his coat and made him put it on. Some time later the man came to return the coat, but Ahmad said, 'A gift cannot be returned.'

***

Ahmad's right hand never knew what his left hand was doing. You will find that his own family knows the least about his deeds and services to other people, but his children recall that he concluded his prayers every night with the words, 'God, please help me to serve people and do good.'

***

There is a popular saying that goes: 'They say that the judge rules and feeds, and we say that if he is able to offer gifts then he should do so.' Ahmad Abdallah Saab proved the saying false. He would conduct

---

1. We have withheld his name so it will not be said that he owes us a favour.

227

people's business and then invite them to his home as his guests. All this from the modest wage he took home, but it was a wage that was wisely spent and properly managed. He would come from Aley to Choueifat and back to Aley on foot, and he would wear simple but suitable clothes, all so that he could spend his money on what he felt was more useful and beneficial. The most striking thing about him was that whenever a poor relative or friend of his was sick or troubled, he would visit him with a sum of money in his pocket that he would offer to give or lend the man. That was the blessing of virtue.

***

One of the achievements that people usually boast about is that they are 'self-made'. Not only was Ahmad Abdallah a self-made man, but he helped his brothers to become self-made men too. He grew up in a home that was rich in everything but money. He began his life as a simple employee, and went on to become a policeman, then a clerk in the Chouf's court, and finally governor of the Arqoub district in Ain Zhalta. He remained its governor until the administrative system was dismantled and the district directorates were abolished. He was then hired as director of the census office in the Aley district, and remained so until he retired in 1948. He started building a house in Choueifat so that he could live the last years of his life among his family, but he died before the house was finished, at the age of 65.

Ahmad Abdallah's rise from a common menial worker to become governor of a district reveals the extent of his self-education. It was doubtless a brilliant accomplishment, but Ahmad's real greatness was in his moral values. He was the firmly rooted mountain that knew no weakness and bent to no wind. He abided by his faith and its requirements and prohibitions during his youth and until the end of his life, whether within Lebanon or overseas, in good times and in bad. He became close to Shaykh Abu Youssef Ali al-Faqih, the famous devout man of religion. They shared a genuine bond of affection and mutual respect, and often worked together for causes of goodwill and reconciliation, and in holding religious ceremonies. When he was not with Shaykh Abu Youssef, Ahmad would be in the company of the lawyer Fandi Hamadeh or the writer Amin al-Gharib. Ahmad's self-education made him no stranger to the worlds of law and literature.

Ahmad's entire life consisted of effort, diligence, decorum, dignity, sacrifice, and giving. His entertainment and leisure consisted of decorous fun and gentle humour. Far-sighted and adroit, he was an intelligent, wise man with sound opinions. His contributions in the areas of opinion and consultation were no smaller than his kind service to all those who sought his help.

***

When my father died in 1943, my Uncle Ahmad was so grief-stricken that he suffered a constriction of the blood vessels. Soon thereafter he suffered a heart attack but survived. One day I told him we wanted him to visit Dr George Khayyat, our doctor and friend, for consultation and treatment. He said to me, 'Life is in the hands of God, and I am thankful that He gave me enough time to raise my children and perform my duties. I am therefore ready for death, however and whenever it comes. I have no need for a doctor.' This is how a good and beneficial life ends, with satisfaction and the assurance that one will meet his fate.

Tanious Zeina and Ali Mahmoud Saab

Tanious Zeina was one of al-Damour's strong young men and he traded in livestock. He would often come to Choueifat, where he had a number of friends and business relationships. One evening in 1928 he came to Choueifat with Nimr Mansour Abu Farraj from Ba'leshmeih and Na'im Nou'man Suleiman Saab and they stayed at the home of Ali Mahmoud Saab. Na'im was the trustee for the properties of Amir Taufiq Arslan in Naa'meh and enjoyed many close relationships in al-Damour. Tanious had two calves with him for sale, and Ali bought them from him on the understanding that they be weighed after being slaughtered in Ali's shop the next morning.

The friends dined and slept at Ali's house, and in the morning they went to the shop and weighed the two calves and Ali paid Tanious for them. But when Tanious reached into his pocket to pull out his wallet and put the money in it, he could not find it. He took Na'im outside the shop and told him he had lost his wallet, and in it were 40 Ottoman liras he had brought to buy a cow from Saeed Hamad al-Qadi of Hay al-Amrousiyya. Na'im played his part by informing Ali of the matter discreetly, and Ali sent his son Shamel to the house to look for the wallet, but Shamel returned without having found it. Ali then went himself, but he too found no trace of the wallet or the money. He sat with his head between his hands, contemplating the predicament in which he found himself.

A wallet with 40 liras in it had been lost, and there was no way of recovering it because it contained nothing to identify its owner. And besides, who would announce that they had found 40 gold liras? What was more, Tanious thought he had lost it, or that it had fallen from him, during the night, meaning in Ali's house. Ali Mahmoud saw no way out except to pay the sum out of his own pocket or run the risk of being accused. He did not think long, but went quickly to Najib Ali Khattar Saab's house. He did not find Najib home, but his wife, Um Adel, had 10 liras on her, so he took the money from her and went on to the house of Abu Shahin Muhammad Hassan Abu Najm Saab. He took another 15 gold liras from Abu Shahin and had enough to cover the rest of the sum himself, so he returned to the shop and gave 40 liras to Tanious. He told Tanious his son had found the wallet and fancied it, so he left it for him but he would later take it from him and send it to Tanious. Tanious went to the home of Saeed Hamad al-Qadi and bought the cow from him, paying the purchase price, and then headed back to al-Damour, arriving home in the evening.

***

Tanious approached his house dragging the cow he had bought behind him. His wife greeted him with the question, 'What is this, Tanious?' He answered, 'It's a cow, woman. Can't you see?' She asked, 'And where did you get the cow, dear?' Tanious said, 'I bought it from Saeed Hamad al-Qadi in Choueifat. I told you about it before.' His wife said, 'And where did you get the money?' Tanious was about to explode when his wife said, 'You left without your wallet, so where did you borrow the money from?' And she gave him the wallet. Tanious felt the world spinning around him and was afraid of falling, so he sat down on a wooden bench in the yard. His wife shouted, 'What is the matter, Tanious?' He raised his head and told her what had happened. She said, 'Hurry to the market and bring a cab while I put my clothes on, and let us go to Choueifat.'

***

Ali Mahmoud had returned home, washed his hands, and asked for his dinner. When his wife asked him about Tanious's money, he said, 'Get dinner ready and I'll tell you the rest of the story at the table.' He fixed himself a glass of 'araq, and soon the table was set. Ali began to tell the story to his wife in a way that would make his own behaviour clear and acceptable to her. He had not yet finished speaking when there was a knock at the door. When his son Shamel got up to open it, he found Tanious Zeina kneeling on the doorstep with his wife standing next to him. A lifelong bond of friendship and brotherhood developed between Tanious and Ali.

Beliefs and Religious Morals

Shaykh Abu Zeineddine Youssef Abu Shaqra

Amir Youssef Chehab (1770–1788) once introduced a heretical innovation never attempted or matched by any of the Lebanese Amirs before or after him. He levied a tax on the turbans worn by the Druze clerics. This provoked outrage among the Druze, who called the tax *qirsh al-shaasha* (the piastre of the white cloth).

When the public was certain of Amir Youssef's resolve to carry out the decree, Shaykh Abu Zeineddine Youssef Abu Shaqra, the chief Druze clergyman, came from Amatour to Dayr al-Qamar to object to the tax and ask the ruling Amir to reconsider. But Amir Youssef remained adamant, and a quarrel ensued between the two men, ending in an exchange of threats with Amir Youssef declaring, 'This country is not big enough for two Youssefs,' which the Shaykh answered with his famous statement, '*al-mazrook yirhal*' (Let the one feeling squeezed leave).[1]

Shaykh Youssef Abu Zeineddine left Dayr al-Qamar in a fury, and when he got to Ammatour he sent men in all directions to mobilize the Druze *ajaweed*. About 7,000 armed *ajaweed* gathered and threatened to march on Dayr al-Qamar, and so Amir Youssef was forced to rescind his decree. Goodwill was eventually restored between the Amir and the Shaykh, but Amir Youssef never forgot the Shaykh's challenge. Soon thereafter he conspired to have him poisoned and the Shaykh died along with one of his relatives, Khattar Najm Nimr Abu Shaqra.[2]

This incident, which illuminates the extent of Shaykh Abu Zeineddine's courage, honour, resolve and effectiveness, does not reveal

---

1. Youssef Khattar Abu Shaqra, *al-Harakaat fi Lubnan* [Movements in Lebanon], p. 167.
2. Abu Shaqra, p. 167.

the full picture of the man. Behind this manhood and wisdom was a modest, humble spirit that sought God and his reward, as the following story shows. One evening, a man entered the Shaykh's council and sat among the audience. The Shaykh did not know him, and after a while everyone left except for the unknown visitor. When the Shaykh asked the man what he needed, he said he was from one of the nearby villages. He had been in Jabal al-Druze with his wife, and on the way back his wife had fallen ill and died. He had buried her under some rocks near the bridge of Jib Jannin in Beqaa, and now he had come to consult the Shaykh about what he had done.

The Shaykh did not answer. He called his servant and asked him to bring him a lantern and a shovel. Then he turned to the man and said, 'Let us go.' The man was stunned and asked, 'Where to, my lord?' The Shaykh remained silent and motioned for the man to follow him. Once they were some distance from the house, the Shaykh said, 'Take me to where you left your wife.' The man had to obey, and so they walked up the mountain together. Before reaching the top, the Shaykh left the shovel in a ditch and they walked on until they got to Jib Jannin, most of the night having passed. The ascent was difficult, and it was a struggle for the two men. The Shaykh was elderly, and the man was already exhausted from the previous day's journey. The road included many difficult parts, not to mention the enveloping darkness in which the light of the lantern could not penetrate beyond the length of a single step.

Yet the struggle to get to the grave was nothing compared to the trip back. The two men had dug the woman's body up from under the stones and were carrying it back with them. They took turns carrying her and stopped to rest from time to time until they traversed the mountain after dawn had broken. When they got to where they had left the shovel, they moved away from the road, and then the Shaykh prayed over the woman's body and buried her. Then they went back down to Amatour.

Fatigue had taken its toll on the man, but what pained him more was his shame at having put the Shaykh through so much toil and trouble. He started to apologize to him, but then his curiosity overcame his awe and he asked the Shaykh the reason for what he had done. Why had he put himself through all that trouble when he could have simply told the man what needed to be done, or sent some of his men to carry out the task? The Shaykh said, 'Listen, my son. I did not want your wife to be buried without prayer, and I did not want her to remain buried near the road in the Beqaa, where people would point to the "Druze woman's grave" as they came and went. As for why I went myself, it was because I saw that

God had led you to me, and through you he had guided me to a good deed that carries merit and reward with the Almighty. I did not want to miss the opportunity by passing the duty on to another. And I did not ask for anyone's help because I wanted to keep the matter a secret, so that not one would know of it except for me and you, beyond God.' But such an incident could not be kept from the public. The Shaykh's kin had sensed his absence, and the woman's husband soon told the story to others.

That was Shaykh Abu Zeineddine Youssef Abu Shaqra, the Druze *shaykh al-'aql*. As for his house, which was the seat of the *mashyakha*, it stood where the house of the retired Captain Nou'man Abu Shaqra in Ammatour stands today.

Qassem S'eifan and his wife Hind

Excessiveness in religious worship and exaggeration in observance of religious requirements exist in all faiths, though to varying degrees. Devout practices like prayer, worship, dervishes, and self-denial through abstinence from good food and a soft bed are really nothing more than going to the greatest lengths to gain God's favour and ask His mercy. This phenomenon occurs in the Druze faith just as it does in others. The Tawhid has its basic beliefs and its spiritual philosophy, and it has its rituals, which are based on promoting the knowledge and enlightenment of the complete mind. Alongside this, the faith prescribes a strict and precise programme for conduct in society and in life. Despite the preciseness and familiarity of this programme, some of the devout still go to extremes in their commitment to it and their observance of its tenets.

The first requirement of the Druze faith is honesty in word (honesty of the tongue). It was once thought that there would be no opportunity for embellishment here, since statements are either true or false. But our *ajaweed* exaggerate even in this regard. They are not satisfied with speaking the truth but include disclaimers with their words, following a statement with a phrase like 'Not on my conscience'[1] or 'And God knows best.' Or they might avoid specifics and speak only in general terms, or conceal part of the story from their listener, out of fear that they might err in the telling. I once heard our uncle, Shaykh Abu Jamil Abbas Hussein Hamad Saab, telling his wife to go to the roof to shoo 'the birds' away from the wheat that was laid out there to dry. The only birds in Choueifat's skies during that season were house sparrows, but our uncle

---

1. Meaning, as far as can be ascertained, 'in good conscience'. [Translator]

avoided saying 'house sparrows' because there was a chance that another kind of bird was among them, and he would fall into sin.

The Druze faith forbade benefiting from illicit gain, so the efforts to interpret what was illicit and what was permissible were numerous and far-flung. The Druze said that the sovereign takes from his subjects rightly or wrongly, so it was forbidden for them to 'eat' the government's money, and by extension it was forbidden to 'eat' the money of an employee who received his wage from the government. Then they disallowed drinking the water from government sources, and some even went as far as refusing to eat fruit that was irrigated with government water. The Druze faith counselled modesty in diet and dress, so some people refrained from eating delicacies and donned the woollen *'aba* and slept on mats and rugs.

***

One of the *ajaweed*'s beliefs is that pain cleanses and disciplines the soul, and that perseverance purifies it and brings it closer to God. The Muwahhidin therefore accept illness and suffering with contentment, submission, and gracious patience, never doubting or complaining and speaking only in gratitude to God and in His praise. So firm was this belief that they saw sickness as God's way of testing His faithful. They said *'Istifqaad Allah rahma'*, meaning that sickness is God's merciful way of telling someone that He cares. Some even deduced that God's not checking up on a person (in other words, that person's not getting ill) is a sign of His anger, or at least the absence of His favour. This is what happened to Qassem S'eifan from the village of Beit Lahya in Wadi al-Taym.

***

Qassem S'eifan took up religion while still in his youth and devoted himself with seriousness and diligence to the requirements of worship, faith, piety, asceticism, and austerity, and his rank rose among the *ajaweed*, and his word was heeded. He was a stickler for rules with himself, his kin, and his brothers in the faith.

He married a woman from Hasbayya named Hind, after verifying her commitment to the requirements and prohibitions of the faith, and she shared his life in full and complete partnership. She took care of all of the housework, cooking, washing, and cleaning, and during the appropriate seasons she would make *burghul, kishk*, and fig preserves.[1] She would also raise a sheep every year to be slaughtered in the autumn, and then she would fill her cupboard with its meat and fat. She would sit with her husband while he recited his daily religious requirements, and attend the religious gatherings on Thursday nights and the ten days of Ashoura,[2] sitting among the village women behind the curtain that separated men from women.

No one doubted the harmony between Qassem S'eifan and his wife Hind. They had been married for seven years and no one had ever heard that they disagreed about anything. The only person to question the completeness of Qassem and Hind's life was Qassem himself. He was concealing a great and dangerous doubt. He had noticed that during the seven years Hind had spent in his home and under his protection, she had never complained of sickness or poor health. 'God was not asking after her,' and that was a sign of His abandonment. Qassem grew anxious. Could he, a most devout clergyman, live with a wife who might not belong with the good people? He did not wish to believe this, so he gave himself some time. But the days and months passed and Hind still did not get sick, so Qasssem's doubts grew. When the year ended, his doubt turned to certainty and he made a momentous decision on a difficult matter. He decided to divorce Hind, even if it meant ruining his own home.

One day he told Hind that it had been some time since they had visited her parents in Hasbayya, and he asked her to prepare for the trip the next day. The couple set out early in the morning, with Qassem riding his donkey and Hind walking behind him. And what a difference there was between what was in each of their hearts! The saying 'The camel is of one mind and his owner is of another' was true in their case. Hind was looking forward to seeing her parents and hopefully seeing that they were fine, and then returning home with her partner in life. Meanwhile Qassem

1. *Burghul* is the bulgar produced from crushed wheat; *kishk* is a dry staple produced from mixing crushed wheat with sour cream, often cooked into a soup. [Translator]
2. Thursday night religious gatherings are probably the most important in a Druze clergyman's week. The ten days of Ashoura are those that precede the Adha religious holiday. [Translator]

was thinking how he would tell Hind's parents about his decision to divorce her, and how he would return home without her and tell his brothers and their sons and daughters what he had done. They all loved and respected Hind. He would have some sad feelings, but he would suppress the whim of his emotions and shut such worldly considerations out of his mind. Qassem was planning for the afterlife.

***

The walk continued and the heat intensified, and Hind's face began to show signs of fatigue and strain. Qassem realized she could no longer keep up with the donkey, and she began to lag behind. He was puzzled and attributed it to the heat. He got off the donkey and invited Hind to ride in his place. She instantly agreed and grabbed the saddle to raise herself up but was not able to. Qassem extended his strong arms to help her and lifted her by her armpits on to the donkey's back. But Hind let out a cry of pain, and then became unconscious and fell forward on to the donkey's neck. Qassem gently lowered her to the ground. He rested her head against a rock and splashed water on her face, and she regained consciousness and her composure.

Qassem looked at his wife's face and saw that it was pale. He asked her what was wrong and she pointed to her side. He asked her to explain and she said, 'I believe it is an *aakila*.'[1] An intense shiver ran through Qassem's body, but he controlled himself and asked, 'When did you start feeling the pain?' She said, 'A long time ago.' He asked, 'And why did you keep this from me?' She answered, 'Aren't you the one who preaches to people and urges them to be patient and hold on only to God?' If a bolt of lightning had struck Qassem and turned him to ashes, or if a tidal wave had swept him into the depths of the sea, or if the ground had opened up beneath his feet and swallowed him into its darkness, his state would have been no worse. He had just learned of his wife's grave illness, and realized the extent of her patience and perseverance and the magnitude of his own error and mistaken belief.

---

1. My grandmother, Um Hamad Wared Fares S'eifan, told me this story, and Qassem was one of her forefathers. She used the word '*aakila*', and the word is still common today. It is known that it was used to refer to some types of cancer.

Qassem S'eifan had anointed himself a ruler and held the scales of good and evil in his hands. He had condemned Hind and doubted her place in the eyes of God. But now the truth was revealed, and Hind had proved to be a faithful, calm, and assured believer, who persevered through her tribulations, and held on to God and accepted His judgements. Who and what was he in the realm of belief and faith compared to this virtuous creature? Qassem's stature shrank in his own eyes before Hind's religious and moral greatness.

Qassem was awakened from his stupor by Hind's voice asking, 'What is wrong, Qassem?' He knew he would have to do much to atone for his error. He wanted to scream out and beg his wife's forgiveness and God's pardon, but he restrained himself and decided to be calm and deliberate. Qassem knew that the path to forgiveness begins with an admission of guilt, so he confessed to his wife about what he had intended to do and told her why. Hind said, 'Qassem, God ordained things to happen as they did, and His will is inevitable, and may He always be praised.' And it was as if nothing had happened. They were still closer to Beit Lahya than Hasbayya, so they decided to go back home. Qassem helped her get on the donkey and they returned to Beit Lahya.

But the days of ease and happiness were gone, and they were not to return. Hind's illness worsened and she was confined to bed. Soon afterwards she passed away. But she died in a gratified state as Qassem and the rest of the family surrounded her with care and attended to her needs throughout her illness, easing her pain and grief with love and affection. After her death she received the blessings and praises of the men of religion as well as the rest of the people.

***

Qassem S'eifan did not cry when his wife died because the faith forbids crying over the dead and calls for patience above all else. But they say he never smiled after that, and his face never showed joy until he followed her to the grave.

Nassif Beik Talhouq and 'Izzeddine Shehayyeb

In the last years of his life, Nassif Beik[1] Talhouq would spend the summer mornings and evenings sitting in front of his house overlooking the courtyard in upper Aley, where the street runs today between the house of Najib Salim al-Faqih and the house of Amin and Afif Milhem Alameh. This was in the late 1860s. One morning 'Izzeddine Najem Shehayyeb passed by and greeted Nassif, who returned the greeting, even though he was not comfortable with 'Izzeddine. He considered him an insubordinate rebel because when dealing with the *mashayekh*, he disregarded the expressions and customs that distinguish their class from that of the commoners. Moreover, he was in the party of his brother Mahmoud Beik Talhouq, the Yazbaki Party, like the rest of the Shehayyebs and Radwans. Nassif's own supporters, the al-Faqih and al-Shmeit families, were Jumblattis.

After a short visit to Mansour 'Obeid, 'Izzeddine returned and greeted Nassif Beik again, but he heard no response. He raised his voice and said, 'Mornings are God's, Beik.'[2] Nasif Beik answered wryly, 'We have returned your greeting. Perhaps you did not hear. Anyway, you have been very cordial with your greetings while going and coming.' 'Izzeddine answered coldly, 'We bid you good morning for breakfast and shake your hand for lunch,' and he quickly walked away. 'Izzeddine Shehayyeb's sarcasm infuriated Nasif Beik. He called the police and ordered them to apprehend and arrest 'Izzeddine for attacking the manager.

---

1. *Beik* is a high rank among the nobility in a class society. [Translator]
2. In an Arab society like Lebanon's, greetings must be answered. Invoking God's name shames the offender who neglects to answer a greeting. [Translator]

As for 'Izzeddine, he did not go to his own house but to that of his relative, Shaykh Abu Muhammad Jaber Shehayyeb, Aley's *shaykh solh*, and told him about his exchange with Nasif Beik Talhouq. The police tracked 'Izzeddine down quickly to the Shaykh's house. When they asked for him, Shaykh Abu Muhammad told them that he would take his relative himself to ask Nasif Beik's forgiveness, and the police left.

Shaykh Abu Muhammad waited for an hour to allow Nasif Beik's anger to subside. When they went before him he said, 'Welcome, Abu Muhammad. As for you, 'Izzeddine, you owe me 10 gold liras, and I ask that you pay it now,' and he produced an old promissory note. 'Izzeddine was not ready to pay the sum at that time, so he got into an argument with Nassif Beik and they shouted at each other. Milhem Beik, Nasif Beik's son, was present, and he liked 'Izzeddine. He had witnessed the morning incident and seen that his father had initiated the unpleasantness and disagreement, so he took 'Izzeddine into an adjacent room and gave him the money to pay the debt and end the trouble with his father.

Nasif Beik Talhouq died around 1870, and people assumed that the incident between him and 'Izzeddine Shehayyeb and its repercussions had come to an end. But God decreed otherwise.

***

About seven years after Nasif Beik Talhouq's death, 'Izzeddine Shehayyeb went on a trip to Damascus. With its beauty, clean air, and pure water, Damascus was the bride of Arab cities. It had the most delicious food, the most beautiful clothes, and the finest furnishings. To this day it enjoys a distinct character of beauty, magic, and splendour.

'Izzeddine was wandering through the famous Hamidiyya Souq when he met his countryman Hassan Mukhaiber Radwan, and they hugged and exchanged greetings of kinship and affection. With Hassan had come his son Mahmoud, who was about 7 years old. Hassan turned to him and said, 'Greet your uncle.' But instead of greeting him the child ran to hide behind his father's *'aba* and said, 'That is 'Izzeddine from Ain 'Ilou [meaning Aley] and I don't like him.' His father said, 'As you command, *beik*.' 'Izzeddine was bewildered. How did the child know his name? And why did Hassan call his son *'beik'*? Hassan invited 'Izzeddine to lunch at his house in Jaramana the next day and promised to explain Mahmoud's behaviour.

In Jaramana, Mahmoud tried to prevent 'Izzeddine from entering his father's house by putting a rock behind the gate, but his father scolded him and 'Izzeddine Shehayyeb entered. After he had rested a little, Hassan Mukhaiber asked, 'Was there ever anything between you and Nasif Beik Talhouq?' 'Izzeddine said that there was and told him the details. Hassan said, 'Then don't be surprised by my son's behaviour because he is the soul of Nasif Beik.' The news of the *naqla*[1] did not shock 'Izzeddine because he was a Druze and believed in reincarnation, and the incident was not the first of its kind. But he could not help but be amazed at how the hatred towards him had carried over in the heart of Nasif Talhouq from one generation to the next.

*** *

Nasif Beik Talhouq 'spoke' [*nataqa*][2] in the person of Mahmoud Mukhaiber as no one before or after him did, to my knowledge. When Hassan Mukhaiber returned with his family from Syria to Aley, the news about his son Mahmoud spread. The child was subjected to the most rigorous tests, examinations, and investigations, but passed them all successfully.

Nasif Beik Talhouq's reincarnation in the person of Mahmoud Hassan Mukhaiber Radwan did not sit well with the Talhouq *mashayekh*, however. It was bad enough that he was a commoner, let alone the son of a poor and simple man. They had claimed that *mashayekh* were not reborn as commoners, though they had never persuaded anyone of this because even they knew in their hearts that God did not divide mankind into *mashayekh* and commoners. They tried to discredit Mahmoud but he convinced them all of the truth of his claim, including his former wife al-Sit Haifa. Many who had not previously believed in reincarnation came to believe because of the truthful, spoken testimonies of Mahmoud Mukhaiber.

Mahmoud Mukhaiber Radwan lived for about eighty years, and until the last days of his life he lived as two very different personalities. He

---

1. Literally 'transfer'; used as a colloquial expression for the transmigration of souls. [Translator]
2. *Nataqa* is a verb whose noun form is *nutq*. It literally means 'spoke', and is used by the Druze to refer to the body's process of recollecting its soul from a previous life. [Translator]

remained poor throughout his life, yet whenever he saw a child of Bani Talhouq he would treat him with kindness and take him to the shop and buy him something with the few piastres he had. And even though he was of the common class, he would speak to the old and young al-Talhouq *mashayekh* as though he was their elder, addressing them by their first names without any title. This did not offend them since his previous incarnation was as one of their forefathers.[1]

'Izzeddine Shehayyeb had been dead for many years by the time Mahmoud Mukhaiber was suffering from his final illness. 'Izzeddine's son Nayef visited Mahmoud and asked, 'Do you recognize me?' Mahmoud answered in the affirmative. Nayef asked, 'And do you like me?' Mahmoud was silent for a moment. Then he said, 'By God, son, our two families are like one. But when I remember your father's retort to me when I was sitting in the square that day, it makes me hate the name Shehayyeb.' At the age of 80, Mahmoud Mukhaiber was still upset over something that had happened 'to him' a few years before he was born.

---

1. The virtuous writer Hani Baz (Radwan) is preparing a scientific religious study of reincarnation, and his most prominent proof is Mahmoud Mukhaiber. Hani Baz recorded the life story of Nasif Beik Talhouq as he took it from Mahmoud.

Hassan Serhal Abu Shaqra and Mahmoud Youssef Saab

Abu Shaqra and Abd al-Samad are among the old and noble Druze families that have played a prominent role in the history of Mount Lebanon over many centuries. Both have given us heroes, knights, men of beneficence and piety, and *mashayekh al-'aql*, as well as poets, writers, and administrators.

As was inevitable in the days of pride and zealous partisanship, however, there was a rivalry between them that often spilled over into conflicts and clashes. There was even a time when people divided themselves into 'Shaqrawis' and 'Samadis', in reference to the two contending families. But when the Jumblatts' foothold in the Chouf was firmly established, and 'they were declared lords over the country, all but a few of the Shaqrawi partisans became Jumblattis, while the Samadis became Yazbakis, with some exceptions.'[1] These designations did not apply to the Druze alone. The Christians too divided themselves along these party lines. In such an atmosphere of partisanship and antagonism, minor incidents were like gunpowder, easily flaring up into confrontations and battles. That is what happened in Amatour in 1854.

***

Saleh Ali Saleh Abd al-Samad was clearing brush on his land in upper Amatour when a fire spread and burned a mulberry tree on the land of his

---

1. Abu Shaqra, p. 26.

neighbour, Najem Ahmad Suleiman Abu Shaqra. A fight broke out between the two men, dragging their respective families into a battle with various types of weapons. The gunfire went on for four hours, with men from neighbouring villages rushing in to separate the two sides and trying in vain to come between the fighting lines. Once the two sides ran out of ammunition, they resorted to hand-to-hand combat. At that point the non-partisans were able to create a buffer between the combatants. Ten men had been killed on the Abu Shaqra side and another five had been wounded. Among the Abd al-Samads and their Mallak allies, ten were dead and twelve were wounded.[1] Twenty men dead and seventeen wounded over a mulberry tree – this is what went down in history as 'the evil of Amatour'.

Horrific and calamitous as the battle was, the defeat of its consequences was extraordinary and glorious. No doubt the equal number of casualties helped to erase the effects of the massacre and made it easier for the peacemakers to restore peace and harmony between the two families. After a short time, each family dropped its claims against the other and a reconciliation meeting was held at the court of Saeed Beik Jumblatt in al-Mukhtara. A second meeting was held at Amatour's *majlis*, where the two families' *ajaweed* conducted their Friday prayers together as though nothing had happened.

Among the fallen victims on the Abu Shaqra side was Hassan Serhal. His brother Yazbek was shot before his eyes, and he had leapt to his aid only to be shot and killed himself.

***

On the same day that Amatour was drowning in blood, with death visiting it and funerals being held in its houses, there were celebrations in the quarters of the Saab family in Choueifat. A male child had been born to Youssef Hamad Mansour Saab, and he had named the baby Mahmoud.[2] But before Mahmoud was four years old, he lost his father to an explosion in the gunpowder storage room in their house.[3] Despite the accident, Mahmoud Youssef inherited the gunpowder mortar from his

---

1. Abu Shaqra, p. 70.
2. The author's paternal grandfather.
3. We have described this explosion in the story 'Najmeh of the Heroes'.

father and took up his trade. He, however, set up the 'factory' in a cave in the valley of Abu Sam'aan between Hay al-Oumara and Hay al-Qoubbeh in Choueifat. The trade in gunpowder was widespread and lucrative. Mahmoud would carry bags of gunpowder to the north of Lebanon, where he developed a bond of brotherhood with some of Youssef Beik Karam's strongmen. His business trips also carried him to the Matn, the Chouf, and Wadi al-Taym.

Mahmoud Youssef was a tall, handsome man with broad shoulders and a sturdy physique. He was also brave, engaging, and witty. His children said that the most precious and valuable things they inherited from their father were his close and intimate ties in various parts of the country. They had 'uncles' in Jouneih, al-Hadath, Kfar Shima, Ras al-Matn, Aley, Baaqlin, and Amatour, as well as in Choueifat and its vicinity and elsewhere.

In Wadi al-Taym, Mahmoud used to stay with the S'eifans, who were originally part of the Saab family. There he met a young woman named Ward, the daughter of Fares S'eifan. He was smitten by her, just as she was by him, and he asked her parents for her hand in marriage. They declined, saying that she was promised to her cousin Ali. They hurried to marry her off to Ali, and the wedding celebrations were held. And weddings then would last days or even weeks. On the third day of the festivities, before consummation of the marriage between Ward and her cousin Ali, Ward sneaked out and met Mahmoud outside her village of Beit Lahya. He sat her behind him and rode to Rashayya, where a number of his friends were waiting with a cleric who carried out the marriage contract. Then the couple headed towards Mount Lebanon, and when they got to Choueifat the family held a wedding celebration for them.

The S'eifan clan accepted the situation after Mahmoud's brother Hassan and his cousin Fandi went to Beit Lahya to assuage their anger and a reconciliation was achieved. Mahmoud and Ward then paid a 'return visit' to Beit Lahya. In the course of the contacts, negotiations, and visits that led to the reconciliation, Hassan got to know Ward's sister Mahmouda, and he took a liking to her. When he asked her father for her hand in marriage, he was accepted without hesitation. Ward was a fine wife for Mahmoud, helping him with his work. She too was endowed with courage, generosity, understanding, and eloquence. They had four sons, but one of them died in infancy, leaving Hamad, Khalil, and Saeed.

***

Despite this rich, productive, eventful life of adventure, in his mind and his memory Mahmoud Youssef lived in the shadow of a previous life. At the age of 3, he had begun to remember that he had a different name. He said he was Hassan Abu Shaqra and that he had a wife and brothers, but that Bani Abd al-Samad had killed his brother and also killed him.

When Mahmoud's parents and uncles recalled the events of Amatour, the history of 'the evil of Amatour', and Mahmoud's age, the picture became clear. The soul of Hassan Serhal Abu Shaqra was the soul of Mahmoud Youssef Saab. There was no great surprise over this, since the *naqla* is among the central tenets of the Druze religion, and *nutq* was already known to exist, especially in cases of sudden death.

In 1888 Mahmoud took his wife Ward to Amatour and explained to her the sequence of the battle of 1854 between the Abu Shaqra and Abd al-Samad families. He showed her where his brother Yazbek had fallen, and how he had jumped to his rescue, and then disappeared from the world.

***

Mahmoud Youssef lived through the 1890s with his family in health, happiness, and prosperity. He was a supporter of Amir Hammoud Arslan and his sons, and Amir Nassib Hammoud was the governor of Choueifat, so no one got in the way of Mahmoud's business in gunpowder. But the situation soon changed. In 1902 Amir Taufiq Majid Arslan became Choueifat's governor, and he was a political rival of his relatives, Amir Hammoud's sons and their backers. His first action on assuming the governorship was to go personally with a police force and confiscate the mortar Mahmoud used to pound the gunpowder. Mahmoud saw him from his house in Mahallat al-Halayej, so he took up his weapons, gathered some provisions, left the house, and set out into the wilderness. A few days later his wife and two sons Hamad and Saeed met up with him and they all fled to Jaramana near the Damascus oasis. As for his son Khalil, he had gone to Beirut and joined the police force.

Mahmoud and his family remained in rural Syria for three years and then returned to Beirut and lived in Wata al-Musaytiba. Before long Mahmoud developed the symptoms of heart disease, and he returned with his family to Choueifat so that he could die there. That was in April 1907.

***

On the fated day, Abu Hamad Mahmoud sat in his bed in his cousin Masoud Hussein Hamad's guest-house. His wife Ward sat on one side of him and his sister Hisn on the other. Mahmoud felt the end approaching but was not afraid. He touched his strong forearms and said, 'Isn't it a shame that worms will devour these forearms?' He was only 53 and still very strong and sturdy.

He felt the pain coming, and distant images and scenes began to dance in his imagination. He turned to his wife and said, 'Um Hamad, I came from Amatour to Choueifat, and now it's time to travel once again, but who knows where to?' He then spoke the names of his two sons, Hamad and Khalil, who were in America. The pain in his chest intensified, and he extended his arms and pulled his wife and sister tightly to his chest. Then he began to shout as if he was answering someone's call, ' I'm coming ... I'm coming ... I'm coming ...' And he surrendered his spirit. But where to?

Shaykh Nasib Makarem and George Shirer

The house of Makarem in Aytat is a branch of the Makarem family of Ras al-Matn. Ken'aan Makarem came from Ras al-Matn to Aytat early in the eighteenth century and settled there. He maintained contact with his relatives through mutual visits. Among those who regularly visited him was his relative Hammoud Zeineddine Makarem, who was a pious *juwayyid* (clergyman). Hammoud got to know the people of the Gharb and mingled with them, and soon he married Arfeh Adballah (Abdleih) from Aytat and returned with her to Ras al-Matn. Arfeh was his equal in goodness, piety, and devotion. (We have talked about her and her religious status in our discussion of the Raydan clan.) They were blessed with a single child whom they named Suleiman.

***

The days and the years passed, and political and military events unfolded in Lebanon. Then the Egyptians entered the country under the leadership of Ibrahim Pasha. In 1835 Amir Fares Abu al-Lam' started to try to recruit the Druze of the Matn to serve in the Egyptian army, pursuant to the orders of Amir Bashir II. He asked Hammoud Makarem to present his son Suleiman for service. Hammoud waited for nightfall, then he packed his belongings and travelled with his wife and son to Baysour. They stayed there for some time before moving to Aytat and settling there. The Talhouq *mashayekh* accommodated them in their *majlis*, in view of their

252

piety. He remained in the *majlis* until he had built a house for himself in Aytat.

Mahmoud's wife Arfeh attained an exalted rank in religion and worship, earning the title 'al-Sit Arfeh'. It is said that when she died the Talhouq *mashayekh* alone carried her coffin. Shaykh As'ad Talhouq was not able to participate in carrying the coffin because he was an old man, so he sufficed with touching it as a blessing.

As for Ken'aan, he had moved to Choueifat and married his son Abbas to the Saab family. Abbas joined the Saab family, and he and his progeny carry their name. Suleiman remained in Aytat, and all of the Makarems in Aytat are his descendants.

***

Suleiman followed in his parents' footsteps in his devotion and adherence to the rules and requirements of the faith, and he too enjoyed a lofty status and reputation. He also raised his sons Muhammad and Saeed along the same lines. And that is how devotion, piety, pure morals, and honesty in word and deed became innate traits of the Makarem clan of Aytat from generation to generation. All of these good qualities and others were manifested in the person of Nasib Saeed Makarem.

Nasib did not receive his religion from the *ajaweed*[1] because he was never without it, from his birth until the hour of his death. He began to memorize the scripture as soon as he was able to speak. When he gained understanding and discretion, his father taught him to abide by the teachings of goodness and justice, to always speak the truth, and only to utter polite words. He memorized and obeyed, and never told a lie or used an indecent word in his life. (They say that if one of his childhood friends cursed him, he would get his brother Najib to return the curse.)

Nasib's father died when he was 14 years old, so he had to leave school to help support his eight brothers, all of whom were younger than him except for Najib. He learned carpentry and excelled at it, but his destiny was elsewhere. He inherited good penmanship and an enthusiasm for it from his mother Azba, the daughter of Suleiman Younis from Aynab. She

---

1. Any person wishing to become a Druze clergyman must receive the blessing of the established clergy in his home town. To receive such blessing, he must, among other things, be at least 18 years old and show piety and devotion. [Translator]

was a graduate of the English School of Shimlan and a famous calligrapher. He dedicated himself with his heart, mind, and fingers to this fine art, crafted holy verses, and embellished lowly passages that inspired, and continue to inspire, joy and awe through the ages. But we are not writing a biography of Shaykh Nasib Makarem, and this is not the place to discuss his artistic genius. We are introducing a story that illuminates the features of his moral genius.

***

Shaykh Nasib did not seclude himself and worship his God far away from work and social interaction. Instead, he left the retreat and the village for the cities and their complicated, developed lives. In his conduct of worldly matters and his participation in contemporary society, he carried with him his religion, his religious attire, and the teachings of the faith. In his inclination towards worship and prayer he practised moderation, tolerance, and openness. He taught penmanship in Beirut's universities and schools wearing a navy-blue garment, a dark jacket, and the white Druze turban, bright as snow. In those days – the 1920s, '30s, and '40s – we would delight in the sight of two of our *mashayekh* – Shaykh Abu Shahin Amin Ali Hamzeh from Abey and Shaykh Nasib Makarem from Aytat – going to Beirut, because of their elegance and radiant appearance.

***

Shaykh Nasib was generous and charitable, not out of a desire for status or a love of recognition, but in fulfilment of religious commandments. One of the brothers once came to him in need. When Shaykh Nasib heard his story, his empathy brought tears to his eyes. When the man was about to leave, the Shaykh gave him all the money he had in his pocket. After he had walked out, the Shaykh called him back in and gave him some more money he had found in the drawer of the cupboard. The man thanked him again and left, only to be called back once more when the Shaykh found some more money in his wife's drawer.

His son Sami, who witnessed all of this, asked his father why he had gone to such lengths to help the man. He replied that he was following the teachings of his religion. The *Hikma*[1] requires a man to help his deserving brother to the extent necessary to keep him from having to ask for help from someone else. Sami said, 'But if you go on that way, you will become poor yourself.' Shaykh Nasib replied, 'He who brought me here will not abandon me.'

Over and above Shaykh Nasib's readings and recitations from God's book, he formulated his own special prayer and would always recite it. It went: 'Dear God, I implore you by all means not to make me speak a word, cast a look, take a step, do a deed, or think a thought that does not meet with your approval.'

***

Among the principles followed by the committed clergyman is sincerity of intentions. When one says something, he is understood to mean it and to remain bound by it no matter what the cost, even if the circumstances change. Something like this happened to two members of this class of *ajaweed*, one from the Chouf and the other from the Gharb. Each of them happened to set out on foot to visit the other on the same day and they ran into each other at Jisr al-Qadi. After they had exchanged greetings and spoken for a while, each of them learned what the other's intention was. They sat together for an hour to inquire about each other's health and then each of them continued on his way to the other's house to fulfil what he had intended to do.

Something similar occurred between Shaykh Nasib Makarem and George Shirer, the new principal of the Souq al-Gharb school at the time. Shirer had succeeded Oscar Harden as principal, and both were American citizens. Harden was a man of honesty, integrity, and fairness. He shared a firm bond of friendship with Shaykh Nasib and they often exchanged visits. Thinking that Harden's successor would be like his predecessor, Shaykh Nasib wanted to get to know George Shirer and so he paid him a visit.

Shirer returned Shaykh Nasib's visit, and at the Shaykh's home he noticed a valuable Persian carpet. He asked, 'Will you sell me this carpet?' The Shaykh answered in the affirmative. Did Shaykh Nasib ever refuse the request of a guest? Shirer asked, 'How much do you want for it?' The

---

1. The *Hikma* is the Druze book of scripture. [Translator]

Shaykh fulfilled his duty of hospitality towards his guest and said, 'As much as you wish.' Shirer said, 'You are strange. What if I paid you 2 liras: would you sell it?' Shaykh Nasib Makarem replied, 'I said "As much as you wish", and I do not go back on my word.' So Shirer paid Shaykh Nasib 2 gold liras and took the carpet and left without batting an eyelid.

Shaykh Nasib Makarem did not believe that the successor of Oscar Harden, a missionary and school principal, could be so exploitative. He still doubted the seriousness of Shirer's behaviour. Surely he had been joking. The carpet was of sentimental value to the Shaykh. He waited for some time and then went to visit Shirer. After conversing for a while, Shaykh Nasib pointed to the carpet that Shirer had taken from him for 2 liras and said, 'Would you sell me this carpet?' Shirer answered, 'Yes. How much will you pay for it?' The Shaykh thought the joke was about to end, so he said, 'Two liras'. But Shirer refused. The Shaykh then offered 3 liras, but Shirer still refused. He raised his offer to 4, and then 5 liras ... but Shirer would not accept. Shaykh Nasib knew the value of the carpet, and he realized that in order to get it back he had to buy it. He began to exceed the real price of the carpet until he reached 40 liras, but Shirer still refused. Shaykh Nasib did not have more than this sum, so he stopped the auction and left Shirer's home.

***

The flame of religion, whose brilliance was diminished and whose light was dimmed in many of the Druze villages and homes by contemporary intellectual upheavals and modern social developments, continued to gain intensity and brilliance in the house of Salman Mahmoud Makarem. The green banner – the banner of Tawhid, righteousness, and piety – continued to pass among them from one master to another. What Shaykh Nasib had taken from his forebears, expanded upon, and practised in a manner appropriate to the requirements of the day he handed down to his son Sami to reinvent once again. Sami not only inherited his father's beliefs, morals, and good reputation but also a library that included all of the *Hikma*'s treasures and its interpretations. Being a doctor of philosophy, he devoted himself to it with seriousness and rigour, and soon he began to uncover its splendid truths and reveal its buried jewels. Nothing less suffices in these times – times of expansive and precise learning and advanced, open education. It is also important at this juncture to mention the similar gallant efforts exerted by the other great writer Abdallah al-Najjar and the brave attempt undertaken by Najib al-'Israwi in Brazil.

Taufiq al-Zein and Elias Najm

Taufiq Abd al-Fattah al-Zein is from Saida. I do not know him personally, but based on what I have heard, I have known many like him in Beirut in times past. I have known them to utter the *shahada*, to pray at the five designated times of the day, to fast during the blessed month of Ramadan, and to carry out the *hajj* if they have the means to do so. Once they have performed the *hajj*, they forsake all their other titles to be called 'al-Hajj' and suffice with it as a title. They give *zakaat*, and give for the sake of charity and for the sake of God, never turning anyone away.[1]

I remember some of them, especially in the evenings in Ras Beirut. They would close their shops just before sunset to go to the mosque and perform the *maghrib* (sunset) prayer and then return to their work until the *'isha'* (dinner) prayer time, all the while repeating God's verses and citing *hadith* and *du'a'*.[2] I cannot forget Abu Muhammad, the municipality worker who would go around lighting the city's street lanterns and invoking God wherever he went – 'Dear God, give us your approval; dear God, give us your pardon'; 'Please facilitate and don't obstruct'; 'Assure parents' forgiveness' – as much as Abu Muhammad had been able to memorize, as he was illiterate.

---

1. These are the five pillars of the Islamic faith. A Muslim must profess the *shahada*, meaning bear witness that there is no god but God, and that Muhammad is His messenger; perform the *hajj* (pilgrimage) to Mecca; pray five times a day; pay *zakaat* (alms) to the poor; and fast during the month of Ramadan. [Translator]
2. The *hadith* is the collection of the Prophet Muhammad's sayings and *du'a'* is the invocation of God's name. [Translator]

When they told me about Taufiq al-Zein, I remembered them all. Those are the true Muslims of the religion of Muhammad.[1] But Abu Adnan Taufiq al-Zein was distinguished from the majority of them by his nature and by his ethics. He is now 109 years old, and no doctor has made any money out of him – not a physician, an eye doctor, or a dentist. Taufiq al-Zein only eats if he is hungry, and never allows himself to get full. When his digestive system is upset, he treats it by only eating yogurt or carob syrup, as the case requires. When healthy he eats lots of fruit, especially oranges. He washes his eyes daily with boric acid, and still reads and writes without glasses. As for his teeth, he rubs them with vinegar, and they are healthy and white. Taufiq is a first-rate calligrapher. He sits cross-legged with a sheet of paper in the palm of his hand and writes with a quill, producing immaculate tracts. His body has extraordinary strength. Some people once threw a huge watermelon at him from a high balcony and he caught it with his outstretched fingers.

***

Taufiq al-Zein was generous by nature. In 1938 he purchased a plot of land in one of Adloun's quarters. The plot was called 'al-Nabi Saadi' (and contained a shrine to this prophet) and measured 772 dunums (a dunum is 1,000 square metres). Because of special circumstances, Abu Adnan had to share ownership of the land with a partner, Elias Najm from the village of Shwaliq. Elias came to Saida and paid Abu Adnan half the price of the land and took a written acknowledgment from him to that effect, and then he returned to his village.

After Elias left, it occurred to Taufiq to count the money again, and he found that Elias had given him 100 Lebanese liras (20 gold liras) more than he was entitled to receive. He became uneasy and could not go to bed. There was no means of communication between Shwaliq and Saida at that time, so he sent his son Adnan out on foot to Shwaliq. Adnan walked 7 km through the night to return the extra money to Elias, and only then was Abu Adnan able to sleep in peace.

Elias Najm and his wife moved to the farm to oversee its operation. God did not bless Elias and his wife with any children, but they were

---

1. The literal meaning of Muslim is one who has surrendered himself to the faith and submitted to the will of God. [Translator]

called Abu Najm and Um Najm out of respect. Taufiq al-Zein and his son Adnan would visit the farm from time to time to help Elias supervise the affairs of the farm and the *fellahin*.

In 1941 the partners realized that they needed to repair the threshing ground and lower it. When the work began, the workers discovered a pit. As they dug deeper, they found five steps leading to a door made of dried mud and gravel. Finding historical ruins was and still is a normal event in the area around Saida. Adnan was curious and wanted to continue the excavation, but his father prevented him, saying that the room was either infested with snakes or contained historical artifacts that must be reported to the government and would thus cause a serious headache. He ordered the workers to fill the pit and resume their work on the threshing ground. And so the matter was closed.

A few months later, Elias left Saida on a trip to Aleppo, leaving his share of the work to his wife. He was gone for a long time and when he returned a year later he was suffering from a serious illness that confined him to bed. When his condition worsened he sent for his partner, and Taufiq and his son Adnan went to visit him. They found him at death's door, so they sat by his bed to console him.

Elias summoned his strength and looked at Abu Adnan and said, 'I have wronged you, my partner. Do you remember the pit under the threshing ground? I opened it in your absence and found a small coffin of polished tiles. It contained twenty-four snakes made of pure gold and a small gold statue, about 30 cm in length, studded with turquoise. I took them secretly – without telling even my wife. I pretended to have business in Aleppo and sold the treasures there at the cheapest prices. I still made 800 gold liras. Then I went after my own pleasure and leisure and catered to my appetites, and I spent all the money. Now I have nothing to show for it but this disease, which undoubtedly will be the end of me. And now I have but one wish left in this life. Having confessed my great misdeed to you in front of my wife and your only child, is there any chance that I might gain your forgiveness and your pardon?'

All ill feelings ceased in Taufiq al-Zein's heart. There was no hatred, blame, or reproach, and he was overcome with feelings of empathy for his partner Elias. Tears came to his eyes and he said, Abu Najm, everything in this world is transient. Of course I forgive you, and I ask God to forgive you and to heal you.' Elias's face relaxed and a pale smile came over him. He took a deep breath and surrendered his soul like someone setting out on a pleasant journey.

Anecdotes

The Delayed Death

Abu Muhammad Hassan Abu Barakeh was one of the big landowners in
Bakkifa near Rashayya al-Wadi. He owned vineyards and fields of olives,
peaches, almonds, and pomegranates. He also owned a large piece of land
in the same plain with its dark soil. He used this land to grow wheat and
barley.

Wheat is the most beneficial plant for mankind. It provides the
essential elements of nutrition for hundreds of millions of the Earth's
inhabitants. Rice and corn prevail only where wheat does not grow. That
is why mankind has surrounded wheat with a halo of esteem and sanctity.
The first thing we learned before we outgrew the foolishness of childhood
was to honour bread and not throw its crumbs to the ground. If a piece
of bread happened to fall to the ground, we were taught to pick it up, kiss
it, and touch it to our foreheads. If a piece of bread was soiled, we were
taught to put it in a high place where feet could not tread on it. For the
Lebanese, sharing a meal with a guest or a host creates a bond and a
relationship. The Lebanese illustrate this by reference to bread. When two
people exhibit intimacy and loyalty, the common refrain is that there is
bread and salt between them.

The wheat plant is magnificent despite its small size and marvellous
despite its frailty. It consists of a few leaves on a stalk that is not even
strong enough to withstand the wind, bending with the breezes in
whatever direction they blow. Yet it continues to grow until it is fully
formed, and then it opens its cells to the sun and absorbs its light, heat,
and energy which it stores in its seeds, all the time crowning its head with
a golden spike. Wheat in Wadi al-Taym is growing in its original habitat,
since it is said that mankind first discovered it around the foothills of

Jabal al-Shaykh (Mount Hermon) and then took it from there to other lands and regions.

Abu Muhammad loved wheat farming and showed a great interest in it. He would always take great joy in the harvest. He used to supervise the process himself and spend the harvesting days with the workers. On the last day of the harvest he would hold a feast for them. His wife Ghaliya would join him and prepare a cauldron of *hriseh*.[1] The men and women would gather under a terebinth tree in a corner of the land and pass around clay platters full of rich food. They would eat and chat, and then would wish Abu Muhammad and Um Muhammad continued blessings and pray to God to keep them all alive until the following year.

***

One year everything proceeded as usual and the last day of the harvest arrived. Um Muhammad went out with the full complement of equipment and utensils she needed to prepare the *hriseh*. She cut the meat into pieces and broke up the bones. Then she mixed them with wheat and water, added salt and pepper, and lit the fire under the cauldron. Once the heat was flowing through the mixture, she began to stir it with a wooden utensil to keep the meat from sticking to the bottom. After about two hours of hard work, Um Muhammad knew that her work was almost done. She reduced the heat under the *hriseh* and left it to simmer until fully cooked. She stepped out on to the plain to breathe the fresh air and enjoy the sight of the piles of wheat on the threshing floor. She talked with Abu Muhammad for a while and then returned to prepare the plates and utensils, since it was almost lunchtime.

When Um Muhammad went back under the tree, she picked up her spoon and approached the cauldron. When she looked into it, the blood froze in her veins: a huge snake was floating on the surface of the *hriseh*, immersed in the melted fat. She quickly regained her composure and tried to scoop the snake out of the food with the spoon, but its flesh was already fully cooked. As soon as she moved it, it disintegrated and dissolved into the *hriseh*. It seems the snake had been attracted by the smell of the food and intoxicated by the aromatic steam emanating from the cauldron, so it fell from the tree into the *hriseh*.

---

1. *Hriseh* is a peasant dish made of meat, bone, and wheat. [Translator]

Lunchtime had arrived and the harvesters were collecting their sickles and what remained of the wheat. There was no time or opportunity to prepare any more food. They would either eat the *hriseh* or nothing at all. Being a daughter of the countryside, Um Muhammad knew that many kinds of snakes were not poisonous. And she was certain that a snake's poison is not harmful if it is ingested through the mouth, unless there is a cut through which it happens to seep into the bloodstream. She had also heard that some peoples ate snakes.

That is why Um Muhammad felt, after overcoming her initial shock, that there was no reason to worry because no one would suffer any harm from eating her *hriseh*. It was just the thought and the idea, and the effect on the appetite, so she decided to keep it to herself and depended on God. The harvesters gathered and ate, as did she and her husband (and what God has written will come to pass), and nothing happened.

***

A year went by and another harvest season came, and Um Muhammad prepared the *hriseh* for the harvesters as she did every year. But this time she made sure not to go far from the cauldron. As she was stirring the food, one of the harvesters passed by. She did not know who he was but had heard her husband call him 'Abu Suleiman'. He greeted her and she returned the greeting. She waited for him to leave, but fate had it that he stayed and talked with Um Muhammad. He commended her cooking ability and told her he had never in his life tasted a better *hriseh* than the one she had made the previous year.

Um Muhammad remembered the snake and laughed. He asked her why she was laughing and she said, 'Last year a snake fell from the tree into the cauldron of *hriseh*, and we ate it with the meat and the wheat.' Abu Suleiman gasped and fell to the ground. Um Muhammad screamed and the men rushed and grabbed Abu Suleiman and tried to sit him up, but he would not rise. They sprayed water on his face but he did not wake up. One of them opened his eye and looked into it. Then he let go and stood up, telling his companions, 'May God compensate with your well-being. Abu Suleiman has died.'

Better to be a Shaykh than a Pasha

Throughout the history of modern societies, migration from the village to the city has been regarded as a departure from a narrow sphere to broader horizons, and as an indication of energy and ambition. This is so because almost without exception the systems of government mankind has established have been highly centralized, concentrating authority, wealth, and cultural and economic activity in the urban centres and leaving rural areas in their weak and needy state. Nevertheless the village still holds much of the beauty of life, where many of humanity's roots and branches extend. Kinship, friendship, and rivalry remain intimate and retain their value, significance, and distinct flavour.

We have all heard the story of when Julius Caesar, the great Roman Emperor, was visiting one of Italy's provinces and the people of the village came out to greet him led by the town chief, who was walking with an air of pride and self-importance. One of Caesar's aides whispered to the Emperor, 'Look at this man, walking as though he is the master of the universe.' Caesar answered, 'Let him do so. It is his right. I would rather be the top man in this village than the second man in Rome.' Rome was the master of the world at the time. The story of Mar'i Shahin Salman reflects the same preference.

***

We have included elsewhere in this book the story of the life and work of Shaykh Shahin Salman. In describing his mind, keen perceptiveness, and

266

far-sightedness, we mentioned that he educated all his children at the finest institutions of their time. His son Milhem received the greatest share of education and culture. Milhem was born in 1859, and after he learned the principles of reading, writing, and arithmetic in Choueifat, his father enrolled him in the National School in Beirut, the school of the great educator Boutrous al-Bustani. There he studied Arabic and English, and then went on to the Abey school, where he completed his education and learned the science of inheritance allocation, metrics, and the principles of poetry. After leaving school, he opened his own school in Wadi Abu Jmeil in Beirut with the help and guidance of his mentor, Boutrous al-Bustani. When the Ottoman administration founded a public school in Milhem's home town of Choueifat, he became a teacher there and then established a school of his own and educated many of the town's children, including the Amirs Shakib and Nasib Hammoud Arslan.

In the early 1880s the British were dealing with the question of Sudan, having occupied Egypt and made the city of Suakin a centre for their military leadership and a base for their campaign against the rule of the Mahdi. They hired a number of administrators and translators through the British consulate in Beirut, including the translators Saeed Shqeir and Mar'i Shahin Sarhan from Choueifat. Saeed and Mar'i demonstrated their competence and ability, and soon they received recognition from the British authorities and were decorated by Queen Victoria for their excellent service. New horizons then opened up before them.

Amid all this activity, and with Mar'i having spent some time in administrative work, and still possessing a good deal of determination and drive, a letter arrived from his family in Choueifat. In it they said that his success in Sudan was a great achievement, and that they were confident he would continue to progress and gain the highest of ranks. But what benefit did his family in Choueifat derive from his success and progress in Sudan? They said that a man's good deeds should be for the benefit of his family, and concluded by informing him that a majority of the town's notables wanted him to be the town's *shaykh solh*, as his father had been before him. They expressed their wish that he would leave Sudan and return to Choueifat. The curious part of the story is that Mar'i did not disappoint his family and friends. He resigned and returned to Choueifat and was elected its shaykh during the reign of the *mutasarrif* Wasa Pasha in 1887.

As for Saeed Shqeir, he remained in Sudan, and when the British occupied Khartoum he worked in the finance department of the British-Egyptian administration. Soon thereafter he attained the title of pasha, and then the British government bestowed a knighthood on him (so that he now had the title 'Sir').[1] It is beyond doubt that had Mar'i Shahin Salman remained in Sudan, he would have gained the same recognition as Saeed Shqeir. Saeed Shqeir himself used to say, 'Mar'i Shahin Salman forsook the status of pasha to be the village shaykh.'

***

Mar'i Shahin Salman served as Choueifat's *shaykh solh* for six years before he resigned because of poor health. But during those six years he fulfilled the job's requirements capably, and the sons of Choueifat saw his intelligence, understanding, equitableness, integrity, fairness, and faithfulness. They re-elected him in 1903, and he remained the shaykh for seven years. He was again re-elected in 1914, when he brought together two posts, that of *shaykh solh* and shaykh of religion.

***

In early October 1918 British forces entered Lebanon by way of Palestine, passing through Choueifat by way of Beirut. The British were the Arabs' allies, and their conspiracies and secret agreements and intentions had not yet been revealed, so the public received them as friends and allies. The people of Choueifat went out and lined both sides of the Beirut–Saida road to observe the British soldiers marching through, their officers riding on the backs of large European horses. On that day, Shaykh Mar'i remembered the days of Sudan and the British and wished to return to them in his mind. He took the medal he had been awarded by Queen Victoria out of his chest and wore it around his neck, and went with a group of his relatives to welcome the British army as it passed by.

The solemnity of Shaykh Mar'i's religious attire attracted the attention of the passing British officers, and they quickly noticed the medal around his neck. Some of them dismounted from their horses and shook his hand, and others gave him the official military salute. The people of Choueifat

---

1. Only two Lebanese have ever attained this rank: Saeed Pasha Shqeir of Choueifat and Fuad Beik Hamzeh of Abey.

were amazed and recalled the saying of Saeed Pasha Shqeir about Shaykh Mar'i Shahin Salman. A few days later, Shaykh Mar'i left his position as *shaykh solh* and retired completely from public service. He moved with his family from Choueifat to Beirut, where his sons were engaged in commerce. He died on 5 March 1932.

Amir Mustafa Arslan and Suleiman Jumblatt Abu Hassan

Suleiman Jumblatt Abu Hassan from Choueifat was known for his recklessness and bravery as well as his light-heartedness and sense of humour. He worked as a carriage driver for Amir Mustafa Arslan and then for Nasib Beik Jumblatt, until finally he acquired his own carriage and went into business for himself.

During the time of Amir Mustafa's *qa'emmaqamiyya*, Suleiman was still a young man, and the slightest provocation would anger him and cause him to fight impulsively. When he was in the service of Amir Mustafa, people would complain to the Amir about him and the Amir would reproach and scold him. Suleiman would ask the Amir's forgiveness and promise not to cause any more trouble.

One day when Amir Mustafa was busy with some important matters at his court in Ain 'Inoub's government house, someone came to him and complained of a transgression by Suleiman Jumblatt. The Amir was enraged and shouted to his clerk to summon Suleiman. When Suleiman arrived, he found the Amir pacing the room, his face showing no sign of approval. He decided on caution and approached the Amir discreetly. Without warning, Amir Mustafa abruptly stopped his pacing, opened his hand, and brought it down towards Suleiman's cheek. But Suleiman had anticipated such a gesture and quickly bent his knees and lowered himself to the ground. The slap missed his face and struck his fez, which fell to the ground. Suleiman turned to run away, but the Amir shouted, 'Come back and take your fez.' Suleiman turned back and answered, 'I left it for you to buy yourself some *qadhaami*.' (*Qadhaami* is a well-known snack made of toasted and ground chickpeas. Bartering pieces of metal and old fezzes for *qadhaami* was common among the poor and middle classes at the time and continued until the early twentieth century.) Amir Mustafa laughed, which was a rare occurrence, and those present laughed as well.

Amir Mustafa Arslan, Shaykh Khalil al-Khouri and Khalil Qassem Saab

One sunny March day, a horse-drawn carriage approached Ain 'Inoub. The sight of the pastures and fields on both sides of the road was of heart-stopping beauty. The land was covered with robes of silk and adorned with blue and red poppies, giving it the appearance of a Persian carpet. The air was scented with the fragrance of saffron, wild lilies, and cyclamen. It was springtime, and the season had begun to sweep through Lebanon, beginning at the coast and moving into the mountains.

Riding in the carriage were Khalil al-Khouri[1] and his family on their way to Ain 'Inoub to visit the *qa'emmaqam*, Mustafa Arslan. Shaykh Khalil al-Khouri was the head of the Arabic department in the *mutasarrifiyya* and was bound to Amir Mustafa by a close friendship as well as by shared political views. Shaykh Khalil lived in Sibneih, south of Baabda.

The carriage passed through Choueifat's residential areas and then its fields. The green almonds were just in season, and almond trees lined both sides of the road. Before the carriage had reached the top of the hill, the driver brought it to a stop on the side of the road to allow the horses to recover from the fatigue of the climb up into the mountains. Shaykh Khalil and his wife and children got out of the carriage to stretch their legs. The sight of the green almonds hanging from the branches enticed them, so they helped themselves to a few.

Almost instantly, the guard's voice boomed out from the top of the hill and he came down towards them, having 'caught them in the act'. The guard was Khalil Qassem Saab, and he was from a house whose men were

---

1. The father of Shaykh Bechara al-Khouri, the former President of Lebanon.

known for their religiousness, piety, honesty, and integrity. Shaykh Abu Qassem Ibrahim, the brother of Khalil, the protagonist of this story, made his house a *majlis* (centre for prayer and worship). He was appointed Choueifat's *shaykh solh* for a period of time. The *majlis* remained a part of the home throughout the life of his son, Shaykh Abu Adib Qassem. The most remarkable aspect of the story of Shaykh Abu Qassem Ibrahim Qassem Saab and his descendants is people's absolute confidence in their honesty and integrity. This trust was unblemished by suspicion from any quarter or from any friend or foe. They were objects of trust, and their chests were depositories of confidence.

But Khalil, though he did not depart from the values of the house, was of a different mould in his perception and his traits. He was impetuous, rash, and impulsive, so, in his case, integrity turned into narrow-mindedness and conservatism turned into extremism. And that is how Shaykh Khalil al-Khouri and his family found themselves on the receiving end of severe reproaches and serious threats for a handful of green almonds. Each almond became a lump in their throats and their mood turned from joy and glee to dejection and gloom. Amir Mustafa noticed their perturbed state and insisted they tell him the reason, so Shaykh Khalil told him about the 'theft' of the green almonds and the scolding they had received at the hands of the guardian of Choueifat's fields.

***

The next morning Amir Mustafa sent for Khalil Qassem, so Khalil went to Ain 'Inoub and entered the council of the *qa'emmaqamiyya*. We have discussed in more than one place in this book Amir Mustafa's reputation and the terror and dread he inspired when angered. Men would tremble when he summoned them to answer for some offence they had committed. But the guard Khalil Qassem Saab, thinking he had done something that earned him a reward, walked into Amir Mustafa's council calm and reassured.

Amir Mustafa asked, 'What did you do yesterday, Khalil?' Khalil responded, 'Me, my lord? I did not do anything.' Amir Mustafa said, 'Khalil, what did you do to the family that had picked a handful of almonds?' The guard answered, 'Oh, yes. Yes, sir. They stole the property of others, so I really gave them a hard time!' Amir Mustafa, now showing signs of bewilderment, said, 'How dare you, Khalil! They are people of high status ...' But Khalil interrupted him, saying, 'If you want the truth, my lord, mischief always comes from those of high status.'

Khalil Qassem Saab's retort to Amir Mustafa was a bombshell and became the talk of the town, as people would repeat the story and laugh when they got to Khalil's remark. People are not usually interested in what the consequences were, however, and narrators differ as to the rest of the story. Some say that Amir Mustafa imprisoned Khalil for a few days, while others say he just smiled and ordered his men to remove Khalil from his council and was satisfied with that. In any case, the outcome is of no importance.

Nasib Beik Jumblatt and Shahin Muhammad Nader al-Jurdi

Shahin Muhammad Nader of the al-Jurdi family from Choueifat made his living hunting birds with birdlime. He would hunt quails, starlings, and blackbirds, and migrating birds such as brown- and black-caps, and wheat birds for food. He would capture goldfinch and nightingales and raise them as songbirds, satisfying his own needs and then selling whatever remained. The occupation of hunting with birdlime became more widespread in Choueifat than in any other Lebanese village because of its location and the size of its municipal jurisdiction. Choueifat's outskirts are larger than Beirut's, and it is on the path used by migrating birds that spend the summer months in Anatolia and the winter in Africa and the Arabian peninsula.

Though the trade did not yield much income, it did not require any capital or entail any mental or physical hardship. The hunting equipment consisted of a few cane cages and a few bundles of sticks of birdlime. The birdlime sticks would be placed in fruit trees or in the skeletons of dead trees. When the birds landed on the birdlime branches they would get stuck, and then the hunter would take them alive. To attract the birds, some seasonal birds would be placed in cages nearby so their brethren would respond to their call. Birdlime is a sticky substance made from the fruit of the sebesten tree and then coloured green to match the leaves of the trees. Dry mulberry-tree branches are then dipped in it and made ready for use.

The fun of the profession made up for its lack of profitability. It offered the pleasure of living with nature through all its seasons. Hunters were exposed to various climatic conditions, from heat to cold to wind, and they enjoyed the changes for the benefits to their health and fitness.

But the greatest pleasure of the pastime is the euphoria that derives from the triumph over the prey, which is a species of gambling, since it involves an element of luck.

Let us return to Shahin. He was a drunkard who would spend every evening in the coffee-house of Saeed Habib Hanna in Hay al-Amrousiyya and drink as much '*araq* as he could get his hands on. When the alcohol crept into his head, he would get carried away with glee and merriment. If things had gone no further than fun and jests, it would have been no problem. But when Shahin got drunk he would get on to politics and partisanship, and call on those present to drink a toast to Amir Mustafa and curse Nasib Beik Jumblatt. Nasib Beik was the Chouf's *qa'emmaqam* at the time, and his offices in government house faced Saeed Habib's coffee-house. His house was also nearby.[1]

Among the patrons of Saeed Habib's coffee-house were a number of Nasib Beik's supporters. They did not appreciate Shahin's behaviour, but rather than confronting him they went to Nasib Beik and reported what Shahin had said and done. Nasib Beik did not know Shahin. He asked those close to him about Shahin and was told he was from the Jurdi family. Nasib Beik had an ardent supporter in the Jurdi family in Mansour Mahmoud al-Jurdi, who owned and ran a coffee-house, with a stage for singers, in the place where the building of Dawoud and Taufiq Wehbeh stands today.

Nasib Beik sent for Mansour Mahmoud, and when he came he asked him about Shahin. Mansour said that Shahin was one of his closest relatives. Nasib Beik asked Mansour to bring Shahin to him because he wanted to meet him. Nasib Beik loved songbirds and had a number of them in cages of wire or cane, including canaries, nightingales, and goldfinches. When the visit took place, Nasib Beik received Shahin amicably and they talked enthusiastically for a long time about their common interest in birds. Nasib Beik benefited greatly from his guest's intimate knowledge of the subject. After seeing the *qa'emmaqam*'s birds and hearing them sing, Shahin began to rearrange the cages to make it easier for the 'ignorant' birds to learn from those that could sing. Then Nasib Beik asked Shahin to catch a feast of birds for him. The visit ended

---

1. Nasib Beik Jumblatt built a house (*hara*) with his own money on land that belonged to Abdo Beik Shqeir. Nasib Beik lived in the house, and when he left the *qa'emmaqamiyya* it became the property of Abdo Beik, and then his son Halim Beik and after him his grandson George. George sold the house to the sons of Saeed al-Qadi al-Jurdi, and they tore it down and built a modern home in its place, where Aref and Ibrahim Saeed al-Qadi al-Jurdi live today.

and Shahin bid Nasib Beik farewell. When he kissed his hand, Nasib Beik placed a gold lira in his palm. Shahin's heart filled with joy.

Once Mansour and Shahin were some distance from the house, Mansour took the lira from Shahin and asked him to meet him in the town square the following morning so they could go to Beirut together to buy Shahin some suitable new clothes. In Beirut, Mansour bought Shahin a pair of trousers, an open broadcloth, a cashmere vest and belt, a shiny pair of shoes, and a Moroccan fez. They returned to Choueifat with some change.

When Shahin got home he took off his old clothes, put on the new ones, and then headed down to the *souq* and went from one shop to the next in his new clothes. A little after sunset, his wandering brought him to the coffee-house of Saeed Habib Hanna. But this night was different from all the others. Previously Shahin would always drink on his friends' tabs, but now he was ordering drinks for his friends and paying for them himself. Those in attendance worried where this would lead. Shahin was drinking heavily, and soon he would begin to talk about politics. If the past were any indication, the drinking would lead him to leave nothing unsaid. Then suddenly, and as always, Shahin stood up and raised his drink above his head, shouting to those present, 'Gentlemen, to Nasib Beik Jumblatt …'

Amir Sami Arslan and Hassan Wehbeh al-Khishin

The prominent Arslanis of recent times were known for their keenness to own land and acquire property. Amir Mustafa Arslan accumulated vast properties in Beirut, Choueifat, Ain 'Inoub, al-Na'meh and elsewhere, and became known for his love of purchasing land and keeping it under his ownership and for his aversion to selling it, so much so that no one dared ask him if he was interested in selling. Amir Shakib owned lands in Khalde and numerous estates in the Choueifat desert, and Amir Taufiq Majid acquired property in Aley, Mahallat al-Ghadir, the Choueifat desert and Khalde.

However, not all their children and grandchildren followed their example. Some squandered a large part of these fortunes. Nothing remained of Amir Shakib's properties, including the house he had inherited from his father and grandfather. The lineage of Amir Hassan Fakhreddine Arslan came to an end with the death of his son Shakib. Of Amir Mustafa's huge fortune, only a small part survived in the hands of his grandson, Amir Muhammad Amin Arslan.

Among those who liked to sell and hated to buy was Amir Sami Abbas Arslan.[1] He began at an early age to sell the estates he had inherited, one after the other, according to his financial needs. His relative Amir Nasib Hammoud Arslan (1868–1927) was the governor of Choueifat at the

---

1. Amir Sami ibn Abbas ibn Salim ibn Mansour ibn Abbas ibn Fakhreddine al-Arslani was a member of the adminstrative council that Jamal Pasha appointed during the days of the First World War, and a member of the Lebanese Senate from 1926 to 1927. Then he became an appointed member in the first parliament, which lasted from 18 November 1927 to 13 May 1929.

time.[1] Amir Sami would authorize him to sell the properties he wanted to dispose of, so Amir Nasib would hold a public auction and the estate would go to the highest bidder.

Amir Nasib's house at the top of Hay al-Oumara in Choueifat was the seat of government, housing the governor's council, the police headquarters, and the goal. But above all, it was the town's social gathering place, where family notables would meet to discuss public affairs with the governor and to spend their evenings and talk, both for their benefit and for their amusement and entertainment.

Amir Nasib's gatherings were always enjoyable. He was a poet and writer who had immersed himself in the study of the Arabic language and had become an expert. He composed a work about Arabic terms that were subject to differences of opinion, but died before he was able to publish it, and the manuscript was lost with his library and the library of his brother, Amir Shakib. However, Amir Shakib collected his brother's poetry and published it in a collection he entitled *Rawdh al-shaqiq fi al-jazal al-raqiq* [The Brother's Garden of Gentle Poetry]. He also included an illustration of the Arslani genealogical record with extensive explanations and footnotes.[2]

In addition to his literary achievements, Amir Nasib was bold, dignified, tall, and well-built, and he admired manliness, appreciated people of virtue, and enjoyed the company of distinguished individuals and tellers of jokes, both of the private and public varieties. Those around him would often plan practical jokes on one another, and he would take part in the fun. Such things made people see him in a different light to Amir Mustafa or Amir Shakib.

Among those in whose presence and company Amir Nasib was comfortable was Hassan Wehbeh al-Khishin (1858–1918), which was not surprising since Hassan was bright, intelligent, far-sighted, and good-natured. Hassan made his living by hunting birds and fishing, and what he made off his few estates. But this time he was planning a hunt of a

---

1. Amir Nasib remained Chouiefat's governor for ten years, from 1892 to 1902, i.e. throughout the period of Na'oum Pasha's rule in the *mutasarrifiyya* of Mount Lebanon.

2. I have a copy of Amir Nasib's collection, and no doubt others have other copies too. But where is the original Arslani record? It is a historical document of great importance, and many historians have relied on it, including Amir Haidar Chehab, Tanious al-Shidiaq, and Ibrahim al-Aswad, though there are those who dispute its contents. It would be a great disappointment for the record to be lost in these days of enlightenment and science after surviving thirteen centuries through ages of ignorance and darkness.

different sort. He saw that Amir Sami was selling off his properties one after the other, and he knew all the lands that the Amir owned. He set his sights on a particular orchard and asked Amir Nasib to buy it for him if Amir Sami put it up for sale.

It was not long before the orchard's turn came and it was offered for sale at a public auction. Interested buyers began the bidding and the price reached 5 gold liras. Amir Sami accepted the offer, but Amir Nasib did not honour the sale and announced instead that the orchard would be sold to Hassan Wehbeh al-Khishin for the same price. No one could object to the order of the Amir. That evening Hassan went to Sami and gave him 3 gold liras as a down payment and thanked him and kissed his hand. They agreed that Hassan would pay the remainder of the purchase price when the sale was recorded.

***

Some time after the sale, Amir Sami went on a leisurely stroll through the orchards of Hay al-Oumara with Nasib Mahmoud al-Musharrafiyya (1875–1943). On their way to the mountain-top, a lush green orchard resplendent with almond and apricot trees and grapevines caught the Amir's attention. It was obviously fertile and well taken care of, and it impressed the Amir. When he asked Nasib who owned it, Nasib answered, 'That is the orchard that belonged to you and you sold to Hassan Wehbeh.'

Amir Sami was stunned. He slapped his forehead and began to curse his agent Dawoud Shibley al-Musharrafiyya for not preventing him from selling it. He headed back to town and stormed into the house of Amir Nasib. He told the Amir that he wanted to get back the vineyard he had sold to Hassan Wehbeh and was prepared to pay 6 gold liras, instead of the 3 liras he had received, to be released from his promise.

Amir Nasib said, 'Sami, I would advise you against going back on the sale after agreeing to it. And I would not suggest that you get caught up in a problem with Hassan Wehbeh when your position is not correct.' But Amir Sami insisted, and so Amir Nasib sent someone to summon Hassan Wehbeh. Hassan came in the evening after returning from hunting and found the council in session and Amir Sami sitting next to Amir Nasib and showing signs of anger.

Hassan took his place among those present. Amir Sami said, 'Hassan, I do not deny that I sold you the orchard in the highest reaches of Hay al-Oumara, but now I want to keep it, and I am willing to pay you 6 gold liras, though you only paid me 3.' Hassan was not surprised by the Amir's overture, for he had anticipated such a change, but he had prepared for the situation. He said, 'I will not oppose your wish, Amir Sami. But I ask that you give me just the same as I gave you.' Amir Sami was relieved and said, 'I will give you twice what I took from you.' But Hassan repeated, 'I want you to give me just the same as I gave you.'

When the misunderstanding and the difference in intentions between the two men became evident, the matter became clear to Amir Nasib and he understood Hassan's plan and design. He remembered that Hassan, who would never even kiss the hand of his own mother, had kissed the Amir's hand when they agreed to the sale. He turned to his relative and said, 'Sami, Hassan is asking you to return what he gave you, no less and no more. He gave you 3 gold liras and kissed your hand. Are you ready to give him the same as he gave you?' Amir Sami leapt from his seat and left the council. After some time, the sale of the land was recorded, and Amir Sami received the 3 gold liras.

***

The orchard still belongs to Hassan Wehbeh's descendants. His sons Kamel and Nadim divided it between them, giving each of them about 2,500 square metres of land in the higher orchards of Hay al-Oumara in Choueifat.

Postscript

The old government records of the Druze-owned property in Choueifat for the year 1301 Hijra (AD 1884), prepared by Choueifat's deputy-*shaykh solh* at the time, Shaykh Abu Qassem Ibrahim Salim Saab, indicate that the Arslanis owned 46 per cent of all the Druze-owned properties in Choueifat. If we assume that the Christians owned land in proportion to their numbers, meaning one-third, then the Arslani properties during that year were about 30 per cent of all of Choueifat's lands.

Qizhayya al-Nakouzi and the Five Pine Trees

In the summer, Qizhayya al-Nakouzi would always chop some firewood from the forest land he owned in al-Mrouj and al-Mtein and store enough pine and oak wood in his house to last him through the winter. Although Qizhayya was illiterate, he had inherited enough property from his father to sustain his family as long as he managed the property well. The property included a forest of 200 pine trees. Qizhayya was very attached to his land and spent his youth as well as his adult years tending it. He was one of those who built Mount Lebanon with their care, hard work, and seriousness, loved the land because it provided their shelter and sustained their health, and considered its blessings sacred because it was the fruit of the sweat of their brow about which the holy book spoke.

The writer, the manufacturer, and the merchant work and toil to earn their profit or wage and then use it to buy their necessities in food, clothing, and other materials. They do not feel any connection between their labour and their sustenance. The farmer, on the other hand, takes his bread from the yield of his threshing floor, eats his fruit from the branches of his trees, and drinks his milk from the udder of his goat. He therefore savours them all and is satisfied, feeling as if he has no need for the world beyond his farm and being his own lord and master. An affinity develops between the farmer and his crop to the point where he feels as though it is a part of him and cannot bear to see it damaged or harmed.

When he chopped his wood, Qizhayya al-Nakouzi would cut down the dry trees and weeds, and trim the fruit trees so that they would prosper and grow. His son Sha'ya, however, did not know these principles. During the summer of 1936, Sha'ya noticed that his father, who was now an old man, was unable to collect enough firewood for the winter supply, so he decided to carry out the task himself before going to his school in Baabdat. He hired a worker and went with him to the pine forest near their house. He chopped down the five trees and left them on the ground to dry, and instructed the worker to come back a week later to chop them up and take them to his father's house. Out of modesty, Sha'ya decided not to talk about what he had done, so he left al-Mrouj for Baabdat without telling anyone about it.

Someone noticed the fallen trees and reported the matter to the police, so the head of the police station and one of his men went to Qizhayya's house to denounce him for chopping down forest trees without permission from the Ministry of Agriculture. Qizhayya was angry. It was not enough that he had lost five pine trees – the police were accusing him of a crime he had not committed. He asked that the rural warden be summoned, since he wanted to know who had committed this crime, but the warden knew nothing. So Qizhayya filed a complaint against an unknown person and assigned the blame to the poor warden. And so the matter became complicated.

After a two-week absence, Sha'ya returned to spend the weekend at home. His father greeted him and then immediately began to tell him about the distressing incident. Sha'ya was startled and said to his father, 'I cut down the pine trees to provide you with wood for your hearth in the cold winter nights.' Qizhayya lowered his head for a moment and then raised it again. Tears were rolling down his cheeks as he said, 'You, you, my son, did this? ... Those pine trees lived off my sweat and blood, and the sweat and blood of my father before me ... How could you cut them down, Sha'ya?'

At that moment, Sha'ya realized the sanctity of the bond between a man and his trees. His father was crying like someone who had lost a loved one. There was nothing unusual about this, for the Lebanese had climbed into their mountain to the point where trees grew, and they had built their lives there. The trees were their building material, their source of nutrition, their shade in the summer, and the fuel for their hearths in the winter. If it was mankind that had brought the trees to those altitudes, then the trees were the reason to remain there. Even the grass of the pastures that separate the trees from the barren high mountains had a role in human life, for on and from the pastures lived the livestock that the Lebanese raised and from which they derived their meat, dairy products, and wool. This symbiotic relationship between man, animal, and plant was the basis of life in Mount Lebanon.

Shibil Ghostin and Milad Salameh

Shibil Ghostin was a man who had attained wealth and power. He emigrated to America and then returned to Lebanon with a fair amount of money, and became mayor of al-Mrouj and Wata al-Mrouj. He owned vast lands in the high mountains and set out to build a silk factory there, but then he changed the building into a hotel, which became known as the Bologne Hotel.

In 1952 construction of the building was well under way, and the dressed and undressed white limestone blocks were spread out on both sides of the road. Milad Salameh came by leading a huge herd of goats back from the coast where he had spent the winter to escape the cold and snow of the high mountains. Shibil looked out and saw the goats stepping on the white bricks and urinating and dropping excrement on them. He was incensed and shouted to Milad, 'Hey goat-herder! You animal! Get your goats away from the bricks! They're soiling them!' Milad hurried his goats along without saying a word in response.

The sun and wind of the high mountains, their cold and heat, their peaks and valleys, and Milad Salameh's struggles through all their difficulties had not only conditioned his body but his spirit as well. They had taught him patience and tolerance and instilled in him a sense of discipline and perseverance. And the open environment of al-Mrouj and its plains and pastures had given Milad clarity of mind, keen vision, and awareness. When Shibil Ghostin insulted Milad, Milad immediately recognized that it was not the proper time to respond, since it would only subject him to harsher and greater insults. But he swore to himself that he would avenge the insult in a memorable way to defend his dignity. Moreover, Milad did not want to get into trouble with the law.

The lands Shibil owned in the mountains had no water in the summer, so they were only suitable for grazing animals. He would therefore lease them to goat owners for meagre sums. But if he could get water to irrigate them in the summer, Shibil could turn the lands into orchards of apples, plums, pears, and other expensive fruits.

Once Milad had settled in the mountains and refurbished the barns and sheds, he set out to implement his plan. He told some of his friends in the town of al-Mrouj that he had discovered a river of water passing under the land of the *khawaja*[1] Shibil, and that it was his dog that had led him to the place from which the river could be seen. One hot day, he said, his dog went off for a while, and when it came back it was all wet. Then another time when the weather was even hotter, he kept an eye on the dog and saw it going into an underground cavern and coming back out soaked in water. So Milad went down himself, and there he saw a flowing river and tasted its sweet water. Milad knew that a village could not contain a secret, and that the news would quickly reach his adversary. His assumption proved correct.

A few days later, messengers came from the *khawaja* Shibil and asked Milad whether the story was true. He cursed the people for not being able to keep a secret and confessed that the news was true. They asked Milad, 'Why don't you show the *khawaja* where the water is? He would give you a valuable reward.' Milad said he could not do so because the river feeds into the fountain of the Mar Moussa Monastery, and if the *khawaja* used the water he would deprive the monastery's land of it, and then the wrath of Mar Moussa would befall him.

They asked Milad to prove that the water he had discovered flowed to the Mar Moussa Monastery. Milad told them that later that day he would put some hay in the river he had discovered, and all they had to do was watch the fountain of Mar Moussa the next day and see the hay appear in the water. So they went the next day, and indeed the hay appeared in the fountain of Mar Moussa. But what they failed to realize was that Milad had placed the hay in the cavern of Mar Moussa's fountain itself in the area of Za'rour.

Shibil had grown anxious and agitated. He would not be deterred from pursuing and pressuring Milad, since the discovery of water on his land would make him the king of his day. The *khawaja* Shibil visited Milad at

---

1. *Khawaja* is an Egyptian word, used here to mean roughly 'the gentleman'. [Translator]

his home in al-Mrouj, bringing him a box of Bahsali sweets.[1] He asked about Milad's mother, who was ill, and then began negotiating about the water, but met with Milad's concern about affecting the fountain of Mar Moussa. Milad invited Shibil to visit him in the mountain for a taste of the water he had discovered, and he set 15 August of the following summer as the date for the visit.

***

Shibil Ghostin continued to try to persuade Milad. He would pass by in his car on Saturdays and take Milad with him from his residence on the coast to al-Mrouj, flattering him and humouring him all the while. Finally he offered him a large sum of money that made Milad's mouth water, making him wish he really had discovered water on Shibil's land. But Milad refused on the pretext of his concern for the welfare of Mar Moussa. He told Shibil, 'Our appointment is on 15 August, and after that we will see what God will arrange, *khawaja*.'

The appointed day, 15 August 1953, arrived and Shibil drove with his cousin Ni'matallah Ghostin to the bottom of the mountain. From there they climbed on foot up the hard, treacherous land carrying gifts for Milad. Milad welcomed them but said apologetically that he could not do as he had promised because he could not find anyone among the goat herders to look after his goats in his absence. He said someone was available to cover for him the next day, so he would be able to go and bring the water then.

Shibil did not accept the apology and volunteered to look after the herd himself during Milad's absence. Milad said the female goats would run away from him and the male goats would attack him if he was not dressed like him, so Shibil suggested that they exchange clothes. He would wear Milad's *'aba*, *kaffiyya*, and *'aqala* and carry his pouch around his neck. So Milad taught Shibil how to say *'taq taq'* and *'hir hir'* to the goats, and then took his bucket and bowl and charged up the mountain. The revenge he was exacting was giving him a sense of power and pleasure.

Milad was gone for two long hours and then returned with a bucket of sweet cold water. He had previously placed some water in a jar in the

---

1. Bahsali is an old sweet bakery in Beirut. [Translator]

shadow of a mound of rocks, and then he had slept by it for a while and come back with it in his bucket. Shibil tasted the water and liked it, and he shared it with his cousin Ni'matallah. But the trip was fruitless because Milad would not budge from his position due to his fear of the wrath of Mar Moussa.

***

Before the summer ended, Milad went to al-Mrouj and sat in the square of the Bologne Hotel. Shibil was there, as were many of the town's people, and Milad began to lecture Shibil. '*Khawaja* Shibil, how did you like goat herding? To attain your dream of an abundance of water, you have to purchase the goats from me, and take off your American clothes and wear the '*aba* and the *kaffiyya* like me, and carry the pouch and share your food with the dog, and sleep on the thistles like me, and know the taste of freedom and be honoured to be called a goat herder.' Milad was delighted, for he had finally avenged his dignity. They say the *khawaja* Ghostin still dreams of the river running beneath his land in the heights of the forts of rock in the foothills of the Sannin mountain.

Scenes

Al-Naqqash

The people of many of the villages of the Chouf and Aley districts carry the names of various wild and domesticated animals. They say that a man called 'al-Naqqash' (the inscriber) wandered through Lebanon. He spent some time in every village and then gave its people a nickname after observing their behaviour and studying their traits. They say he was knowledgeable about people and had a keen sense of observation.

This supposition could not be further from the truth, however, for not a single one of these nicknames applies accurately to its subject. They are no more than metaphors suggested in a spirit of jest and banter. I recommend that those who do not readily appreciate or forgive jokes and jests, or are uncomfortable with them or cannot tolerate them, especially if they come from one of the villages afflicted with an unsavoury nickname, should bypass this chapter of the book and avoid reading it.

***

The story goes that al-Naqqash went from town to town on his mule, staying in each place until he came up with a suitable name for its people. First he is said to have visited the Gharb, then the Chouf, and then the Arqoub, before finishing his tour in the Jurd. When he got to Ain Dara he saw a group of children playing. He liked to talk to children to extract from them the secrets of their elders, so he stopped his mule and leaned his chin against his hand and asked them where their fathers were. They answered that they had gone to gather two-pronged branches to use in

291

supporting chins. (Two-pronged branches are used to support dangling branches.) When al-Naqqash heard the children of Ain Dara mocking him, he uttered his famous sentence, 'Its monkeys are in its hills and its plenty is on its coast.' Then he rode away. But where to?

It is said that he went to Sharoun, and that its people had heard the nicknames he had given to the people of other villages and were not amused, so they killed him. Others say his blood is on the hands of the people of Ain Dara because he called them bears. Then there are those who say he was not killed at all but simply disappeared.

***

Nobody knows who al-Naqqash was, where he was from, what became of him, or when he lived and died. Some of the stories suggest that the nicknames have been around for quite a long time. Has the passage of time since al-Naqqash's life erased his biography from memory? There are some who say that al-Naqqash was an imaginary figure, and that people exchanged these nicknames after they became common and supported them with the story of al-Naqqash. They say the name 'Naqqash' was derived from the word *naqash* (to inscribe) in reference to his fashioning of these epithets. I am inclined to agree with this view, for the reasons explained below.

It does not seem possible that a man could roam the villages, bestowing nicknames upon their people in this way, without anyone recalling his origin or background. Nor does it seem possible that a person would devote himself to roaming the length and breadth of the county to categorize people in this way just for his own amusement. We find nicknames in Kiserwan and Wadi al-Taym similar to those in the Chouf, though there are fewer of them. Is it possible that al-Naqqash went there too? I cannot imagine that al-Naqqash, especially in those days, could have walked safely out of Choueifat, 'Einbal, Jdaideh, and other towns after bestowing them with his blessings.

There does not necessarily have to be a particular 'Naqqash' behind these nicknames. People, as individuals or as groups, often give each other nicknames and epithets as jokes, in retaliation for a prior offence, or for other motives. These nicknames and epithets then become established, giving rise to a type of popular literature in times of depression. Whatever and wherever their origins, it is a social and historical reality that the people of a number of our villages carry the names of animals and birds as nicknames, and we do not want them to be lost because they are a part of our heritage. In what follows I will document the nicknames that have reached me.

Perhaps the most noteworthy fact about al-Naqqash's nomenclature is the wonderful spirit in which people have accepted them. The Lebanese have joked and laughed about al-Naqqash's nicknames for many generations, and I have not heard of one incident where they gave rise to anger or antagonism. I hope that the reader takes this chapter of the book in the same spirit.

The Aley district

Aghmid:	The Coyotes
Bshamoun:	The Herons
Ba'werta:	The Lizards
Benneih:	The Foxes
Dayr Qoubel:	The Terebinth Birds
Choueifat:	The Tapeworms
Abey:	The Crows
Aytat:	The Gypsies
Ain Ksour:	The Chickens
Ain 'Inoub:	The Frogs
Kfar Matta:	The Frogs

The Chouf district

Jahliyya:	The Frogs
Jba':	The Calves
al-Jdaideh:	The Dogs
Harat Jandal:	The Grasshoppers
al-Khreibeh:	The Young Billy Goats
Dayr al-Qamar:	The Bee Eaters (Birds)
Dmit:	The Coyotes
Dayr Kousheh:	The Crabs
Dayr Baba:	The Mother Hens
Ghouara:	The Calves
Amatour:	The Roosters
'Einbal:	The Young Donkeys
Bater:	The Cats
Baarouk:	The Lunatics
Batloun:	The Baby Birds
Brieh:	The Chicks
Bshatfeen:	The Cats
Baaqlin:	The Sheep

Ba'daran:	The Foxes
Kahlouniyya:	The Gypsies
Mukhtara:	The Wolves
Ma'aser al-Chouf:	The Bald Heads
Mristeh:	The Squirrels
al-Mazra'a:	The Cows
Niha:	The Bedouin
Warhaniyya:	The Monks
Atrin:	The Donkeys
Ain Zhalta:	The Gypsies
Ain Qani:	The Misers
Ain Wazein:	The Gypsies
Gharifeh:	The Fire Pokers
Kfar Nabrakh:	The Misers
Kfar Heem:	The Chicks
Kfar Qatra:	The Bats
Kfar Faqoud:	The Mice

The Kiserwan district

Ashqout:	The Coyotes
Ajaltoun:	The Dogs
Mazra'at Kfar Zibian:	The Bears
Rayfoun:	The Bald Heads
Ghostah:	The Lions
al-Qulay'aat:	The Gypsies

A Few Anecdotes about al-Naqqash's Nicknames

Fouad al-Khishin and Ramez Abu Saab

The poet Fouad al-Khishin is from Choueifat, whose people al-Naqqash favoured with the nickname 'The Tapeworms'. Ramez Abu Saab is from Aytat, whose people al-Naqqash dubbed 'The Gypsies'. They say he chose this nickname for the people of Choueifat because of their large numbers, and their frequent movements up and down the mountain. As for the people of Aytat, they earned their nickname because of their fast manner of speaking and their habit of travelling before noon rather than before dawn.

Fouad al-Khishin received a gift of honeydew[1] from a friend in Iraq and shared a portion of it with his friend Ramez Abu Saab, accompanying his gift with the following verses of *zajal*:

Mann al-samaa' *is a piastre a drop*
and it's fragranced with crimson roses.
It comes from one who's a tapeworm
and goes as a gift to a gypsy.

Kamal Beik Jumblatt, Na'eem al-Fatayri, and the People of Ba'tharan

During the revolution of 1958 a number of men from various Lebanese villages, including a group from Ba'tharan, gathered in al-Mukhtara. One day a dispute broke out between some young men from the Baz and Khattar families, both from Ba'tharan. The matter escalated into an exchange of gunfire, leaving one man from each family slightly injured. The people of Amatour, who shared ties of neighbourhood and kinship with the people of Ba'tharan, immediately formed a delegation to try to settle the dispute and reconcile the parties, but they were not successful. So Shaykh Abu Hassan Na'eem al-Fatayri[2] from Jdaideh tried to mediate between the two families. He had better luck than the group from Amatour and managed to reconcile the combatants.

After the reconciliation the two sides went with Abu Hassan to visit Kamal Beik Jumblatt in al-Mukhtara. After some serious discussion, Kamal Beik could not help but make a comical remark about the incident. He told the people of Ba'tharan (The Foxes), 'Al-Naqqash's theory proved correct in your case. The people of Amatour (The Roosters) tried with you, but you were not scared and you disappointed them. But when the son of Jdaideh (The Dogs) squeezed you, you gave in right away.'

---

1. In Arabic, honeydew is known as *mann al-samaa'*, which literally means the blessing of the heavens. [Translator]
2. Shaykh Na'eem al-Fatayri was one of the community's devoted *ajaweed* and important heroes. He was killed in an ambush by a group of bandits on the road to Kfar Heem after killing one of them in the struggle.

Wadi' Talhouq

A council in Suwaida once brought together the man of letters Shaykh Wadi' Talhouq and two of his friends, one from Atrin and the other from Jdaidet al-Chouf. The conversation turned to friendly banter, and the son of Jdaideh (The Dogs) said, 'We would be willing to trade our name with any other village except Atrin (The Donkeys).' The son of Atrin answered, 'We see you just as you see us.' The discussion became heated and they appealed to Shaykh Wadi' to settle it. He said, 'The truth is that we have no interest in your trade, but if you do exchange titles, then let us, the people of Aytat (the Gypsies) know, because we cannot do without either one of you.' It is well known that the gypsies depend on donkeys for their transportation and on dogs for their protection.

Patriarch Boulous Mas'ad and Ahmad Fares al-Shidiaq

Boulous Mas'ad was born in Ashqout in 1806. He ascended the ranks of the Maronite clergy, and in 1854 he was elected Patriarch of Antakia and the rest of the East and remained so until his death in 1890. He was a scholar and a historian, and played a prominent part in Lebanon's political history over a long period of time.

Boulous had a cousin from Ashqout named Fares al-Shidiaq. Fares was two years his senior, and they studied together at the Ain Waraqa school. Fares had a brother named As'ad, who left the Maronite Church to join the Anglican faith, so the Maronite Patriarch persecuted him, and he died in Qannoubine. Fares emigrated from Lebanon to Egypt, where he studied classical literature and excelled in the Arabic language and its principles. He went on to Malta, London, Paris, and then to Tunisia, where he converted to Islam and became known as Ahmad Fares al-Shidiaq. He finally settled in Istanbul, where the Sublime Porte entrusted him with editing the empire's official publications. He also published a number of his own works, the most famous of which is *al-Saaq 'ala al-Saaq Fima Huwa al-Faaryaaq*.

***

In 1867 the Patriarch Boulous Mas'ad travelled to Rome to participate in the Western celebrations for Saints Peter and Paul. From there he travelled to Paris and then to Istanbul, where he was received as a guest of the Ottoman government. Ahmad Fares al-Shidiaq had some influence in Istanbul, so he requested that the Ottoman authorities give Patriarch Mas'ad a warm and generous reception. They did so, and the government hosted him in a palace overlooking the Bosphorus. As luck would have it, the palace was near the home of Ahmad Fares al-Shidiaq, but Ahmad never visited and the Patriarch was not aware that Ahmad lived in the same neighbourhood.

As with all the sons of the mountain, it was Patriarch Boulous's habit to wake up early. He would step out on to the palace's balcony and enjoy the glorious view of the Bosphorus. His cousin Ahmad was no different in this regard. He too would wake up early and go down to the garden of his home and recite some of the Syriac hymns he had learned at Ain Waraqa.

***

Day after day the Patriarch would hear these hymns and not believe his ears. Finally he spoke to the bishops accompanying him and said, 'I do not know if I am dreaming or awake. Every morning I hear chants in the Syriac language coming from the nearby house. Have any of you heard this?' The bishops knew of Ahmad Fares al-Shidiaq's presence in the nearby house and knew what he had done for their delegation with the Ottoman government, but they felt it would be inappropriate to speak his name because he was an apostate from the Church. But now that His Eminence the Patriarch had asked the question, the opportunity had presented itself, so one of them said, 'Our lord, it must be some old coyote.' His Eminence recalled that the coyote was the name given to the sons of Ashqout, and in the blink of an eye he said, 'Is it Fares?' They answered, 'Yes, and he would like to kiss your hand. Would you permit it?' So Fares was granted an audience with the Patriarch, and the key was the nickname of the people of Ashqout.

Akhwat Shanay[1]

When one of my friends from the mountain heard that I was going to write a chapter about Akhwat Shanay he said, 'Why write about Akhwat Shanay? Everybody knows his stories.' It is true – almost every person in the Chouf and the Matn has heard at least one story about Akhwat Shanay, and to this day they tell these anecdotes and enjoy them, despite the passage of 105 years. A man of such consequence deserves to go down in history and have his stories and anecdotes recorded lest they be lost, distorted, or altered through oral transmission.

I have not come across anything in writing about Akhwat Shanay, except for the incident with Shaykhs Hammoud and Nasif Abu Nakad, narrated below. Everything else about him comes to us by way of a chain of oral transmission. There is no doubt that the man must have been a strange and unusual phenomenon for his memory to endure in people's minds and for his name to remain on their tongues all this time. His name was linked with that of Amir Bashir II. Moreover, the village of Shanay was never known for anything as much as it was for its 'Akhwat', even though it is a beautiful village and its inhabitants are among the best of people.

People called him 'Akhwat', which is a colloquial term denoting some malfunction in thought and behaviour that does not reach the level of madness. No one ever said Akhwat was mad, except for Youssef Khattar Abu Shaqra in his telling of the above-mentioned anecdote involving Shaykhs Hammoud and Nasif Abu Nakad. Youssef Abu Shaqra referred

---

1. *Akhwat* is a colloquial word meaning 'crazy man'. Akhwat Shanay was nicknamed the 'Crazy Man of Shanay', Shanay being his home town.

to him as 'Majnun Shanay' (the madman of Shanay), but I believe he used the word 'Majnun' not because it applied to Hassan Muhammad Hamzeh but because the word 'Akhwat' is not a proper Arabic term. This choice would be consistent with the rest of Abu Shaqra's work, which is characterized by a splendid use of the Arabic language, with an eloquence rarely matched in historical writing.

***

Akhwat Shanay is the nickname of Hassan Muhammad Hamzeh from the town of Shanay, just east of Bhamdoun in the district of Aley, who lived during the first third of the nineteenth century. He married one of his relatives and was blessed with four children including two daughters, Mdallaleh and Mayyaseh, one of whom was married to Ain Zhalta and the other to Baysour. As for the boys, they were Muhammad and Abd al-Salam. They both married and their progeny live in Shanay to this day.

Hassan Hamzeh's marriage and that of his children are evidence of people's acceptance of him as a normal person without defect or deformity. Moreover, none of his sons, grandsons, or descendants exhibited any mental or physical abnormality. Yet some of his words and deeds suggest some kind of aberration that appears at times and disappears at others. The nickname people gave him, 'al-Akhwat', is proof of this aberration.

***

It appears from the man's history that he held a certain position in the Chehabi security apparatus. Amir Bashir II, who ruled the country and its citizens with two iron fists, must have had a highly competent intelligence network. He had eyes and ears throughout the land, keeping abreast of all that went on and all that was said. And what eyes could be better than those of an 'Akhwat', whom people loved to see and to whom they opened their homes? He would sit with them and their guests and mingle with the servants and guards, listening and observing. They would assume that his understanding was limited and would not exercise caution or conceal their secrets in his presence.

Hassan Hamzeh would constantly wander from town to town and from place to place, attending the councils of the *mashayekh* and notables, going to the 'arenas' and joining the spectators at contests and wrestling matches, and socializing with horsemen, servants, and slaves and hearing what they said. Then at the end of the tour he would return to Beiteddine, the seat of Amir Bashir's rule, and relate all that he had observed.

Hassan Hamzeh was an integral part of Amir Bashir II's entourage, and the Amir would not have had a jester in his entourage unless he served some other purpose. Members of the Hamzeh family say that some of them have seen a copy of Amir Bashir's will at the home of Muhammad Beik Taqieddine in Baaqlin. Apparently it contained a provision giving Hassan Muhammad Hamzeh an income for as long as he lived, and providing for his family after his death. And God knows best.

Let us now leave Hassan's stories and anecdotes and tell the reader more about him. They say that birds of a feather flock together, and that humans find comfort in their peers, and that those with handicaps or physical infirmities tend to empathize with one another. It is said that, like Shanay, Shbaniyya in al-Matn had its own 'Akhwat'. A friendship and affection developed between Akhwat Shanay and Akhwat Shbaniyya. They would exchange visits and talk at length. Akhwat Shbaniyya lived with his mother in a modest house.

Once Hassan visited his friend in Shbaniyya, and the latter treated him graciously. Akhwat Shbaniyya's mother prepared a meal for them, and they ate and then sat together to talk. Suddenly the mood changed. Akhwat Shbaniyya said to Akhwat Shanay, 'Hassan, I'd like to live near you so I can see you every day. If I give you half my house, will you agree to live in it?' Hassan gladly accepted. So the two friends divided the room, with Hassan taking the inner part and Akhwat Shbaniyya taking the outer part, meaning the part with the door. Each of them sat in his part of the house and they resumed their conversation, each calling the other 'neighbour'.

Time passed and the sun was about to set, and it was time for Hassan to leave Shbaniyya so he could reach Shanay before dark. He stood up and was about to leave, but Akhwat Shbaniyya would not let him pass through his part of the house. The discussion became heated and they locked arms, but Hassan was still not able to get out of the room. Each of them returned to his base. The mother tried to intervene with her son, but he would not allow her to mediate and insisted that Akhwat Shanay had no right to pass through his property.

Then Hassan suddenly regained his awareness and shrewdness. He said to his friend, 'Brother, we forgot something important.' Akhwat Shbaniyya said, 'And what is that?' Hassan answered, 'We forgot to divide the roof between us.' So Akhwat Shbaniyya got up and Hassan went with him to rectify this oversight. They stepped outside into the yard, and Akhwat Shbaniyya leaned a ladder against the wall and climbed up to the roof ahead of Hassan. But instead of climbing after him, Hassan waited until his friend was on the roof and dragged the ladder off the wall and threw it to the ground. Then he set off quickly towards Shanay.

***

It is said that the wedding ceremony of Hassan's daughter Mdallaleh took place according to custom and tradition, and Hassan's behaviour was normal. The ceremony ended and the groom's relatives went off, taking the bride away on the back of a thoroughbred horse. But as soon as they got outside the village, they heard Hassan shouting to them and saw him running behind them. The convoy stopped to see what Hassan wanted. When he caught up with them, he said, 'People! Our relatives! Please, I beg your pardon. We have fallen short in our duty to you. We forgot to put kohl on the bride's eyes, and a bride's eyes are supposed to have kohl.' He took an applicator out of his pocket and handed it to his daughter. The people shook their heads and said, 'Well done, Hassan. May all your days be joyful,' and they went on their way.

***

One day Bhamdoun was fortunate enough to receive a visit from Hassan. As usual, the town's young men gathered around him and started to joke with him and listen to what he said. They were near the church, so Hassan asked, 'Do you worship God in the church?' They said, 'Yes'. He asked, 'And if I prayed in it, would God listen to me?' They replied, 'Of course, Hassan.' So he left them and ran to the steps of the church, climbed on to its roof and began to recite the *fatiha*[1] repeatedly in a loud voice.

A shaykh from Majdel Ba'na happened to pass by and hear him. He shouted, 'Hassan! What are you doing?' Akhwat Shanay said, 'I'm reciting the *fatiha*.' The shaykh said, 'Do you know where you are, Hassan?' He answered, 'Yes, Shaykh. I'm standing on the roof of the church, and I'm reciting the *fatiha*, and those like yourself who understand know that I'm reciting the *fatiha*, and those who do not think I am just babbling. What do jackasses know about eating ginger?'

***

Hassan's legs also took him to Ain 'Inoub, where he attended the *majlis* of Mallak Qaed Bey.[2] Mallak was wise and intelligent, and Hassan was taken with his words and said to him, 'Mallak, I wish God had given me your mind and taken ten years of my life.' Mallak said, 'May God preserve your mind, Hassan.' Hassan said, 'If you like my mind, then take it and give me yours.' The audience laughed, but they admired Akhwat Shanay's understanding and his good opinion. Up to this point all was fine with Hassan. But what happened after that was that every time Hassan was in Ain 'Inoub, he would stand above the town and call out in his loudest voice, 'Mallak!' When Mallak answered, Akhwat Shanay would shout, 'Mallak, I wish that what is yours was mine and what is mine was yours!'

***

Although the Hamzeh family in Shanay and the Hamzeh family in Abey are related, the Abey Hamzehs are Jumblattis and the Shanay Hamzehs are Yazbakis. Thus Hassan was a Yazbaki. One day, he happened to be in Mukhtara, the Jumblatti centre and stronghold, when he ran into a friend of his. The friend wanted to put Hassan on the spot, so he asked

---

1. The *fatiha* is a Qur'anic verse frequently recited by Muslims. See also the footnote about the *fatiha* in the chapter 'The Battle of Wadi Baka'. [Translator]
2. The grandfather of Fayez As'ad Qaed Bey.

him, 'Hassan, are you a Yazbaki or a Jumblatti?' Hassan answered, 'Wait until we are beyond the shadow of the palace.'

***

They say that Amir Bashir had a thoroughbred horse, blue in colour, with a beautiful face and build, and that he was fonder of this horse than all the others in his stable. The horse became ill, which greatly upset the Amir. He brought the best-known veterinarians in the land to treat it and asked his servants and slaves to give it special care and attention. He threatened them with grave consequences if they let the horse die.

But what good is caution in warding off fate? The horse died, and the servants were dismayed and worried. None of them dared bring the bad news to Amir Bashir. While they were in this quandary, Akhwat Shanay arrived and found the horse lying on its back and the servants in a state of confusion. He asked what the problem was and they explained that none of them dared go to the Amir and inform him. Hassan reassured them, saying, 'Just leave it to me.' He went to the Amir and greeted him. The Amir asked Hassan how he was and about the state of the country and what people were saying. Hassan replied, 'My lord, the country is well and secure in the shadow of Your Excellency. The people all wish you long life and lasting glory. I even saw your blue horse today with its legs praying to God to keep and protect you.' The Amir shouted, 'God have mercy on you, Hassan! The mare has died!' Akhwat Shanay said, 'I did not say that, my lord. You did.'

***

A group of Amir Bashir's loyalists turned against him, but then gave him their allegiance again. The Amir treated them leniently and mercifully, contrary to his usual ways, but this did not sit well with Akhwat Shanay. He wanted the Amir to take his revenge because they were traitors. But the Amir did not do so, and Hassan reluctantly held his tongue.

A few days later, some of the palace's men went out to hunt for quail. They used a female quail as bait, putting it in a cage on the ground, so that when it chirped the male quail would respond and fall prey to the hunters. The hunt began, and the men opened fire on the wild quail. But Hassan aimed his rifle at the female and killed it. The men returned to the palace and told Amir Bashir what Hassan had done. The Amir summoned Hassan and asked him, 'Why did you kill the bird?' Hassan replied, 'It betrays its own species and draws them to their death. And a traitor must be killed.' The Amir understood what Akhwat Shanay was getting at.

***

We come now to the anecdote that has immortalized Akhwat Shanay. It is told a number of different ways, but the meaning is the same. Amir Bashir II's greatest development project was bringing the water of the Safa spring to his capital of Beiteddine through a channel 15 km long. He carried out the project through unpaid forced labour, imposing 80,000 days of toil on the people of his emirate. Each man had to work one day a year without compensation. The work began on 10 July 1812 and continued for a period of two years without the Amir spending anything from his treasury on the project. When it was finished he held a grand festival to celebrate its completion.

The people attribute the idea of forced labour to Akhwat Shanay. They say that Amir Bashir held a meeting around the Baarouk spring to study the project and its implementation. He listened to the opinions and views of his men and advisors but did not care for any of them. The pastor of the village of Bmihreih insisted that the project was impossible. The Amir grew tired of all the talk and argument.

Akhwat Shanay was in the entourage, so the Amir sought some comic relief from the serious discussion by joking with him. He called him and asked, 'And you, Hassan – what is your opinion?' Hassan answered in a confident tone, Amir, can you be the master of the land and the ruler of its people and not be able to bring water to Beiteddine? Have each of your subjects dig the length of his grave and the water will get there.' Amir Bashir said, 'By God, Akhwat Shanay's opinion is better than that of the pastor of Bmihreih.' And the project came about as Hassan had decreed.

***

We move finally to the story of Akhwat Shanay with the Shaykhs Hammoud and Nasif Nakad, as told by Youssef Khattar Abu Shaqra in his book *al-Harakat fi Lubnan* [Movements in Lebanon], published by his son, Aref Abu Shaqra:

'It is said that the two of them [Shaykhs Hammoud and Nasif] had carried out the execution of Jirjis Baz in secret, without anyone discovering what they had done. Then they walked together to Jbeil, pretending to be on a mission from the Amir [Bashir II]. When they reached Jounieh they encountered the madman of Shanay. He said, "Mercy on your souls! You killed Jirjis Baz in the monastery, and now you are coming to kill his brother Abd al-Ahad in Jbeil too." The two shaykhs were worried that their deed had been discovered and that someone had brought word of it to Abd al-Ahad Baz, so he would be expecting them to be coming for him and would be plotting to kill them. They went back and asked around but found that it was a just a coincidence. So they went on to Jbeil and carried out their assigned mission.'

I doubt the truth of this story. First, it is known that Jirjis Baz and his brother Abd al-Ahad were killed on the same day, 15 May 1807. The sources say that it was the 'Imadis and the Talhouqis who killed Abd al-Ahad in Jbeil. Second, we know that in 1807 Shaykh Nasif was no more than 15 years old. It does not make sense for him to be commissioned at such a young age with a task like killing Abd al-Ahad Baz in Jbeil.

Horsemanship

The horse is the noblest of all the domesticated animals. It combines beauty of features, purity of skin, and proportionality of body parts with power, agility, and gallantry. It is distinguished by its awareness, intelligence, and honour, so its fine qualities of character complement the beauty of its physical appearance. The horse is always ready to serve. It rarely sleeps and it labours in all regions and climates. Although it prefers the open plains, it climbs heights with firm and stable steps and wades through rivers and marshes. It can live in the burning desert as well as in the snow and ice of cold countries. One of the oddities of its constitution is that it is immune to the common cold. I do not know the scientific reason for that.

The horse is the strongest and most capable of runners. Some animals might outrun the horse over a short distance, but only the horse can withstand kilometre after kilometre and hour after hour of running. A horse might weigh half a tonne or more, yet it can carry one, two, or three people and walk and run until the riders tire. The horse's sense of honour runs so deep that it continues to run if prodded, not only to the point of fatigue but to the point of death. Is there anything more honourable? There are many testimonials to this quality of the horse.

In 1475 Amir Ali, the son of Amir Ahmad Qassem Chehab, escaped from his uncle's prison in Hasbayya, mounted a horse and rode it towards the Chouf. The horse kept on running until it crossed the Beqaa valley and reached the foothills of the Western Mountain, where it collapsed beneath him and died. The Amir then took a mare and went on to

Baaqlin.[1] There is also a story that Amir Ali, the son of Amir Fakhreddine al-Ma'ni, was killed after his horse died beneath him from exhaustion.[2]

Furthermore, the horse will throw itself to its death if its rider pushes it to do so. A horse might not realize that it is exposed to mortal danger when its rider leads it into the heat of battle, amidst the lightning of weapons of steel and the deafening blast of explosions. It might not comprehend the fact that the spears pointed at its head and chest can kill it and that the bullets fired at it can penetrate its belly. But what animal does not sense its fate when it jumps or is pushed from a towering height? Instinct teaches animals about the dangers of leaping into the unknown, so they do not do so — except for the horse, which, when pushed by its rider, will jump to certain death. We all know the story of the Mamluk[3] who escaped the massacre of Muhammad Ali Pasha by jumping with his horse over the wall of the citadel in Cairo. I do not know how much truth there is in that story, but here is a similar story whose truth is beyond doubt.

During the first disastrous developments in Mount Lebanon in 1842, a group of fighters under the leadership of Ali Beik Hamadeh went deep into the mountains around Amatour to escape their enemies. They took a passage in the mountain that was not wide enough for their horses. Ali Beik refused to save himself and leave his horse to be booty for the Christians. He peered over the edge of the high boulder and poked the flank of his horse with his spur. The horse leapt forward and fell off a sheer cliff and died. Ali's leg was broken and he was unable to move until the next day, when his kin heard what had happened and took him to Baaqlin.[4]

We might ask how the steadfastness, speed, and perseverance of the horse compares to that of the camel, which is known for its extensive, seemingly limitless perseverance. I found the answer in a news item I read in a foreign magazine. It states that early in this century in Australia a race was held between a horse and a camel over a distance of about 177 km. The horse beat the camel but died at the end of the journey. As for

---

1. Ibrahim al-Aswad, p. 248.
2. Piaget De San Pierre, *al-Dawlah al-Durziyya* [The Druze State], translated by Hafez Abu Muslih, p. 74.
3. The Mamluks were the class of soldier-slaves who came to rule Egypt during the fifteenth century. They were defeated by the Ottomans in the sixteenth century to resurface later and finally be finished off under Muhammad Ali. [Translator]
4. Abu Shaqra, p. 56.

the camel, after a full night's rest it went back the same distance the next day in the same amount of time it had taken to come.

The beauty, intelligence, strength, perseverance, and noble qualities of Arabian horses make them the finest horses in the world. We do not know the reason for this superiority. The Arab world is not the horse's original habitat. It was brought here from Central Asia, where it originated. Does the climate account for this, or was it the kind treatment the Arabian horse received that allowed it to develop these distinguished traits? The Arabs' avid enthusiasm for their horses led them to keep records of the horses' genealogies, documenting their traits and their descent from thoroughbred fathers and mothers. Perhaps this attentive care helped to improve the species by selecting the very best of each generation.

Equestrians and horse lovers were adamant about the pure lineage of the horses they chose. They believed that heredity was the dominant factor in a horse's make-up and character, and that a defect might surface in its descendants even after several generations. They would attest to the truth of this theory with the following famous story. There was a man who owned a thoroughbred mare. He was very proud of it and would show it off to his peers in the field. Once it stumbled and fell forward. Its owner opened a 'historical investigation' into the matter and found that the horse's 'great, great ... grandmother' had once done the same thing. Stumbling is an obvious defect in a thoroughbred horse. We recall that our uncle Qassem Saab's horse once stumbled during a spear-throwing contest in the upper square of Hay al-Oumara. Qassem reacted by drawing his gun, and he would have shot the horse had his relatives not restrained him. He sold it the very next day.

***

In the Arab world, thoroughbred horses were traditionally the most valuable and prized possessions. Glory and good fortune were associated with their ownership. And on the backs of horses developed the noblest moral order for men – the order of chivalry, which became an expression of bravery, generosity, and other moral virtues. The people of Europe followed in the Arabs' footsteps in the Middle Ages, giving horsemanship the highest order among their social virtues and distinguishing between horse riding as an art form and the moral system that governs it. In this chapter I am using 'horsemanship' in its original sense, meaning proficiency in horseback riding, and its use in running and racing and in war and peace.

As for the families and individuals that gained fame in horsemanship in Lebanon before and after the advent of the car, they are too many to list. But I wish to record here the names of some of those I have heard about. Among these families were the Hamadehs in Hirmel, al-Moneitra, and Bsharri; the Hobeishs, Hamiyyas, and Harfoushes in the Baalbeck valley; the Dandash Aghas in Akkar; the 'Imads in parts of Aqoura; and the 'Imads, Hamadehs, Abd al-Maliks, Abu Shaqras, and Abd al-Samads in the Chouf. In the south they included the Asads and Fransises in al-Qulei'a near Marj 'Iyoun; the 'Iryans in the western Beqaa; the Hashishos in Saida; the 'Izzes, Arabs, and Ltoufs in Beirut; and the Ma'loufs in Zahle, including Najib Beik, who performed extraordinary feats before the German Emperor in 1898 and presented him with his horse's saddle. The Arajis in Qub Elias were also renowned.[1]

***

In Choueifat, Halim Beik Shqeir was known for his skill and agility on horseback. It is said that he would grab a running horse by the neck and throw his body underneath it. Then he would turn his body around until he was in the saddle. Nayef Qassem Saab was also well known. He would balance a spear on his head and ride around the field on the back of his horse without letting the spear fall. He would also run his horse from the heights of Choueifat down the hill to the Saida road, including part of the hill that was paved with stones and bricks.

***

But the pinnacle of skill, boldness, nerve, and daring was 'the operation' of Rafi' Abd al-Samad in Dar al-Mukhtara. It happened that his son Hassan stabbed Iskandar Shahin Ltayf. Hassan was arrested and placed in Beiteddine prison. It also happened that the *mutasarrif* of Mount

---

1. From a study prepared by the Lebanese broadcasting station in Beirut.

Lebanon, Na'oum Pasha, paid a visit to Nasib Beik Jumblatt in al-Mukhtara and delegations came from the villages to participate in his reception. Rafi' Abd al-Samad, with his reputation for bravery and horsemanship, seized the opportunity to plead with the *mutasarrif* for his son's release. He steered his horse towards the entrance of the palace and began to climb its broad steps. The people gathered around the square and waited to see what Rafi' would do. He reached the landing of the outer first floor and they thought he would stop there. Instead he rode the horse into the first floor, leaving the main staircase, and entered a small room connected to the roof of the second floor (where the *mutasarrif* and Nasib Beik were sitting with the country's notables) by an outer staircase suspended in the air and fastened to the wall. He went out on to the staircase through a narrow door, bending his body flat along the horse's back. Then he climbed the narrow staircase that hung about 15 metres above the garden. The horse and its rider went up to the roof. Rafi' wanted to go back down the same way, but the *mutasarrif* and Nasib Beik would not allow it.

The staircase is still in its place, and every visitor to the palace hears the story of Rafi' Abd al-Samad and looks up at the towering staircase, secured only by an iron railing no higher than 80 cm, not even the height of a horse's belly. Men still stand in amazement at the incredibly dangerous feat and the remarkable skill it required. Rafi''s wish was granted – the *mutasarrif* ordered his son's release.

Hassan inherited his skilled horsemanship from his father. An eyewitness told me that on one occasion in Baaqlin, forty horsemen of the Abd al-Samad and Abu Shaqra families came from Amatour, each riding his own horse. In front of them was Hassan Rafi' Abd al-Samad, performing tricks with his horse at the head of the delegation.

***

Ahmad Salloum Murad of Bshamoun's skill in horsemanship could be compared to that of Abd al-Samad. He was an equestrian of the first order, and would jump with his horse from one rooftop to the next. Like Rafi', he performed a feat that required much daring and skill when he climbed the steps of Baaqlin's government house on the back of his horse.

***

Then the automobile arrived, and the horse disappeared from sight. At one point in our modern history, the 'fashion' of wearing boots came back, prompting the writer Saeed Taqieddine to make his famous statement, 'Horsemanship is gone, and nothing remains of it but the boots.' But recently, the desire to ride horses has returned among the well-to-do, and a number of clubs have been established for this purpose.

Wild Animals in Lebanon

It may seem strange to include a chapter about wild animals in this book, but I am convinced that it is necessary. Knowledge is always preferable to ignorance, and the people in Lebanon know of the existence of wild animals in some areas. If these facts are not recorded they will doubtless be lost with the passage of time. The earliest information we have about wild animals in Syria and Lebanon is from the Old Testament. In the Song of Songs (4:4–16) of King Solomon, we find the following: 'Come from Lebanon, my bride, come from Lebanon, come! Descend from the top of Amana, from the top of Senir and Hermon, from the haunts of lions, from the leopards' mountains.'

We know from al-Mutanabbi's poem in praise of Badr ibn Ammar ibn Isma'il that there were still lions in the Jordan valley in the tenth century AD. We also know from the memoirs of Usama ibn Munqith, who lived at the time of the Crusades, that the lion, the tiger, and the mongoose were among the animals known in Hama in Syria. And Saleh ibn Yahya tells us in his book *Tarikh Beirut* [The History of Beirut] that Amir Zeineddine Ali al-Tanoukhi slew a lion near Aramoun in the Gharb area. That was towards the end of the thirteenth century. Mondrel mentions that when he passed through Beirut in 1696 he saw a lion's den at the palace of Amir Fakhreddine al-Ma'ni in the north-eastern part of the city. Were Fakhreddine's lions from Lebanon and Syria, or were they from Africa? We do not know. Then we hear nothing further about lions.

As for tigers, in the 1890s, Zeineddine al-'Indary from 'Oubadiyya killed a tigress that used to prey on livestock. It lived in the mountain above the town, and to this day the place is still known as the ridge of the tigress. In 1898 Khalil Mahmoud Saab was transporting a bag of

312

gunpowder from Choueifat to Aley just before dawn. Khalil was 13 years old at the time. When he got to the upper orchards of Choueifat, he saw a tiger standing on top of an embankment overlooking the road. There was a carriage behind him on its way to Ain 'Inoub. He quietly slipped behind the carriage and grabbed hold of the back of it, and hung on until he got to Ain 'Inoub after daybreak. (Hanging on to the backs of horse-drawn carriages was one of the most enjoyable adventures for children. The companions of a child who had managed to hang on in this way would shout to the driver, 'Behind you, driver,' and the driver would hit the back of the carriage with his long whip.)

In 1937 someone gave Fawzi Beik al-Traboulsi, the commander of the Lebanese national police, a small tigress as a gift. In 1948 two men from the Marj 'Iyoun police force were on a mission in the Hajeer valley near Majd Silm when a huge animal jumped out in front of them and then ran into a bush on the side of the road. They opened fire and killed the animal, and then found that it was a tiger. During the Ramadan War of 1973, the newspapers mentioned that the fierce battles in the Golan brought the tigers out of their dens.

***

As for bears, they were found in abundance in Lebanon and Syria until the beginning of the twentieth century. But it has been a long time since we heard of bears appearing in Lebanon, though it is possible that there are still some in the mountains of Syria. In the museum of the American University of Beirut, there is a bear that the Rev. James Crawford killed in the Bloudan mountains of Syria early in the century.

On a moonlit night in 1915, Hani al-Qontar encountered a family of bears, consisting of a male, a female, and two cubs, frolicking in the fields of Mtein. Hani was carrying his hunting rifle and the female bear confronted him, so he shot and wounded it. The male and the two cubs ran off, and a fight ensued between the wounded bear on one side and Hani and his cousin on the other. The fight went on for more than an hour as they attacked and fled and struck and gave chase, until finally the two men killed the animal. Hani took its fur, and the townspeople divided its meat among themselves. It was a time of war and scarcity, and bear meat made acceptable food since bears live on grass and fruit.

313

In 1922 George Beik Thabet and Shaykh Muhammad Attalah were hunting for partridges in the mountains of Ain Dara when they spotted a bear. Shaykh Muhammad Attalah opened fire and hit the animal but did not kill it. The bear ran off, and the Shaykh followed it to its lair and finished it off with his dagger. Only Shaykh Muhammad would have undertaken such a dangerous adventure.

***

With the extinction of lions and the scarcity of tigers, the *sheeb* emerged in Lebanese stories and legends as the fiercest wild animal. It is a cross between a hyena and a wolf, and it is ferocious and vicious. People believe it was called a *sheeb* because it '*yashib*', or leaps, which is used in the vernacular instead of '*yanshub*'. We have mentioned elsewhere that around the middle of the nineteenth century, Abu Hussein Ali 'Izzeddine Abd al-Khaliq killed a *sheeb* near Majd al-Ba'na with his bare hands.

In 1844 Hanna Ibrahim Khalaf and his wife Saada, who lived in Ain al-Rommaneh near Aley, heard a ruckus coming from their open-air chicken coop. Saada went out of the door and ran towards the chicken coop and Hanna looked out of the window. They saw that there was a *sheeb* in the chicken coop. When it saw Saada it was ready to pounce, but before it could do so Hanna jumped through the window and grabbed its jaws and pulled them apart. A fierce struggle ensued between man and beast, and it did not end until Hanna was able to grab an axe and strike his adversary. The *sheeb* had wounded Hanna's neck and so he was taken to Dr Iskandar Baroudi. The doctor was able to stitch up the wound, but the scar remained. Hanna skinned the *sheeb* and presented its fur as a gift to Wasa Pasha, the *mutasarrif* of Mount Lebanon at the time.

The story has an amusing subplot. They say that Hanna's brother Louis was having dinner while his brother fought with the *sheeb*. When they called him, he apologized because of the *hirmat al-'aysh* (the sanctity of food), and so he did not get up. But Louis claims that he was confident in Hanna's strength and bravery and knew that his brother did not need any help.

***

As for wolves, foxes, hyenas, jackals, hedgehogs, and badgers, there are still plenty of them in Lebanon. But with man's expansion on the land and his progress in the craft and machinery of fighting, they too are on the path to extinction.

In the mid-1960s hyenas began to appear in large numbers in the southern part of Lebanon. They say that these animals had escaped from the swamps of al-Houleh, where the Israelis were reclaiming the land. On 2 February 1975 a female wolf intercepted a car full of passengers between Mijdlayya and Zgharta and attacked it. One of the passengers shot the animal and killed it. They found that it weighed more than 100 kg and was about 20 years old.[1]

It is worth mentioning at the end of this chapter the commonly held belief that the digging of the Suez Canal severed the path of animals that used to come from Africa into Palestine, Syria, and Lebanon.

---

1. *Al-Nahar*, Wednesday 5 February 1975.

Snow on the Coasts

At midday on Tuesday 10 February 1920 the rain stopped falling but the sky remained overcast. When we returned from school at four in the afternoon, we went out to play in the road now known as '*tal'at al-amercan*' (the ascending road of the Americans), just west of the American University in Ras Beirut. We were three children: myself, Ali Najib al-'Oud, and Mustafa Abd al-Rahim Qoleilat. The wind gathered strength, and it grew very cold, so we split up and went home. Before I entered the house, I saw a white flake falling from the sky to the ground. I took it in my hand but did not know what it was. I asked my mother and she said, 'These are snowflakes.' Of course, I did know what hail was.

We awoke on the morning of Wednesday 11 February to a sight I had never seen before: the ground was covered with a thick layer of snow, and the branches of the tree were weighed down by its white load. That was the snowstorm of 1920, one of the biggest to reach the coastal areas in that century. It was said that 'The snow reached the boats in the sea.' About 20 cm of snow fell in Beirut, and about half a metre in Choueifat. The weight of the snow caused the olive branches to break, and it was a massacre (of trees) unlike any the people of Choueifat had seen in more than a century. Some estimated the amount of thick wood taken from Choueifat's olive groves after this snowstorm at 20,000 *kantars*,[1] or 8,000 tonnes.

This snowstorm was accompanied by an unusual weather phenomenon. Usually the weather clears up after a snowfall. Hence the common saying, 'It snowed ... it cleared.' But in 1920 it snowed in the

---

1. One *kantar* equals about 250 kg. [Translator]

coastal areas on the night of 11 February and then let up during the day, but the sky remained overcast. On 12 February it rained heavily and swept the snow from the streets and fields. These rains caused a catastrophe in Palestine, where the snow piled up on the mountains around Jerusalem. When the rain fell it melted the snow and swept it away, causing huge floods to descend on the town of Jericho, destroying its homes and killing a number of its inhabitants.

***

I have been observing the weather in Beirut and its surrounding areas since 1920. Whenever there is a cold winter, I hope for snowfall on the coasts so that I can enjoy its beautiful scenery. This observation of over fifty-five years has given me some knowledge of the wind patterns and the succession of violent storms. I would like to share with the reader some conclusions, based on first-hand observations and direct sensory perception, about the falling of snow on the Lebanese coastal areas.

***

After the snowstorm of 1920, I would hear my elders talk about the snow of 1911 and the snow that had fallen in the coastal areas thirty years before that. Thus I learned the first basic fact, which is that snow only falls on the coastal areas once every ten years or more, but not according to any rule or pattern, as will be seen from the following account of what has happened in this regard in the years since.

***

In 1932 Lebanon suffered severe storms and heavy rains in the last third of January, and the harsh weather went on for about two weeks. On 7 February the rain stopped and the wind changed and began to blow from the north-west instead of the south-west. The temperature dropped, and early in the night, snow began to fall on the coast. There was not much of it so none settled on the ground, but in Choueifat there was an accumulation of a few centimetres. Then the weather cleared up and the northerly winds set in.

***

On Tuesday 30 December 1941 the wind blew from the south-west and the sky grew overcast. Then the wind picked up and it began to rain heavily; this continued for four days. When we woke up on Saturday 3 January 1942, the weather had temporarily cleared, but the wind was stronger and its direction had changed from south-westerly to north-westerly. The temperature dropped, and then snowflakes began to fall. At noon the snow came down on the Lebanese coastal areas, and it continued intermittently until midday on Sunday 4 January, by which time 10 cm of snow had fallen.

This snowstorm was accompanied by the largest bird migration that the Lebanese had witnessed that century. Sparrows covered the earth, all of them of the large variety known as *kikh*, and ducks landed in the rivers and streams. We saw the wild hens, starlings, coquette, and other winter birds walking on the white ground. Hunters were few then, and it was also a time of war and so bullets were scarce and expensive. The strange thing is that these birds did not stay in our country for more than one day. By Monday they were all gone.

Then the weather cleared and the northerly wind took over and it grew colder, but I do not remember that the temperature fell any lower than one degree Celsius.

***

In 1950 it snowed twice in Beirut. The first time was in the evening of Friday 28 January. After a few days of heavy rain, the wind had changed direction and it blew from the north-west throughout the afternoon. A little after sunset, snow fell on the coastal areas again, but for no longer than one hour and in two shifts. Then on Saturday the weather cleared. After a few days the southerly and south-westerly winds returned and there was heavy rainfall. At the end of the week, snow began to fall on

Beirut, and it continued for three days, but intermittently, so it did not settle. In and above Choueifat the snow piled up heavily. That was the last snowfall on the coastal areas worth mentioning. Several times after that there were weather conditions conducive to snow on the Lebanese coastal areas, and there were some mild snow showers, but never enough for a considerable snowfall.

These are the times in the last century that snow fell in Lebanon's coastal areas. And it appears that this is what has been happening over the centuries throughout the current period of the planet's history. Here and there we read about Lebanon experiencing a bitterly cold winter or a severe snowstorm. I know of no more comprehensive record of the weather in Lebanon than that of Amir Haidar Ahmad Chehab. He recounts the events year by year, rarely failing to include an account of precipitation, temperatures, and their consequences, especially if there are unusual weather conditions. From time to time we read that 'the snow reached the coastal areas.' Ordinary people use a different expression to mean the same thing. They say, 'The snow reached the decks of the boats.'

It appears that towards the end of the eighteenth and early in the nineteenth century, two snowstorms struck Lebanon that were unprecedented in the annals of recorded or recollected history. According to Amir Haidar, 'In this year of 1778, a tremendous snowfall swept Lebanon, leaving almost 30 cm of snow on the seashore and just less than half an arm's length in Dayr al-Qamar.' This year became an important date in Lebanon's history because it was the year that Shaykh Ali Jumblatt,[1] father of the famous Shaykh Bashir Jumblatt, died.

The second snowstorm, which was apparently even more severe, came in 1813. Here is how Amir Haidar Chehab describes it:[2] 'That year (1228 Hijra), on the twenty-fifth of Muharram, there was a solar eclipse. Then, five days later, there came two days of powerful winds, followed by snow on the third of Safar (5 February 1813). It snowed from Friday morning until Saturday evening. The snow fell for thirty-seven and a half hours without a single hour's interruption. There were two arms' lengths of it on the ground, which was close to a record. In the higher mountains snow

---

1. Shaykh Ali is the one who gave permission to the Catholic Maliki priests to build the Mokhalis Monastery east of Joun and gave them the land and resources to build it and support its priests (al-Shidiaq, p. 141).
2. *Lubnan fi Ahd al-Umara Chehabiyyeen* [Lebanon in the Reign of the Chehabi Amirs] by Amir Haidar Ahmad Chehab, p. 587.

was not known. It was so dry that the snow stuck to the leaves of the trees. It destroyed property in most places and ruined more than half the olive trees. Little remained of the olive and orange trees, and the snow destroyed many buildings in mountain villages. The snow reached the interior of the Houran country and the port of Acre. In the Beqaa valley it left over 2 metres of snow. Most of the inhabitants of Kafra[1] died, and people no longer knew where the village was. No one was able to reach them. Much livestock in the mountain villages died of hunger. In Druze towns,[2] the roads from one village to the next were cut off, and in most villages even the path from one house to the next was lost.'

After that Amir Haidar cites a poem by one of the poets that describes and recounts the severe snowstorm.

***

That is what we have in the way of facts. As for the reasons for discrepancies in weather conditions between one year and the next, they are innumerable and science knows little about them. No one has ever

---

1. Kafra was a thriving village lying on the north-eastern shoulder of the intersection of Kabr Shmoun, between Shimlan, Baysour, and Ain Ksour. It was the Lebanese domicile of the Hamdan family, who were originally Yamanis. After the Battle of Ain Dara in 1711 and the victory of the Qaysis over the Yamanis, the Hamdans left Kafra for the mountains of Houran, where they 'established' Jabal al-Druze (Jabal al-Arab today) and became its masters and rulers until this sovereignty was transferred to al-Atrash family. Like the al-Atrash family, the Hamdans became known for their sound politics, courage, sagaciousness, and generosity. Soon thereafter, many of Kafra's people and other Druze followed the al-Hamdan family to Houran. Kafra was devastated until the snowstorm mentioned above came and wiped it out of existence. It is very regrettable that with all the development in that area in the last twenty years, no one thought to revive the name of Kafra, the town of the Hamdans, being who they are in history.

2. The nucleus of Lebanon – Lebanon the emirate, the two *qa'emmaqamiyyas*, the *mutasarrifiyya*, and finally the republic – is the Chouf, the Matn, and Kiserwan. The Druze dominated these districts as amirs and feudal lords from the first centuries of the second millennium AD, meaning since the time of the Tawhid *da'wa*. The scope of their domain would narrow at times and expand at others, reaching its climax during the reign of Amir Fakhreddine al-Ma'ni. The political name for this unit (Lebanon) was Jabal al-Druze ('the Druze Mountain') or Bilad al-Druze ('the Druze country'). This name remained until the days of Amir Bashir al-Malti, whose rule led to separation, division, and then reunification, but under a non-Lebanese *mutasarrif*. The situation changed, and so did the name.

documented a full year of weather conditions identical to another in all its details and events. Science has yet to discern regular patterns in weather conditions. They say that the weather repeats itself every thirty years. Our late uncle, Abu Ramez Abd al-Halim Saab,[1] undertook to record in his memoirs the weather conditions every day of the year. He found no proof of this theory.

Some time ago I read in an American magazine that meteorologists in the United States were looking into the existence of weather cycles and investigating the theory of the cyclical repetition of weather conditions every forty years. We have not heard anything further about this theory. There are some institutions that venture to predict weather conditions in the coming seasons, but only in a general way.

There is one astronomical factor that is known to influence weather conditions in terms of temperature, which is the tilt of the Earth's axis towards the sun. We know that the line of the Earth's rotation on its axis is not perpendicular to the path of its orbit around the sun, but tilts 23 degrees from a right angle. This tilt causes the four seasons because the Earth's orbit and the varying angles at which its parts face the sun cause variations in the amount of heat they receive from the sun, depending upon their location along the Earth's lines of latitude. But what is pertinent to this chapter of the book is that the tilt of the Earth's axis with respect to its path of orbit around the sun is not constant. It varies from

---

1. Abd al-Halim Qassem Saab is among the outstanding personages in the history of our family and of Choueifat. He was venerable, firm, bold, handsome, well-built, elegant, and precise. He assumed the office of head of the municipality in Choueifat in the town's days of glory, when the new land survey took place in the early 1930s. At this point, I should mention how an important part of Choueifat's jurisdiction and land was almost lost. When Beirut International Airport was built, the businesses and institutions wiped out the border between Choueifat and Bourj al-Barajneh. The municipality of Bourj al-Barajneh began to collect fees for the rental costs of the operators of the airport facility. When the author assumed office as the head of the municipality of Choueifat in 1952, he became aware of this matter and began to study the airport's location on the maps and with the old keepers and property owners and discovered that there had been a mistake. He filed an administrative suit for a determination of where the border was, and it was shown that the airport facility was within Choueifat's municipal domain. The head of the Bourj al-Barajneh municipality at the time was the kind and trusted brother, dear friend, and capable deputy Mahmoud Ammar, and he restored our rights to us in their entirety. The return of the airport provided a valuable source of income for the municipality of Choueifat.

year to year in a random manner. Thus the resulting levels of heat and cold vary from year to year.

***

Let us return now to our main topic, which is snow on the coasts of Lebanon from the perspective of my personal observations over a period of just over half a century. The results can be summarized as follows. First, snow only falls on the coastal areas after a few days of stormy, rainy weather. Second, snow only falls on the coastal areas when the south-westerly winds change to north-westerlies. Third, even when these conditions occur, the temperature does not always fall far enough for snow to form. Or the level of humidity might drop so that only a few snowflakes or showers fall and do not settle on the ground.

***

Mountain people believe that snow is beneficial to plants, and that it kills off harmful insects. They call snow the 'yeast of the earth' because its water melts slowly and goes deep into the soil and the underground basins, nourishing the fountains and springs, whereas most rainwater goes to waste in the rivers and streams, not to mention the fact that it sweeps away the soil and carries it to the bottom of the sea.

Whatever the case, snowfall remains one of the most gorgeous and spectacular of Lebanese sights. Lebanon took its name from its snow because 'Lebanon' is derived from a word of Semitic origin meaning 'whiteness'.

Saabisms

The Saab Family in Choueifat

The written history of the Gharb area in Mount Lebanon recorded only the names of the Arslani governors and rulers and their Tanoukhi relatives. This is the case with historical writing in general, and even more so when the historian is one of these rulers, like Saleh ibn Yahya al-Tanoukhi or the keepers of the Arslani records, or one of their followers like Ibn Sbat al-Aliehi. This leaves the researcher of family histories in this area with oral records as his only available source.

The story that takes memory as its vessel and the tongue as its vehicle, and is transferred from person to person and generation to generation, is like an ocean wave. It begins powerfully, overflowing with energy, and then gradually loses its force and momentum. As occurrences recede further into history, recollections diminish, and images fade in people's minds. But with some attention and effort, we find that the general outline and impression survive.

Many Druze families remember their movements from one town to another in Lebanon, and the circumstances of their arrival from Aleppo and the Jabal al-A'la. But there are other families that settled where they are today many long centuries ago and no longer recall how or when they arrived. That is the case with the Saab family in Choueifat. The inherited belief among the members of this family is that they came from Wadi al-Taym some time in the distant past. As for the reasons for the move and the details of its events, they have been erased from memory by the passage of time.

***

No one has studied the roots and origins of Druze families like the great scholar and meticulous historian Suleiman Beik Abu 'Izzeddine. He spent thirty years collecting and studying documents and records, interviewing knowledgeable sources, organizing data, drawing conclusions, and recording his findings. However, he passed away before he could document the results of his study and research in a book. His death was a grievous loss.[1]

In a page of Suleiman Beik Abu 'Izzeddine's writings, we find the following about the Saab family in Choueifat: 'It is said that the Saab family is one of the oldest Druze families in Choueifat, except for the Arslan family.' Why this exception? The Arslan family did not come alone. Their clans and tribes came in great numbers to what appeared to be almost completely uninhabited mountains and they built on them and lived in them.[2]

Moreover, the belief that we came from Wadi al-Taym accords with the history of the Arslan family in terms of the path that was taken. It is known that they first came to Wadi al-Taym, and then moved to Sinn al-Fil and to Beirut and its suburbs. 'In AD 799 Amir Masoud (Arslan) moved with his clan to Choueifat, built residences there, and took up residence himself. Choueifat was part of al-Bourj at the time, and it had no buildings. The Amir built it into a sizable village.'[3] The Saab family's conviction about the depth of their roots and origins in Choueifat is reinforced by their status in Choueifat society. No one, including the Arslans, has ever denied this seniority. Our houses were being built in the earliest times in and around the houses of the Arslans.

We were also the wealthiest Choueifat family after the Arslans in the times when fortunes were estimated in terms of the numbers of weapons, horses, and properties that people owned. I have found a document dating back to 1301 Hijra (AD 1884) that lists the distribution of property taxes (*mal amiri*) among the Druze of Choueifat on the basis of the number of dirhams each person possessed. The document, which I have reproduced as a novelty, authorizes the *shaykh solh* of Choueifat, Shaykh Abu Qassem Ibrahim Qassem Salim Saab, to collect the required money. It bears the signatures of Mansour Ahmad (Saab), Amin Daher Assaf

---

1. The data and documents collected by Suleiman Abu 'Izzeddine are now in the custody of his niece, the scholar of history Dr Najla Abu 'Izzeddine. They are therefore preserved in a safe place, and we can hope to benefit from this treasure trove of history, and from the research of Dr Najla.
2. Tanious al-Shidiaq, pp. 235, 495 and 496.
3. Tanious al-Shidiaq, pp. 235, 495 and 496.

(Saab), Najm Suleiman Hassan (Abu Hassan), Dawoud Suleiman Ahmad (al-Musharrafiyya), Mer'i Shahin Salman and Hamad Shahin Abbas (al-Souqi), Shahin al-Shami and Ali Khattar Suleiman (Saab), Mansour Muhammad Hassan (Sha'ban), Faraj al-Jurdi, Amin Shdid al-Souqi, and Khalil Hussein Arbid. The dirhams were distributed as follows: the Arslan family: 1,103 dirhams; the Saab family: 338 dirhams; the Jumblatt family and various endowments: 205 dirhams; and another 584 dirhams distributed among more than twenty families.

As for ownership of horses, the wife of our uncle Fandi Hussein Hamad Saab (Ward, the daughter of Salman Ataya) told us that at her wedding in 1886, the Saab delegation that went to bring her from Abey to Choueifat included twenty horsemen. All of the horses were offered to the bride to ride, but the privilege went to Amin Daher Assaf Saab because he was the groom's neighbour. They used to present the bride with a *seibeh*, a ladder with three steps, so she could mount the horse without assistance.

***

This does not mean that we believe in the continuity of the name and the purity of blood in our family since those olden times. The tribal order did not automatically transform into the family order with the transition from shacks and tents to houses and dwellings. This process undoubtedly required a lengthy period of time. The name may have changed several times, and the family structure never ceased to evolve and change with the introduction of new elements through marriage or giving shelter, and entry into kinship and the departure of other elements through extinction or emigration. But there are some basic foundations that remain constant: the general consistency of blood, the common history, the consistent bonds of intimacy and good neighbourliness, and the partnership of interest for the sake of earning a living and the preservation of the name and identity.

The trajectory of a large family through the generations and the centuries is like a river flowing through valleys and plains. Some new water enters through springs and streams, and some water is lost to canals and waterways. But the river remains the same in its name, its traits and characteristics, and its path through the land. As for branches and relations, what is beyond doubt is that the origin is found among the Saab of Choueifat, and to our knowledge there are only two branches.

The first branch was in Beit Lahya in Wadi al-Taym, but the name of its founder, who had to leave Choueifat for reasons we do not know, has been lost. His descendants increased in number, with some of them carrying the name S'eifan and others the name Khaireddine. The S'eifans were greater in number, and they gained status and developed bonds of kinship through marriage with the al-'Iryan family. Some of their men became famous in the wars of Ibrahim Pasha. But they died out at the beginning of the twentieth century. The only survivors from their lineage are the branches. As for the Khaireddine family, two of them remained – Ali and Hani, the sons of Mahmoud Ali Khaireddine, who returned to Beirut and reassumed the family name.

The second branch of the Saab family are the Hajalis in the Mashqouq area of Jabal al-Druze. The founder of this branch was Muhammad Saab, who killed a man in Choueifat and had to leave the town as a condition of the reconciliation. He went to Jabal al-Druze and settled in al-Qrayya, where he married a woman named Hajaleh. He died there, and his three sons became known by their mother's name. Then the family moved to Salkhad, and from there to al-Mashqouq, where they settled. There were, and still are, among them men who became known in the fields of administration and justice and heroes who participated in the national movements.

Other than these two branches ... nothing, despite the many families that carry the name of Saab in Lebanon and Jabal al-Druze, whom we mention with all due respect and appreciation.

***

That leaves the emigration of modern times. It is a known fact that today Lebanese emigrants and their descendants outnumber the residents of Lebanon. This applies to the Saab family as well. There is a large community of Sa'bs today in Venezuela, and another in Mexico. There are also some of us in the United States, Brazil, Argentina, Africa, and the Arab countries. Many of us died in foreign lands, and we do not know how many of the rest will return.

The Magic Turns on the Magician

Mansour Ahmad and Qassem Hussein were among the pillars of the Saab family, and were prominent figures and famous men of the Gharb in the nineteenth century. They were both men of wise opinion, grace, and distinction, and were counted as heroes. They were veterans of many battles and wars in which they were in the vanguard. Once a dispute occurred between them for a reason that no one recalls, and it led to a severing of relations, despite their bonds of kinship and ties of good neighbourliness.

The news of the disagreement spread, and it attracted people's interest because of the status and influence the two men enjoyed in public affairs, both social and political. The news saddened their relatives and friends but it pleased their adversaries and those who envied them. Efforts were made – efforts to reconcile the two men as well as efforts to exacerbate the situation – with each party working to serve its particular biases and interests. The sons of the Saab family and their friends initiated efforts of peace and goodwill, while those who harboured hatred and resentment tried to fan the flames of conflict and strife. What is strange is that the negative forces were quicker to mobilize and take the initiative to exacerbate the disagreement between Mansour Ahmad and Qassem Hussein. And what is even stranger is that the magic turned on its magician, and evil intentions produced beneficial results.

One evening two men[1] from Hay al-Amrousiyya came to visit Qassem Hussein at his home in Hay al-Oumara. Abu Fandi received them properly, and they sat down to talk. In the course of the conversation the

---

1. We shall withhold their names.

two men brought up the subject of his disagreement with Mansour Ahmad. They told Qassem that they supported him against Mansour, and that he could depend on them if the need arose. Abu Fandi realized the true intention behind their visit. He thanked them and expressed appreciation for their concern, and the two men left.

They did not return to Hay al-Amrousiyya but went instead to Mansour Ahmad's house and resumed their evening at his place. They went through the same routine, offering Abu Ali their support in his dispute with Qassem Hussein. Mansour thanked them for their concern, and the two men departed. They were happy with what they had done and convinced that they had succeeded in fuelling the fire that was burning within the Saab family.

***

It was four o'clock in the morning and Abu Fandi had gone to bed when he heard a knock at the door of his house. He rose and listened, and he heard the voice of his servant responding to the visitor and opening the door. Then he heard the voice of Mansour Ahmad asking the servant, 'Is your master here?'

Qassem did not know the purpose of Mansour's visit at this late hour of the night, given that relations between them had been severed. And Mansour's strength was unlimited and his courage went beyond reason, so Qassem started to reach for his weapons and to take his time about coming out of his room. Mansour understood what Abu Fandi was thinking, so he called out to him, 'Come out, Abu Fandi. I have come to visit you.' When Abu Fandi appeared, Mansour said, 'Strangers have come into our home, and I want us to make up in their honour.' Abu Fandi said, 'By God, Abu Ali, you have beaten me to it, in reconciliation and righteousness.'

The following afternoon, Mansour Ahmad and Qassem Hussein went to Hay al-Amrousiyya together. Their tour was a return visit to the two notables with two faces and two tongues.

The Cutting Proof

Hussein Ahmad Mansour Saab was pious from an early age. He abided by the religious teachings in word, deed, and appearance, and stayed clear of the youthful adventures for which his brother Youssef became famous. He dedicated himself to religiosity and worship, and became known for his honesty, integrity, scholarship, and gentleness.

Abu Abbas Hussein was strongly attached to the land and its yields. He would tend personally to the orchards of grapes, figs, almonds, and apricots he had established in Wadi al-Halayej and the olive groves in Mahallat al-Bahsasa. As he had adopted religious customs, he would wear a striped robe, a white turban, and sturdy boots. He would also carry a strong, thick cane of oak.

One morning, Abu Abbas went to the square in front of the bakery in the heights of Hay al-Oumara in Choueifat. There he met one of the town's sons, and they exchanged greetings and conversation. Abu Abbas was ready to be on his way, but our friend stopped him. He pointed to the stick Abu Abbas was carrying and said, A person who carries such a stick should be able to use it.' Words failed Abu Abbas, and he raised his stick and brought it down on the man's head and shoulders. The man was injured, a ruckus arose, and the men came running out of the bakery and the nearby shop to restrain Abu Abbas and calm him down. One of them asked him why he had beaten the man. Shaykh Abu Abbas answered, 'He said something ... and I was just proving to him that he was right.'

The Reawakening of Blood

Mahmoud Youssef Saab and Abdallah Mansour Saab[1] shared ties of kinship and good neighbourliness. Abu Hassan Abdallah lived in the house that now belongs to his grandsons, Fouad and Suhail, and Abu Hamad Mahmoud lived in the house that is now the home of Khalil Nasib Saab in Hay al-Oumara in Choueifat. Neighbourliness is sacred and kinship has its obligations. But they can also be a source of friction and a point of departure for numerous and various disputes. That was the case with Mahmoud and Abdallah. Each would make personal and financial sacrifices for the other through difficulties and disasters. From time to time they would have verbal altercations, but these would always end well.

On one occasion, however, the reproach grew into a quarrel, and anger overcame them. Each man grabbed his cane and raised it above his head and ran towards the other until they were within striking distance. Then, as fast as a bolt of lightning, Mahmoud threw his cane behind his back and shouted at his cousin, 'I've thrown it down.' With the same speed, Abdallah also said, 'I've thrown it down too.' And they embraced instead of hitting each other.

---

1. Mahmoud Youssef is my paternal grandfather, and Abdallah Mansour is my wife Najla's paternal grandfather.

The Pride of Youth

Khalil Saber Saab was 15 years old, but despite his youth, he had a rebellious spirit and a heart that was open only to the causes of pride and haughtiness. His father had died when he was still young, and he grew up without supervision and developed a strong tendency towards independence and liberation.

It happened one day that Khalil got angry with his sister and hit her, so his mother went and told his uncle Mansour Ahmad Saab. Mansour summoned his nephew and reprimanded him for hitting his sister, and was unable to keep himself from slapping the boy. Khalil's world turned upside down and he felt troubled and distressed. He made a decision, so he turned to Mansour and said, 'You are my uncle, and the eye cannot rise above the eyebrow. But I am leaving Choueifat, and I promise you that I will not return as long as you are still alive.'

No one could deter Khalil from emigrating. He left Choueifat without saying goodbye to anyone and went towards Wadi al-Taym. First he settled in Ain Ata, and then he moved to Meimis. Then he entered the Turkish army, and his job carried him twice to the holy lands in Hijaz. His life was a series of dangers and adventures (and he married seven times). But the home to which he always returned was Wadi al-Taym, and he came to own property in Meimis.

Khalil never returned to Choueifat during the life of his uncle Mansour. This self-imposed exile lasted about forty years. Whenever he missed his sisters and his family, he came to the al-Ghadir area and sent for them. What is strange is that even after the death of his uncle Mansour, he still hated living in Choueifat or staying there – so much so that when he came in 1909 with a delegation from Wadi al-Taym to attend the funeral of Amir Muhammad, the son of Amir Mustafa Arslan, in Ain ʿInoub, he passed through Choueifat without even getting off the back of his horse. But when he fell seriously ill and felt that death was approaching, he returned to Choueifat and died there on 17 August 1915.

***

Khalil had two sons – Asʿad and Jaber. Jaber grew up and lived in Choueifat, and then moved to Beirut. As for Asʿad, he married a woman from the Madhi family in Meimis and lived there. Then he moved to Thibin in Jabal al-Druze and established a second home there. Two sons – Maʿrouf and Wadiʿ – were born to Asʿad. Maʿrouf received the house and property in Meimis, and Wadiʿ received the house and property in Thibin.

A Killing Postponed

In 1913 Hamad Mahmoud Saab[1] was a policeman in Beirut. It happened one day that he was passing through a street that branched off al-Khandaq al-Ghamiq and he saw one of Beirut's strongest and most dangerous outlaws of the time, wanted for a number of robberies and murders.[2] When the outlaw spotted the policeman, he turned around and ran off as fast as his legs could carry him. Hamad raced after him with his gun drawn, but the outlaw was beyond the range of his gun, so the chase continued.

By coincidence, Khalil, Hamad's brother, was in Beirut that day. He had purchased a quantity of guns and ammunition and stowed it in his horse's saddle, and was walking with it towards the Choueifat road. (Khalil was a gun trader in the manner of the time.) Suddenly there appeared before him a man who was running fast. Khalil stopped his horse and asked him, 'What is wrong?' He did not know the man. The man answered, 'The police are after me.' Khalil decided to have some fun, so he said, 'Go this way and I will save you.' He directed him to an alley on the right. The man went, and as soon as he disappeared from sight, Hamad appeared, running with his gun drawn. When he saw his brother he asked him, 'Did you see so-and-so?'

The outlaw was famous for his crimes and assaults, and Khalil did not want to save him from justice. But he had promised the man that he would help him get away from the police, so he said to his brother, 'He went that way,' pointing in the opposite direction to the alley. Hamad ran

---

1. Hamad was the author's uncle, and Khalil was his father.
2. We will not mention his name.

and kept on running for some time until he got tired and weary and returned to the station. When he realized that his brother had tricked him, he became angry with him. Hamad said that had he brought back the outlaw dead or alive he would have got a promotion or a commendation, and that Khalil had squandered the opportunity for him. Khalil said, 'Next time might be better, God willing.'

In 1914 Khalil quit gun trading and joined the police force, and Hamad retired and went to Mexico. Soon thereafter the First World War began.

***

In 1920 Hamad Mahmoud was still in Mexico with his younger brother Saeed. As for Khalil, he had become a police deputy. One night during the summer of that year, Khalil and his partner Shaykh Youssef Hobeish were with a police force on a mission in Ras Beirut when they came across a band of outlaws. A battle broke out in which Khalil was able to kill the leader of the group after the latter had killed the deputy, Youssef Hobeish.[1]

Upon returning to the station, it became clear that the slain outlaw was the same man Khalil had helped to escape from his brother Hamad seven years earlier. The outlaw had progressed in his profession during those years, and the number of his victims had increased. When the news reached Abu Anis Hamad in Mexico, he wrote to his brother Abu Mahmoud Khalil saying, 'You saved him from me to slay him yourself. I hope he had become fatter and juicier.'

---

1. We have recounted the story of this incident elsewhere under the title 'Hobeish Police Station in Beirut'.

Flour Trading

Ali Mahmoud Saab spent his life in trade, working in villages and rural areas. During the First World War, he owned a shop in Hay al-Oumara in Choueifat where he sold hundreds of items, supplies, and nutritional goods. He was also a barber and a butcher. These are the village shops – the rural supermarkets that naturally differ from the city stores and are distinguished from them by their simplicity and modesty.

Before sundown on 30 September 1918, Hamad As'ad al-Khishin passed by Abu Salim Ali and told him that on that day, following the advice of one of his friends from Beirut, he had gone to Qmatiyya and bought a bag of flour for 125 Turkish piastres per *ratl*.[1] Ali was surprised by the news because the price of a *ratl* of flour in Beirut was 150 piastres. He asked Hamad about the quality of the flour and Hamad said it was good.

The next morning, Ali Mahmoud rented two muleteers and took a donkey to ride on. He collected whatever money and bags he had and closed his shop to go to Qmatiyya to buy flour. As he was preparing to leave, two of his relatives – Hamed Abdallah Sharafeddine and Aqil Saeed Waked – arrived and asked him where he was going. He did not think it appropriate to conceal his destination, since they were his relatives and had a right to know even the secrets of his trade. When they heard about the cheap price of flour in Qmatiyya, they asked him to take them along so they could buy some too. He did not turn down their request, so they went away and then returned with money and bags.

---

1.   A *ratl* is an old measurement weighing 2.5 kg. [Translator]

The caravan set out with God's blessings and the group reached Qmatiyya before noon. Aqil was a strong young man, and so he bought 30 *ratls* of flour and put it in a bag and carried it on his back. Hamed was not able to carry more than 20 *ratls*, so he was content with that amount. Greed got the better of Ali, however, and instead of buying what the muleteers' donkeys could carry he bought two more bags, loaded them on to his donkey, and returned on foot. The men did not complain of fatigue, and they returned safe and successful. Saving a quarter lira per *ratl* on flour was worth more trouble than they had endured.

They reached Choueifat in the afternoon and Aqil and Hamed went home. Ali went to his shop and opened it and unloaded the donkeys. He put the bags in their places and paid the muleteers their fees, not forgetting to tip them, since the transaction would be profitable, God willing. Ali sat at the door of his shop to rest and thank God for his safety and success. Less than an hour had passed when one of the neighbourhood's sons came by. The man had just been in Beirut, and without even bothering to greet Ali first he said, 'Uncle Ali, I bring you good news. The war is over and a *ratl* of flour in Beirut is selling for quarter of a lira ...' Ali's heart beat fast because of this good news. One day of peace had just cost him more than what he had made in many months of war.

***

What had happened was that once it was confirmed that the war had ended, the Beirut merchants who had been hoarding the people's food released it on to the market all at once, so the price took a sharp fall.

Ali Mahmoud closed his shop and went to his house in Hay al-Qoubbeh, feeling as if the world was closing in on him. He had just arrived home when he heard a call. It was Amir Amin Mustafa Arslan, and he had come to gather the Chouiefatis to attack the troops of the Turkish army, which had just been defeated by the British. Ali took his rifle and went to the gathering place in the government house square in Hay al-Amrousiyya. Perhaps on the battlefield he would be able to forget about the horrors of trade.

Sultan Abdel Hamid

The drainpipe enjoys a special status in village life. It ensures the drainage of rainwater from the rooftops, and this is called the roof drainpipe. Another kind of drainpipe is the fountain drainpipe, which collects the spring water and guides it to the basin. There are certain proverbs and sayings connected with both types, and they are still heard today. When someone develops a reputation for being disagreeable, they say he is 'like someone who breaks the fountain's drainpipe'. If someone denies benefits to his relatives and bestows them on strangers, they say 'his drainpipes empty to the outside'. If a person evades an evil only to fall into a harsher and more disastrous one, they say he is 'like someone running from under a drip to end up under a drainpipe'. They also call the winter days when the land does not produce plants and people must resort to their stored crops 'the time when the drainpipe is depressed'.

As for the structural benefit of the drainpipe in the village, it transports rainwater from the roof to the outside so that it does not run on to the walls, putting pressure on them and leaking from them into the house. A drainpipe is nothing more than a tin pipe, and when no tin is available it is made from wood. When heavy rainfall threatens to damage the terraces, the drainpipes would be turned outwards towards the narrow streets, making it almost impossible for people to pass through the streets during rainfall.

**

In 1932 the Choueifat municipal council made a decision requiring people to alter the drainpipes that poured water on to the streets by extending them all the way down to the ground so that they did not pour like waterfalls on to passers-by. The head of the municipality was Abd al-Halim Qassem Saab, and he asked the clerk Tanious Shaker Nasr to prepare three copies of the decision. He then sent them with the municipal policeman, Najib Amer Wehbeh, who posted them on the shop doors — one in each of Choueifat's three neighbourhoods.

***

The next morning, Abd al-Halim's older brother Salim Qassem Saab looked out of his window and saw a man atop his wall on the side of the house abutting the road. He stepped out on to the balcony and saw that it was Najib Faysal, a plumber who worked for the municipality as a supervisor in charge of water, busy putting together extensions to the drainpipe.

Najib hastened to greet him, and Shaykh Salim returned the greeting and then said very calmly, 'I beg your pardon if I intrude and ask you, when did you buy this house?' Najib answered, 'God keep the house for its owners, Uncle Abu Fouad ... but the head of the municipality, your brother, sent me to extend the spout to the ground ... Haven't you heard about the municipality's new decision on this matter?'

Shaykh Salim said, 'So Abdel Hamid sent you to fix the drainpipes at my house.' Najib Faysal looked at him in surprise, thinking that Shaykh Salim had incorrectly stated the name of his brother, Abd al-Halim. As if realizing what was running through Najib's mind, the Shaykh continued, 'Yes, my son. This is Sultan Abdel Hamid, and there is no disobeying his order, so get on with your work.' And he went back into the house.

***

When relatives and friends recounted this story, Abu Ramez Abd al-Halim would say, 'By God, I could not certify a citation to a single person if my own kin did not comply with the stipulations of the law.'

Trustworthy People

In 1927 Labib Dawoud Saab, who was seven years old at the time, was playing with his cousins, Hassan and Mahmoud, around the home of Sami Fandi Saab on the Saida road in Hay al-Oumara in Choueifat. Uncle Sami had not yet built his new house. The property was still as it was when he bought it from his relative Hamad Mahmoud. In front it was a big carob tree that passers-by would sit under for shade and rest in the summer days.

The carob trees in the coastal plains grow and age like the oak trees of the mountains, though their wood is not as sturdy as that of the oak. A number of these trees became famous in Choueifat. There was the 'Gharb carob tree' in Hay al-Oumara, under which Choueifat's *shaykh solh* Shahin Salman and Isber Afandi Shqeir met with the leader of the French troops in 1860. Near the 'Gharb carob tree' was the 'gypsy carob tree', under and around which the gypsies used to camp. And in Hay al-Amrousiyya was the 'carob tree of As'ad Saba' on the bend of the old Choueifat road near the house of As'ad Saba. The carriage drivers used to park their carriages in its shade to give their horses some rest before the ascent into the mountain.

Labib stood under the carob tree and saw Kamel Ammar Saab, a mounted policeman, approaching on horseback from the direction of the village. When Kamel reached the Beirut–Saida road, which was paved with pebbles and dirt, he turned his horse's head towards Beirut and nudged it, and the horse jumped and went running. The horse's sudden motion caused Kamel's gun to fall out of his holster. Kamel did not notice that it had fallen, and Labib ran and picked it up. He called to Kamel, but Kamel was already some distance away and did not hear him. So Labib took the gun, and without being seen he hid it in a bush behind the house and returned to play. A short time later, Kamel returned on foot looking at the ground. Labib knew that he was looking for his gun, so he ran and fetched it and gave it to him. When Labib went home, he told his mother what had happened and she commended him and told him to always return things to their owners and never to covet others' belongings.

***

By 1935 Labib had reached the age of fifteen and was working as a carpenter's apprentice in the shops of Ghifrail and George Rabbat in the Carpenters' Souq in Beirut. A few others from Choueifat worked with him in the same factory: Shamel Ali Mahmoud, Taufiq Abd al-Halim Wehbeh, and Hassan Youssef Hassan from the Saab family, and Saeed Halim Abu Na'im and Ajaj Khalil Fares al-Musharrafiyya. Labib's weekly wage was 150 Lebanese piastres, or a quarter of a lira (Lebanese pound) a day. He used to pay 10 piastres each day for his transportation back and forth in a horse-drawn carriage. Of course, he and his friends would take their lunch from among the leftovers at home.

One stormy, rainy day Labib stood at his place of work watching the heavy rain from behind the glass door. He saw a man running to avoid getting soaked, and reaching into his pocket for a handkerchief to put over his head to protect himself from the rain. When he took out the handkerchief, a bill of money came out of his pocket and fell to the ground. Labib opened the door and ran and picked up the bill. He found that it was a 100-lira note. He looked up and saw that the man was gone, so he put the bill in his pocket and returned to the shop.

His friends had seen him, so they gathered round him and said, 'You found some money, and we are your partners. So how much is it?' Labib said, 'It is 1 whole lira, and I'll buy some sweets with it and we'll eat them after lunch.' When the rain stopped, Labib went to the shop of Abu Jamil Youssef Homeidan al-Rishani in Martyrs Square and bought 1 lira's worth of sweets. He hid the remaining 99 liras in his pocket. Never before that day had Labib's pocket contained such a fortune.

That evening Labib told his father how he had found the money and what he had done, and he gave him the 99 liras. His father Abu Suleiman asked him, 'Weren't you able to follow the man or make him hear your voice?' Labib assured his father that he had not been able to do so because the man quickly disappeared from sight. His father asked if he had seen the man's face and would recognize him if he saw him. Labib said he could not. At that point, Abu Suleiman reached a formal conclusion on the matter and considered the money a blessing for himself and his family. A few days later he bought a donkey and began using it for work.

***

One morning in 1936, Labib Dawoud left his father's house as usual on his way to his work in Beirut, carrying his lunch under his arm. When he got near the house of Abdallah Ahmad Saab, he saw a bundle on the ground. When he picked it up it was obvious that it contained money. He looked around in all directions but did not see anyone. He put the bundle inside his jacket and continued on his way, but instead of going towards the Saida–Beirut road he headed to the area of the cemetery. There he opened the package and found a wallet containing some paper money and silver and copper coins worth 350 Lebanese liras. In the wallet he found a picture of his relative Kamal Wahid Saab, who was overseas.

Labib did not go to work that day but returned home. He was making 30 piastres a day, and now he had 350 liras in his pocket. But what was Kamal Wahid's connection with the money since he was in America? Labib could not solve the mystery. He related the news to his mother as Um Suleiman was washing the laundry. His mother was calm and nonchalant and said, 'Labib, do you think the bundle fell from the sky?' He said, 'Of course not.' She said, 'And who would carry a picture of Kamal Wahid?' Of course, it had to be one of his relatives, and Labib understood what his mother meant to say.

After a while she asked him, 'Are you prepared to return the money to its owner, Labib? Its owner is certain to appear.' Labib looked at his mother, toiling as she washed the clothes. Then he looked at his sisters, sitting in a corner of the house because they had no clothes other than the ones his mother was washing. He looked back at his mother's face and read her insistence, and so he nodded his head in the affirmative. Labib's younger brother As'ad saw the money, and as usual he began to cry and ask that they give him a piastre. Labib reached into his pocket and took out a pierced penny of his own money and gave it to him.

About half an hour later, Labib heard voices. He looked out and heard his relative Ali Mahmoud Saab saying to his cousin Saeed Jihjah Saab, 'It is people's money, Saeed. How can I rest before I find it?' Labib understood who the money belonged to and he called out to him, 'Uncle Ali, please come by and see us.'

***

In addition to working as a trader, Abu Salem Ali Mahmoud spent the early hours of each day working as a butcher. He would slaughter as many sheep and calves as the market could consume. At about 10 o'clock, the butchery and selling of meat would stop, and he would wash his hands and change his clothes and sit down to sell goods and give haircuts.

Ali used to buy the sheep from Mohieddine al-Tarabulsi. He was conscientious about paying for them in a timely manner, so every night he would put the revenue from his meat sales in a designated drawer in his house and keep it there until it was time to go and pay what he owed. When the payment date arrived, he would take the money with him to his shop so that he could take it to Beirut when he was done with his butcher's work for that day.

On this occasion, he happened to calculate and set aside what he owed two days before the due date. Um Salem saw him put the money in a wallet and a buckskin bag, so she assumed he was going to Beirut the next day. When she woke up and saw that the money was still in the house she thought he had forgotten it, so she put it in a bundle and put the bundle with the clothes she would send him each morning. She sent the clothes and the money to her husband with her young son Adel, and alerted him to the presence of the money among the clothes.

When Adel got to his father's shop, he put the load on the table and opened the bundle of clothes to take out the money, but it was not there. Adel screamed and tried to run, but his father grabbed him and gently and patiently tried to get him to explain. After some sweet persuasion with candied chickpeas, Adel told his father that he had dropped the money. Ali let him go, and then ran to wash his hands and change his clothes. Adel ran home and told his mother what had happened. Abu Salem walked from the shop towards his house while Um Salem walked from the house towards the shop. They met near the house of Salman Mohsen al-Jurdi, without either of them finding any trace of the money. The sum of money was huge by the standards of the purchasing power of the lira at that time.

Saeed Jihjah Saab happened to pass by and learned of the trouble. He invited them to his house for a cup of coffee to clear their minds a little. Once they were at Abu Gharra Saeed's house, Abu Salem could not drink his coffee. He got up and walked quickly out of the house and towards the neighbourhood square saying, 'How can I sit down and drink coffee when the money we lost was someone else's money in our trust?' That is when Labib, as we mentioned, heard him and invited him to the house. There Um Suleiman gave him the bundle and asked him to count the money. Ali refused and said, 'One who returns all is not greedy with part. May God give us more of your likes, Um Suleiman.'

The village cannot keep a secret, so the news spread among the people. A few days later, Shaykh Abu Hassan Hammoud Abu Fakhr[1] paid a visit to Abu Suleiman Dawoud Saab's house and congratulated Um Suleiman on her honourable conduct the day her son Labib found the bundle of money in the road. After Shaykh Abu Hassan's visit, Shaykh Abu Aref Nasib Mahmoud Musharrafiyya[2] also paid a visit to the house of Abu Suleiman to offer congratulations and express his appreciation. This is how the *ajaweed* encouraged people to do good deeds and behave righteously.

***

In 1937 Labib was promoted and began to earn 3 liras a week. This enabled him to buy a locally manufactured hunting rifle, and he started using it to hunt birds on his days off. At the end of February that year, Labib went to hunt in Choueifat's olive groves. His father Abu Suleiman was supervising the ploughing of a piece of land in the Rihana area on behalf of its owner, Amin Rashid Saab. Labib passed by his father, and then he headed to the bank of the Ghadir River. There he saw a flock of the birds known as *sulunj* landing in an olive tree. Labib followed the

---

1. Shaykh Abu Hassan Hammoud Abu Fakhreddine from Hay al-Qoubeh in Choueifat was a devoted man of faith and among the best of people. He was honest and steadfast in his dealings with others, and would spend long hours and exert sincere and noble efforts to solve people's problems and resolve their disagreements. He was patient, understanding, affable, and gentle.
2. Shaykh Abu Aref was another of the honest and pious men of faith, and a perceptive and knowledgable man. He was forgiving, even-tempered, and pleasant, and had an engaging personality.

birds and fired a shot. He managed to hit a number of birds with a single shot. He jumped for joy and ran to where they had fallen and began to gather them up. Among the birds he saw a black leather wallet, so he picked it up. When he opened the wallet, he found stacks of money consisting of 250-lira and 100-lira notes. Labib counted the money and found that the total was 3,500 Lebanese liras. He also found two rings of pure gold. He closed the wallet and put it in his pocket, and then went back to the Rihana and sat on the ground near his father. His legs would no longer carry him walking after birds.

Labib began to think. Why was money finding him wherever he went? And each time a greater sum than the time before. He was seventeen now, and had never managed to save more then 10 liras. But he was finding sums on the roads in the hundreds and thousands. And now he had found a fortune in the heart of the Choueifat groves. Would its owner come forward? And if the owner was not from the family, what would his father have him do?

Labib grew happier with every moment that passed without the money's owner surfacing. But his joy did not last long, for he heard some murmuring coming from the village road. Then he saw Muhammad Ali Qassem approaching with his hands hitting both sides of his head and saying, 'Oh, the ruin of my home. Oh, the humiliation of my children.' Muhammad Ali owned the ox that was used to plough in the Rihana, and he was from Shmistar in the Beqaa. Abu Suleiman asked him, 'What is the matter, man?' Muhammad Ali said that he had lost his wallet, and it contained 7,000 liras. Abu Suleiman said, 'You are in an olive grove. People rarely walk through here. Go and retrace your path and you're sure to find what you have lost.' Muhammad Ali went in the direction from which Labib had come. At that point Abu Suleiman looked at his son's face and noticed that he seemed agitated and had stopped hunting. He said to his son, 'You found the wallet, didn't you?' Labib said, 'Yes, but it only contains 3,500 liras. Muhammad Ali is lying and saying it contains 7,000 liras.' His father said, 'Leave the matter to me.'

Muhammad Ali soon returned. He was slapping his face like a woman and said that he had found nothing. Abu Suleiman grabbed a stick he was carrying and struck Muhammad Ali with it hard. The man was shocked and asked why he was beating him. Abu Suleiman hit him again and said, 'I'm hitting you because you are lying. Where did you get 7,000 liras to lose?' The man was almost in tears. He said, 'It is the price of my house and I sold it yesterday. But the truth is that the sum is only 3,500 liras.' Abu Suleiman turned to his son Labib and said, 'Give him his wallet.'

Labib did so. Muhammad Ali fell at Abu Suleiman's feet and thanked him, and then he opened the wallet and took out 100 liras and a gold ring and gave them to Labib. After Muhammad Ali left, Abu Suleiman said to his son, 'Labib, the 100 liras you have received are more blessed than thousands.'

Scenes of Dignity

What follows are four scenes that occurred in the same place and under the same circumstances. The first was in May 1912 in the government house square in Hay al-Amrousiyya. It was the day of the elections for Choueifat's *shaykh solh*, and there were two candidates for the position – Shaykh Fandi Qassem Saab and Shaykh Salim Qassem Saab. When the door of the government house opened for the voting, the two candidates stood and hugged in front of the people. When the votes were counted, it turned out that Shaykh Fandi had won, and Shaykh Salim hugged him to congratulate him as if nothing had happened.

A few days later, Shaykh Fandi was blessed with a son. It had been decided that they would name the boy Fawzi, but Shaykh Fandi said, 'Fawzi is derived from *faza* [meaning 'to win'], and I fear that some might consider it a challenge to my relative.' The boy was named Chehab.

***

The second scene occurred on 10 April 1921, and again it was election day for Choueifat's *shaykh solh*. The competition was still on between Shaykh Fandi and Shaykh Salim, so Shaykh Salim ran for office and Shaykh Fandi was nominated by his cousin Shaykh Muhammad Isma'il. Shaykh Milhem Shahin Salman was also a candidate. All three men were well suited for the position.

Shahin Salman was Shaykh Milhem's brother and Shaykh Fandi's son-in-law, and Milhem asked him to support his brother. Shaykh Fandi said,

'Listen, Shahin. You are my son-in-law, and to me you are like my son. But I only gave you my daughter in marriage. I did not give you my name and family.' Muhammad Isma'il withdrew, as did Shaykh Milhem Shahin Salman, and so Shaykh Salim won by default. Shaykh Fandi was the first to go into the government house and vote for Salim. Shaykh Salim did not wait for Shaykh Fandi to visit him and congratulate him but went himself with the family's notables and visited Shaykh Fandi in his house in Hay al-Amrousiyya. Shaykh Fandi was older than Shaykh Salim, and when signing proposals, Salim would leave the first signature line blank for Fandi.

***

The third scene occurred on 27 May 1934, again in the government house square. This time the occasion was the election of a new municipal council for Choueifat, and there was strong competition between two groups, one headed by Abu Halim Qassem Saab and the other by Khalil Mahmoud Saab. Before the voting began, Abd al-Halim and Khalil hugged in front of the crowd in the square, and then each went about the business of the election with seriousness and interest.

In the evening, Abdel Hamid's victory was announced. Khalil approached him and hugged him to congratulate him, and everything went back to the way it was before the election.

***

The fourth scene occurred on 7 December 1952, again in the government house square for the election of a new municipal council. The candidates for the presidency were Kamel Jihjah Saab and Mahmoud Khalil Saab. Kamel and Mahmoud were not satisfied with hugging in front of the crowd in the morning, but drove around together in Mahmoud's car to carry out the voting process in Choueifat's three neighbourhoods. When Mahmoud won, his uncle Kamel approached him and congratulated him, and the curtain fell on the battle's beginning and end.

As for the Saab family's kinships through marriage, they are numerous. But in what follows I will record those that I recall, for the benefit of the family's sons, relatives, and friends, and for the benefit of those who wish to study social relations among the Druze, because what applies to the Saab family in this regard applies to the other families as well, though to different degrees. There is a relationship of one marriage or more tying the Saab family to the following families:

Choueifat	al-Musharrafiyya		Rasamni
	al-Khishin		Mowaffaq
	al-Jurdi		Khair
	Sha'ban	Aley	Jamaleddine
	al-Qadi		al-Fiqih
	Haidar		Shehayyeb
	Abu Fakhr		al-Rayyes
	al-Mashtoub		'Obeid
	al-Souqi		Morad
	Na'im	Aynab	al-Sha'ar
	al-Rishani	Abey	Hamzeh
	Salman		Raydan
	Abu Faraj		Ataya
	Arbid	Kfar Matta	Khaddaj
	Abu Aram	al-Benneih	Nasr
	Nasser	Baysour	Melaa'eb
Dayr Qoubel	Younis		Aridi
	'Izzeddine	al-Ramliyya	Salman
	Saeed	Sharoun	al-Sayegh
Ain 'Inoub	Raydan	Me'srayti	al-Sayegh
	Qaed Bey	Majdel Ba'na	Abd al-Khaliq
	Saad	Sofar	Jum'a
	Abu Salman		Makarem
	Homeidan		Talhouq
	Ammar		al-Ja'fari
	Shouja'	Baaqlin	Hamadeh
Bshamoun	Abu Ali		Khudr
	Abu Ibrahim		al-Ghoseini
	al-'Eid		Taqieddine
	Masoud		Ibrahim
	Morad		Salaheddine
Sarahmoul	Nureddine		Abu Ajram
Aramoun	al-Jawhari		al-Qa'samani
	al-Daqdouq		al-Dahouk
al-Fisaqin	Ghosn	'Einbal	Abu Ziki
Aytat	Assaf		Abd al-Baqi

Atrin	Hassan	al-Freidis	Damaj
Gharifeh	Abu Hamdan	Kfar Shima	al-Fata
	Harb	Ibl Saki	Munthir
al-Kahlouniyya	Saab	Hasbayya	Qays
Mazra'at			al-Zagheer
al-Chouf	Zibian		al-Khatib
al-Mukhtara	Qansou	Bakkifa	al-Asal
Ain Qani	Zeineddine		Abu Barakeh
	Hakim	Rashayya	Mohanna
	al-Sham'a		Abu Hojeili
Kfar Heem	Abu Khozam	Meimis	Fadah
	Abu Dargham		Maadi
Kfar Faqoud	Zahreddine	Jabal al-Druze	al-Haili
Dayr Baaba	Abu Ammar		Danout
Kfar Qatra	Barakat		al-Shariti
Ain Zhalta	Zahreddine		'Imad
Brieh	Saghbini		Saghbini
al-'Oubadiyya	al-Najjar		al-Abdallah
	'Indary		Abu Zour
	Rashid		Hamshou
	Thabet		Abu Rislan
	Faraj		Ghazal
Qoubbei'	al-A'war	Ras al-Matn	Makarem
Falougha	al-A'war		Taqi
Bmariem	Shahin		Noueihed
Qurnaeil	al-A'war	Broummana	Maqsad
	Hilal	Beit Miri	al-Najjar
Bzibdin	Mou'dad	Beirut	Qoleilat
	Sarieddine		al-Rifai
Kfar Silwan	Moghrabi		al-Sawwah
Amatour	Abu Shaqra	Jaramana –	
Bater	Hamdan	Damascus oasis	al-Ali
Jiba'	Slim		
Kfar Nabrakh	Abu Ghanem		
	al-Saadi		
	Abu Khair		
al-Barouk	Abu 'Ilwan		